P9-CRF-233

THE GREAT CHICAGO FIRE, 1871

TEXT COPYRIGHT © 2023, 2015 BY DREYFUSS TARSHIS MEDIA INC.
ILLUSTRATIONS COPYRIGHT © 2023 BY DREYFUSS TARSHIS MEDIA INC.

ALL RIGHTS RESERVED. PUBLISHED BY GRAPHIX, AN IMPRINT OF SCHOLASTIC INC., *PUBLISHERS SINCE 1920*. SCHOLASTIC, GRAPHIX, AND ASSOCIATED LOGOS ARE TRADEMARKS AND/OR REGISTERED TRADEMARKS OF SCHOLASTIC INC.

THE PUBLISHER DOES NOT HAVE ANY CONTROL OVER AND DOES NOT ASSUME ANY RESPONSIBILITY FOR AUTHOR OR THIRD-PARTY WEBSITES OR THEIR CONTENT.

NO PART OF THIS PUBLICATION MAY BE REPRODUCED, STORED IN A RETRIEVAL SYSTEM, OR TRANSMITTED IN ANY FORM OR BY ANY MEANS, ELECTRONIC, MECHANICAL, PHOTOCOPYING, RECORDING, OR OTHERWISE, WITHOUT WRITTEN PERMISSION OF THE PUBLISHER. FOR INFORMATION REGARDING PERMISSION, WRITE TO SCHOLASTIC INC., ATTENTION: PERMISSIONS DEPARTMENT, 557 BROADWAY, NEW YORK, NY 10012.

PHOTOS ©: 151 TOP: SCIENCE HISTORY IMAGES/ALAMY STOCK PHOTO; 151 CENTER: STOCK MONTAGE/GETTY IMAGES; 151 BOTTOM: OTTO HERSCHAN COLLECTION/HULTON ARCHIVE/GETTY IMAGES; 152 TOP: INTERIM ARCHIVES/GETTY IMAGES; 152 CENTER LEFT: WORLD HISTORY ARCHIVE/ALAMY STOCK PHOTO; 152 CENTER RIGHT: SHUTTERSTOCK.COM; 152 BOTTOM: CHICAGO HISTORY MUSEUM/GETTY IMAGES; 153 TOP: CHICAGO HISTORY MUSEUM/ALAMY STOCK PHOTO; 153 CENTER: CHICAGO HISTORY MUSEUM, ICHI-063134, WANDSBECK SEITZ, LITHOGRAPHER; 153 BOTTOM: ANDREW FARE/ALAMY STOCK PHOTO; 154 TOP: CHICAGO HISTORY MUSEUM, ICHI-002737, LOVEJOY & FOSTER, PHOTOGRAPHER; 154 CENTER: CHICAGO HISTORY MUSEUM/GETTY IMAGES; 155 TOP: CHICAGO HISTORY MUSEUM/ALAMY STOCK PHOTO; 155 CENTER: INTERFOTO/ALAMY STOCK PHOTO; 155 BOTTOM: CHICAGO HISTORY MUSEUM/ALAMY STOCK PHOTO; 156 TOP: CHICAGO HISTORY MUSEUM, ICHI-002845, COPELIN & HINE, PHOTOGRAPHER; 156 CENTER: SCIENCE HISTORY IMAGES/ALAMY STOCK PHOTO; 156 BOTTOM: ALLAN BAXTER/GETTY IMAGES; 157 BOTTOM RIGHT: SHUTTERSTOCK.COM.

SPECIAL THANKS TO JULIUS L. JONES

WHILE INSPIRED BY REAL EVENTS AND HISTORICAL CHARACTERS, THIS IS A WORK OF FICTION AND DOES NOT CLAIM TO BE HISTORICALLY ACCURATE OR TO PORTRAY FACTUAL EVENTS OR RELATIONSHIPS. PLEASE KEEP IN MIND THAT REFERENCES TO ACTUAL PERSONS, LIVING OR DEAD, BUSINESS ESTABLISHMENTS, EVENTS, OR LOCALES MAY NOT BE FACTUALLY ACCURATE, BUT RATHER FICTIONALIZED BY THE AUTHOR.

LIBRARY OF CONGRESS CONTROL NUMBER: 2022041164
ISBN 978-1-338-82515-2 (PAPERBACK)
ISBN 978-1-338-82516-9 (HARDCOVER)

10 9 8 7 6 5 4 3 2 1   23 24 25 26 27
PRINTED IN CHINA   62
FIRST EDITION, MAY 2023

EDITED BY KATIE WOEHR
LETTERING BY JANICE CHIANG
INKS BY CASSIE ANDERSON
COLOR BY JUANMA AGUILERA
BOOK DESIGN BY KATIE FITCH
CREATIVE DIRECTOR: YAFFA JASKOLL

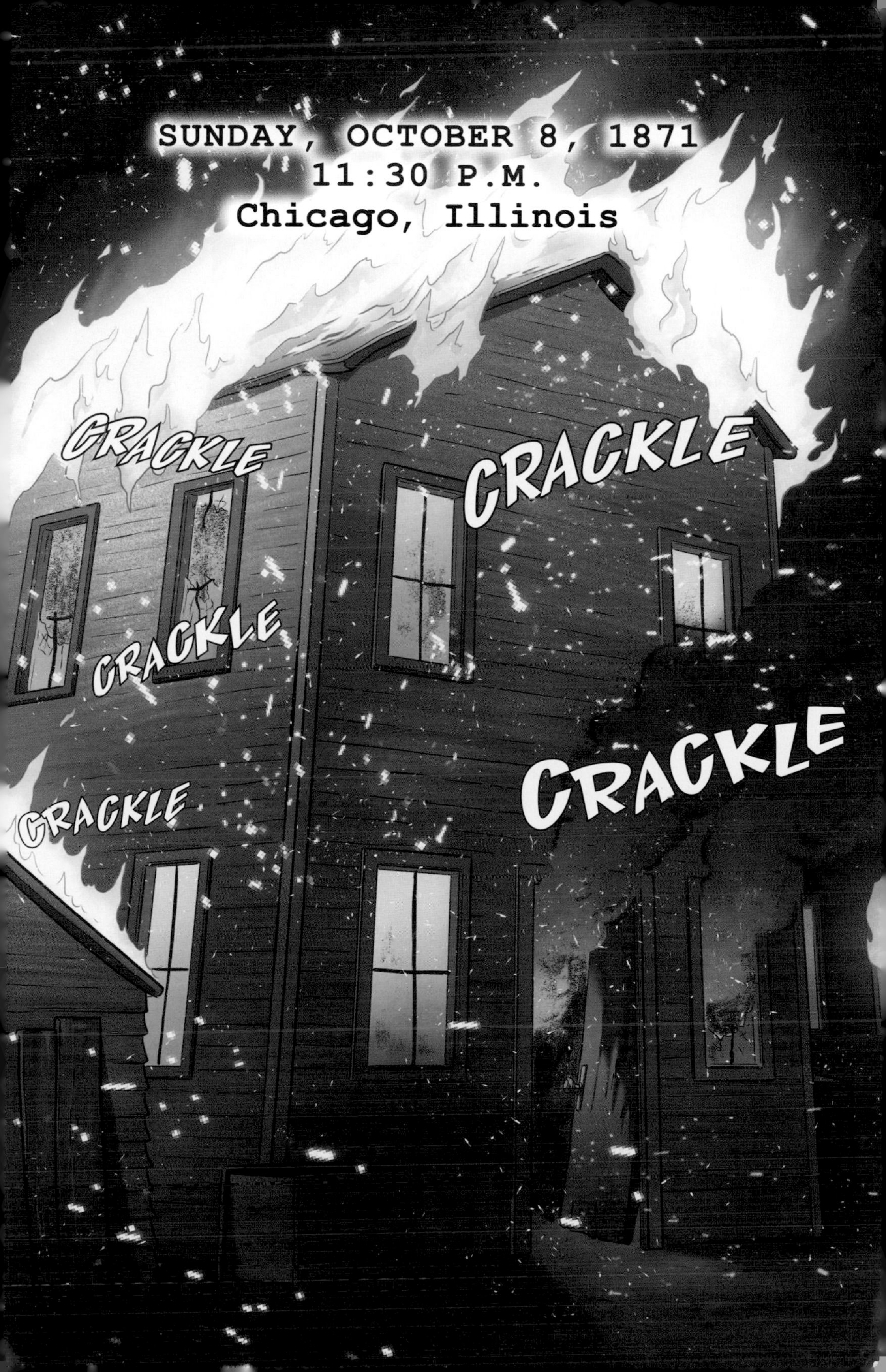
SUNDAY, OCTOBER 8, 1871
11:30 P.M.
Chicago, Illinois
CRACKLE
CRACKLE
CRACKLE
CRACKLE
CRACKLE

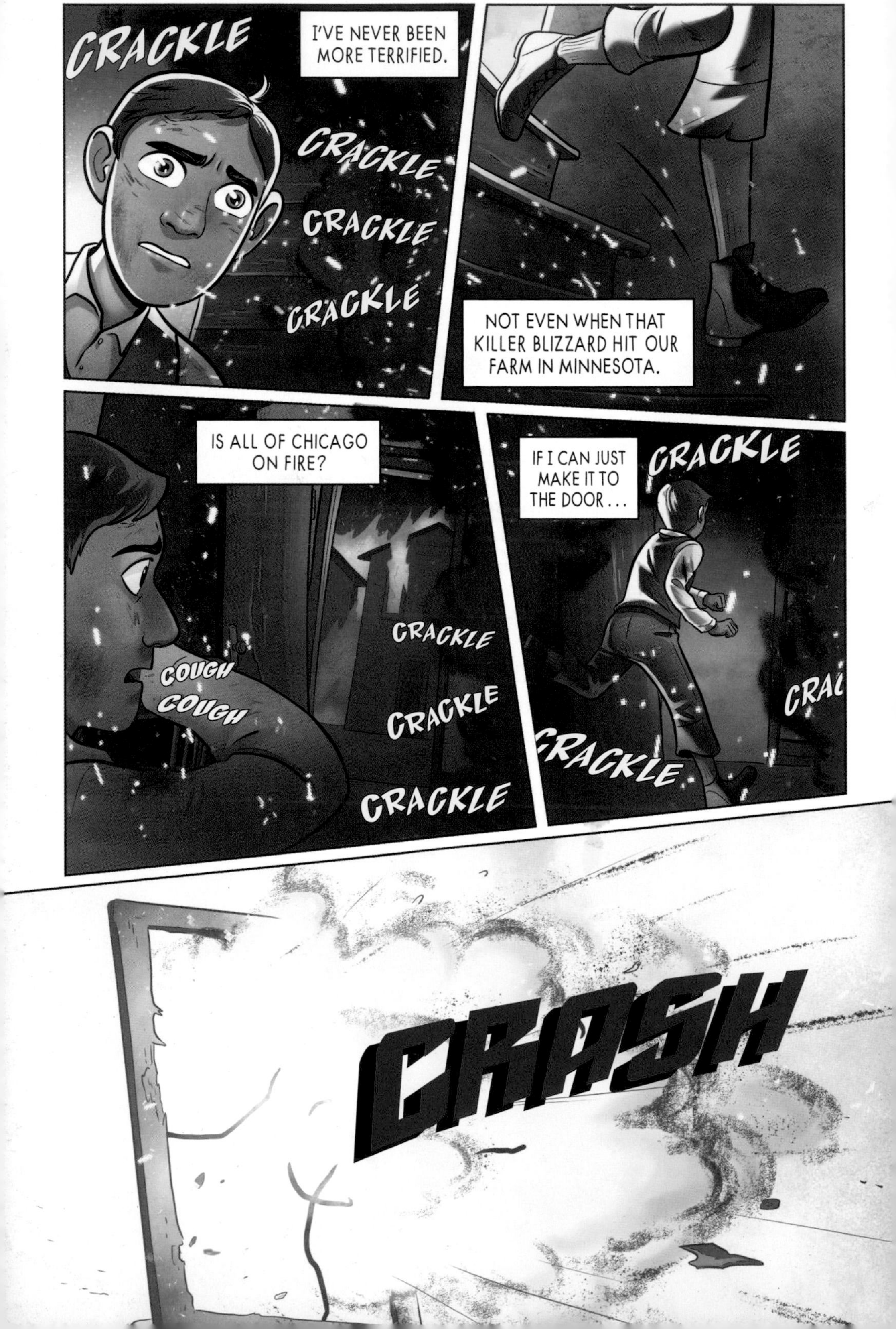
CRACKLE
I'VE NEVER BEEN MORE TERRIFIED.
CRACKLE
CRACKLE
CRACKLE
NOT EVEN WHEN THAT KILLER BLIZZARD HIT OUR FARM IN MINNESOTA.
IS ALL OF CHICAGO ON FIRE?
CRACKLE
COUGH
COUGH
CRACKLE
CRACKLE
IF I CAN JUST MAKE IT TO THE DOOR . . .
CRACKLE
CRAC
CRACKLE
CRASH

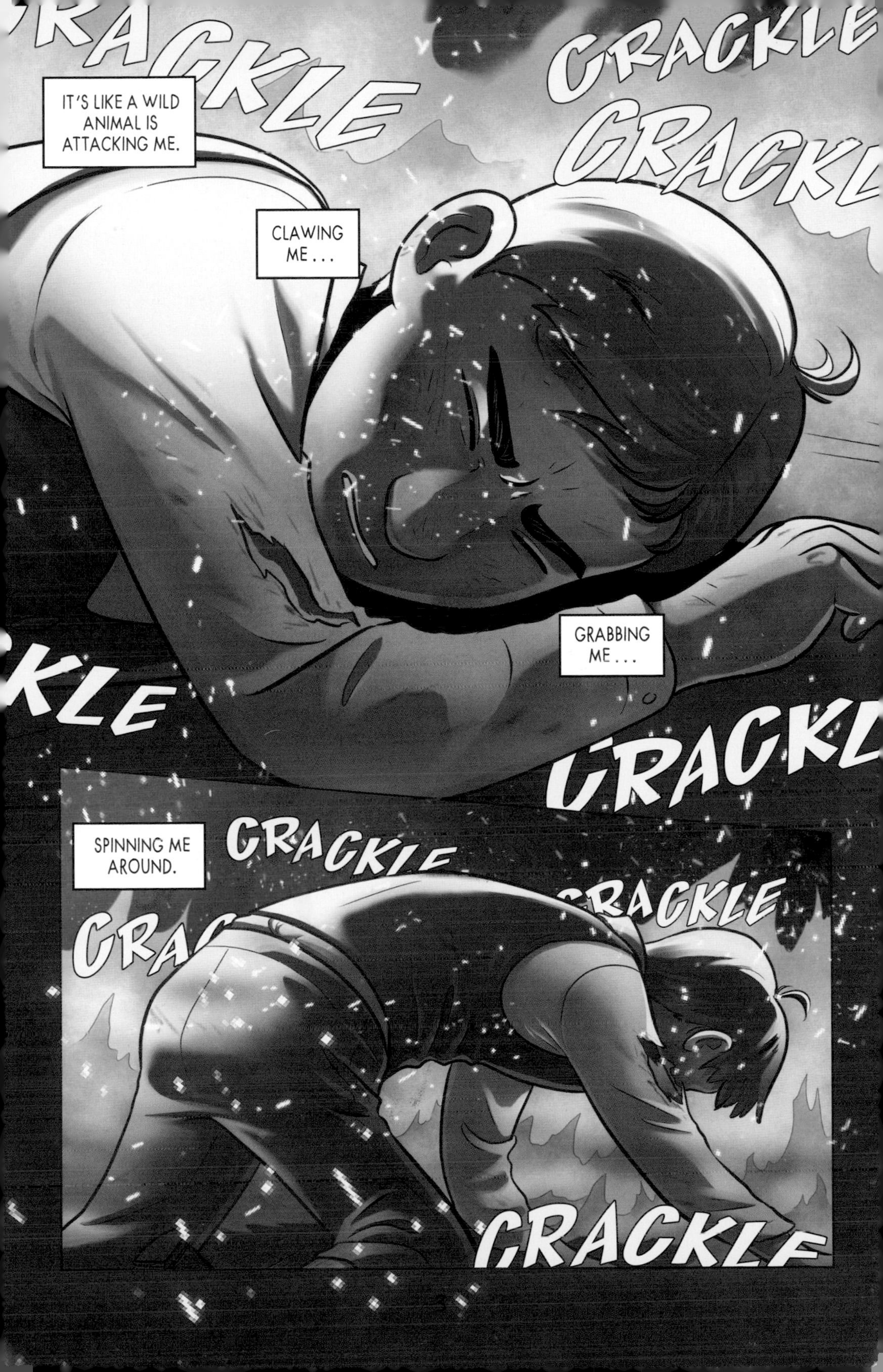
CRACKLE
IT'S LIKE A WILD ANIMAL IS ATTACKING ME.
CRACKLE
CRACKLE
CLAWING ME . . .
GRABBING ME . . .
CRACKLE
SPINNING ME AROUND.
CRACKLE
CRACKLE
CRACKLE

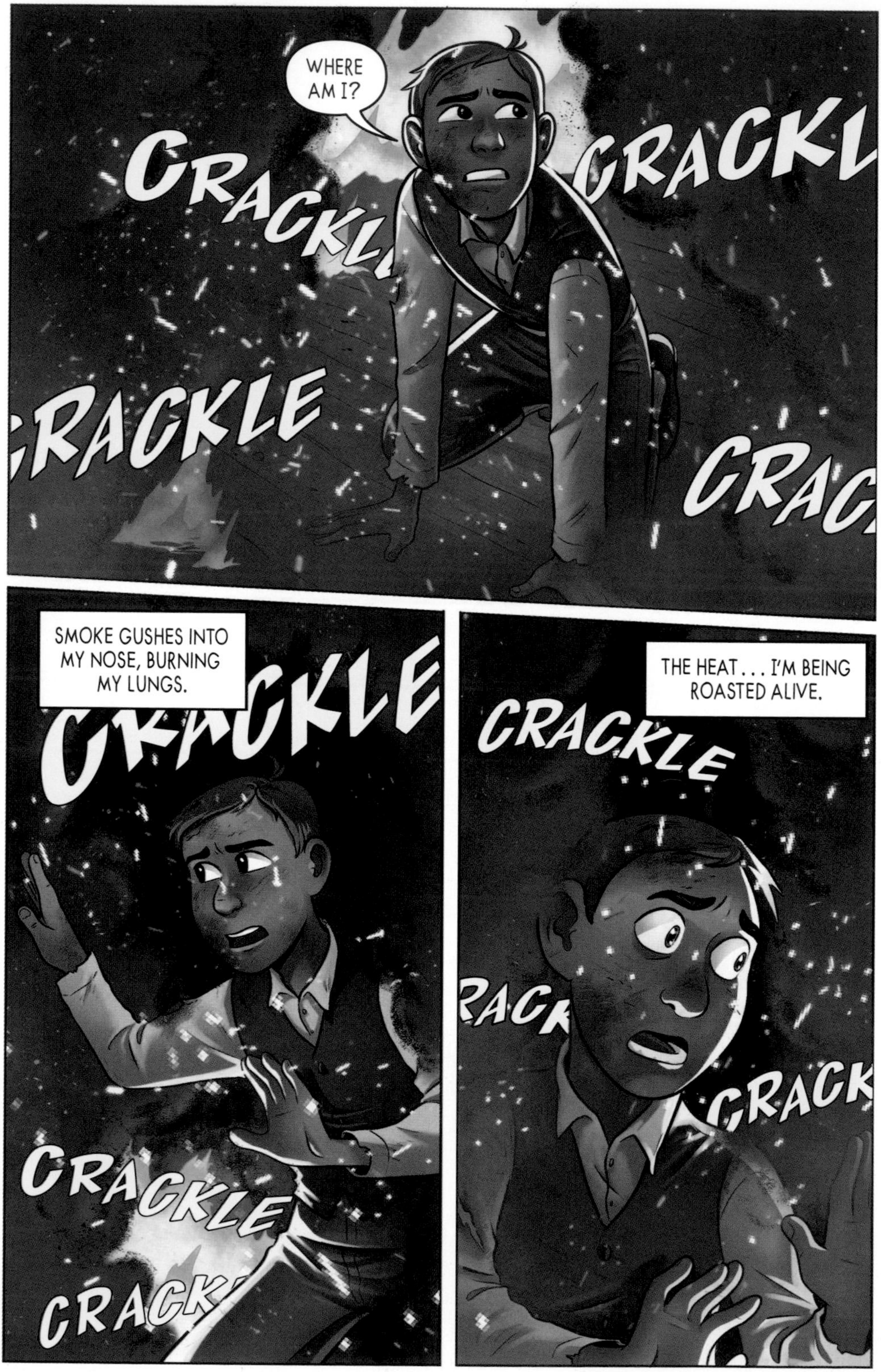
WHERE AM I?
CRACKLE
CRACKL
CRACKLE
CRAC
SMOKE GUSHES INTO MY NOSE, BURNING MY LUNGS.
CRACKLE
CRACKLE
CRACK
THE HEAT . . . I'M BEING ROASTED ALIVE.
CRACKLE
RACK
CRACK

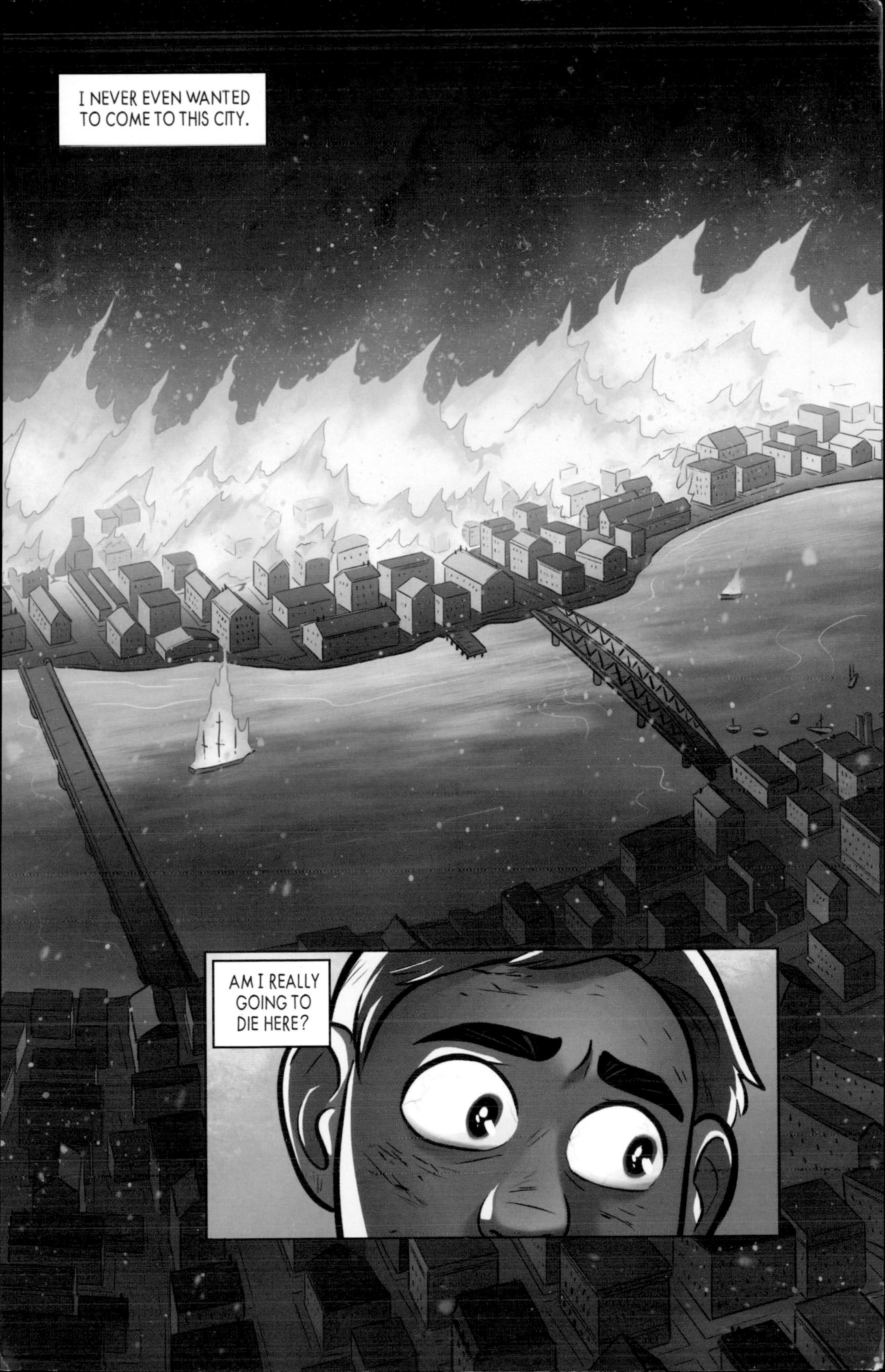
I NEVER EVEN WANTED TO COME TO THIS CITY.
AM I REALLY GOING TO DIE HERE?

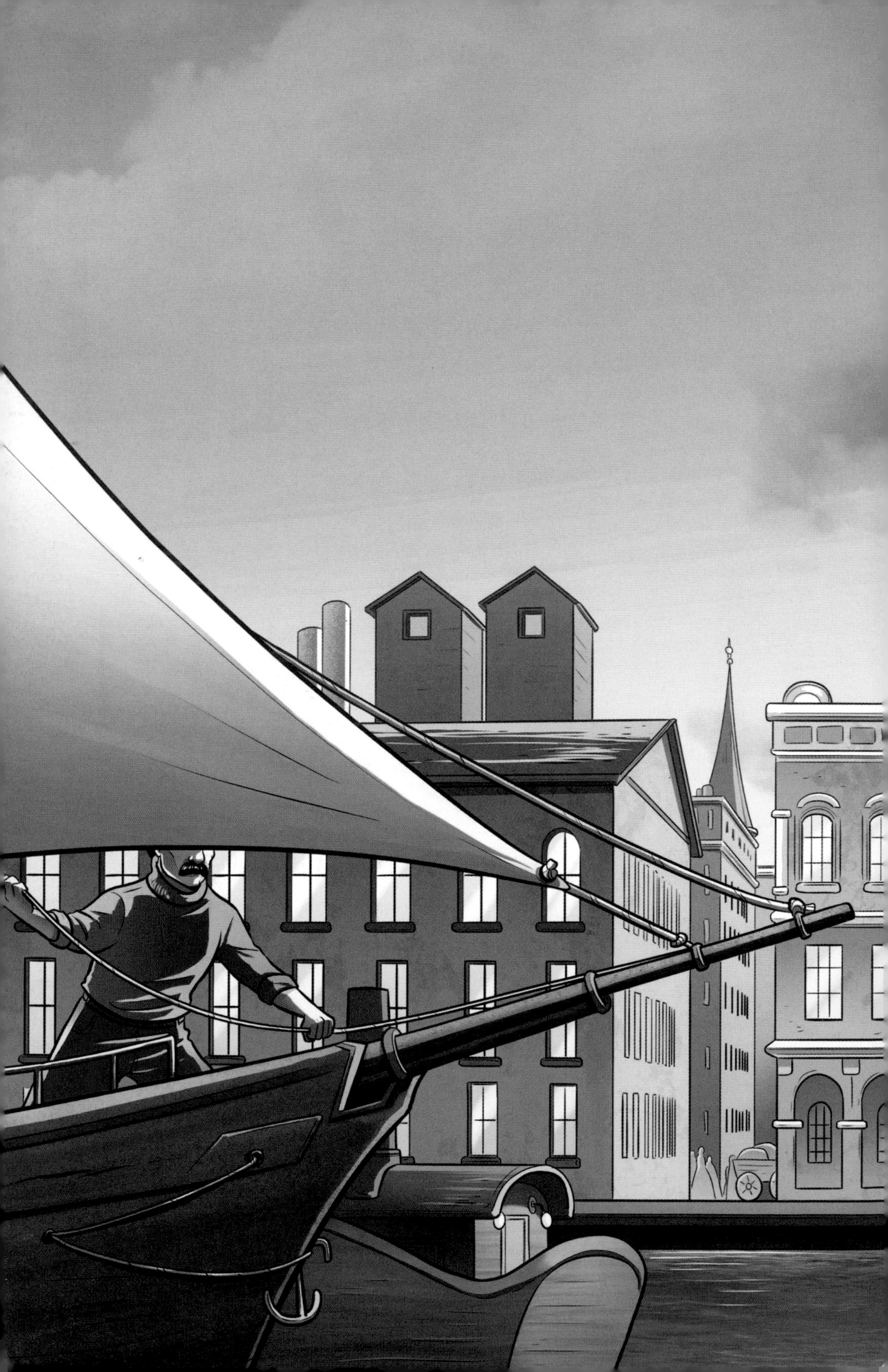

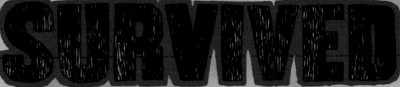

I SURVIVED

THE GREAT CHICAGO FIRE, 1871

BASED ON THE NOVEL IN THE *NEW YORK TIMES*
BESTSELLING SERIES BY LAUREN TARSHIS

ADAPTED BY GEORGIA BALL
WITH ART BY CASSIE ANDERSON
COLORS BY JUANMA AGUILERA

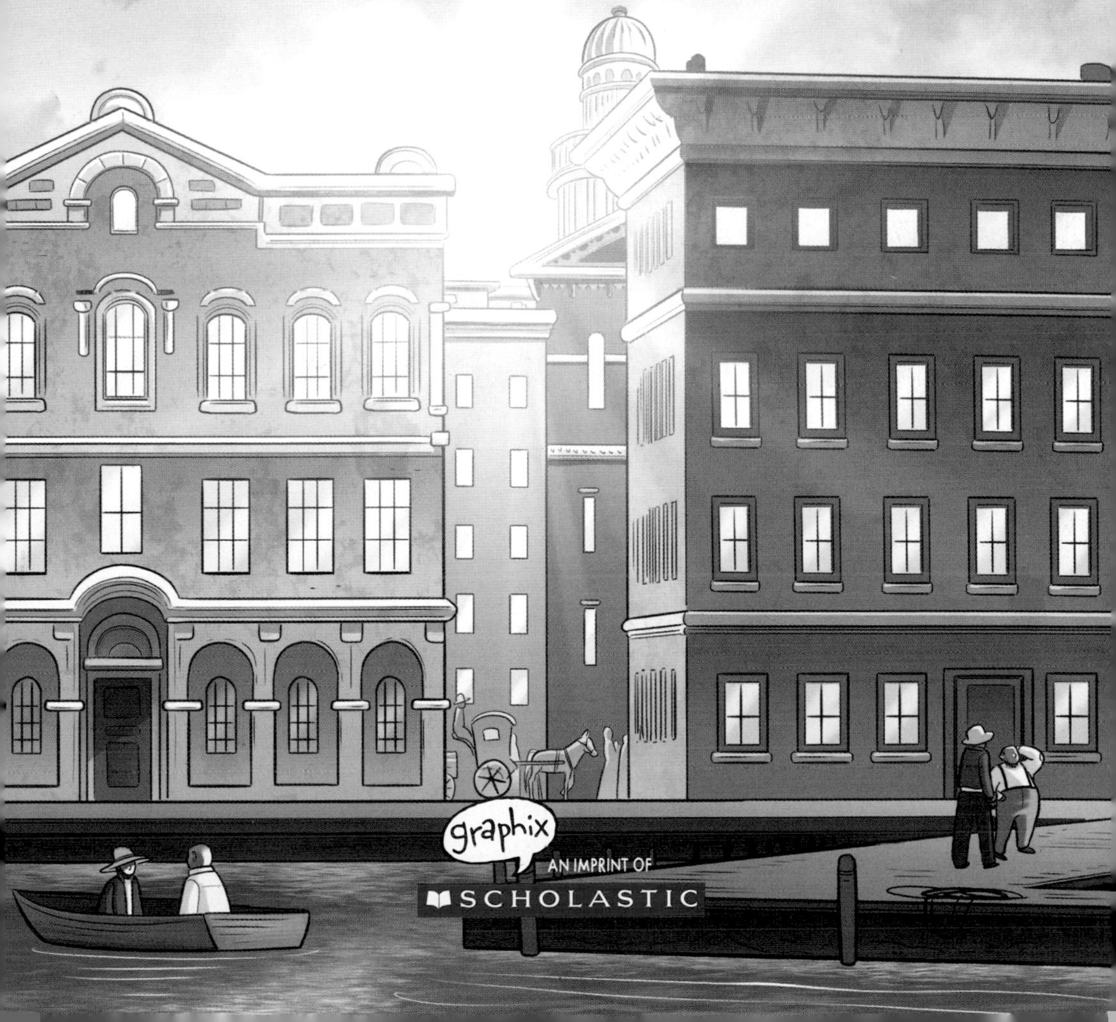

graphix
AN IMPRINT OF
SCHOLASTIC

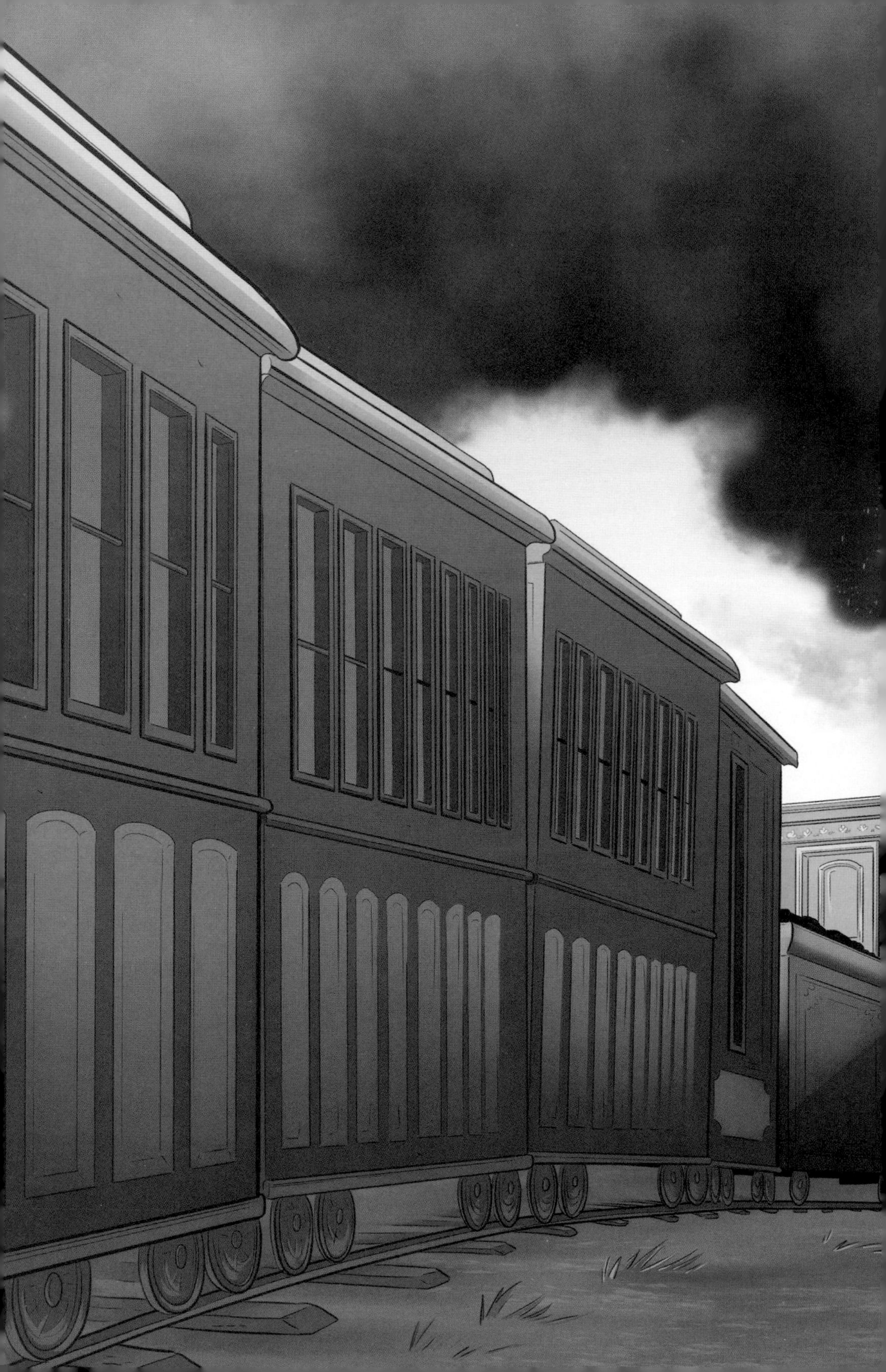

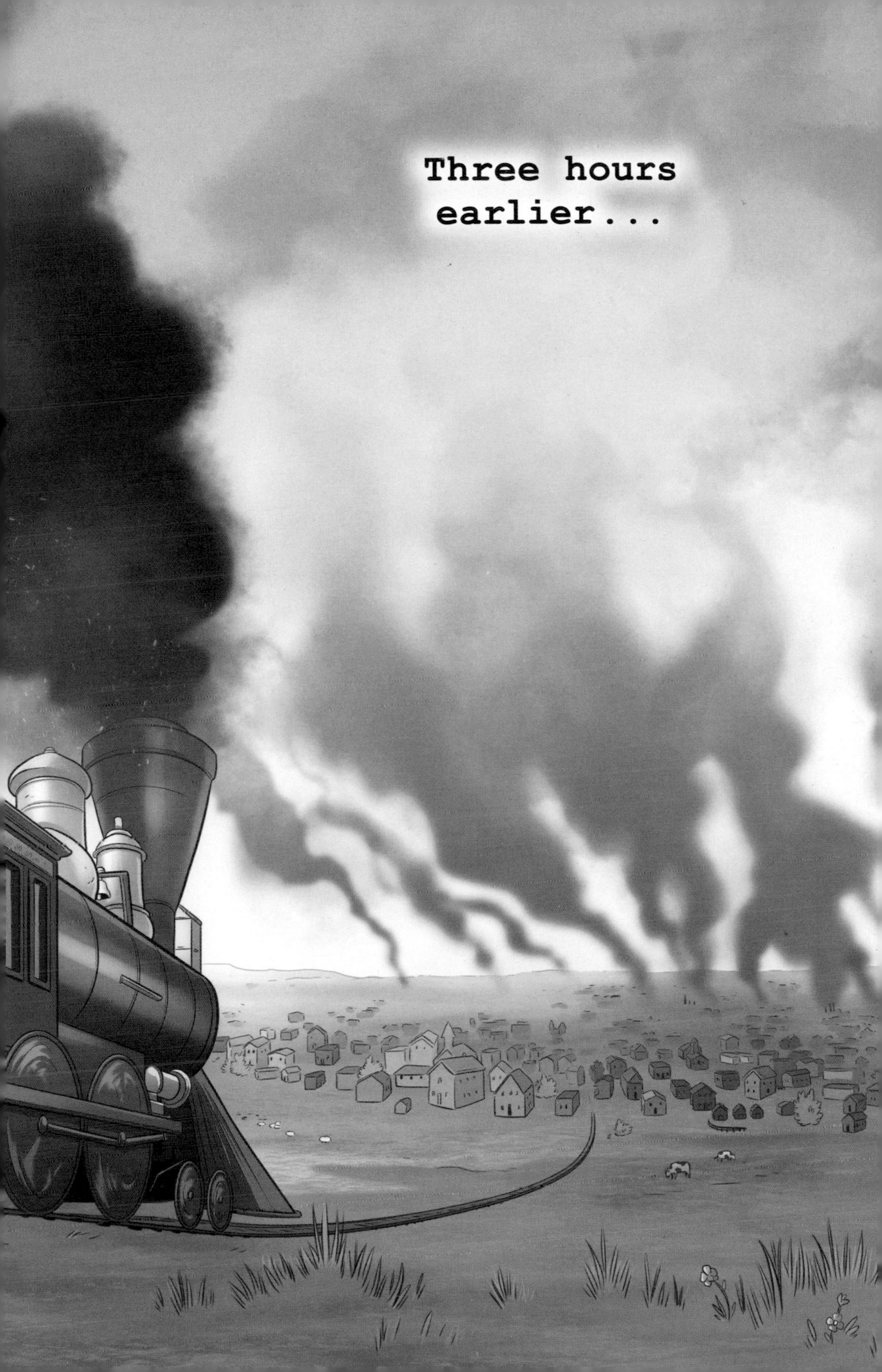
Three hours earlier...

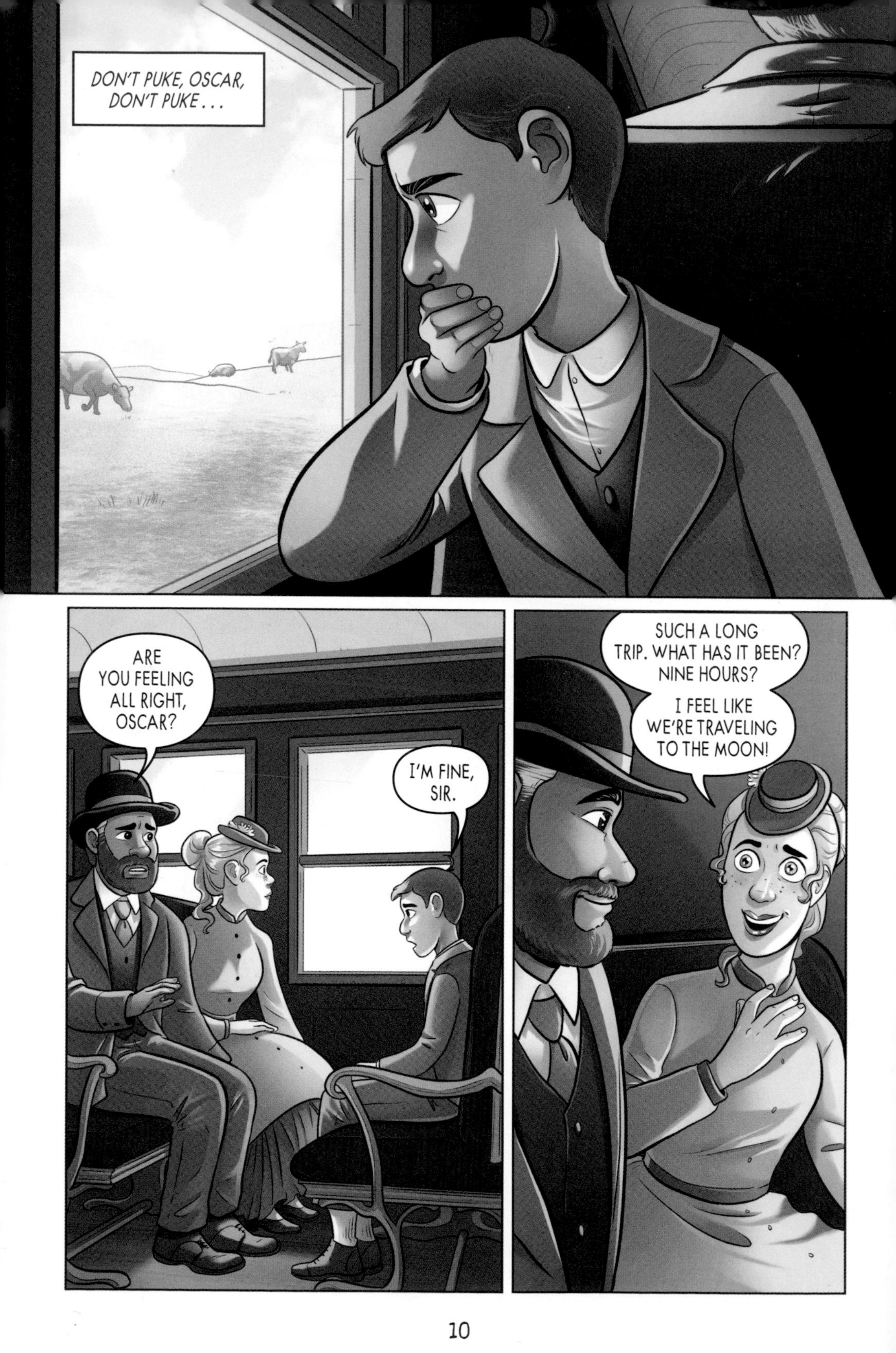
DON'T PUKE, OSCAR, DON'T PUKE . . .
ARE YOU FEELING ALL RIGHT, OSCAR?
I'M FINE, SIR.
SUCH A LONG TRIP. WHAT HAS IT BEEN? NINE HOURS?
I FEEL LIKE WE'RE TRAVELING TO THE MOON!

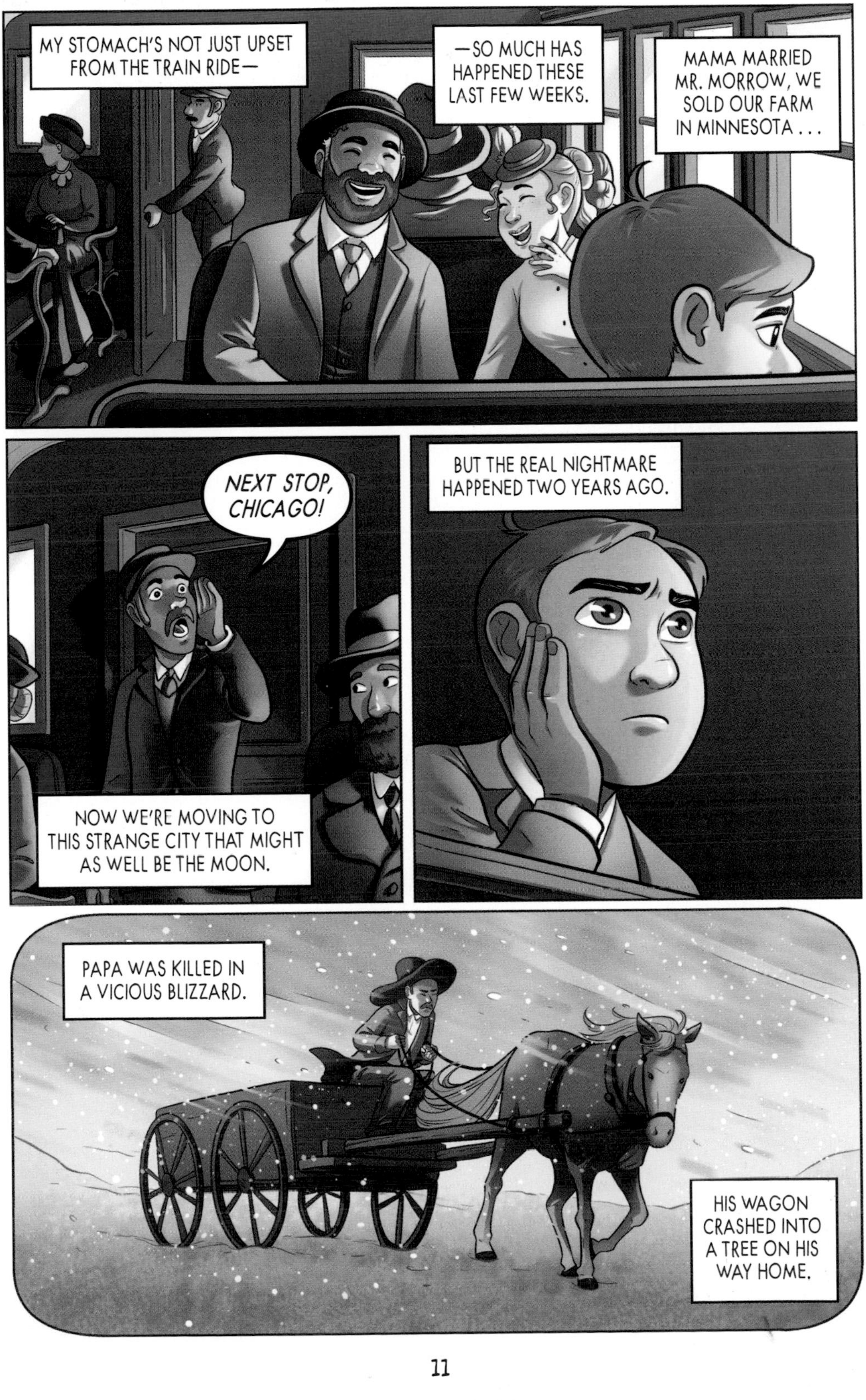
MY STOMACH'S NOT JUST UPSET FROM THE TRAIN RIDE—
—SO MUCH HAS HAPPENED THESE LAST FEW WEEKS.
MAMA MARRIED MR. MORROW, WE SOLD OUR FARM IN MINNESOTA . . .
NEXT STOP, CHICAGO!
NOW WE'RE MOVING TO THIS STRANGE CITY THAT MIGHT AS WELL BE THE MOON.
BUT THE REAL NIGHTMARE HAPPENED TWO YEARS AGO.
PAPA WAS KILLED IN A VICIOUS BLIZZARD.
HIS WAGON CRASHED INTO A TREE ON HIS WAY HOME.

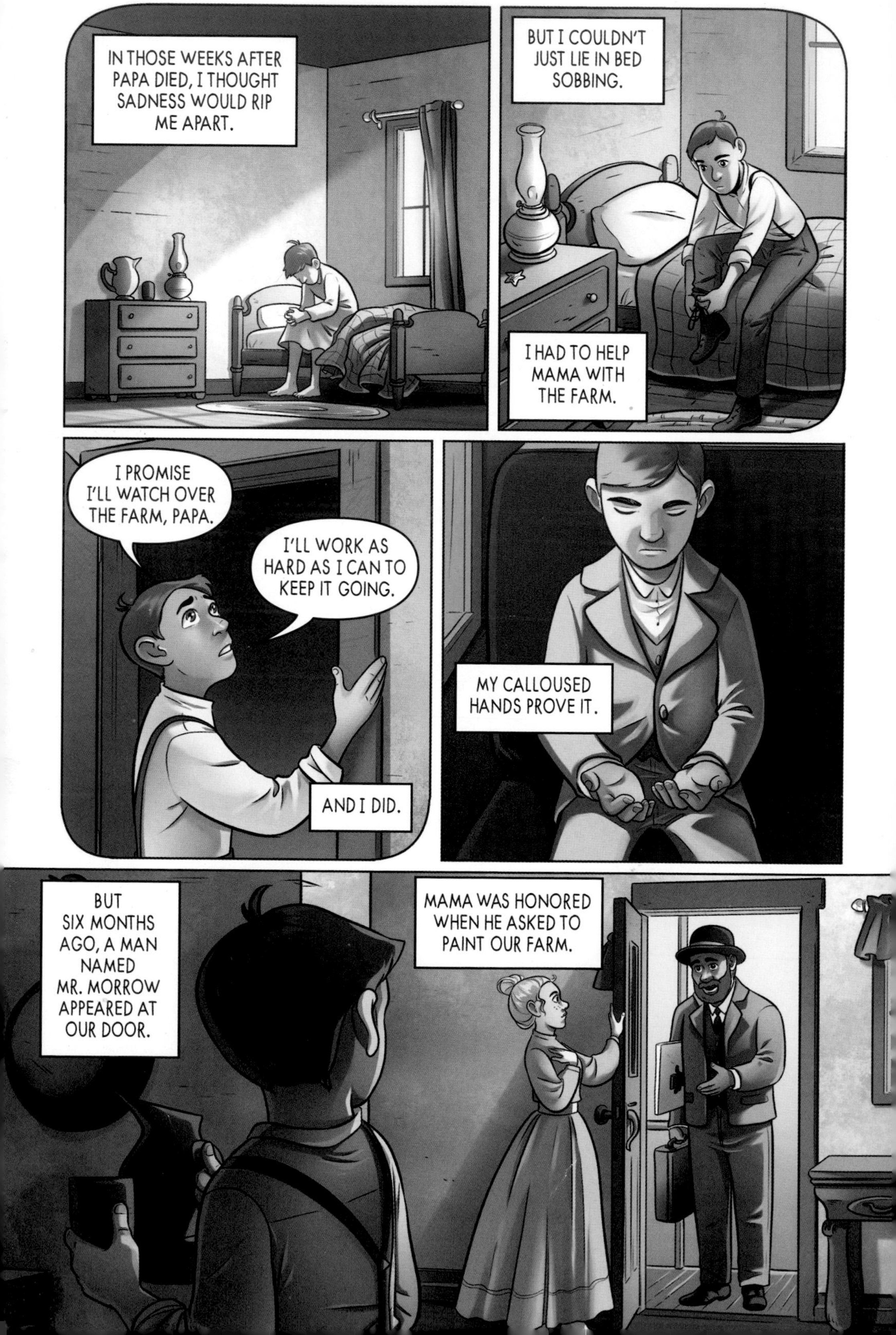
IN THOSE WEEKS AFTER PAPA DIED, I THOUGHT SADNESS WOULD RIP ME APART.
BUT I COULDN'T JUST LIE IN BED SOBBING.
I HAD TO HELP MAMA WITH THE FARM.
I PROMISE I'LL WATCH OVER THE FARM, PAPA.
I'LL WORK AS HARD AS I CAN TO KEEP IT GOING.
AND I DID.
MY CALLOUSED HANDS PROVE IT.
BUT SIX MONTHS AGO, A MAN NAMED MR. MORROW APPEARED AT OUR DOOR.
MAMA WAS HONORED WHEN HE ASKED TO PAINT OUR FARM.

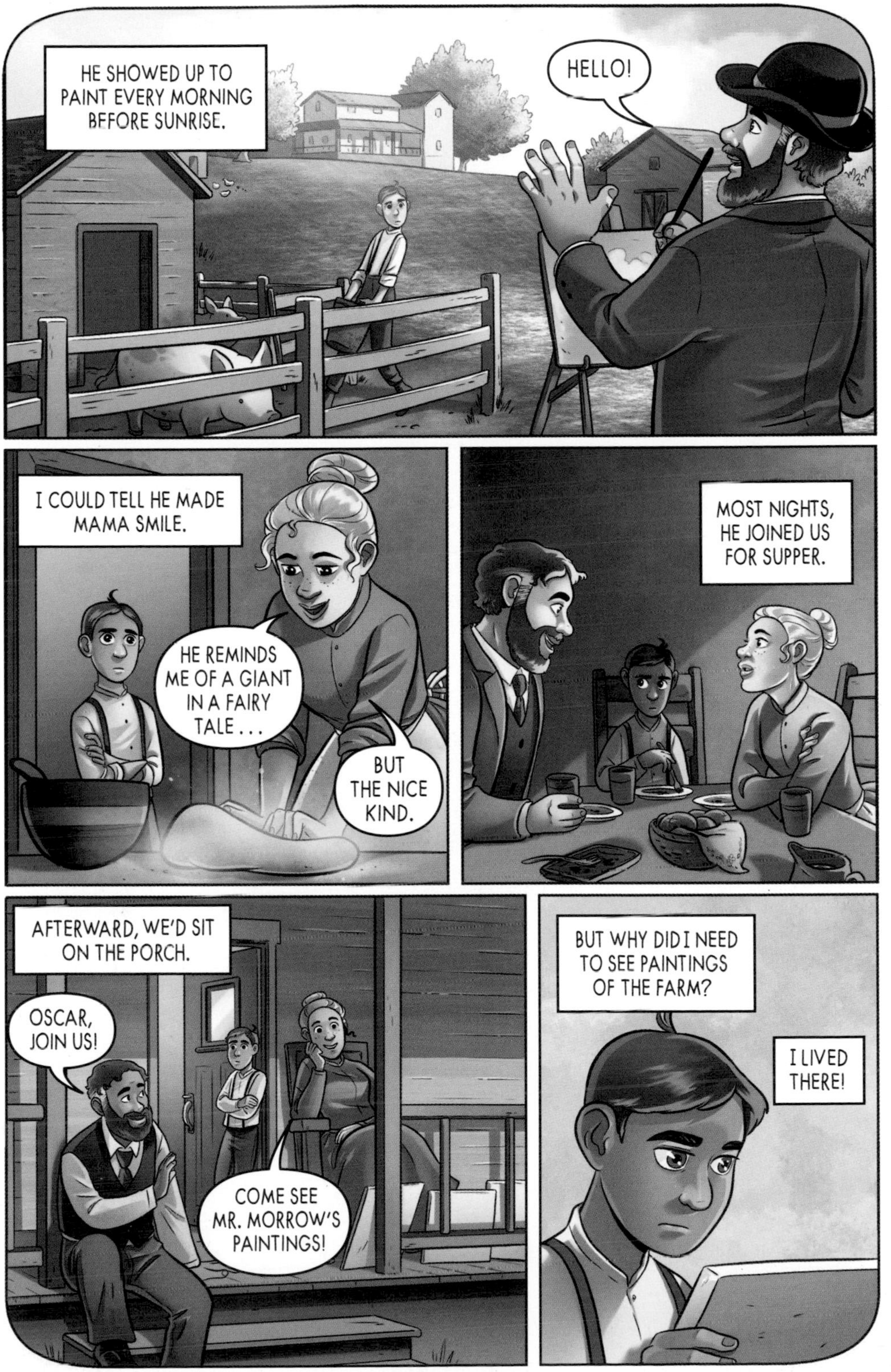
HE SHOWED UP TO PAINT EVERY MORNING BEFORE SUNRISE.
HELLO!
I COULD TELL HE MADE MAMA SMILE.
HE REMINDS ME OF A GIANT IN A FAIRY TALE . . .
BUT THE NICE KIND.
MOST NIGHTS, HE JOINED US FOR SUPPER.
AFTERWARD, WE'D SIT ON THE PORCH.
OSCAR, JOIN US!
COME SEE MR. MORROW'S PAINTINGS!
BUT WHY DID I NEED TO SEE PAINTINGS OF THE FARM?
I LIVED THERE!

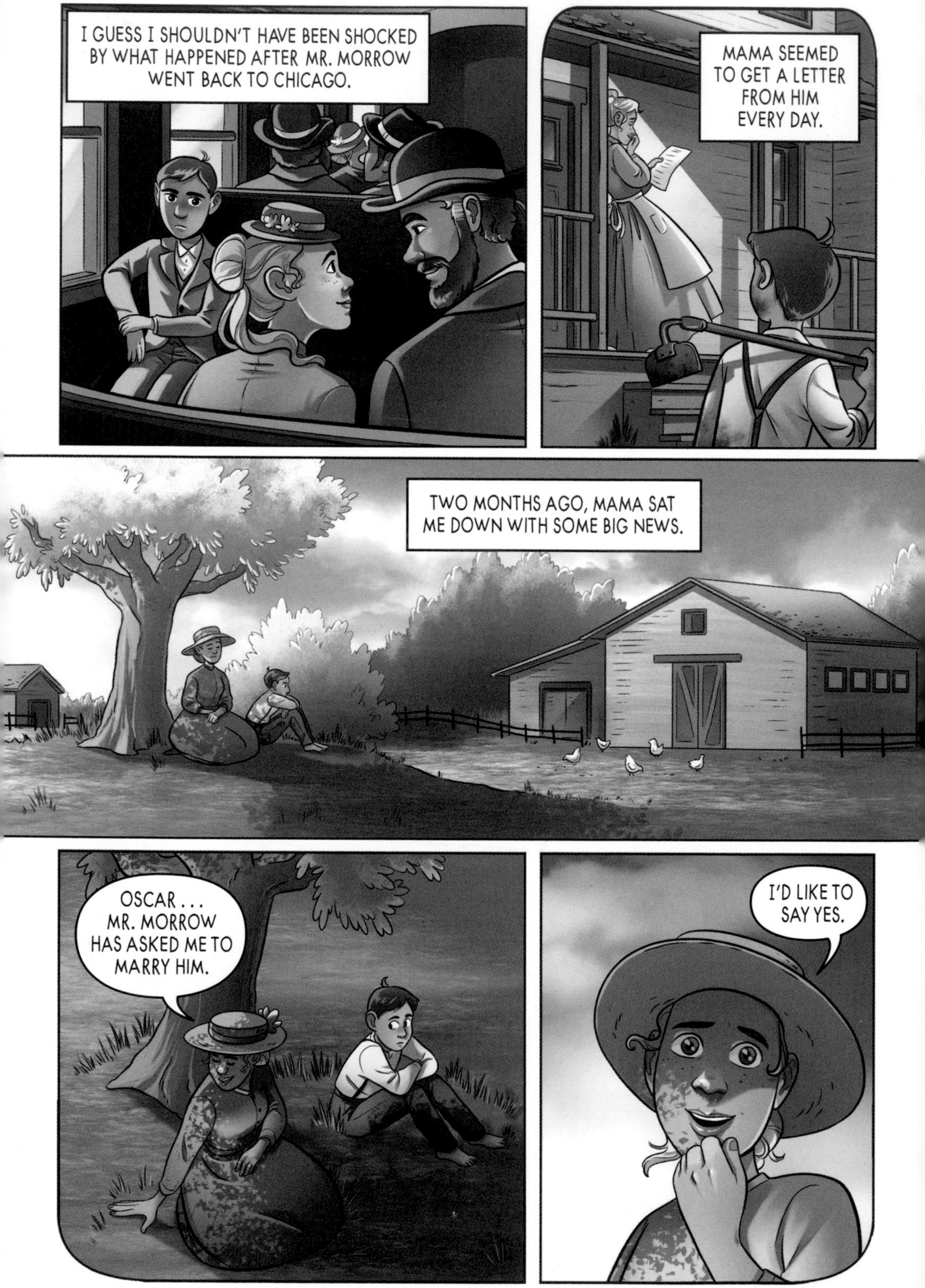
I GUESS I SHOULDN'T HAVE BEEN SHOCKED BY WHAT HAPPENED AFTER MR. MORROW WENT BACK TO CHICAGO.
MAMA SEEMED TO GET A LETTER FROM HIM EVERY DAY.
TWO MONTHS AGO, MAMA SAT ME DOWN WITH SOME BIG NEWS.
OSCAR . . . MR. MORROW HAS ASKED ME TO MARRY HIM.
I'D LIKE TO SAY YES.

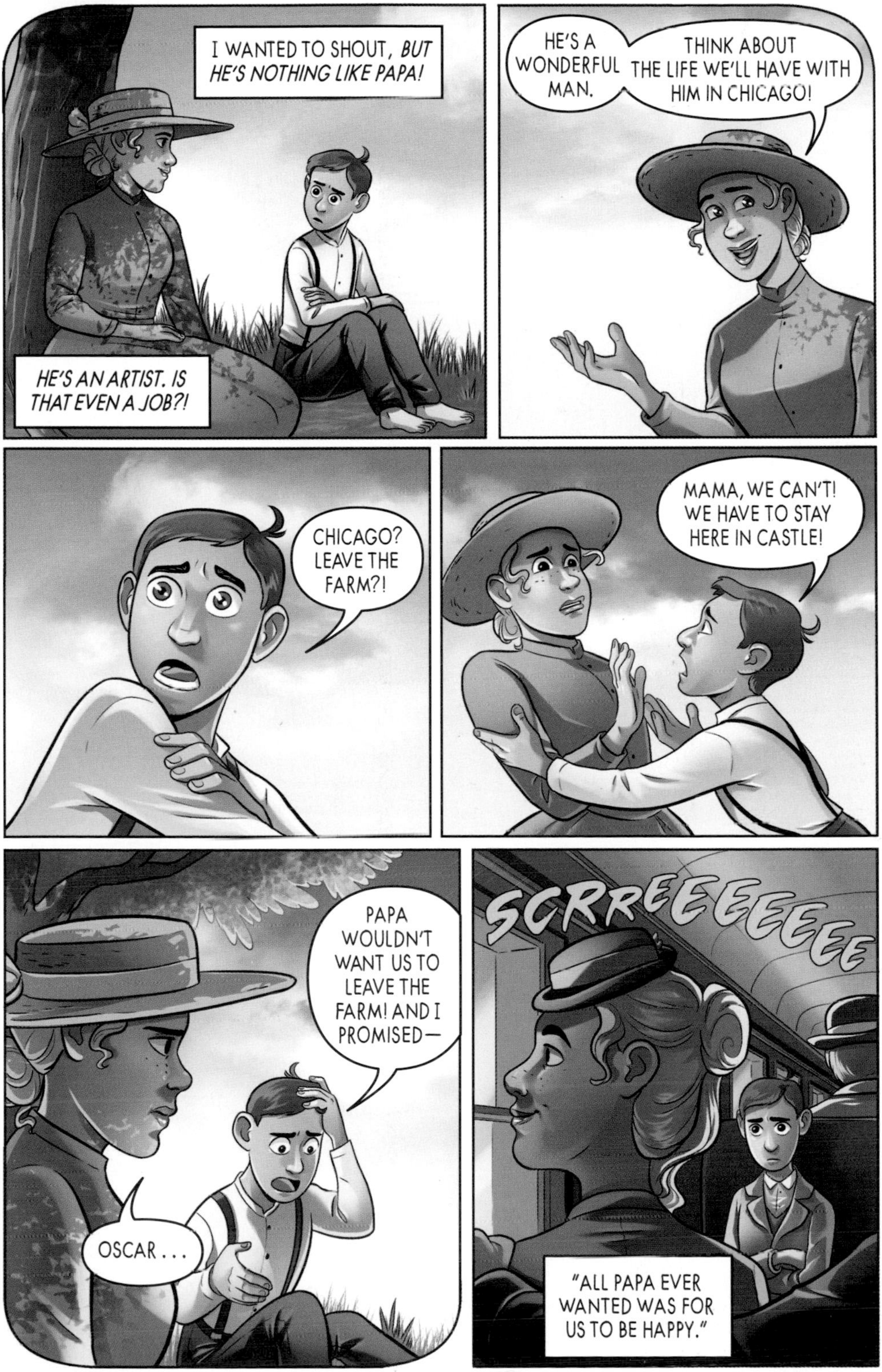
I WANTED TO SHOUT, *BUT HE'S NOTHING LIKE PAPA!*
HE'S AN ARTIST. IS THAT EVEN A JOB?!
HE'S A WONDERFUL MAN.
THINK ABOUT THE LIFE WE'LL HAVE WITH HIM IN CHICAGO!
CHICAGO? LEAVE THE FARM?!
MAMA, WE CAN'T! WE HAVE TO STAY HERE IN CASTLE!
PAPA WOULDN'T WANT US TO LEAVE THE FARM! AND I PROMISED—
OSCAR . . .
SCRREEEEEEEE
"ALL PAPA EVER WANTED WAS FOR US TO BE HAPPY."

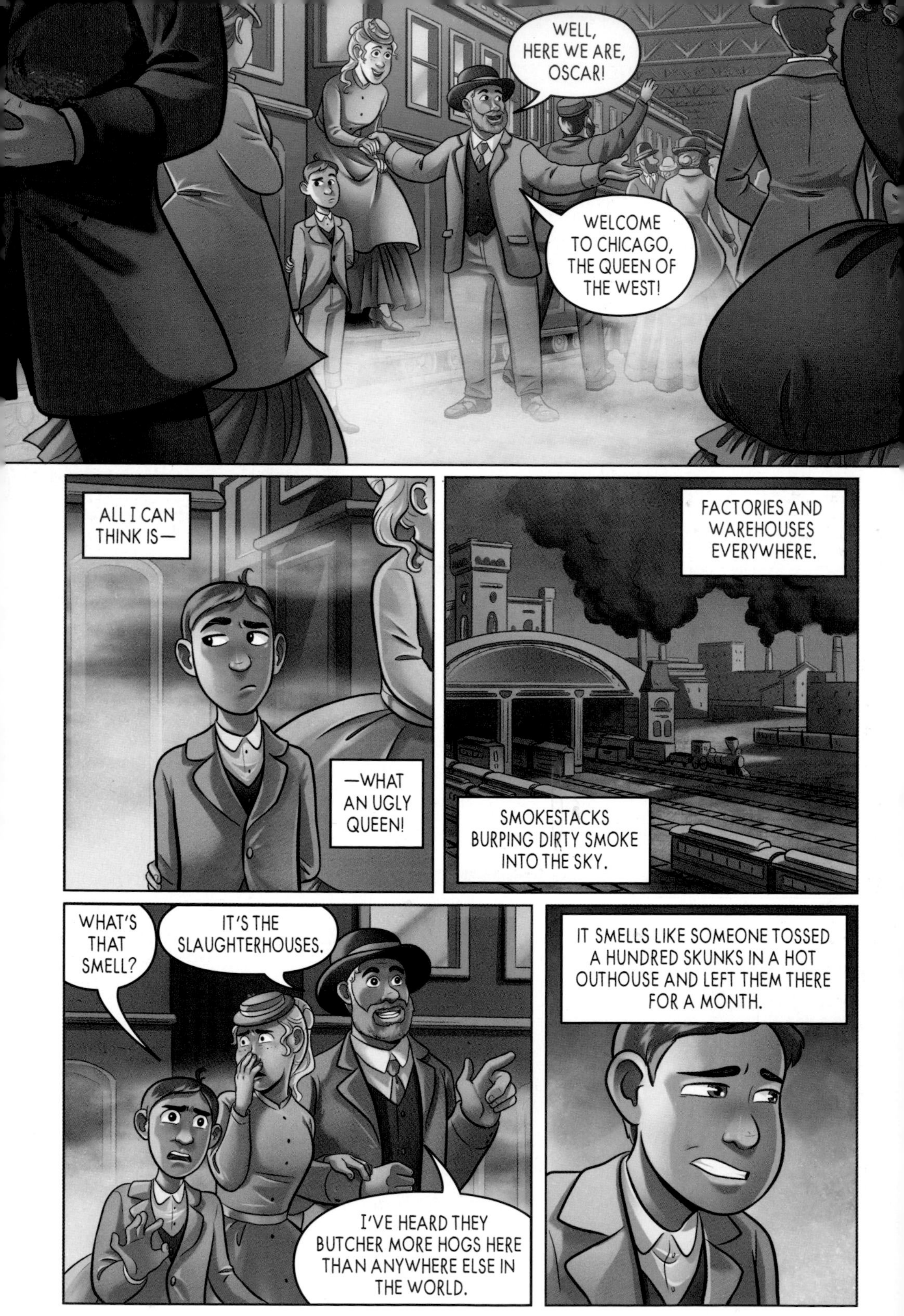
WELL, HERE WE ARE, OSCAR!
WELCOME TO CHICAGO, THE QUEEN OF THE WEST!
ALL I CAN THINK IS—
—WHAT AN UGLY QUEEN!
FACTORIES AND WAREHOUSES EVERYWHERE.
SMOKESTACKS BURPING DIRTY SMOKE INTO THE SKY.
WHAT'S THAT SMELL?
IT'S THE SLAUGHTERHOUSES.
I'VE HEARD THEY BUTCHER MORE HOGS HERE THAN ANYWHERE ELSE IN THE WORLD.
IT SMELLS LIKE SOMEONE TOSSED A HUNDRED SKUNKS IN A HOT OUTHOUSE AND LEFT THEM THERE FOR A MONTH.

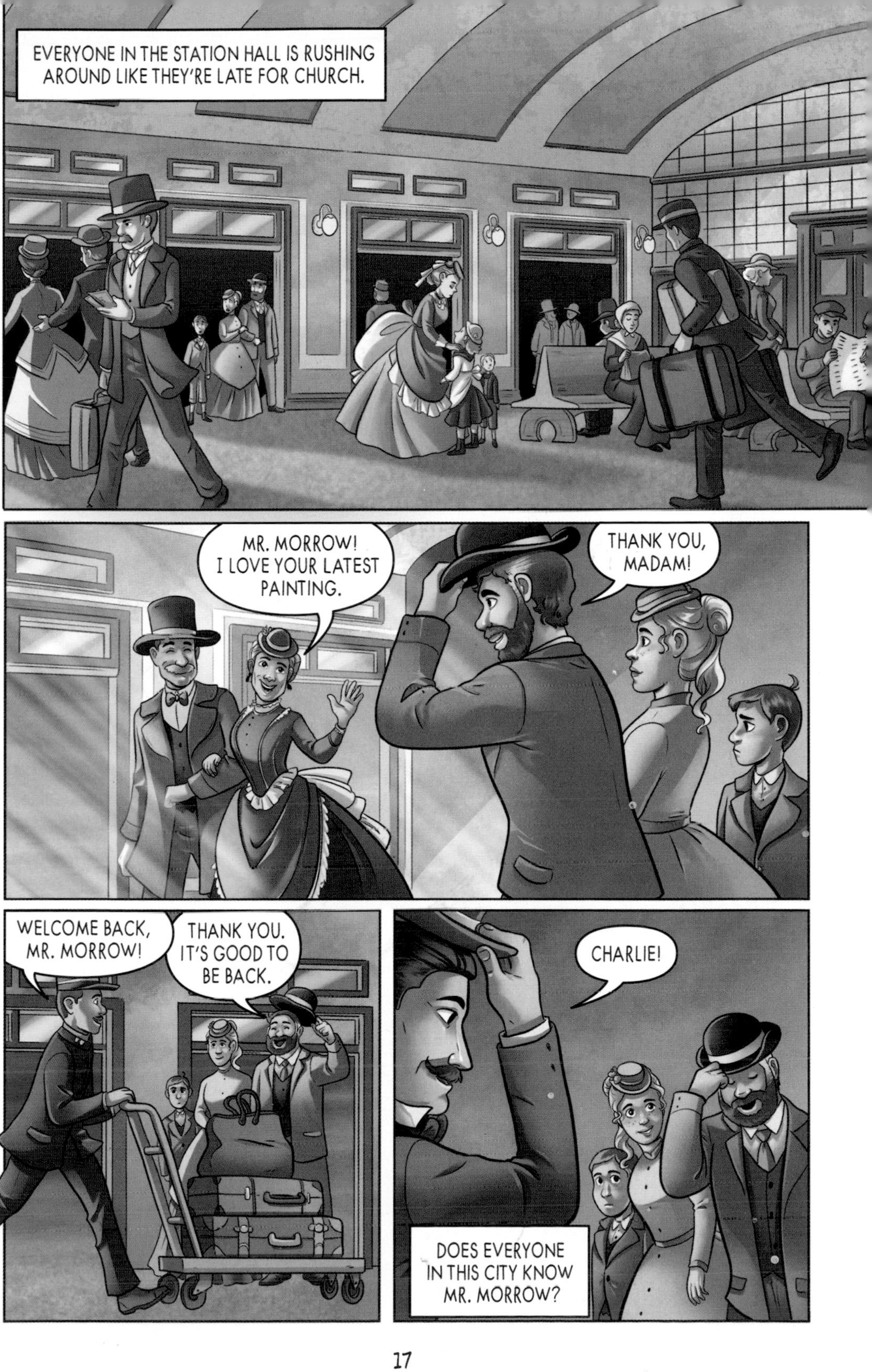
EVERYONE IN THE STATION HALL IS RUSHING AROUND LIKE THEY'RE LATE FOR CHURCH.
MR. MORROW! I LOVE YOUR LATEST PAINTING.
THANK YOU, MADAM!
WELCOME BACK, MR. MORROW!
THANK YOU. IT'S GOOD TO BE BACK.
CHARLIE!
DOES EVERYONE IN THIS CITY KNOW MR. MORROW?

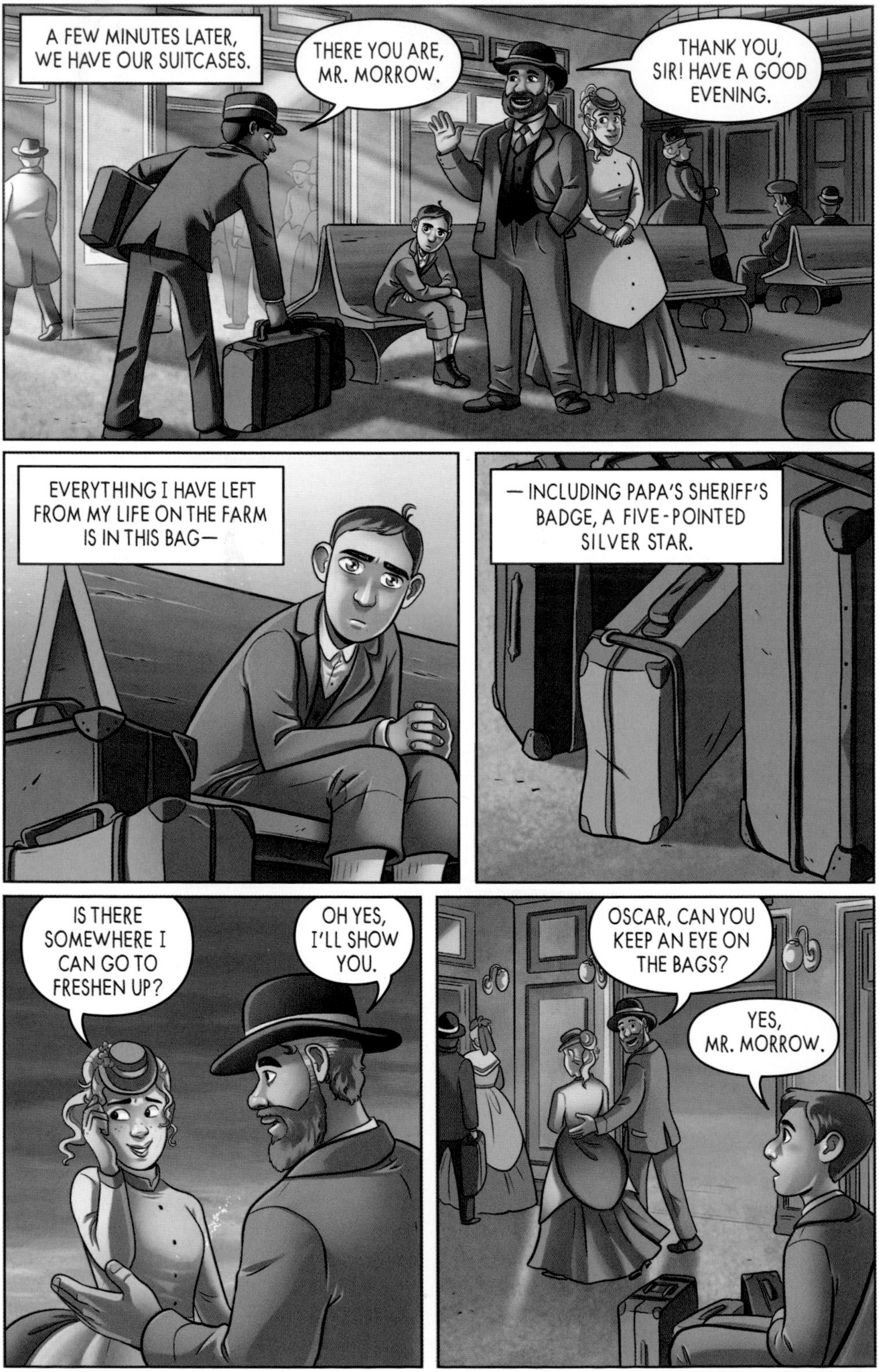
A FEW MINUTES LATER, WE HAVE OUR SUITCASES.
THERE YOU ARE, MR. MORROW.
THANK YOU, SIR! HAVE A GOOD EVENING.
EVERYTHING I HAVE LEFT FROM MY LIFE ON THE FARM IS IN THIS BAG—
—INCLUDING PAPA'S SHERIFF'S BADGE, A FIVE-POINTED SILVER STAR.
IS THERE SOMEWHERE I CAN GO TO FRESHEN UP?
OH YES, I'LL SHOW YOU.
OSCAR, CAN YOU KEEP AN EYE ON THE BAGS?
YES, MR. MORROW.

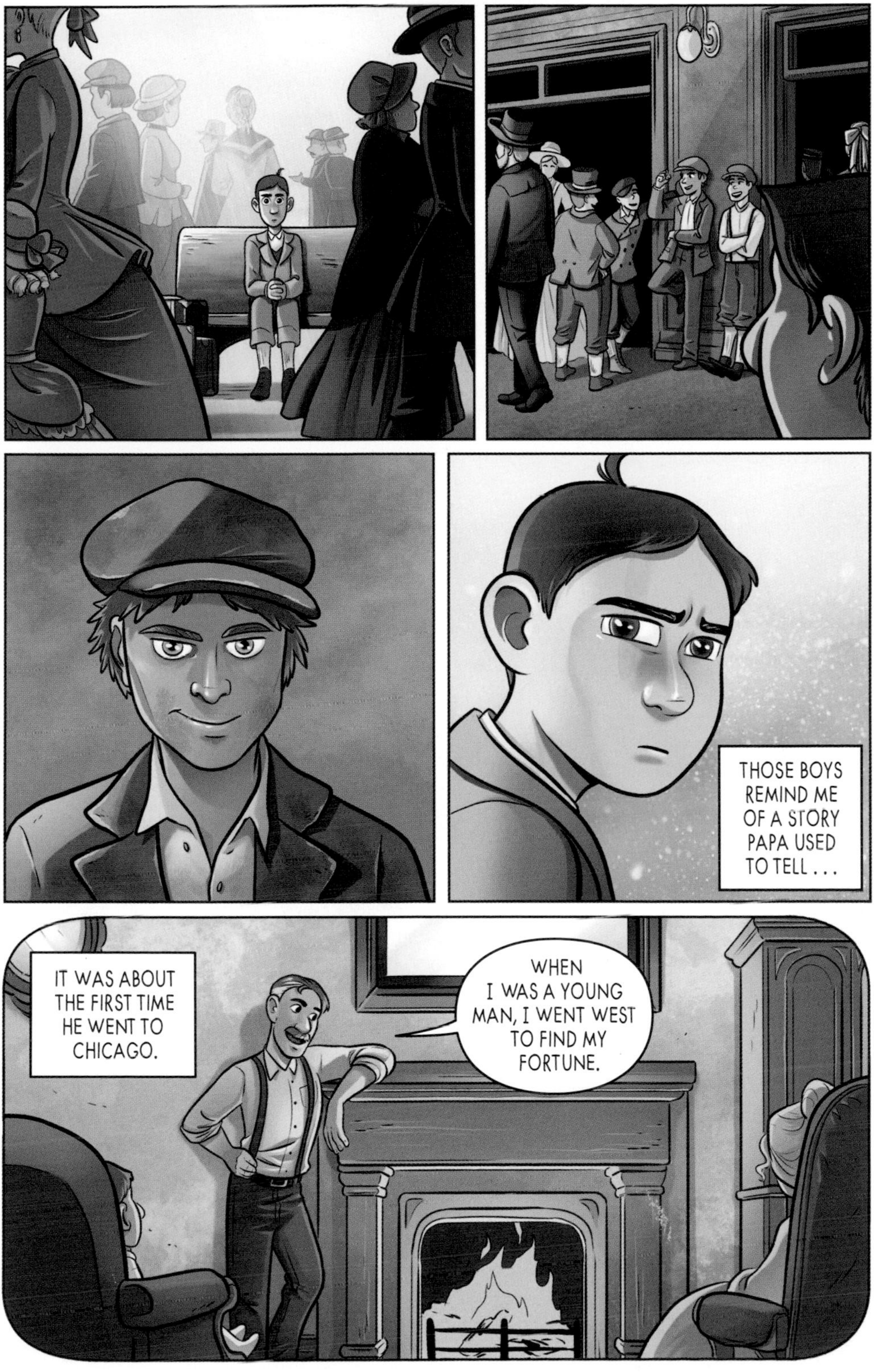
THOSE BOYS REMIND ME OF A STORY PAPA USED TO TELL . . .
IT WAS ABOUT THE FIRST TIME HE WENT TO CHICAGO.
WHEN I WAS A YOUNG MAN, I WENT WEST TO FIND MY FORTUNE.

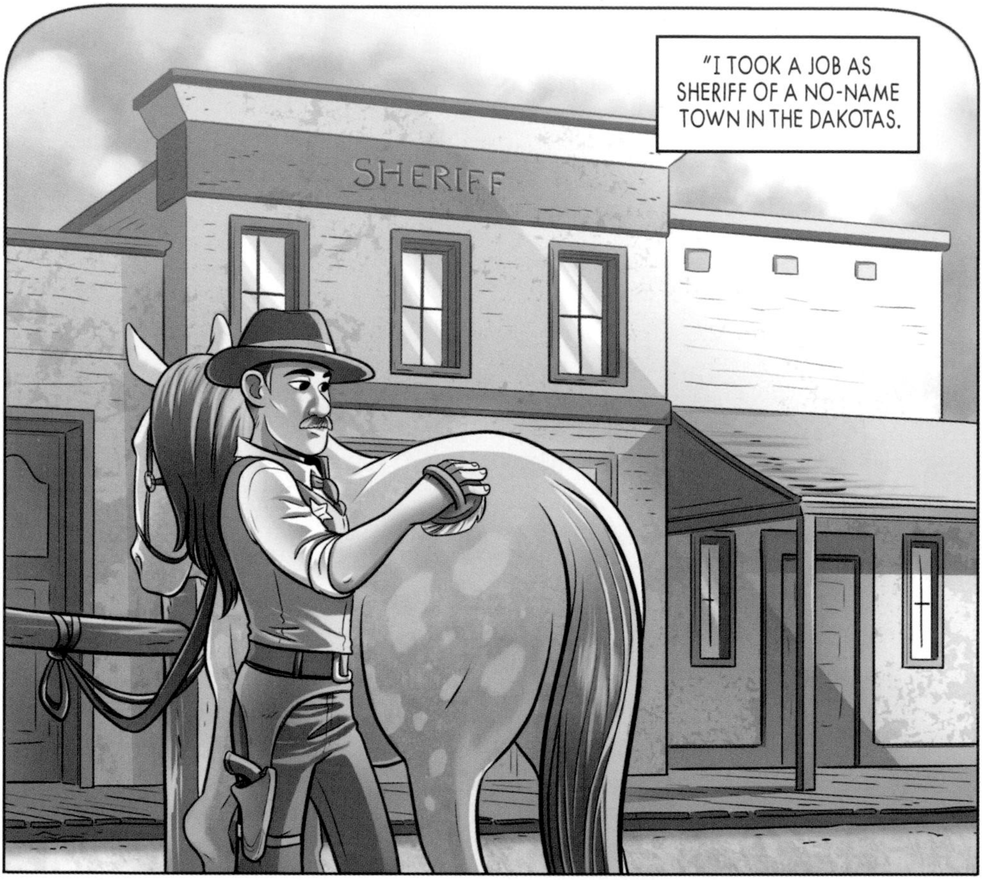
"I TOOK A JOB AS SHERIFF OF A NO-NAME TOWN IN THE DAKOTAS.
SHERIFF

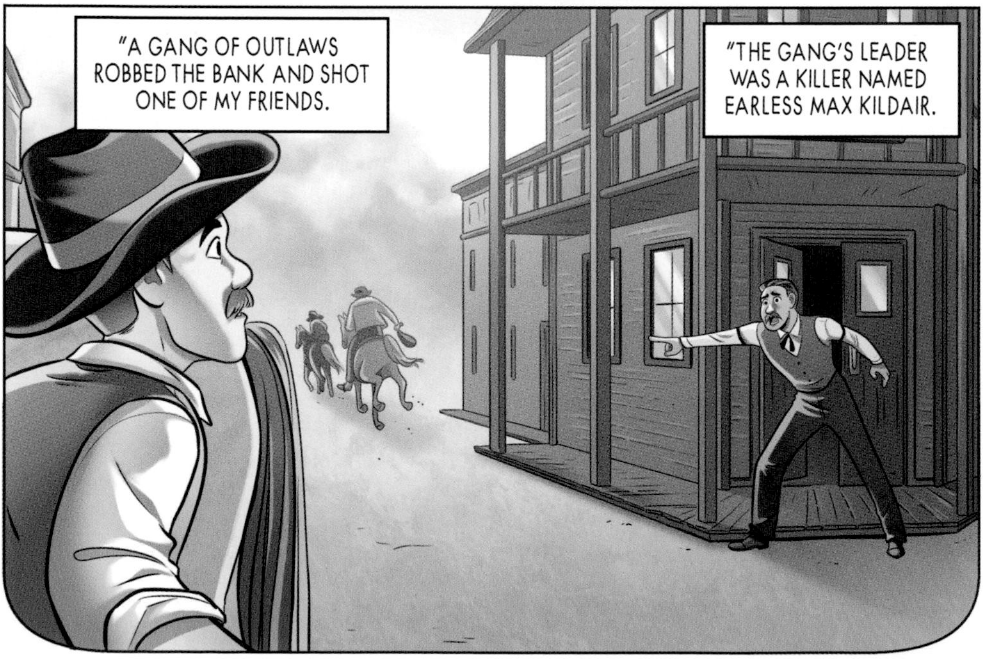
"A GANG OF OUTLAWS ROBBED THE BANK AND SHOT ONE OF MY FRIENDS.
"THE GANG'S LEADER WAS A KILLER NAMED EARLESS MAX KILDAIR.

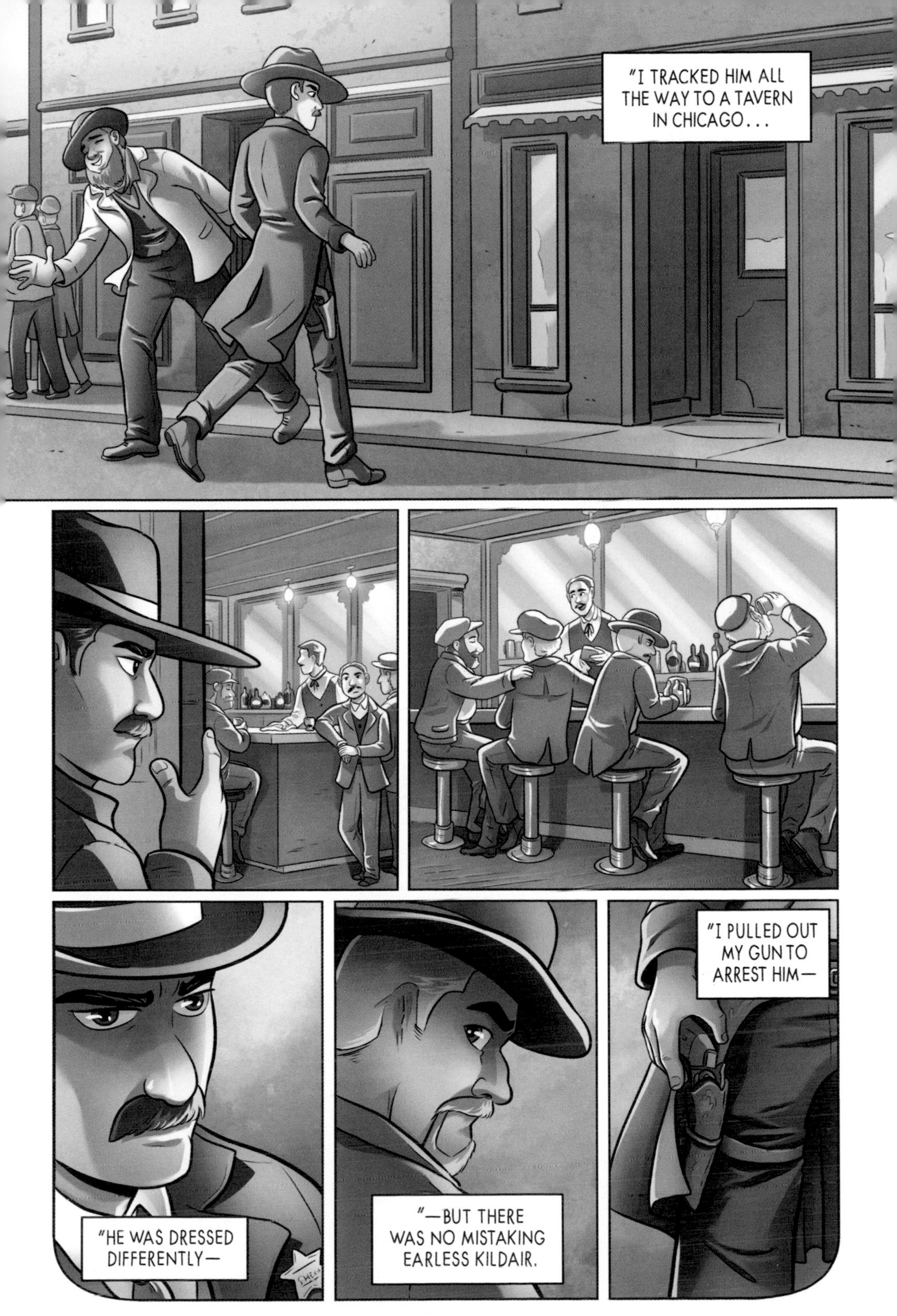
"I TRACKED HIM ALL THE WAY TO A TAVERN IN CHICAGO...
"HE WAS DRESSED DIFFERENTLY—
"—BUT THERE WAS NO MISTAKING EARLESS KILDAIR.
"I PULLED OUT MY GUN TO ARREST HIM—

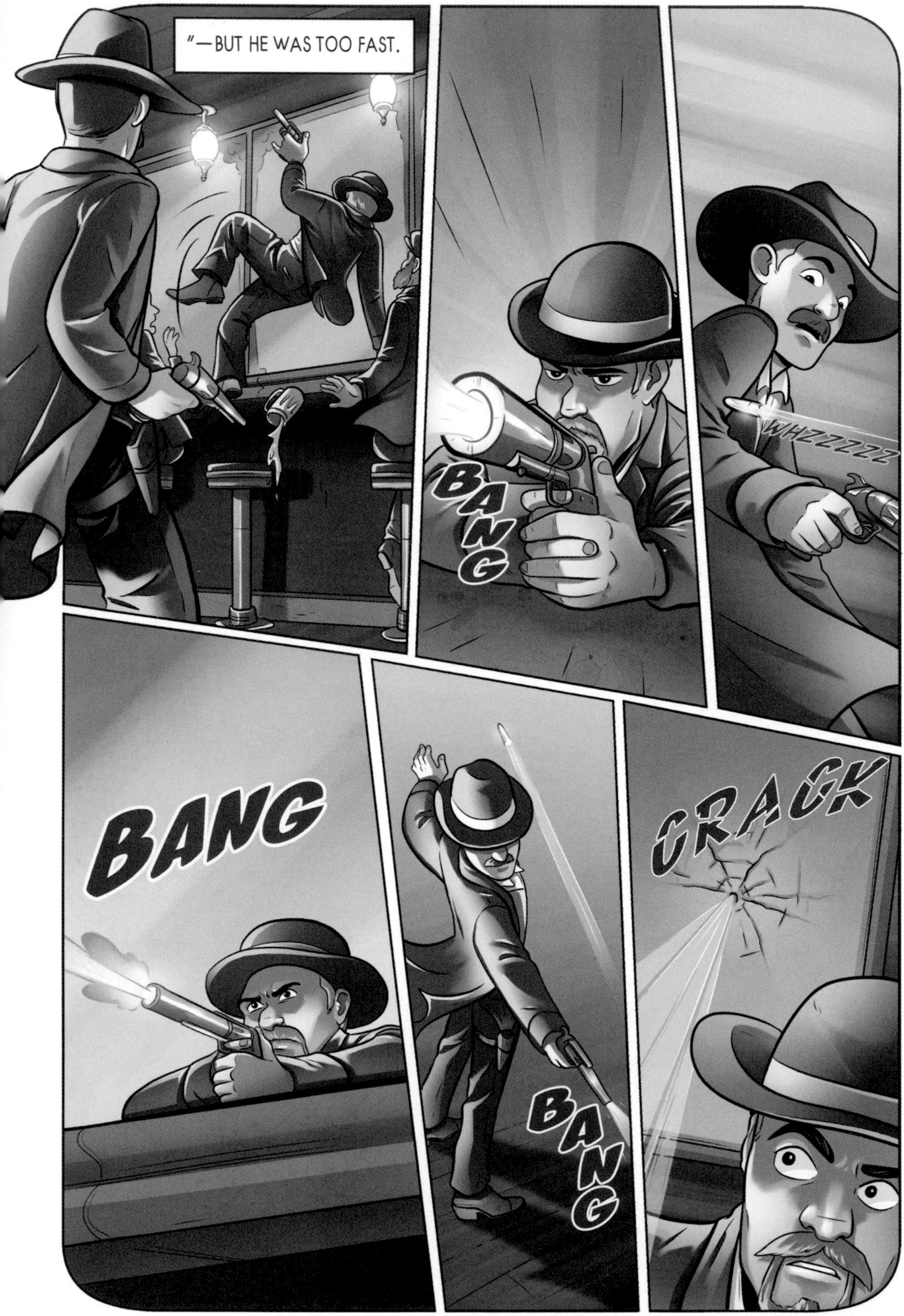
"—BUT HE WAS TOO FAST.
BANG
WHZZZZZZ
BANG
BANG
CRACK

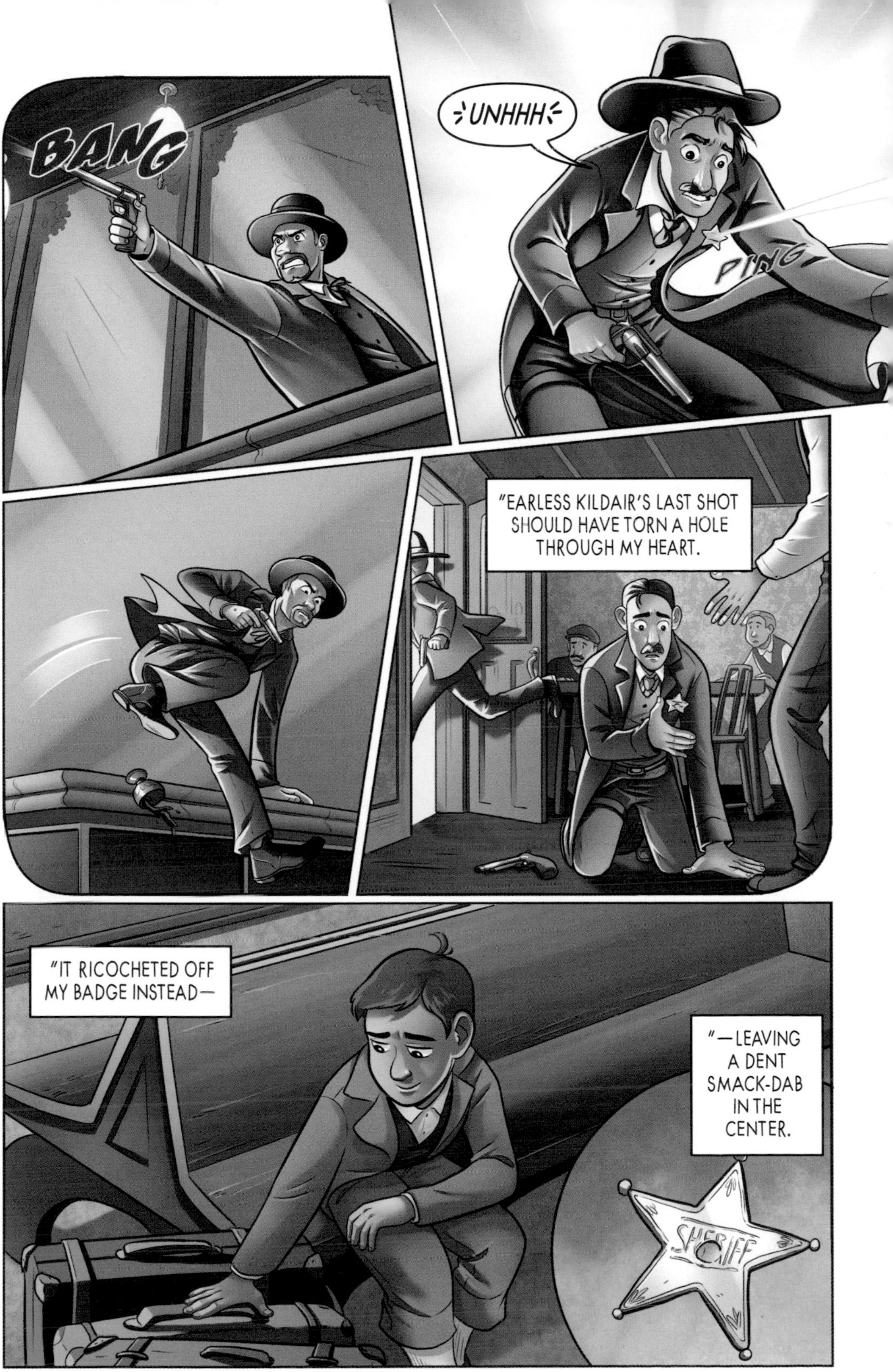
BANG
UNHHH
PING
"EARLESS KILDAIR'S LAST SHOT SHOULD HAVE TORN A HOLE THROUGH MY HEART.
"IT RICOCHETED OFF MY BADGE INSTEAD—
"—LEAVING A DENT SMACK-DAB IN THE CENTER.
SHERIFF

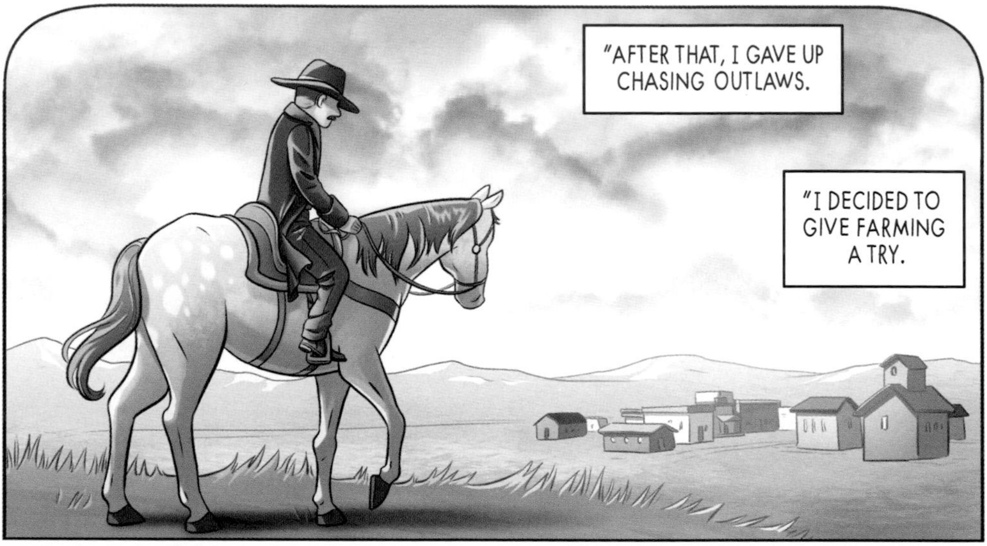
"AFTER THAT, I GAVE UP CHASING OUTLAWS.
"I DECIDED TO GIVE FARMING A TRY.
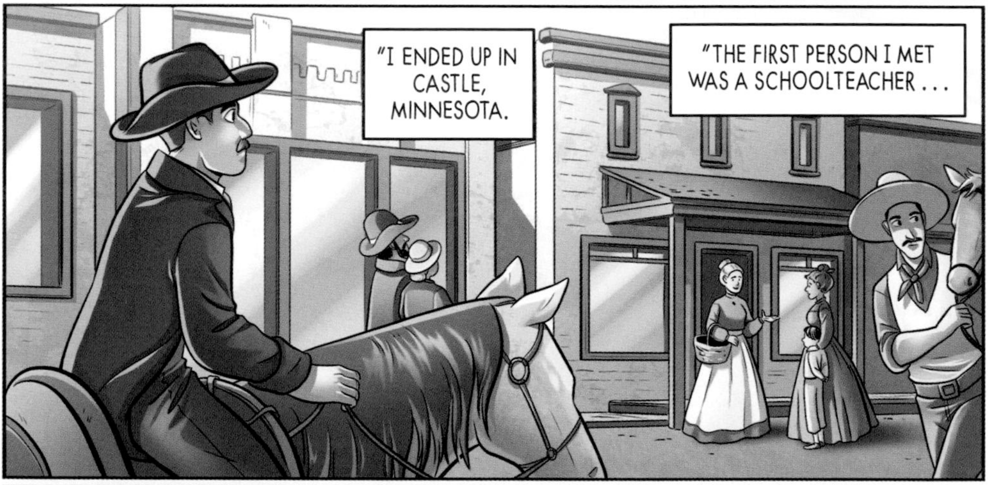
"I ENDED UP IN CASTLE, MINNESOTA.
"THE FIRST PERSON I MET WAS A SCHOOLTEACHER . . .
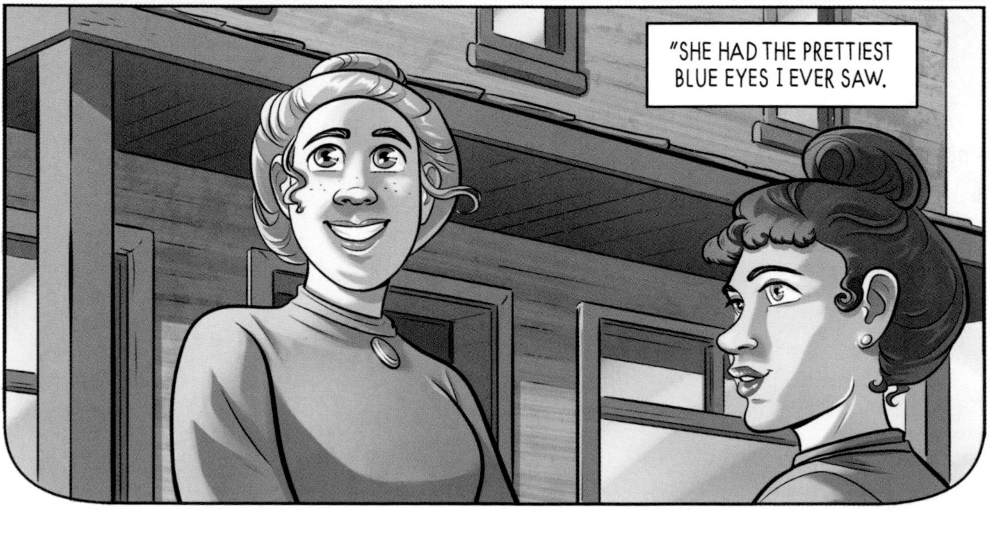
"SHE HAD THE PRETTIEST BLUE EYES I EVER SAW.

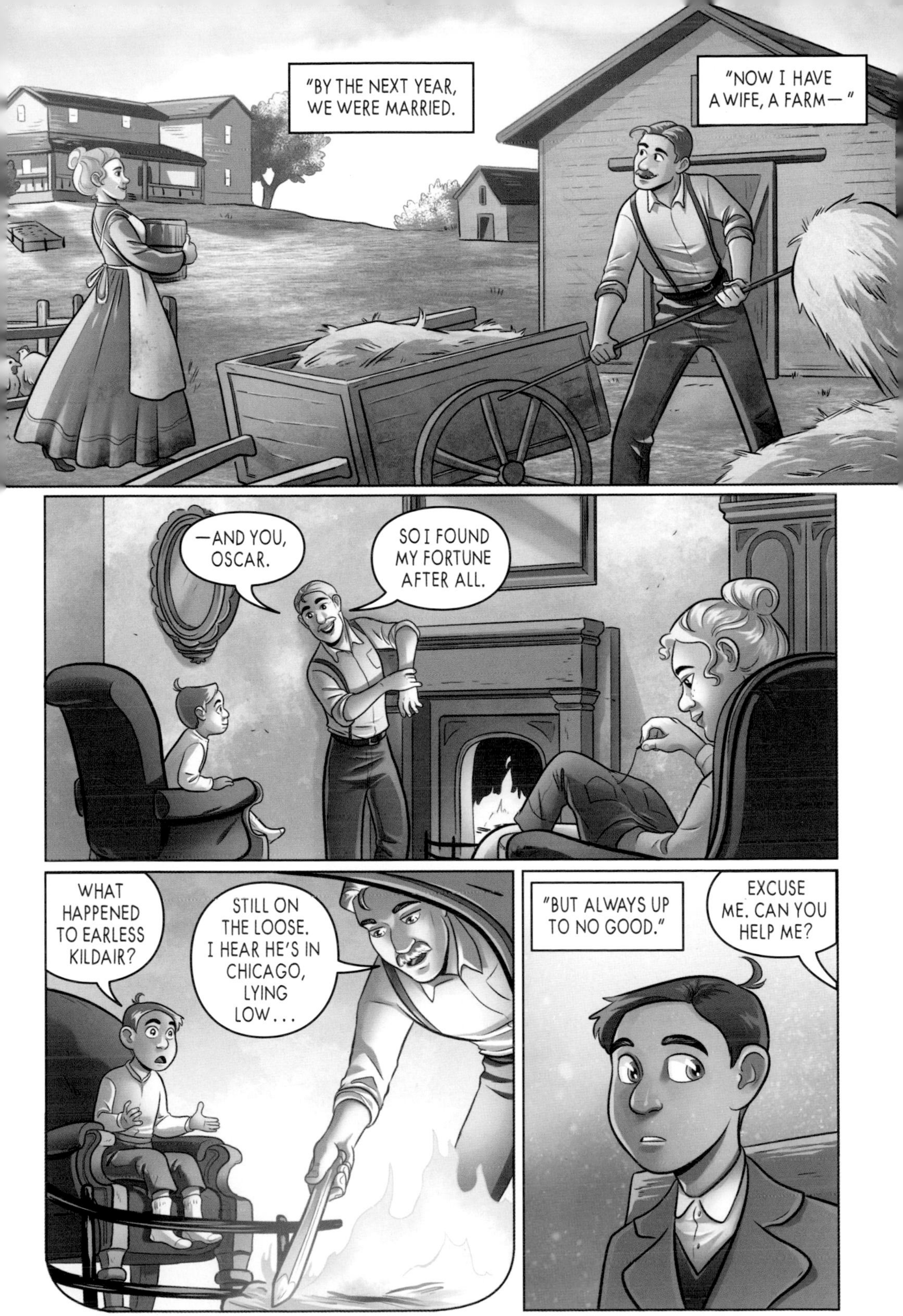
"BY THE NEXT YEAR, WE WERE MARRIED.
"NOW I HAVE A WIFE, A FARM— "
—AND YOU, OSCAR.
SO I FOUND MY FORTUNE AFTER ALL.
WHAT HAPPENED TO EARLESS KILDAIR?
STILL ON THE LOOSE. I HEAR HE'S IN CHICAGO, LYING LOW . . .
"BUT ALWAYS UP TO NO GOOD."
EXCUSE ME. CAN YOU HELP ME?

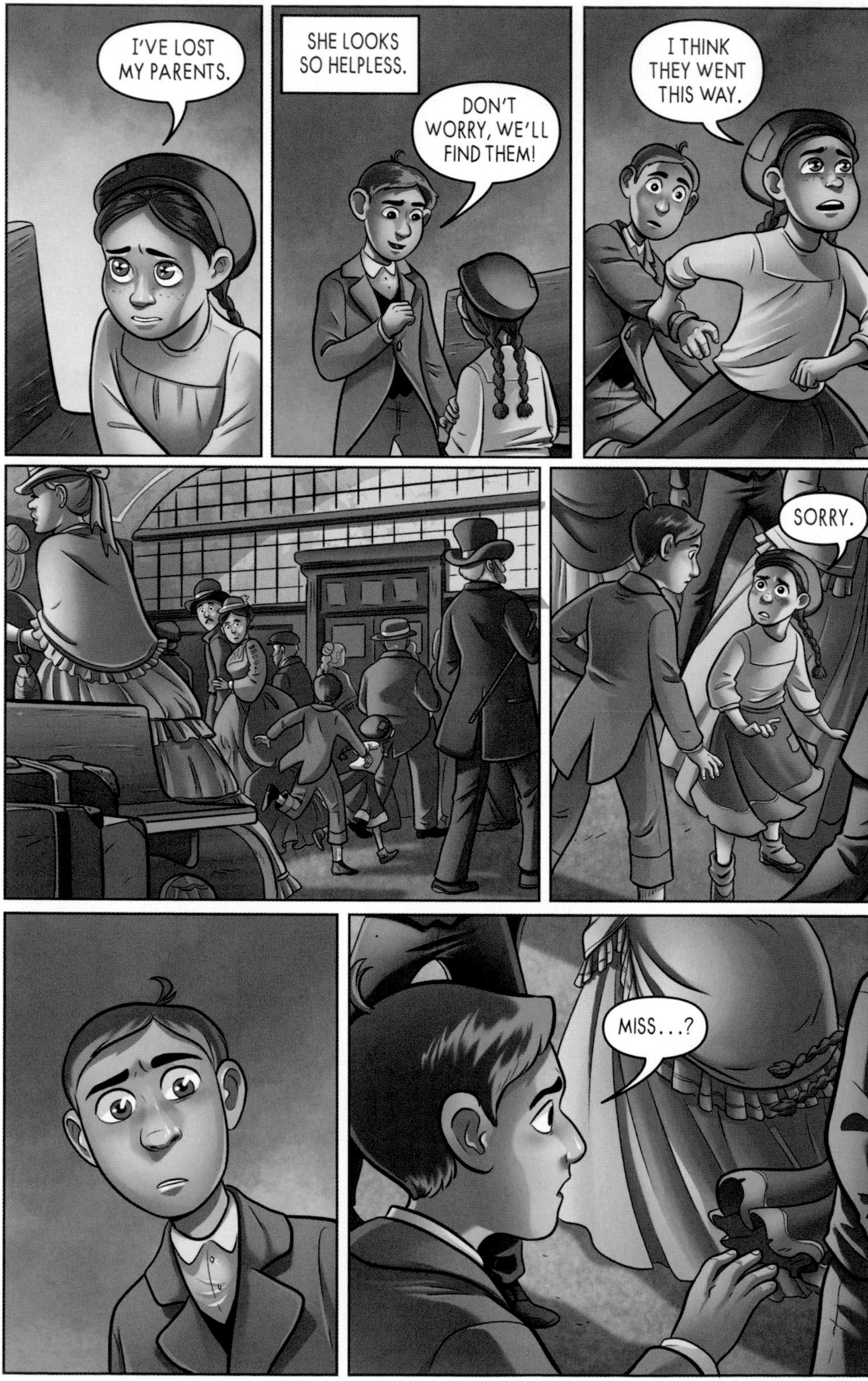
I'VE LOST MY PARENTS.
SHE LOOKS SO HELPLESS.
DON'T WORRY, WE'LL FIND THEM!
I THINK THEY WENT THIS WAY.
SORRY.
MISS...?

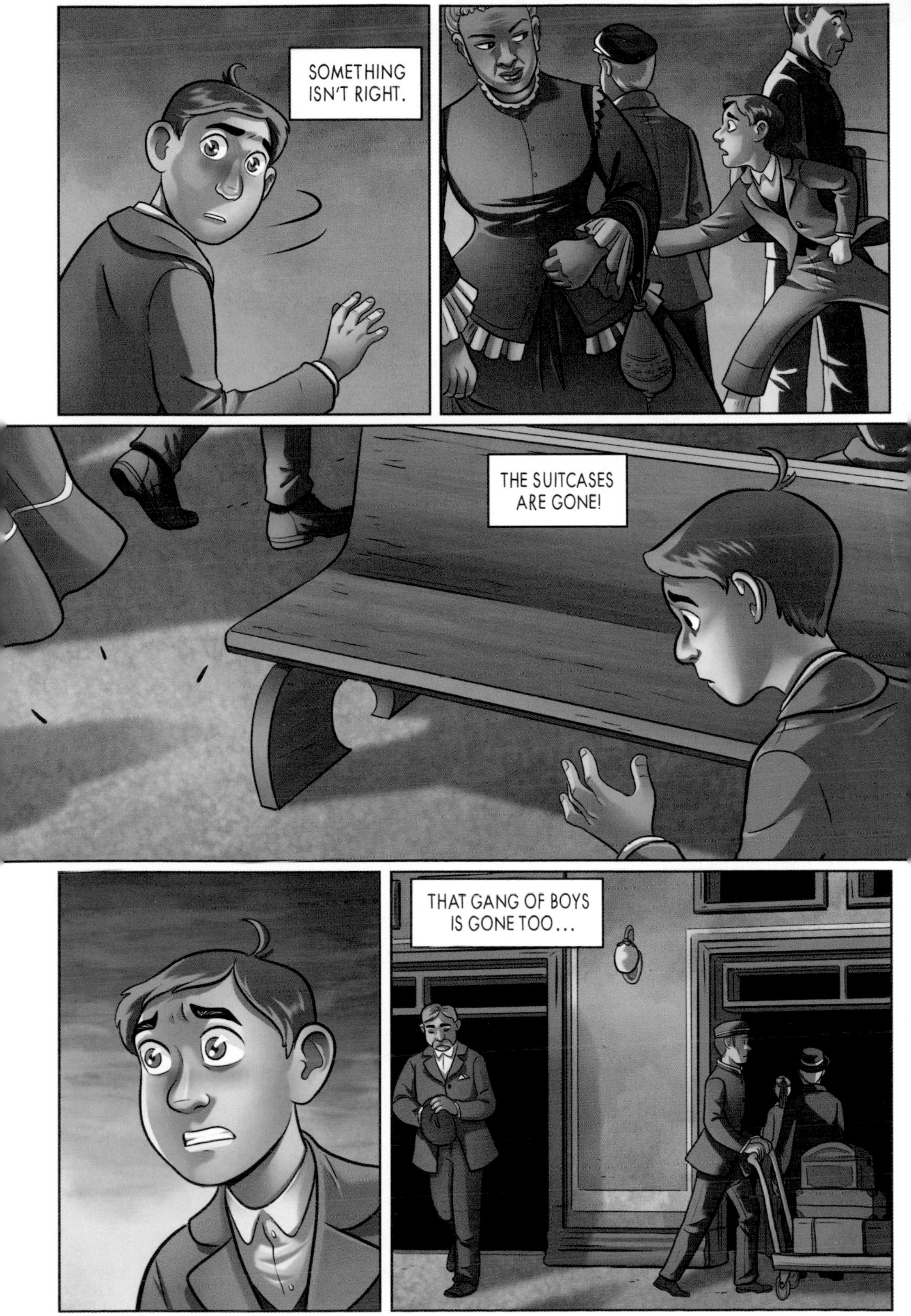
SOMETHING ISN'T RIGHT.
THE SUITCASES ARE GONE!
THAT GANG OF BOYS IS GONE TOO...

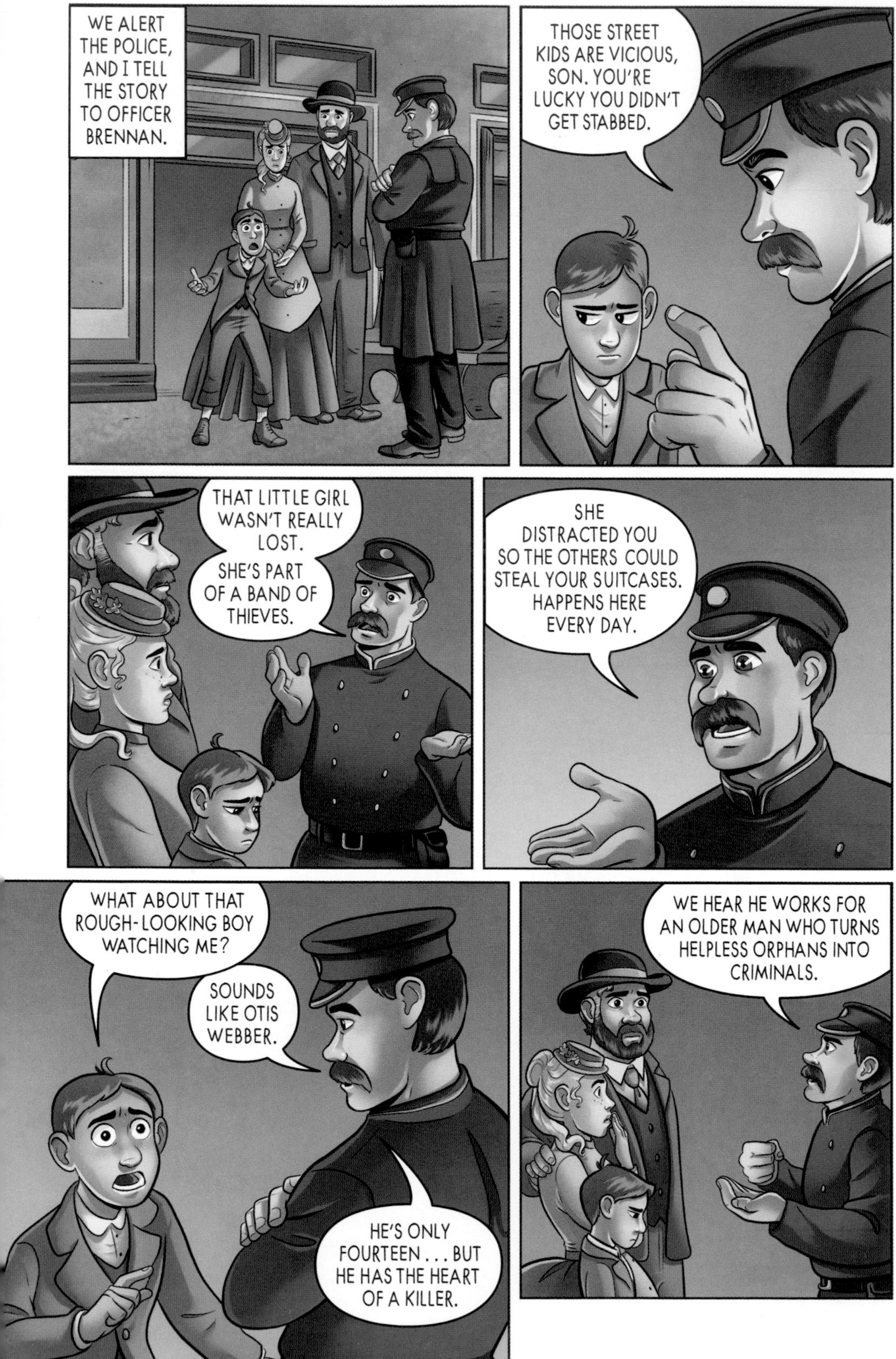
WE ALERT THE POLICE, AND I TELL THE STORY TO OFFICER BRENNAN.
THOSE STREET KIDS ARE VICIOUS, SON. YOU'RE LUCKY YOU DIDN'T GET STABBED.
THAT LITTLE GIRL WASN'T REALLY LOST.
SHE'S PART OF A BAND OF THIEVES.
SHE DISTRACTED YOU SO THE OTHERS COULD STEAL YOUR SUITCASES. HAPPENS HERE EVERY DAY.
WHAT ABOUT THAT ROUGH-LOOKING BOY WATCHING ME?
SOUNDS LIKE OTIS WEBBER.
HE'S ONLY FOURTEEN . . . BUT HE HAS THE HEART OF A KILLER.
WE HEAR HE WORKS FOR AN OLDER MAN WHO TURNS HELPLESS ORPHANS INTO CRIMINALS.

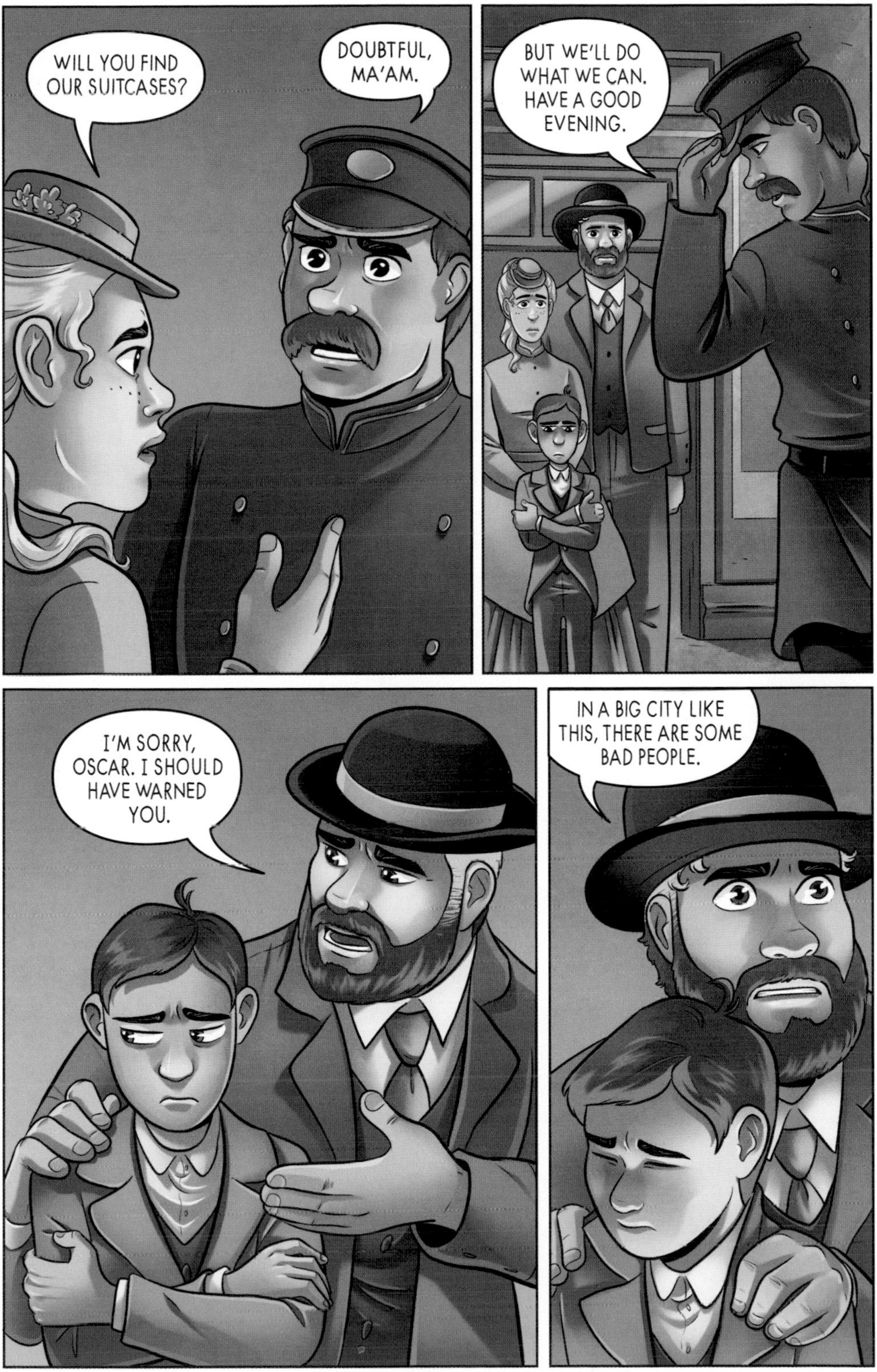
WILL YOU FIND OUR SUITCASES?
DOUBTFUL, MA'AM.
BUT WE'LL DO WHAT WE CAN. HAVE A GOOD EVENING.
I'M SORRY, OSCAR. I SHOULD HAVE WARNED YOU.
IN A BIG CITY LIKE THIS, THERE ARE SOME BAD PEOPLE.

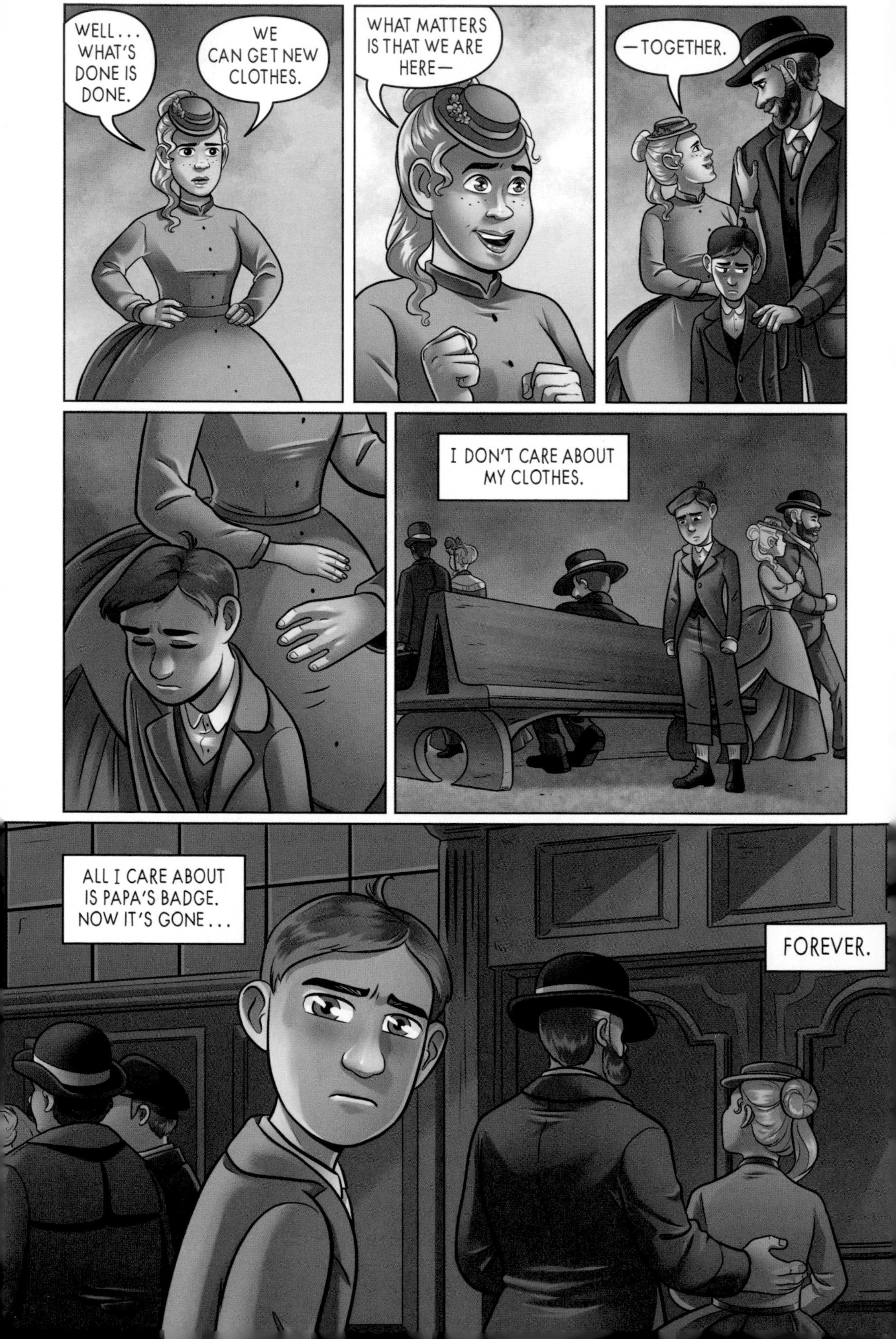
WELL . . . WHAT'S DONE IS DONE.
WE CAN GET NEW CLOTHES.
WHAT MATTERS IS THAT WE ARE HERE—
—TOGETHER.
I DON'T CARE ABOUT MY CLOTHES.
ALL I CARE ABOUT IS PAPA'S BADGE. NOW IT'S GONE . . .
FOREVER.

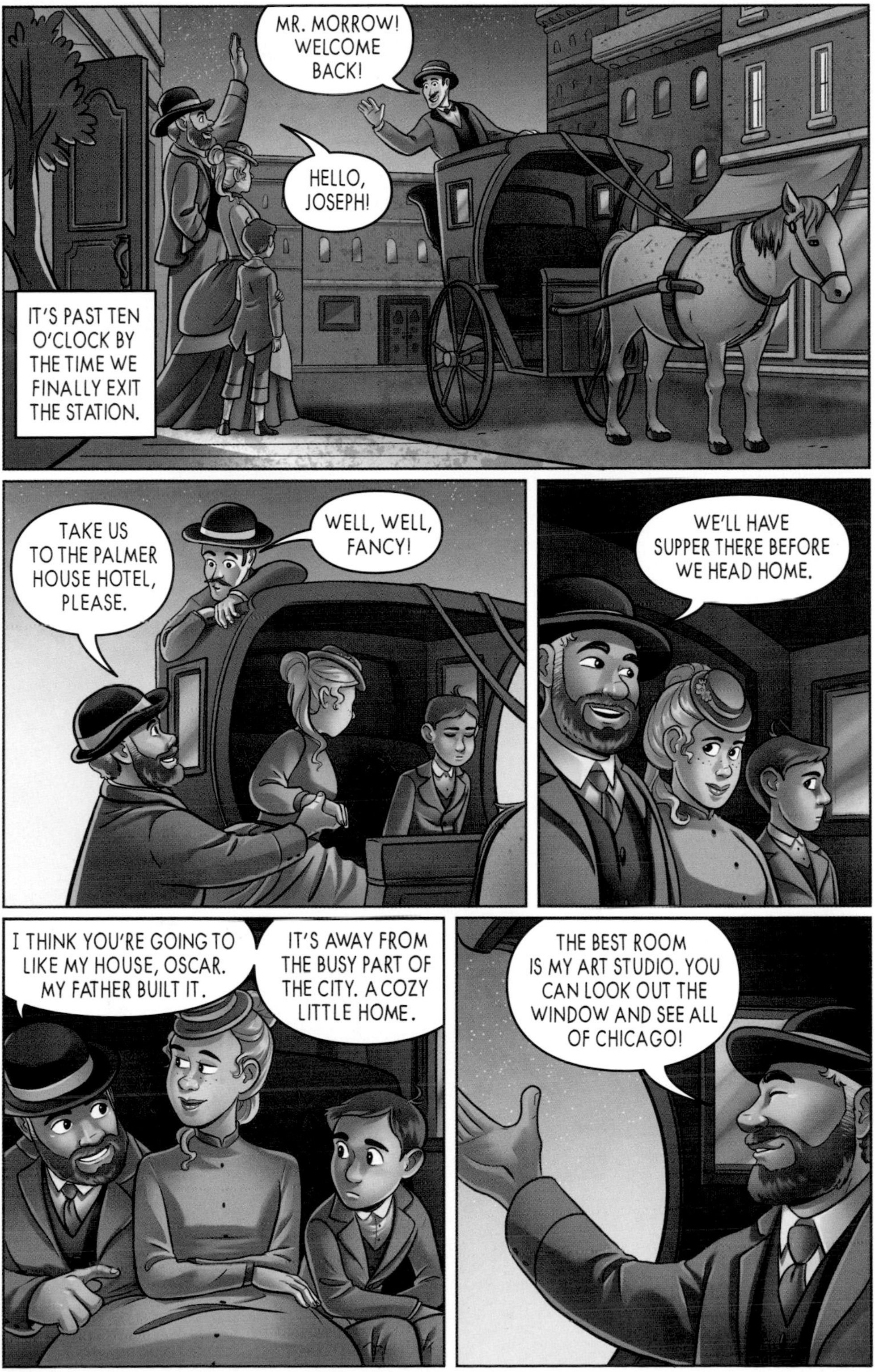
IT'S PAST TEN O'CLOCK BY THE TIME WE FINALLY EXIT THE STATION.
MR. MORROW! WELCOME BACK!
HELLO, JOSEPH!
TAKE US TO THE PALMER HOUSE HOTEL, PLEASE.
WELL, WELL, FANCY!
WE'LL HAVE SUPPER THERE BEFORE WE HEAD HOME.
I THINK YOU'RE GOING TO LIKE MY HOUSE, OSCAR. MY FATHER BUILT IT.
IT'S AWAY FROM THE BUSY PART OF THE CITY. A COZY LITTLE HOME.
THE BEST ROOM IS MY ART STUDIO. YOU CAN LOOK OUT THE WINDOW AND SEE ALL OF CHICAGO!

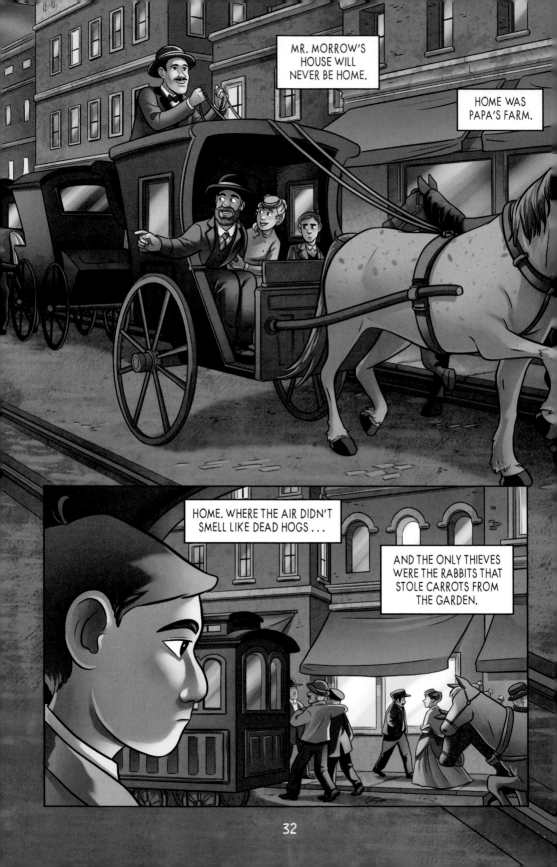

MR. MORROW'S HOUSE WILL NEVER BE HOME.

HOME WAS PAPA'S FARM.

HOME. WHERE THE AIR DIDN'T SMELL LIKE DEAD HOGS . . .

AND THE ONLY THIEVES WERE THE RABBITS THAT STOLE CARROTS FROM THE GARDEN.

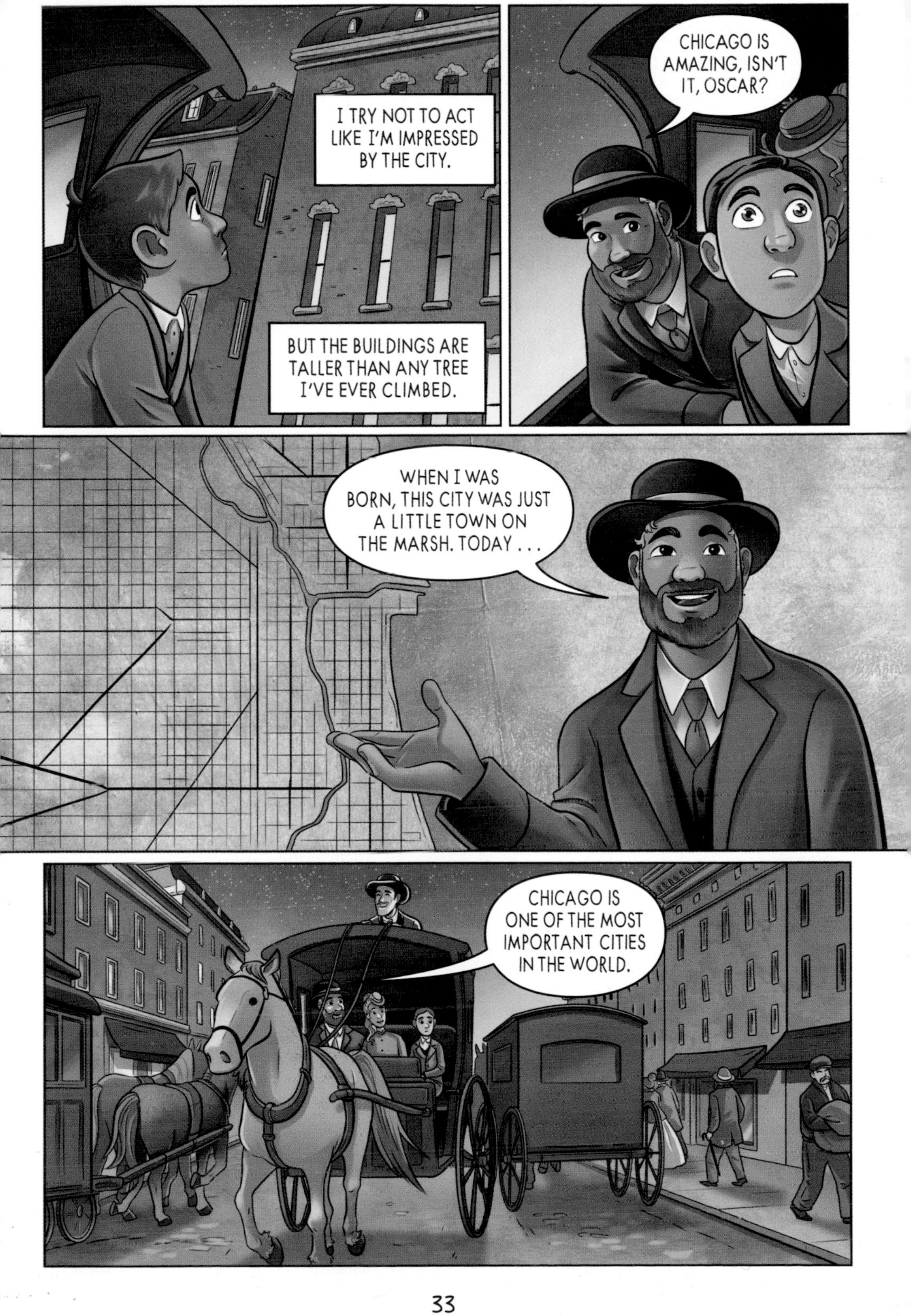
I TRY NOT TO ACT LIKE I'M IMPRESSED BY THE CITY.
BUT THE BUILDINGS ARE TALLER THAN ANY TREE I'VE EVER CLIMBED.
CHICAGO IS AMAZING, ISN'T IT, OSCAR?
WHEN I WAS BORN, THIS CITY WAS JUST A LITTLE TOWN ON THE MARSH. TODAY . . .
CHICAGO IS ONE OF THE MOST IMPORTANT CITIES IN THE WORLD.

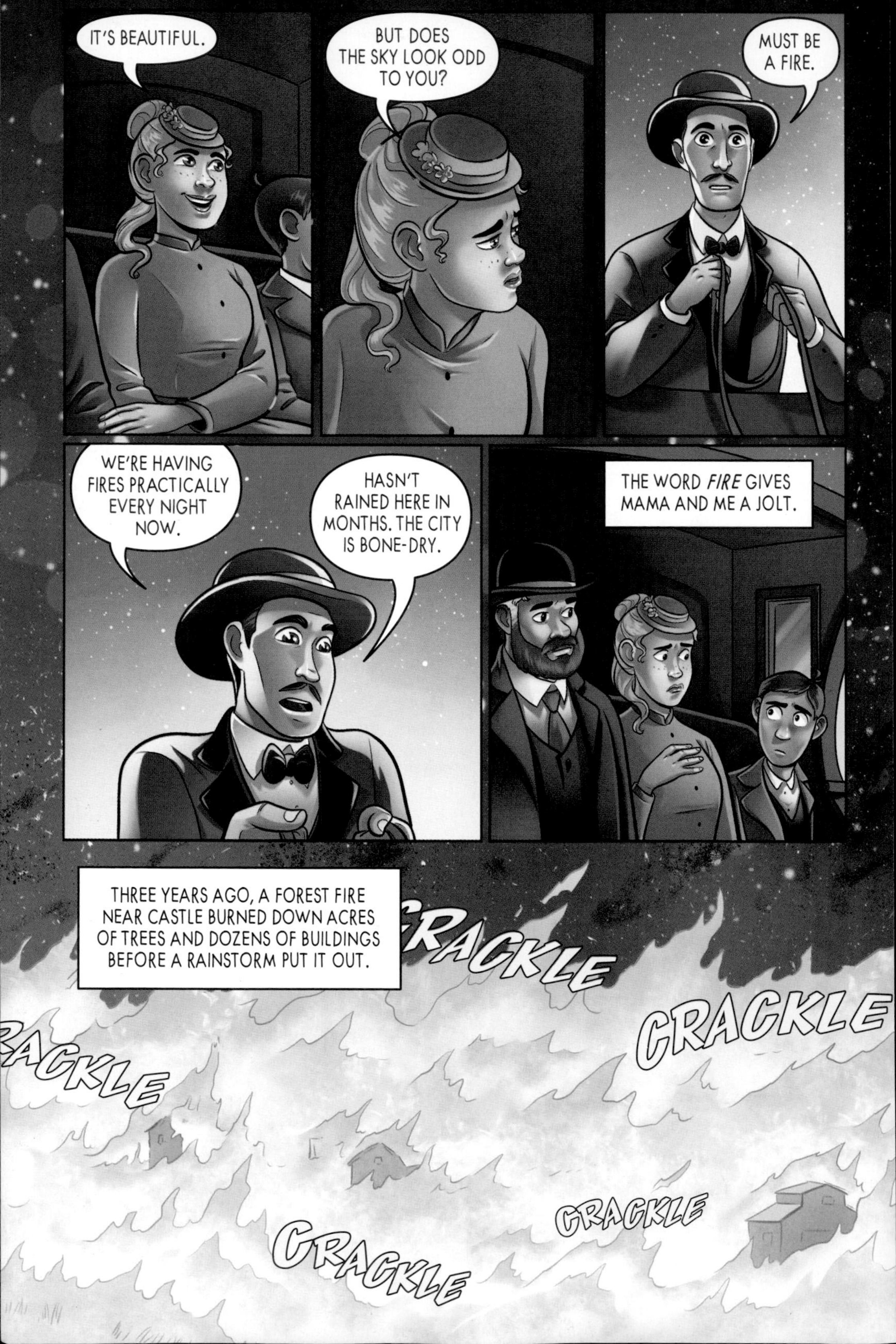
IT'S BEAUTIFUL.
BUT DOES THE SKY LOOK ODD TO YOU?
MUST BE A FIRE.
WE'RE HAVING FIRES PRACTICALLY EVERY NIGHT NOW.
HASN'T RAINED HERE IN MONTHS. THE CITY IS BONE-DRY.
THE WORD *FIRE* GIVES MAMA AND ME A JOLT.
THREE YEARS AGO, A FOREST FIRE NEAR CASTLE BURNED DOWN ACRES OF TREES AND DOZENS OF BUILDINGS BEFORE A RAINSTORM PUT IT OUT.
CRACKLE
CRACKLE
CRACKLE
CRACKLE
CRACKLE

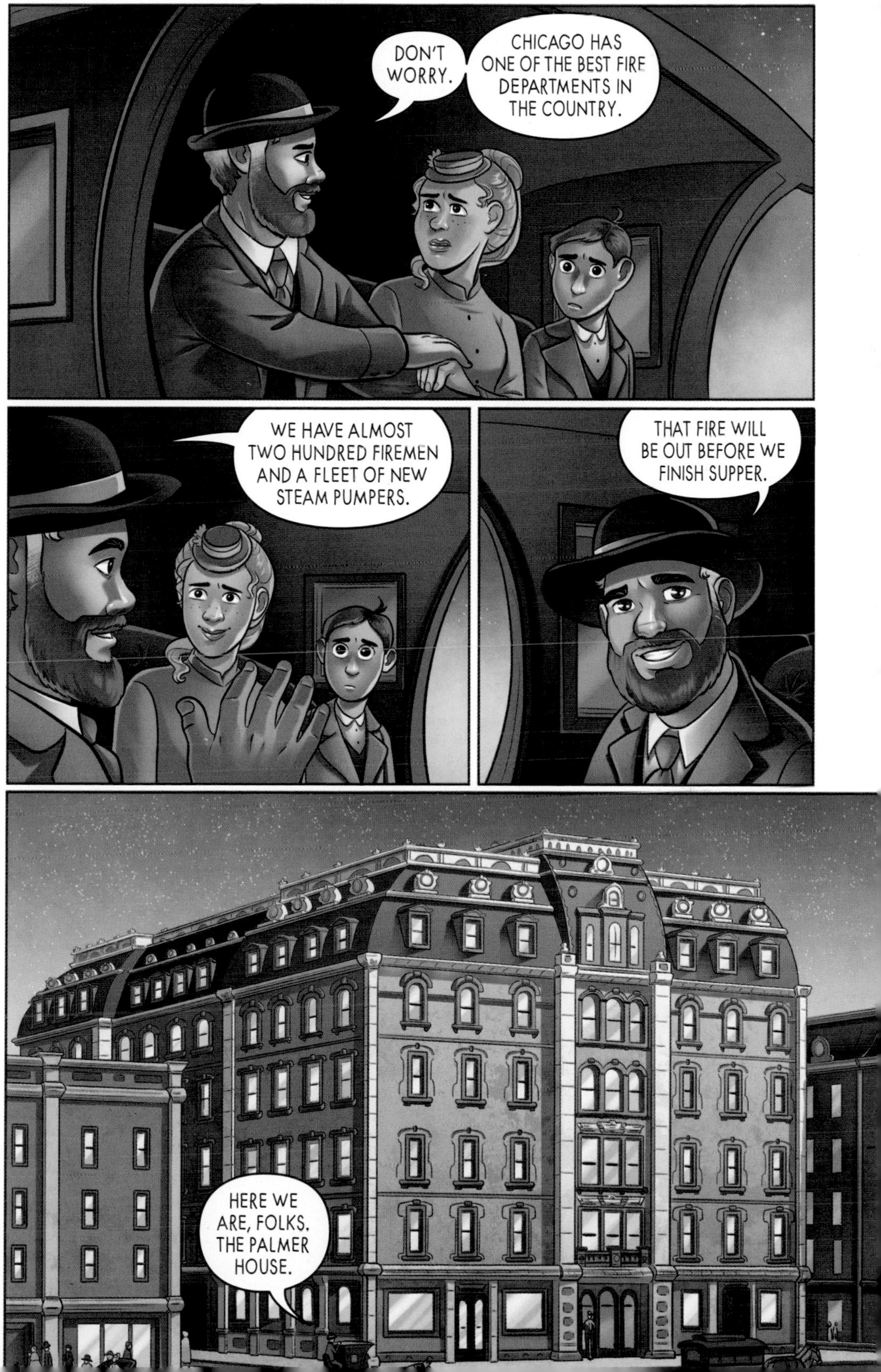
DON'T WORRY.
CHICAGO HAS ONE OF THE BEST FIRE DEPARTMENTS IN THE COUNTRY.
WE HAVE ALMOST TWO HUNDRED FIREMEN AND A FLEET OF NEW STEAM PUMPERS.
THAT FIRE WILL BE OUT BEFORE WE FINISH SUPPER.
HERE WE ARE, FOLKS. THE PALMER HOUSE.

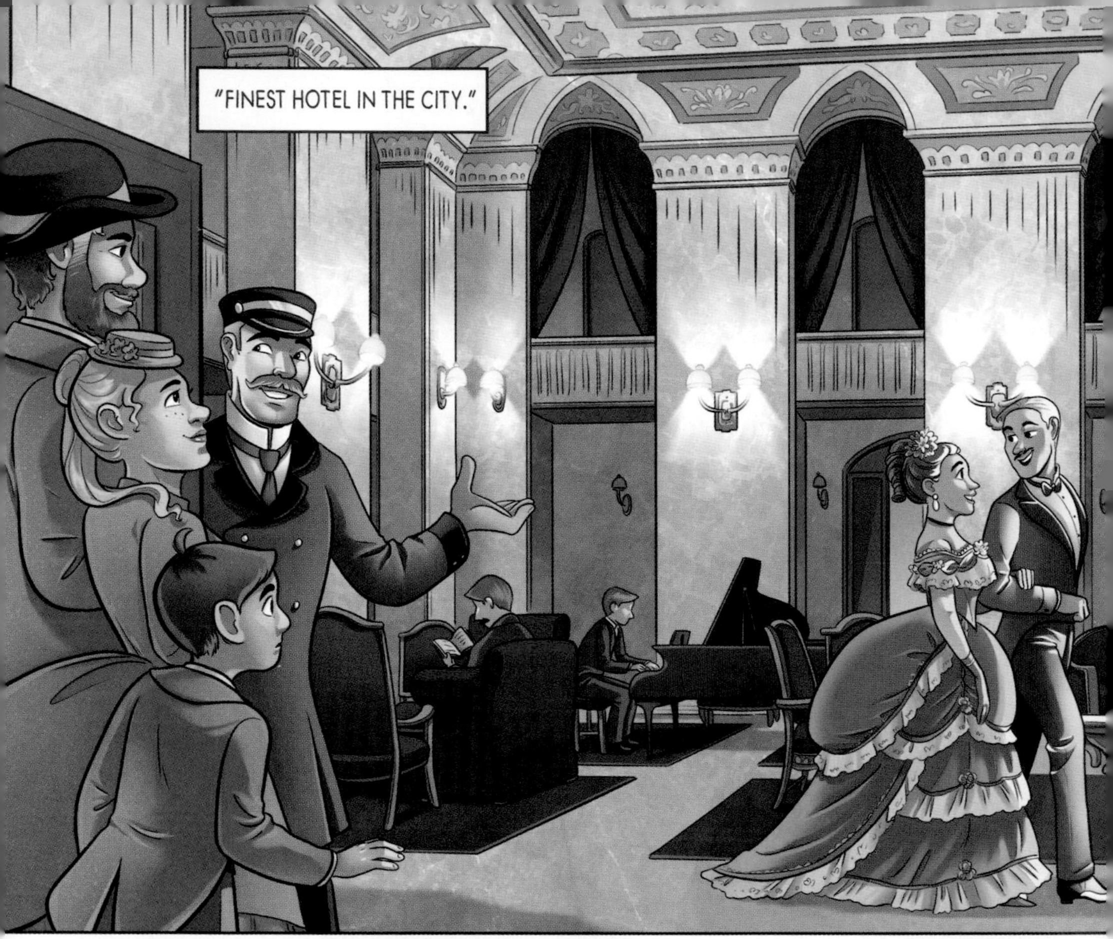
"FINEST HOTEL IN THE CITY."

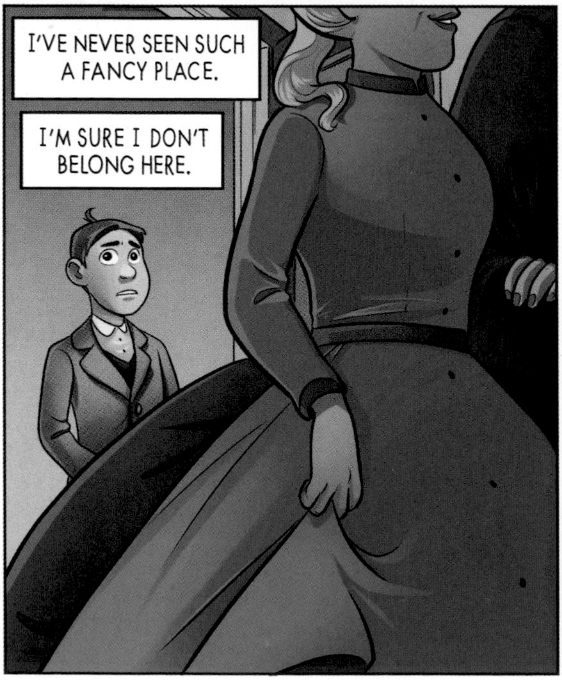
I'VE NEVER SEEN SUCH A FANCY PLACE.
I'M SURE I DON'T BELONG HERE.

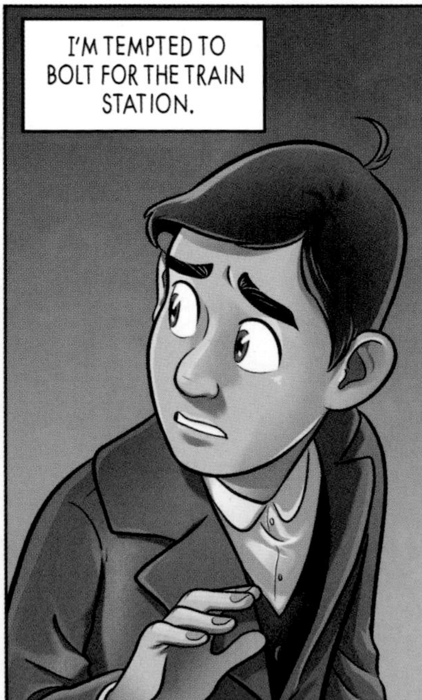
I'M TEMPTED TO BOLT FOR THE TRAIN STATION.

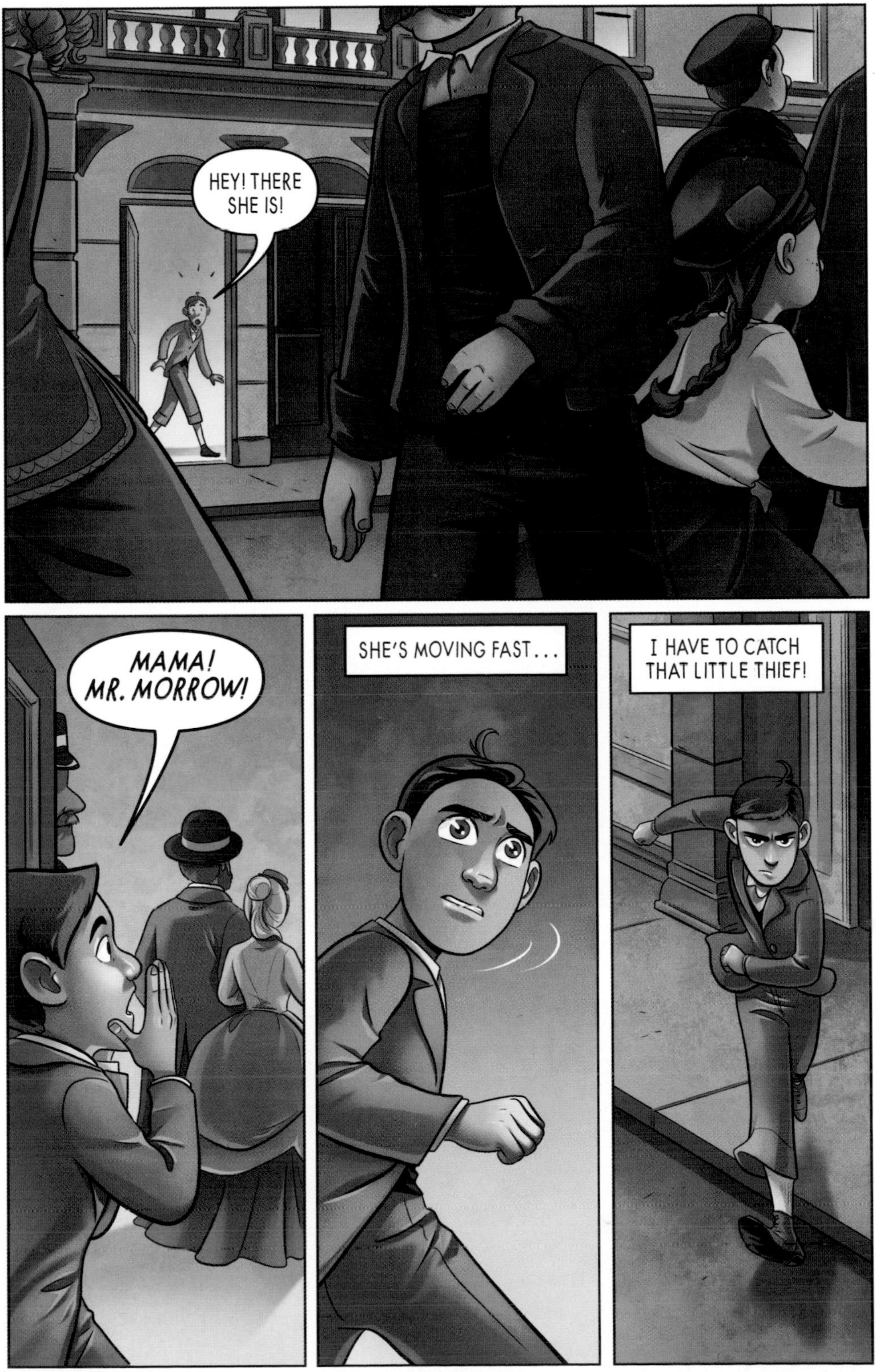
HEY! THERE SHE IS!
MAMA! MR. MORROW!
SHE'S MOVING FAST...
I HAVE TO CATCH THAT LITTLE THIEF!

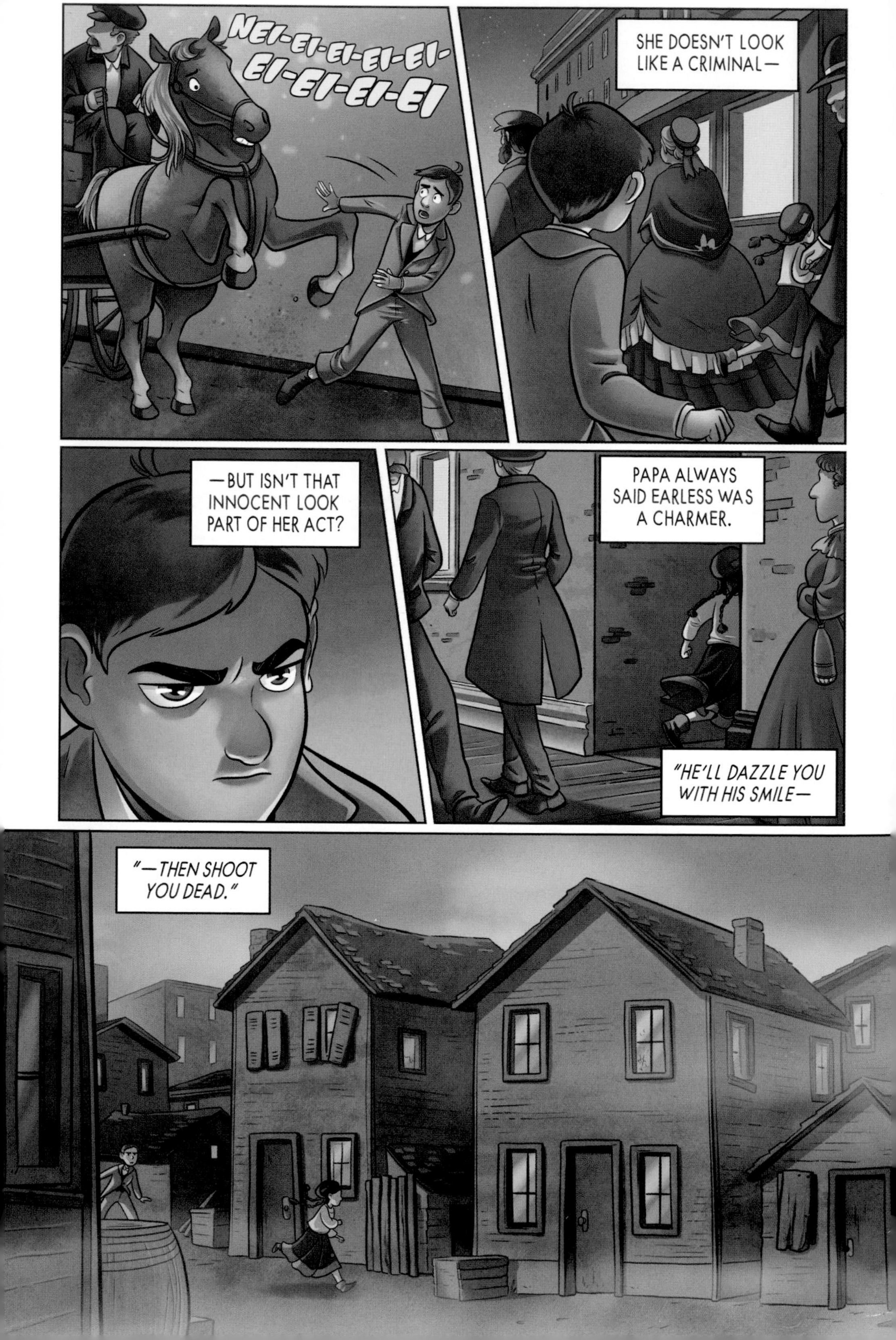
NEI-EI-EI-EI-EI-EI-EI-EI-EI
SHE DOESN'T LOOK LIKE A CRIMINAL—
—BUT ISN'T THAT INNOCENT LOOK PART OF HER ACT?
PAPA ALWAYS SAID EARLESS WAS A CHARMER.
"HE'LL DAZZLE YOU WITH HIS SMILE—
"—THEN SHOOT YOU DEAD."

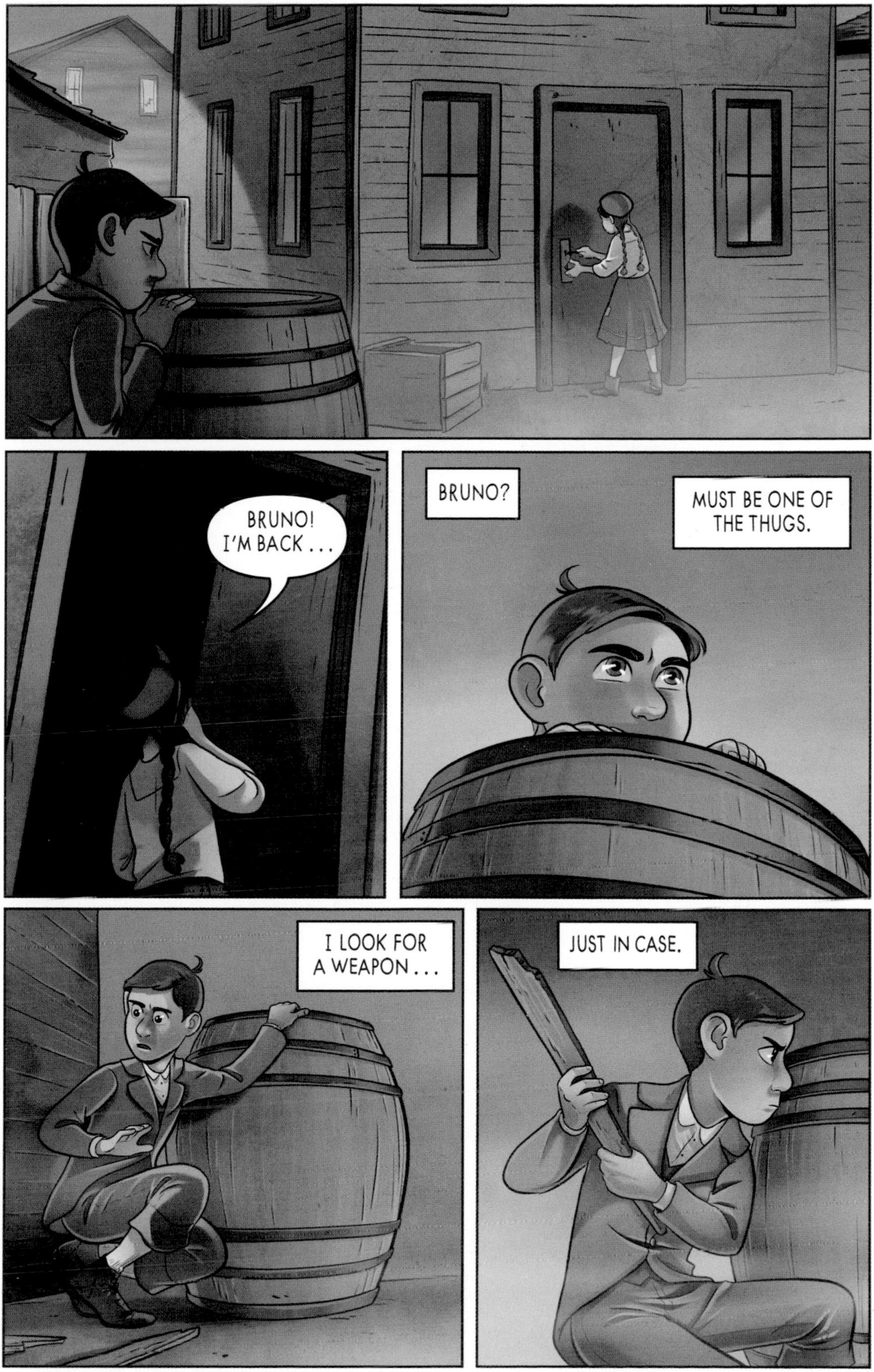
BRUNO! I'M BACK . . .
BRUNO?
MUST BE ONE OF THE THUGS.
I LOOK FOR A WEAPON . . .
JUST IN CASE.

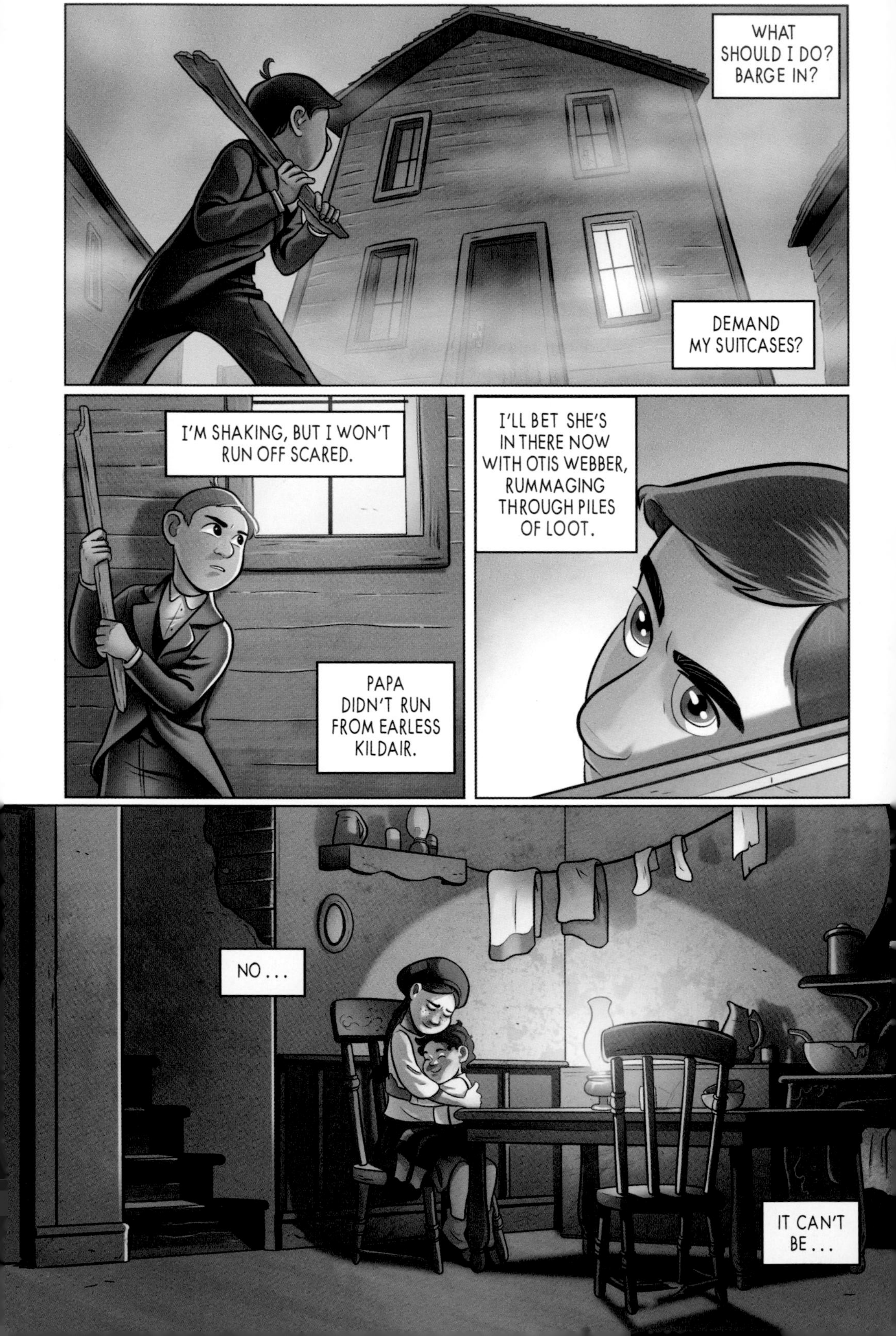
WHAT SHOULD I DO? BARGE IN?
DEMAND MY SUITCASES?
I'M SHAKING, BUT I WON'T RUN OFF SCARED.
PAPA DIDN'T RUN FROM EARLESS KILDAIR.
I'LL BET SHE'S IN THERE NOW WITH OTIS WEBBER, RUMMAGING THROUGH PILES OF LOOT.
NO . . .
IT CAN'T BE . . .

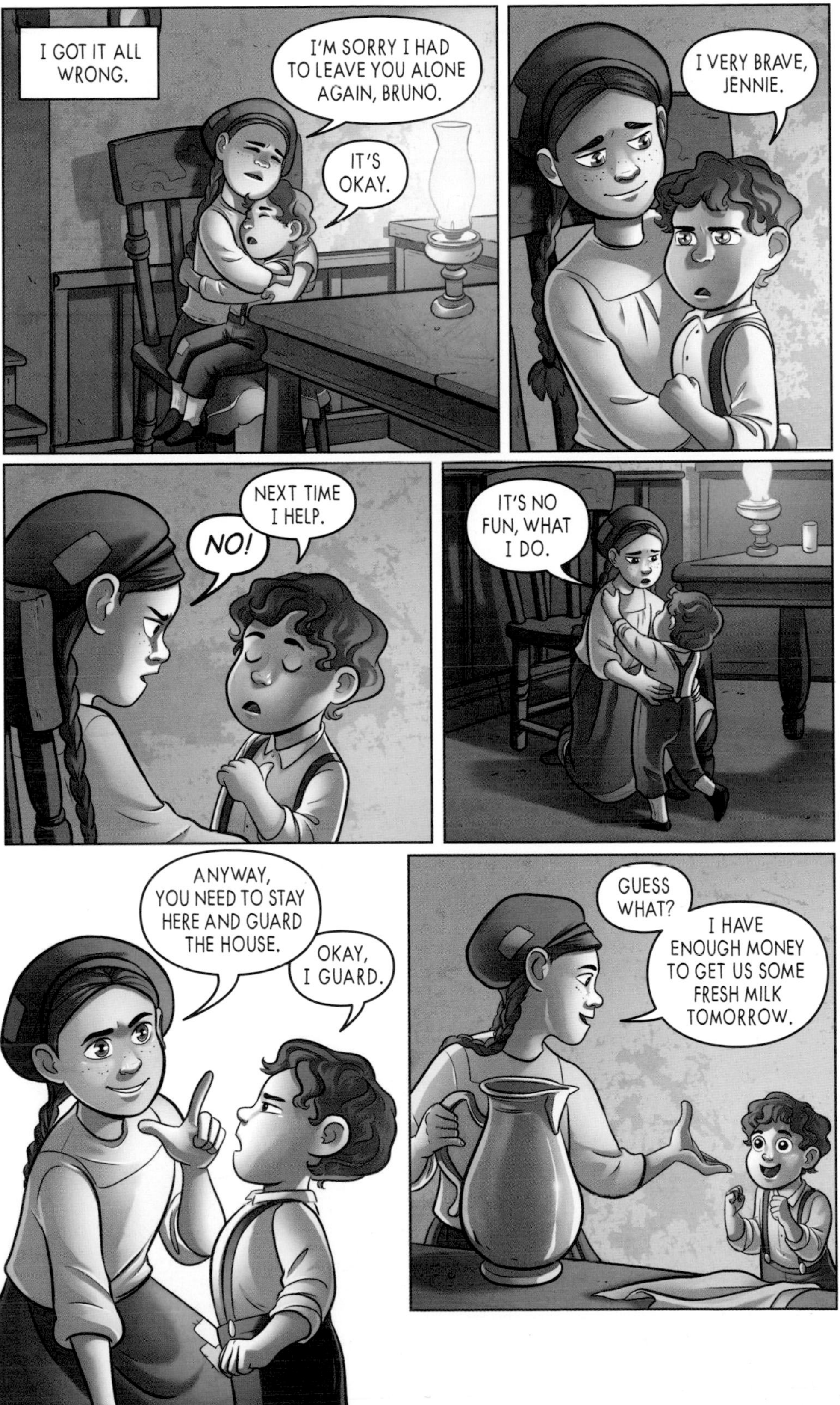
I GOT IT ALL WRONG.
I'M SORRY I HAD TO LEAVE YOU ALONE AGAIN, BRUNO.
IT'S OKAY.
I VERY BRAVE, JENNIE.
NEXT TIME I HELP.
NO!
IT'S NO FUN, WHAT I DO.
ANYWAY, YOU NEED TO STAY HERE AND GUARD THE HOUSE.
OKAY, I GUARD.
GUESS WHAT?
I HAVE ENOUGH MONEY TO GET US SOME FRESH MILK TOMORROW.

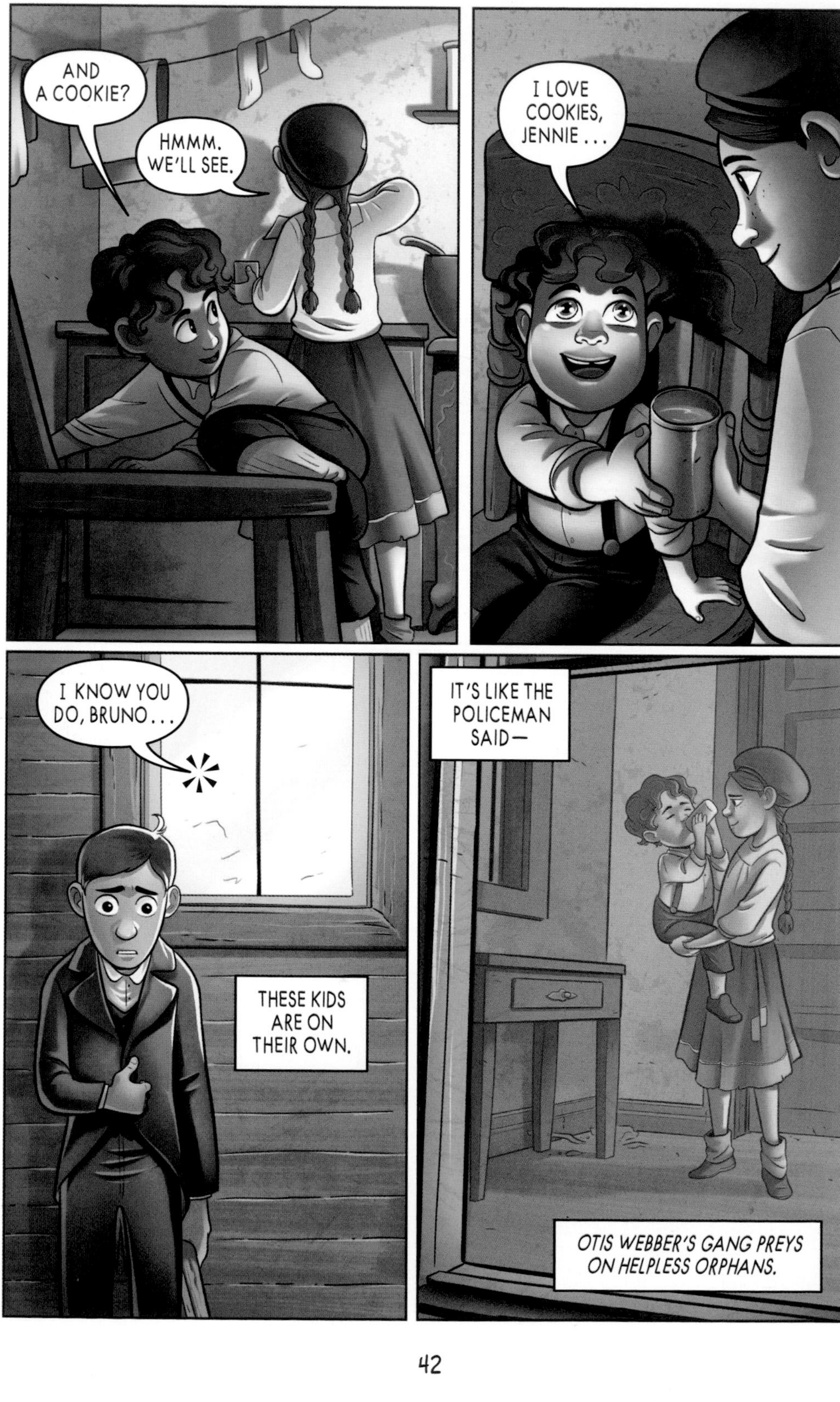
AND A COOKIE?
HMMM. WE'LL SEE.
I LOVE COOKIES, JENNIE . . .
I KNOW YOU DO, BRUNO . . .
IT'S LIKE THE POLICEMAN SAID—
THESE KIDS ARE ON THEIR OWN.
OTIS WEBBER'S GANG PREYS ON HELPLESS ORPHANS.

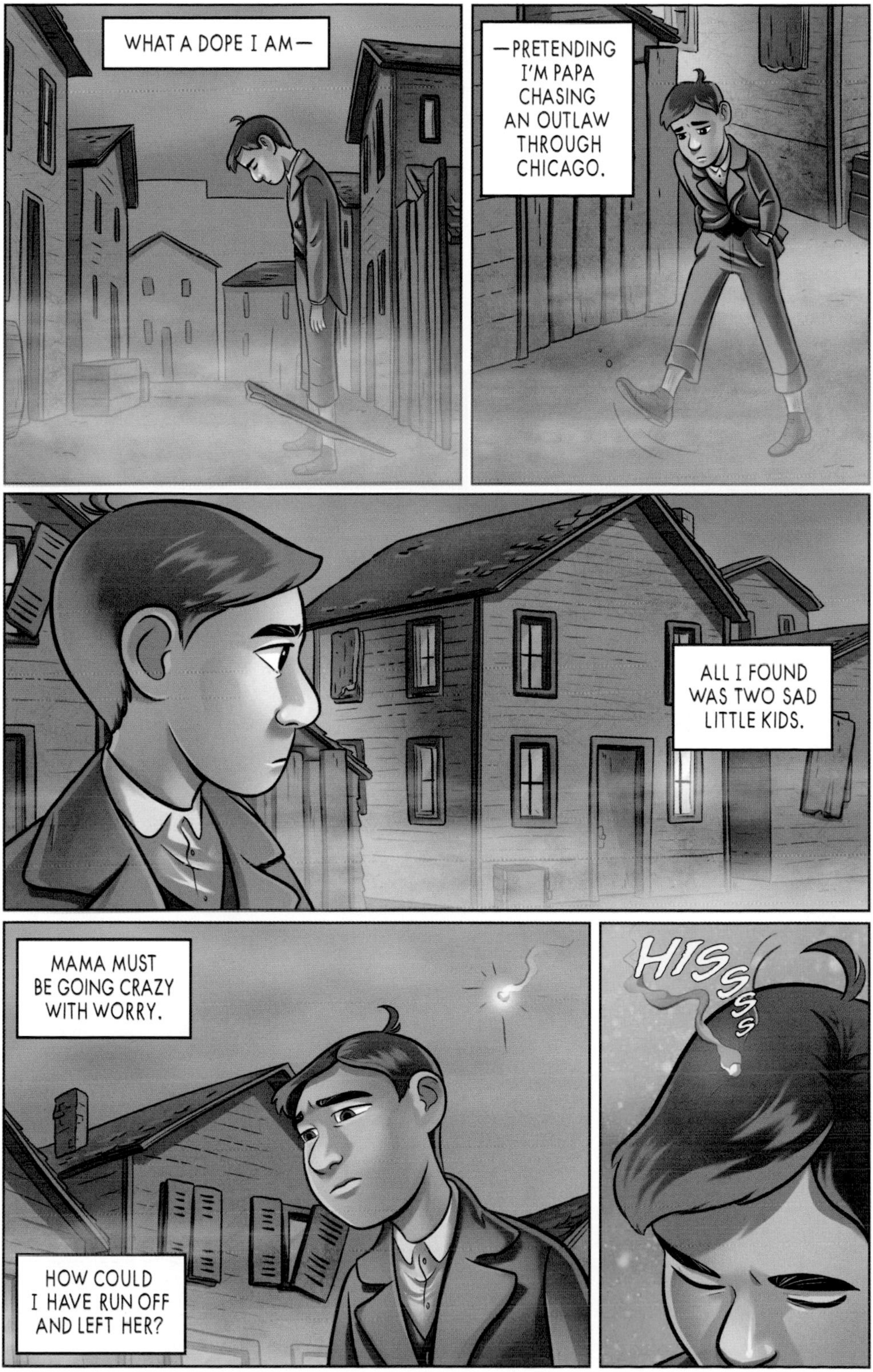
WHAT A DOPE I AM—
—PRETENDING I'M PAPA CHASING AN OUTLAW THROUGH CHICAGO.
ALL I FOUND WAS TWO SAD LITTLE KIDS.
MAMA MUST BE GOING CRAZY WITH WORRY.
HOW COULD I HAVE RUN OFF AND LEFT HER?
HISSSS

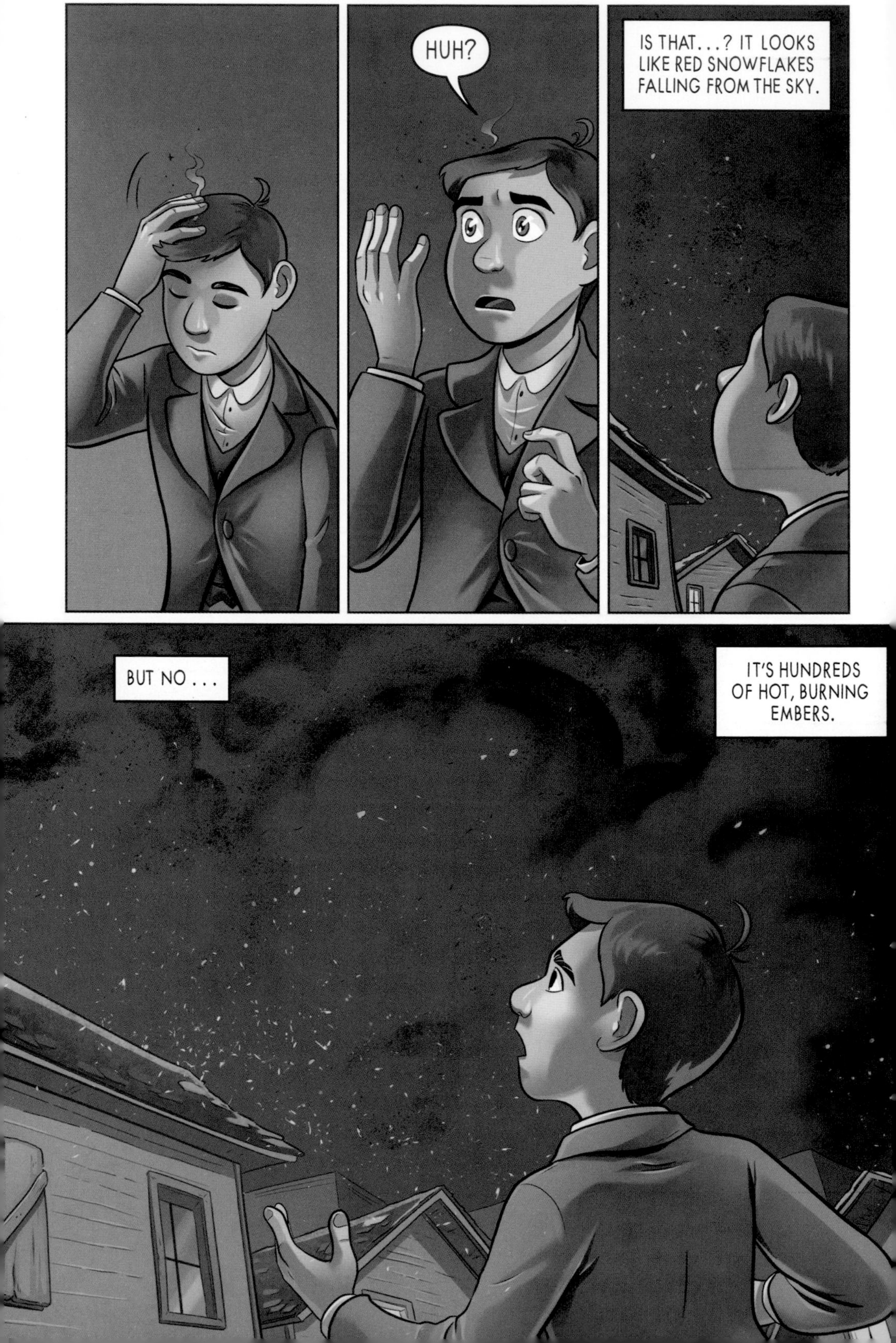
HUH?
IS THAT...? IT LOOKS LIKE RED SNOWFLAKES FALLING FROM THE SKY.
BUT NO . . .
IT'S HUNDREDS OF HOT, BURNING EMBERS.

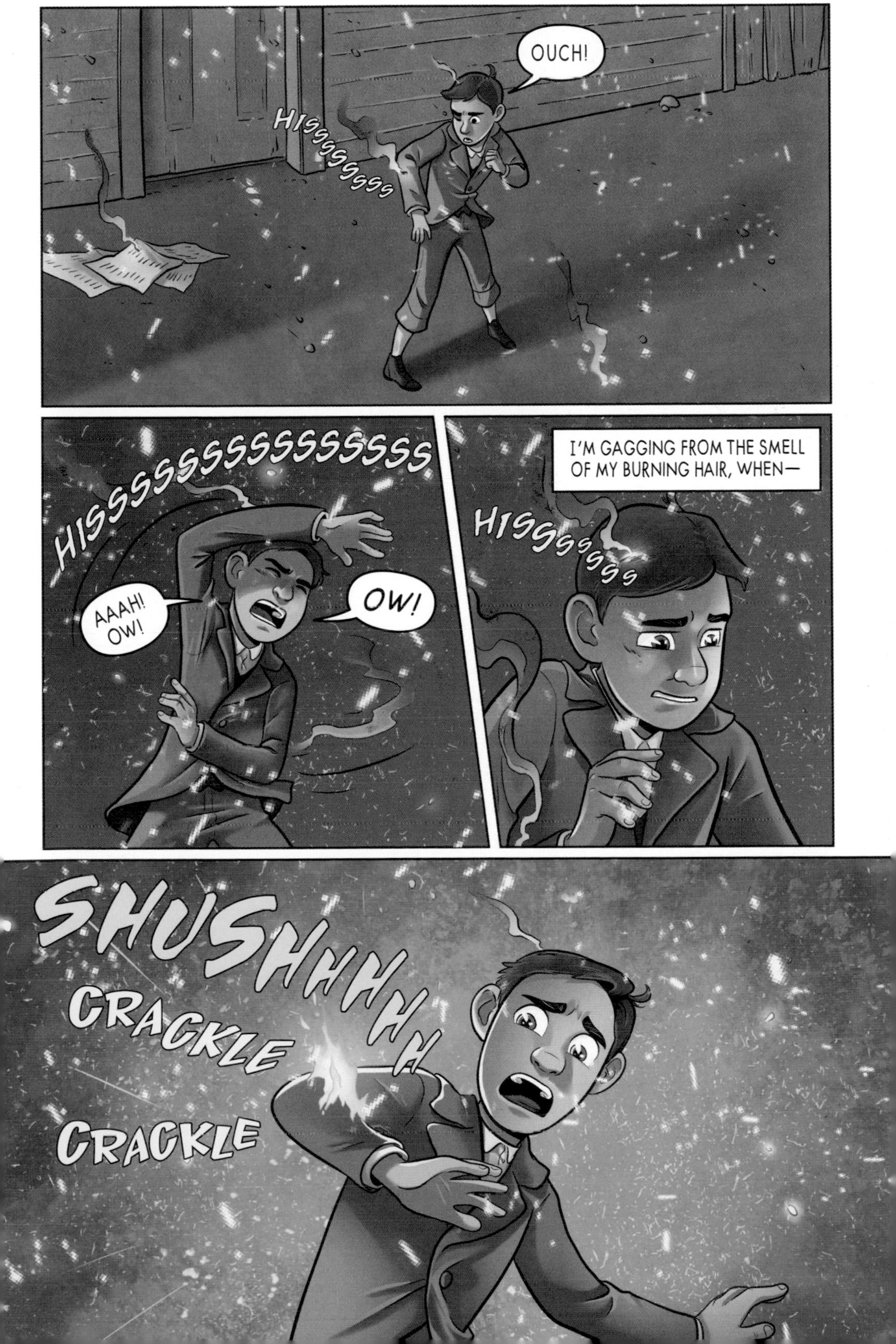
OUCH!
HISSSSSSSS
HISSSSSSSSSSSSSSS
AAAH! OW!
OW!
I'M GAGGING FROM THE SMELL OF MY BURNING HAIR, WHEN—
HISSSSSSS
SHUSHHHHH
CRACKLE
CRACKLE

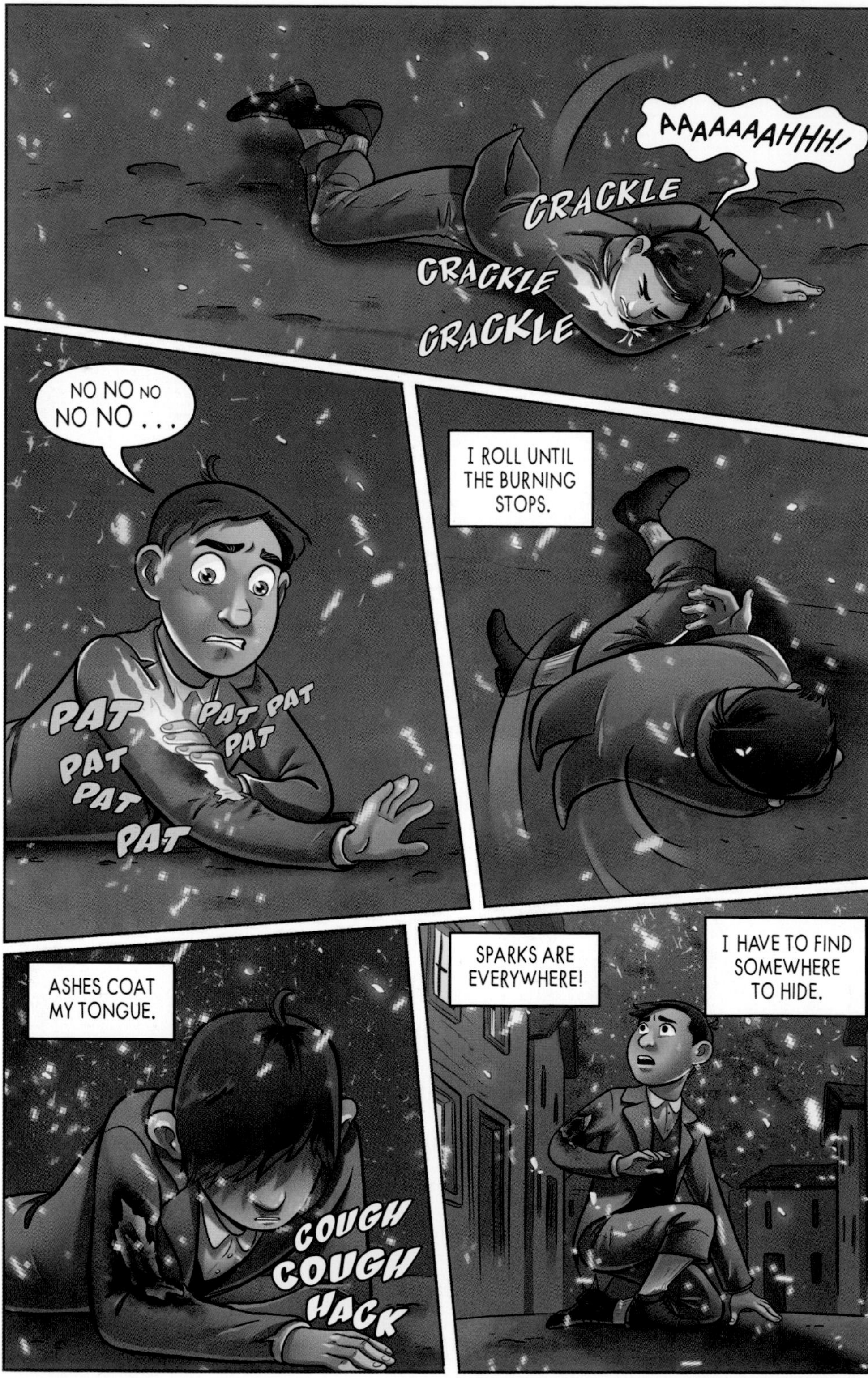
AAAAAAAHHH!
CRACKLE
CRACKLE
CRACKLE
NO NO NO
NO NO . . .
PAT
PAT PAT
PAT
PAT
PAT
PAT
PAT
I ROLL UNTIL THE BURNING STOPS.
ASHES COAT MY TONGUE.
COUGH
COUGH
HACK
SPARKS ARE EVERYWHERE!
I HAVE TO FIND SOMEWHERE TO HIDE.

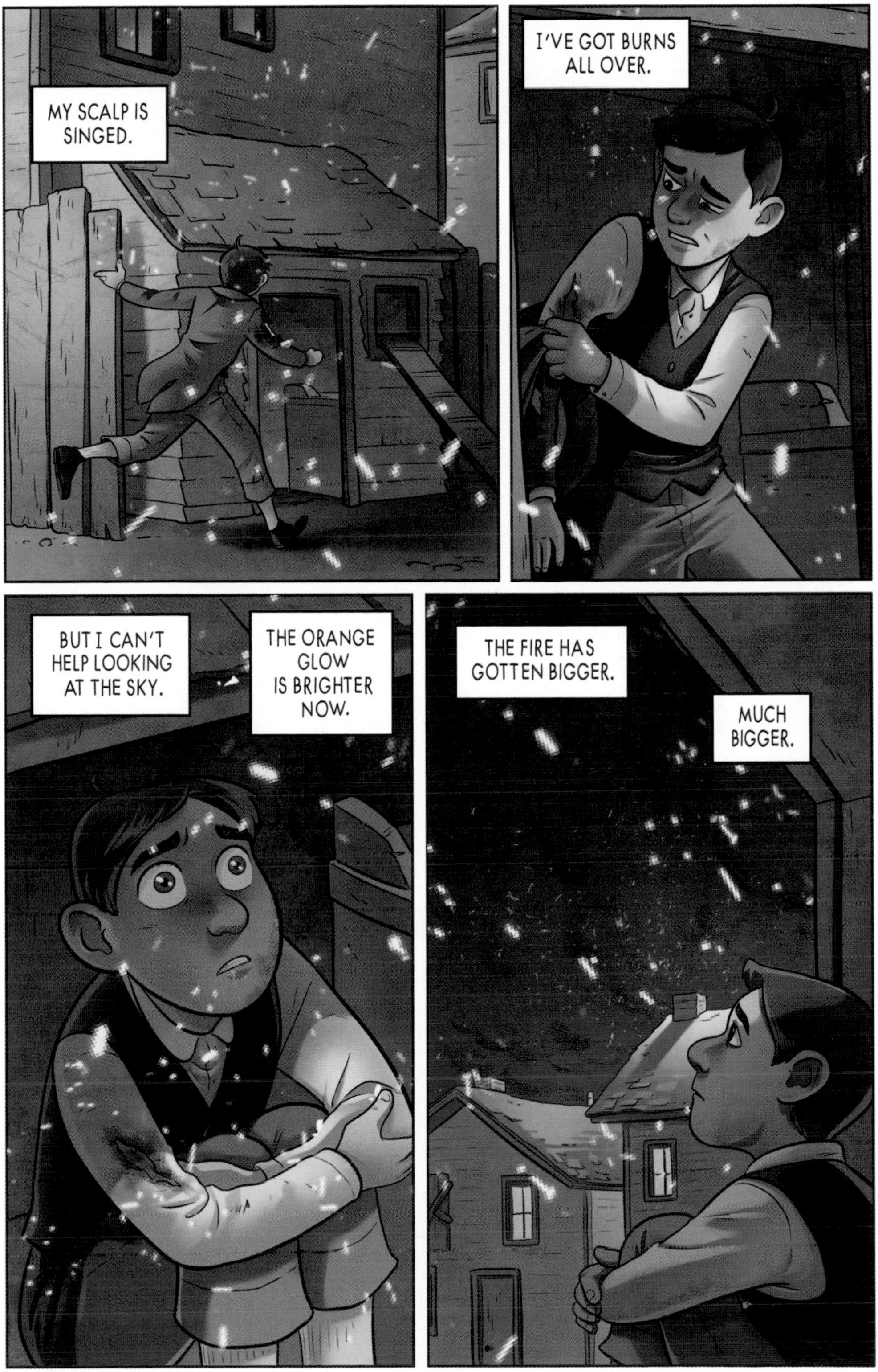
MY SCALP IS SINGED.
I'VE GOT BURNS ALL OVER.
BUT I CAN'T HELP LOOKING AT THE SKY.
THE ORANGE GLOW IS BRIGHTER NOW.
THE FIRE HAS GOTTEN BIGGER.
MUCH BIGGER.

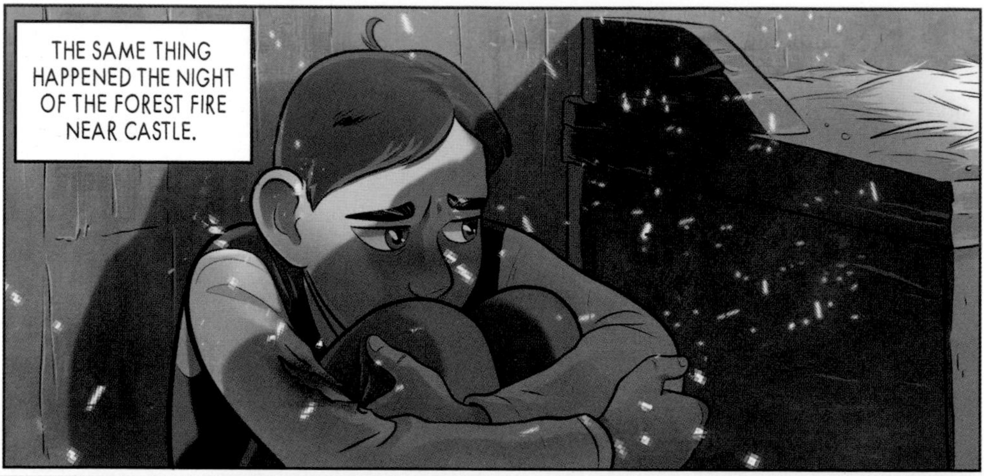
THE SAME THING HAPPENED THE NIGHT OF THE FOREST FIRE NEAR CASTLE.

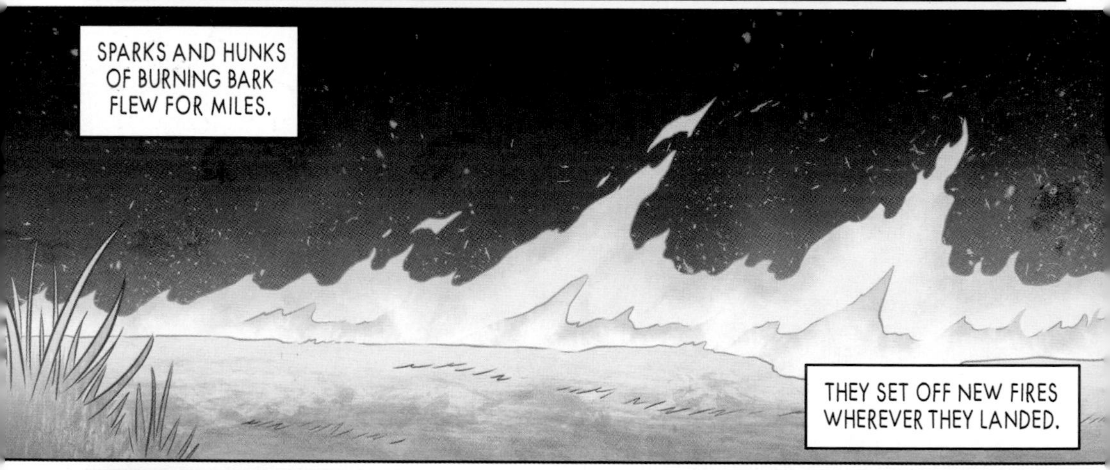
SPARKS AND HUNKS OF BURNING BARK FLEW FOR MILES.
THEY SET OFF NEW FIRES WHEREVER THEY LANDED.

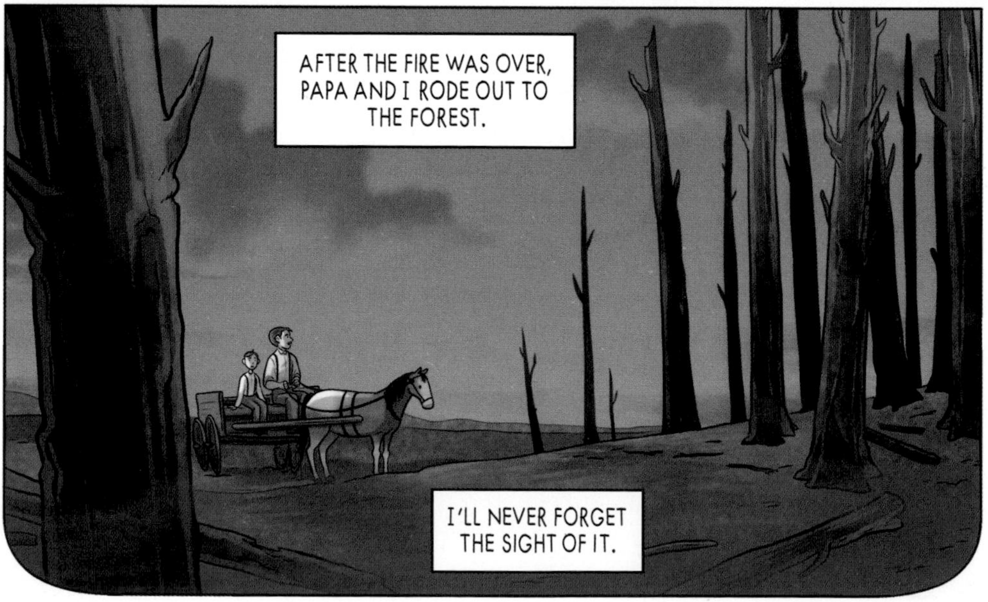
AFTER THE FIRE WAS OVER, PAPA AND I RODE OUT TO THE FOREST.
I'LL NEVER FORGET THE SIGHT OF IT.

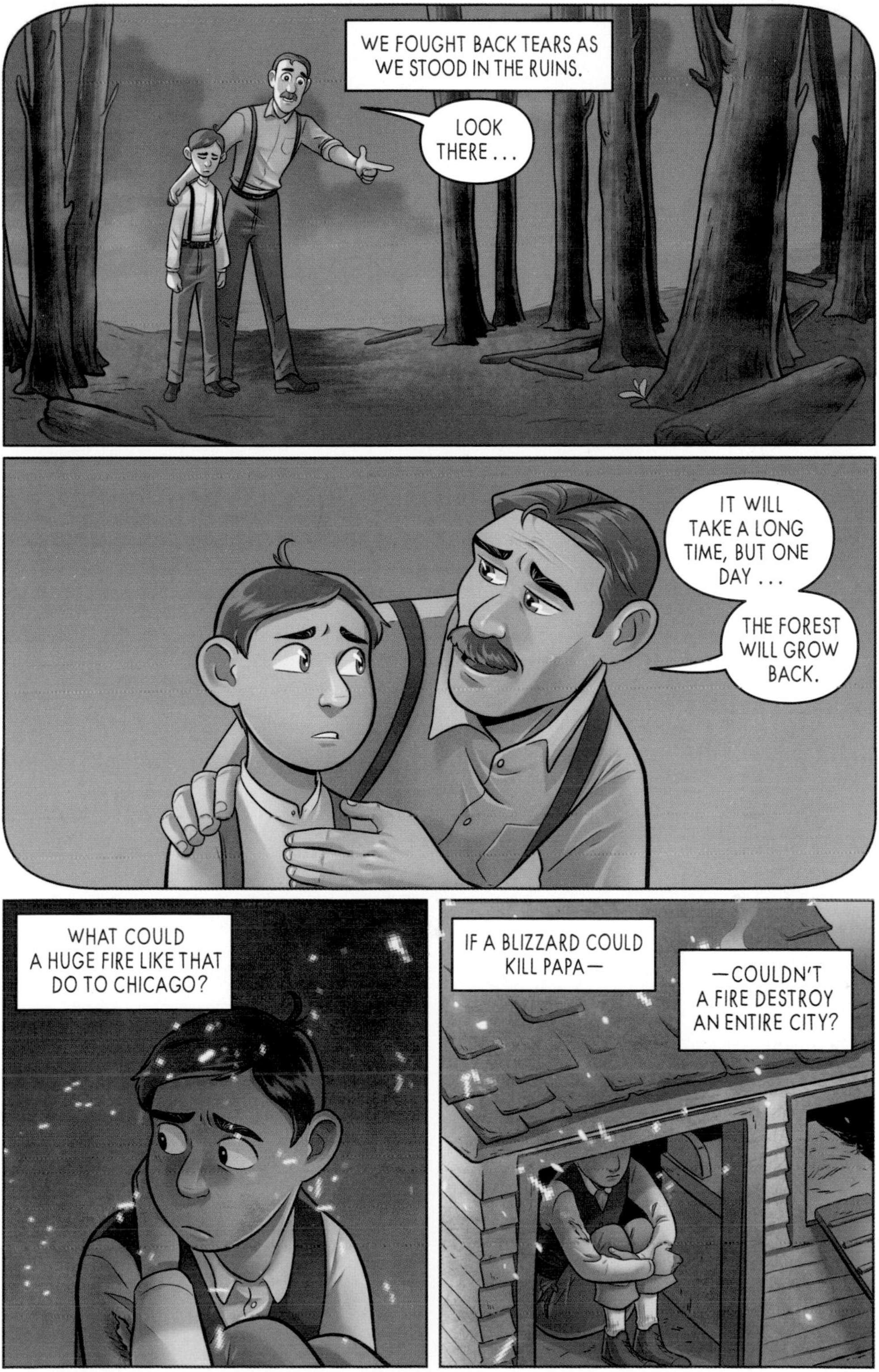
WE FOUGHT BACK TEARS AS WE STOOD IN THE RUINS.
LOOK THERE . . .
IT WILL TAKE A LONG TIME, BUT ONE DAY . . .
THE FOREST WILL GROW BACK.
WHAT COULD A HUGE FIRE LIKE THAT DO TO CHICAGO?
IF A BLIZZARD COULD KILL PAPA—
—COULDN'T A FIRE DESTROY AN ENTIRE CITY?

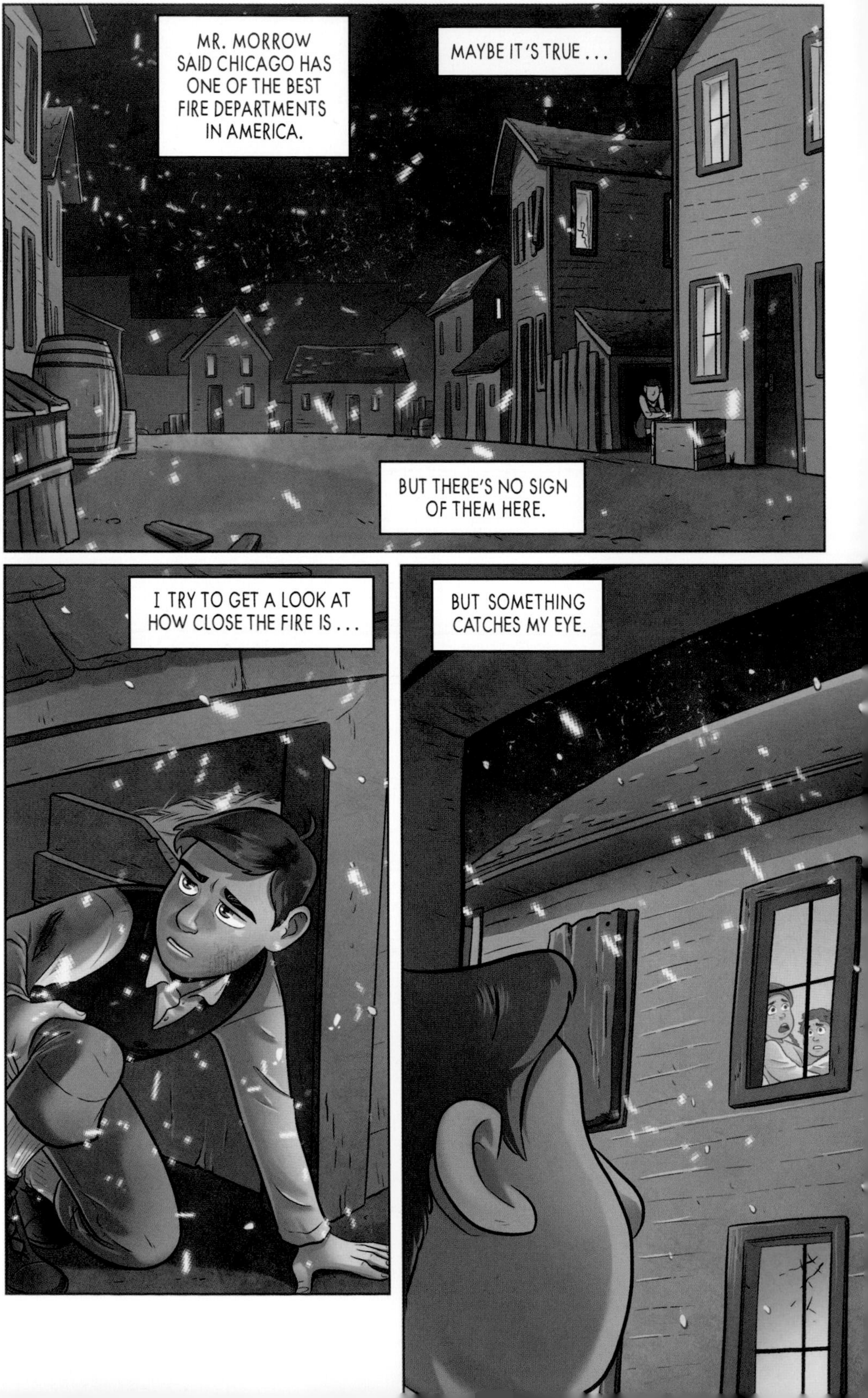
MR. MORROW SAID CHICAGO HAS ONE OF THE BEST FIRE DEPARTMENTS IN AMERICA.
MAYBE IT'S TRUE . . .
BUT THERE'S NO SIGN OF THEM HERE.
I TRY TO GET A LOOK AT HOW CLOSE THE FIRE IS . . .
BUT SOMETHING CATCHES MY EYE.

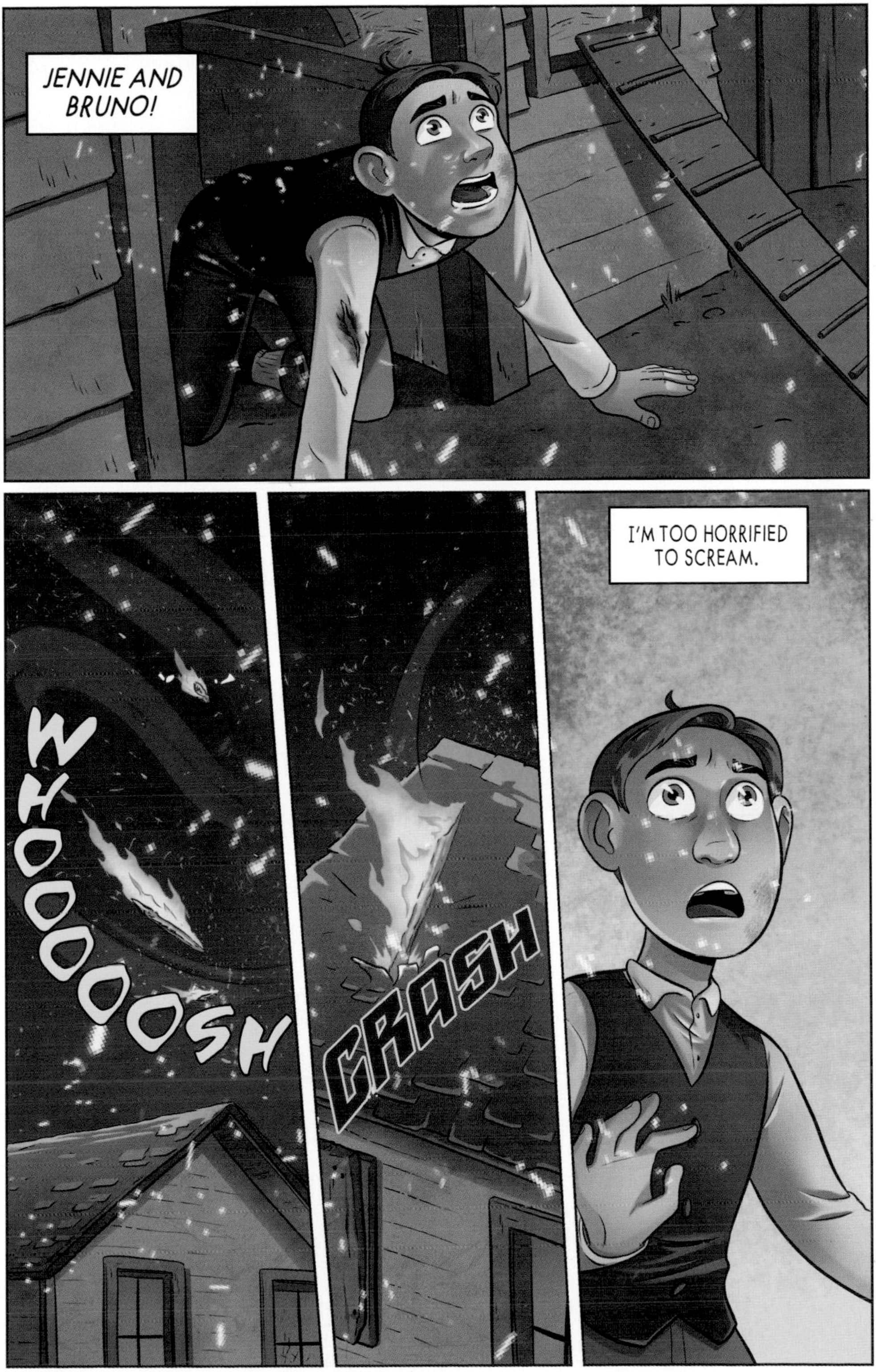
JENNIE AND BRUNO!
WHOOOOOOSH
CRASH
I'M TOO HORRIFIED TO SCREAM.

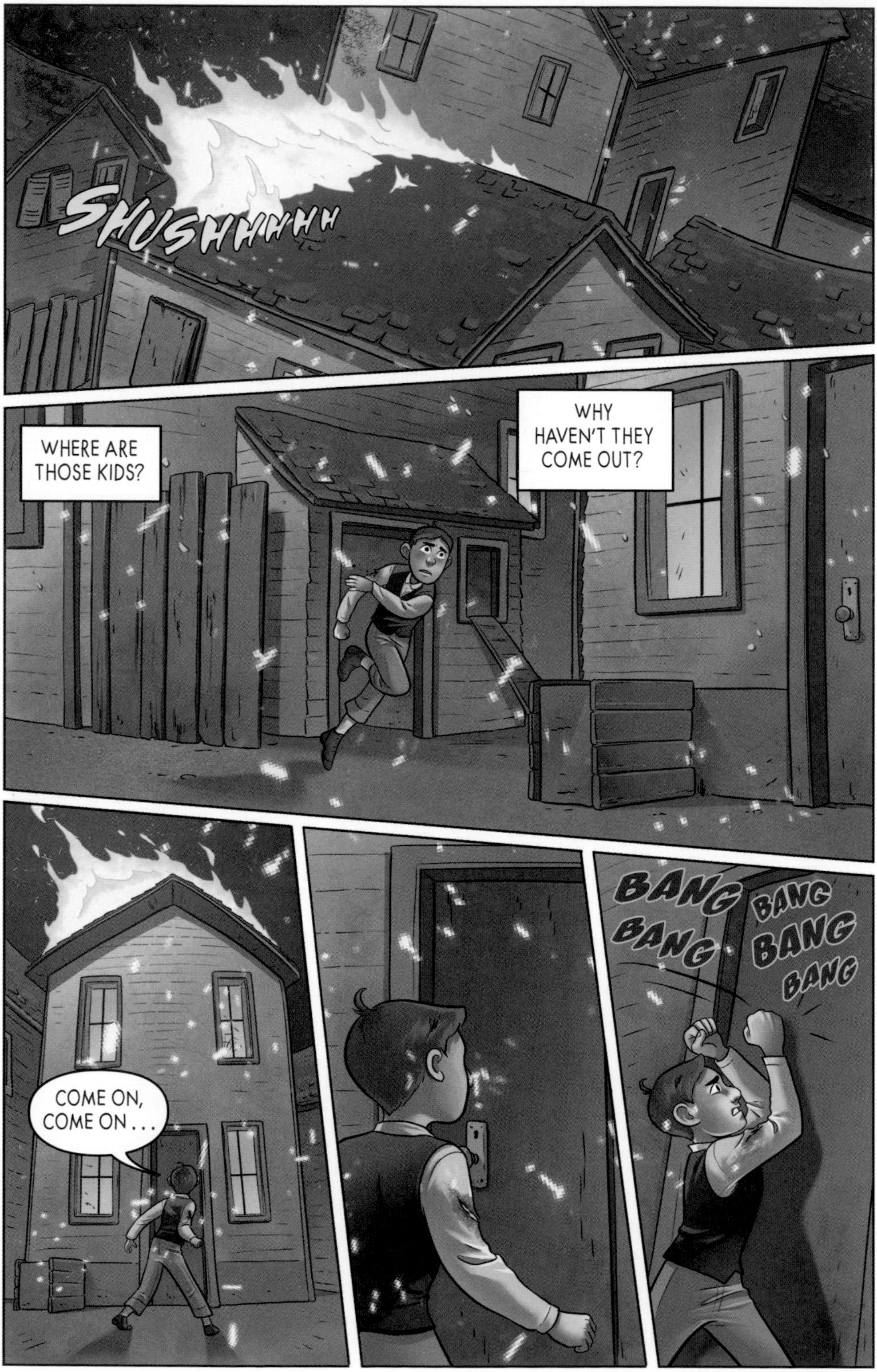
SHUSHHHHH
WHERE ARE THOSE KIDS?
WHY HAVEN'T THEY COME OUT?
COME ON, COME ON . . .
BANG BANG
BANG BANG BANG

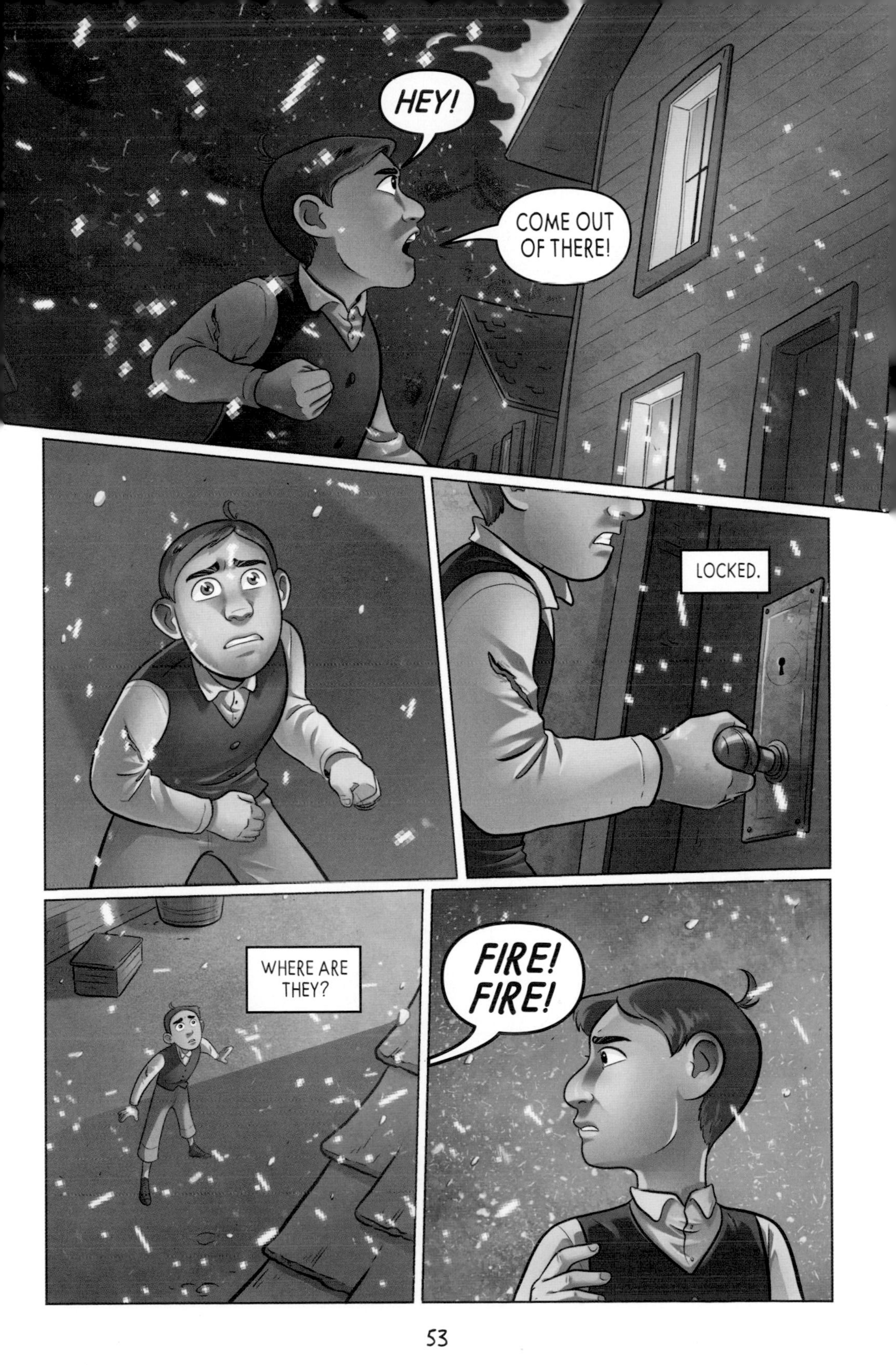
HEY!
COME OUT OF THERE!
LOCKED.
WHERE ARE THEY?
FIRE! FIRE!

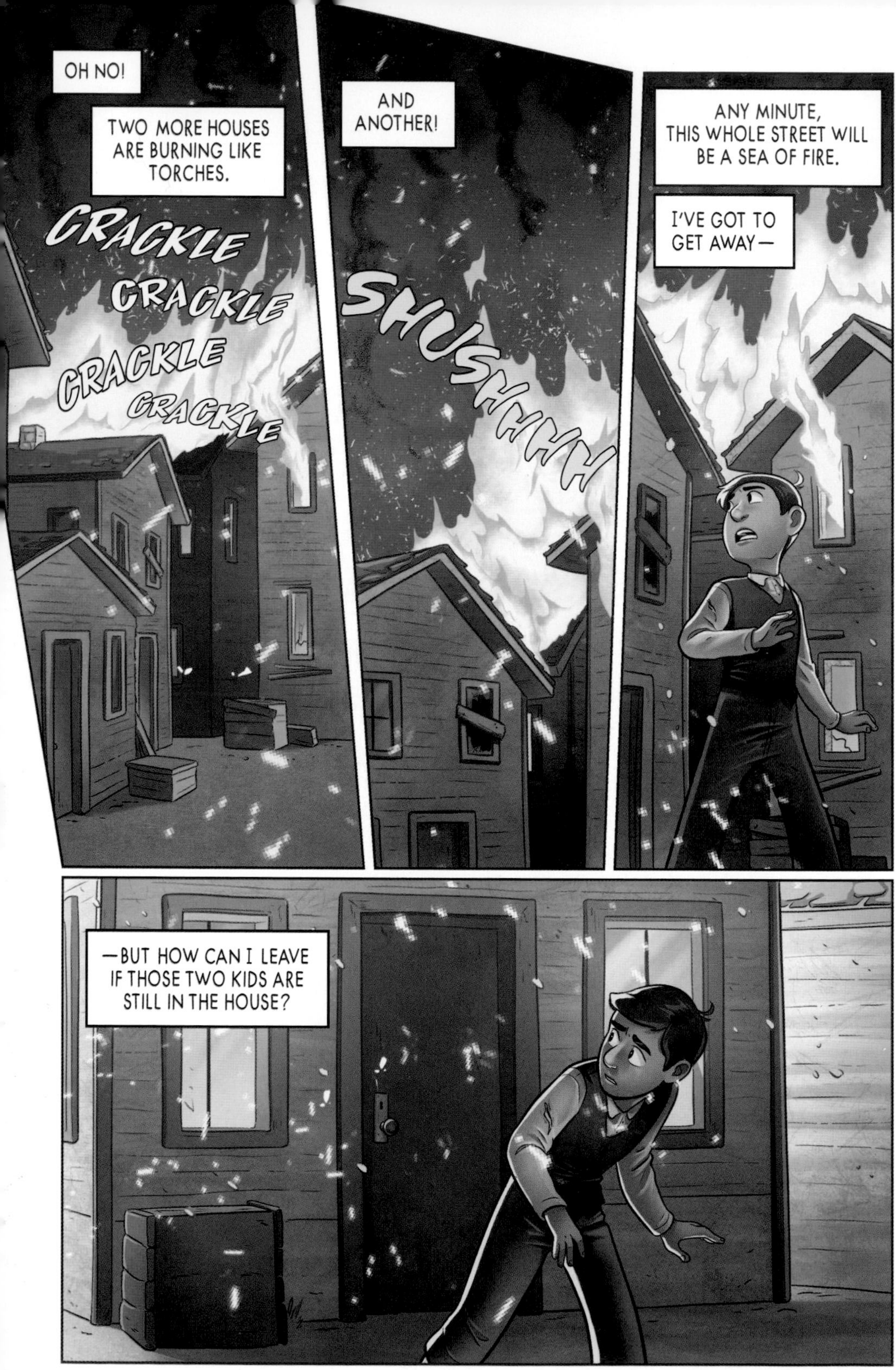
OH NO!
TWO MORE HOUSES ARE BURNING LIKE TORCHES.
CRACKLE CRACKLE CRACKLE CRACKLE
AND ANOTHER!
SHUSHHHH
ANY MINUTE, THIS WHOLE STREET WILL BE A SEA OF FIRE.
I'VE GOT TO GET AWAY—
—BUT HOW CAN I LEAVE IF THOSE TWO KIDS ARE STILL IN THE HOUSE?

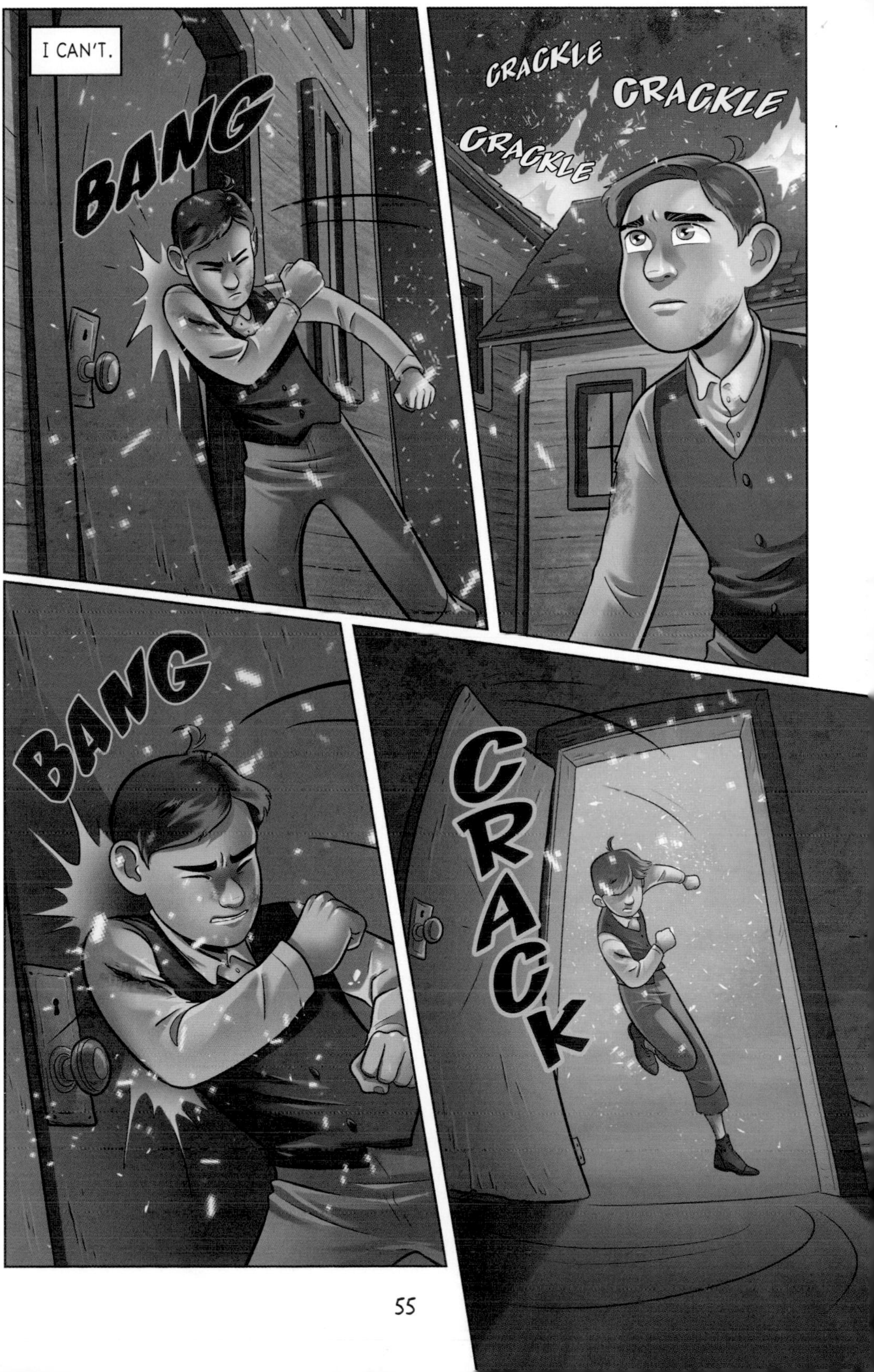
I CAN'T.
BANG
CRACKLE
CRACKLE
CRACKLE
BANG
CRACK

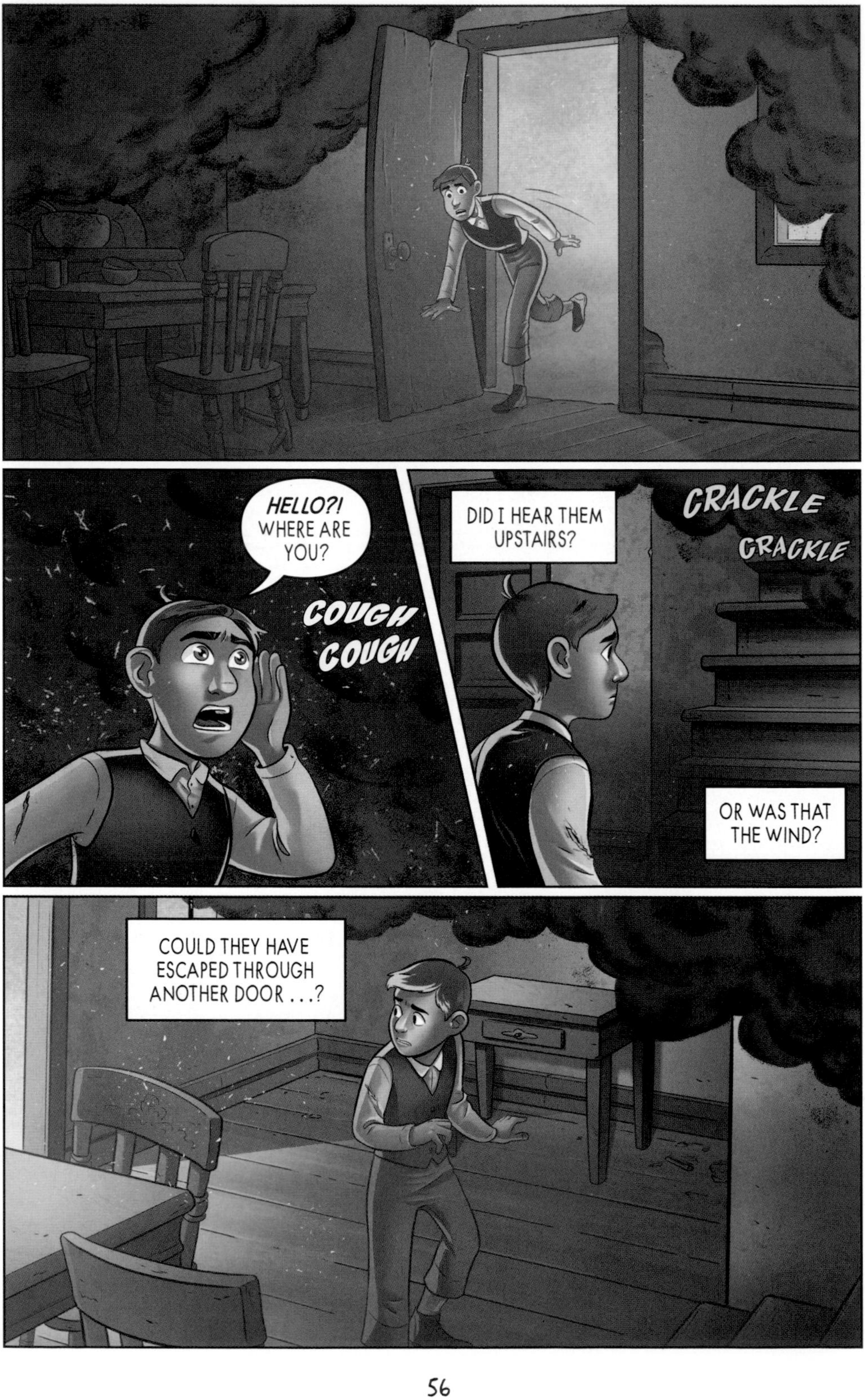
HELLO?! WHERE ARE YOU?
COUGH COUGH
DID I HEAR THEM UPSTAIRS?
CRACKLE
CRACKLE
OR WAS THAT THE WIND?
COULD THEY HAVE ESCAPED THROUGH ANOTHER DOOR . . .?

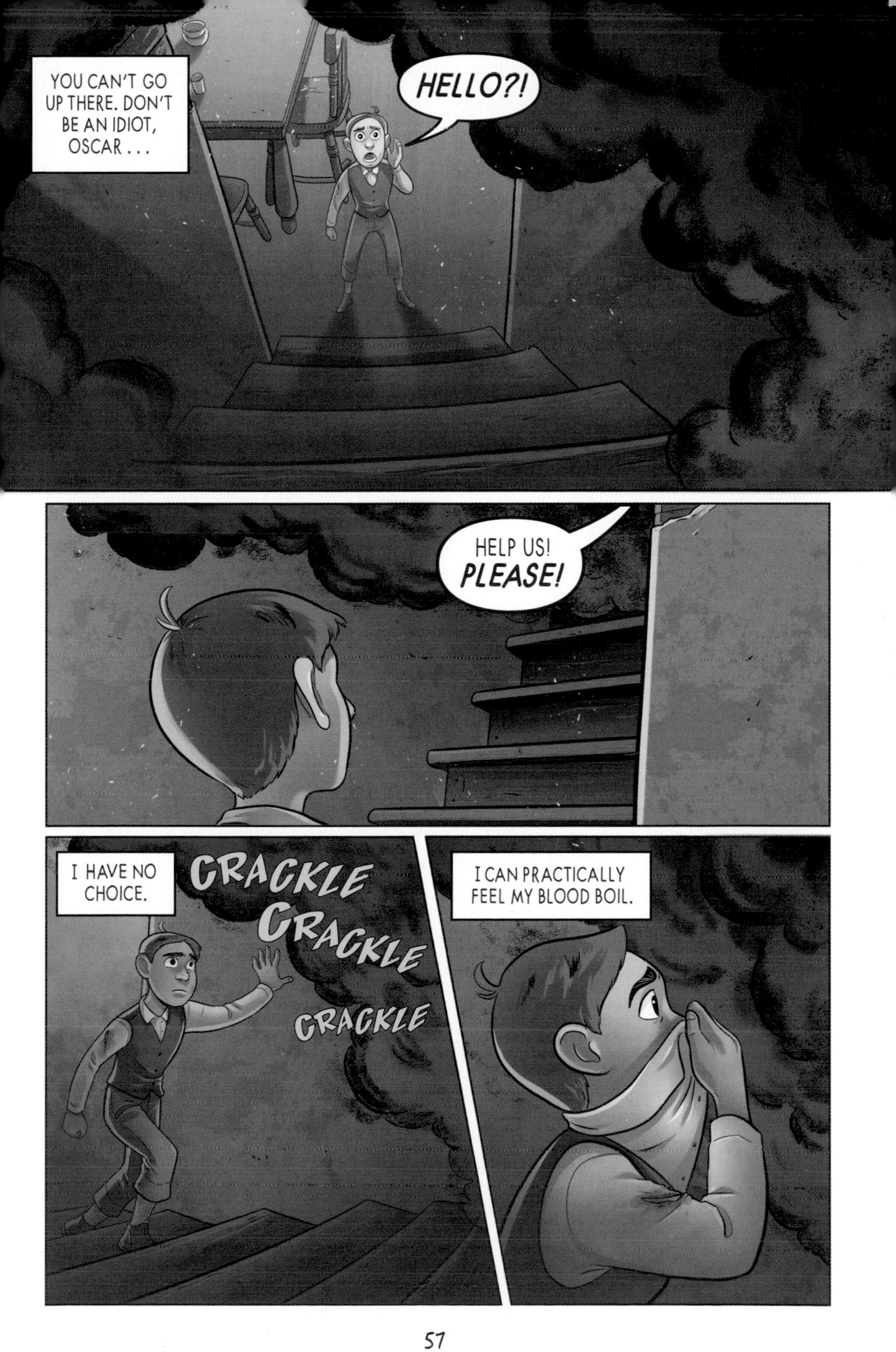
YOU CAN'T GO UP THERE. DON'T BE AN IDIOT, OSCAR . . .
HELLO?!
HELP US! PLEASE!
I HAVE NO CHOICE.
CRACKLE
CRACKLE
CRACKLE
I CAN PRACTICALLY FEEL MY BLOOD BOIL.

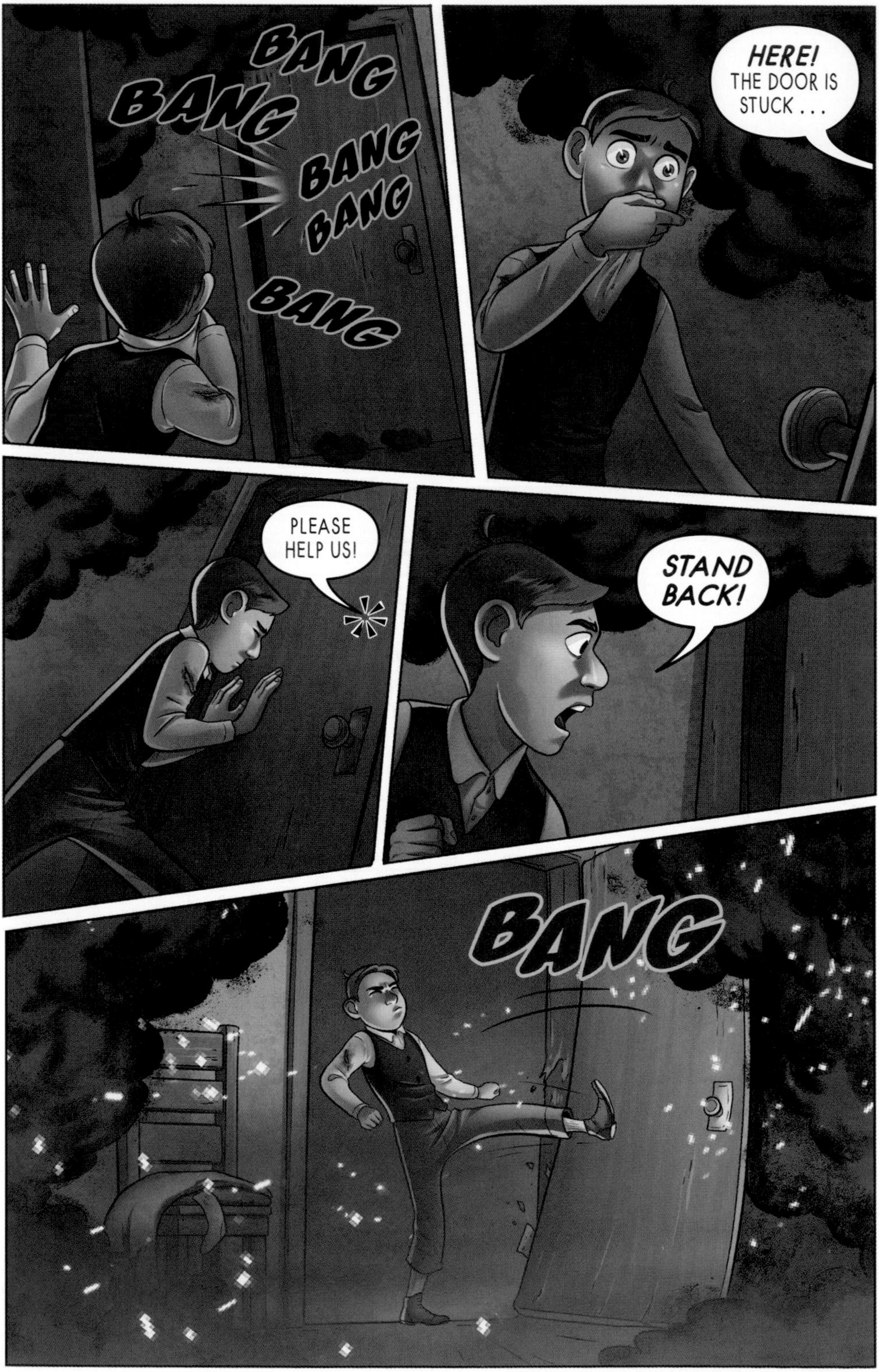
BANG
BANG
BANG
BANG
BANG
HERE! THE DOOR IS STUCK . . .
PLEASE HELP US!
STAND BACK!
BANG

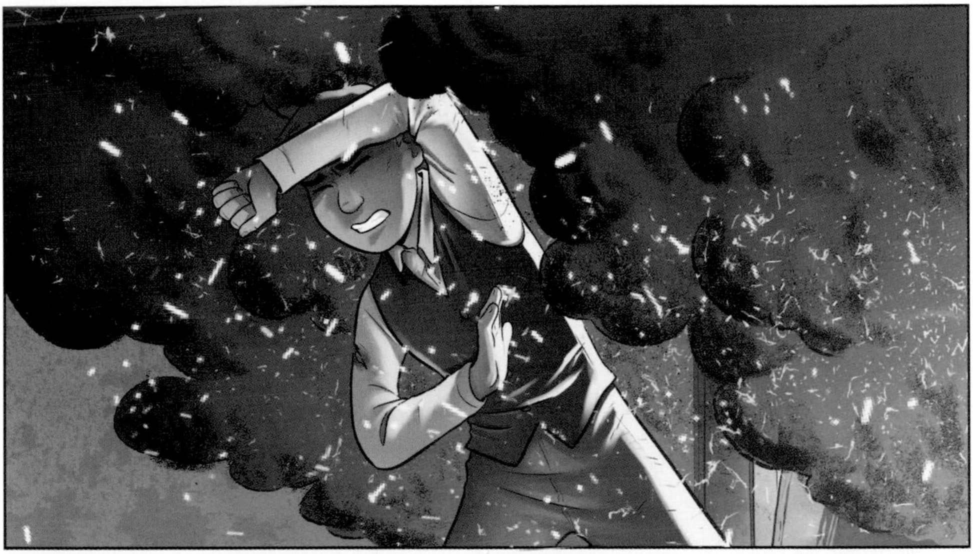

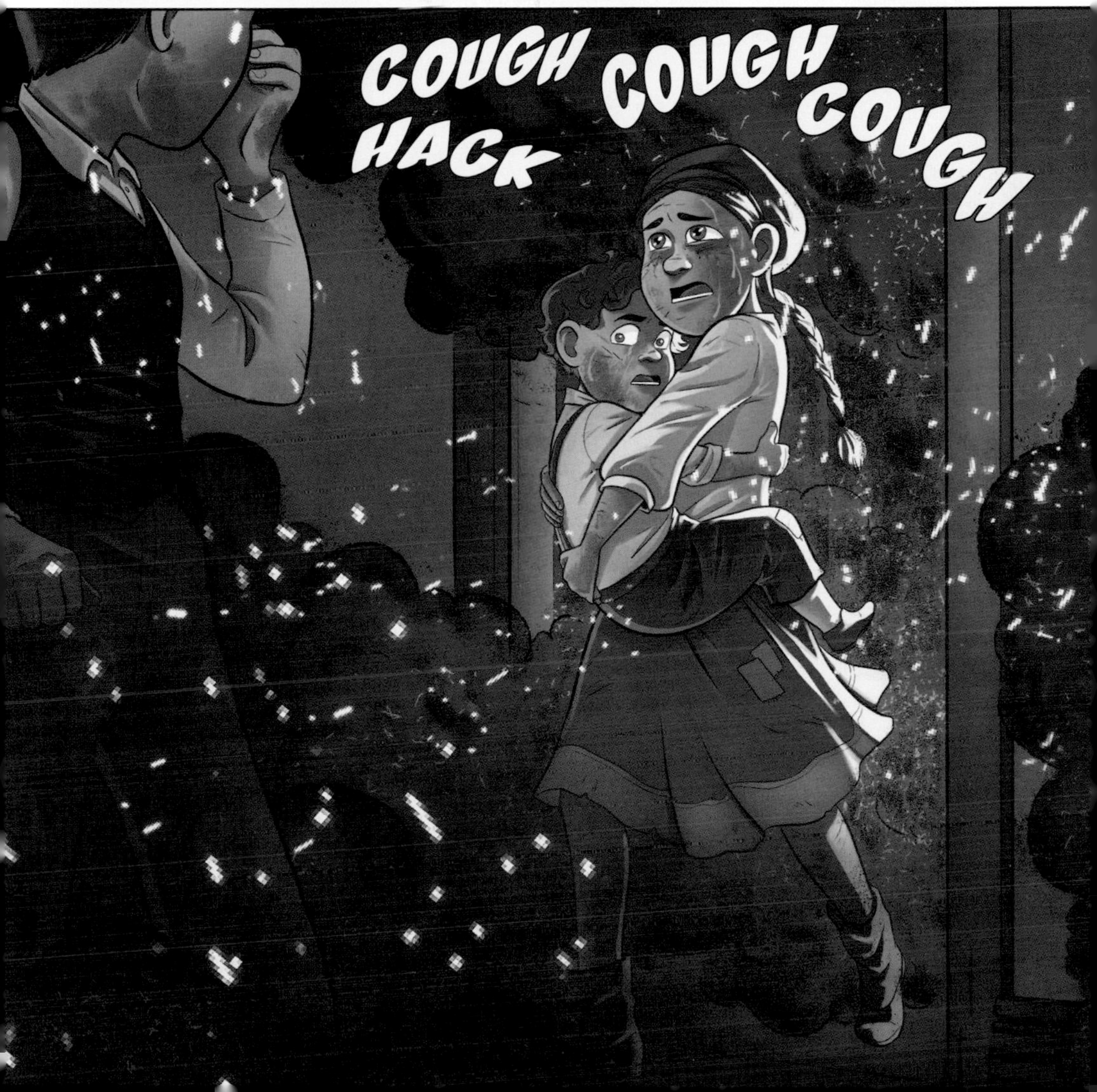
COUGH
HACK
COUGH
COUGH

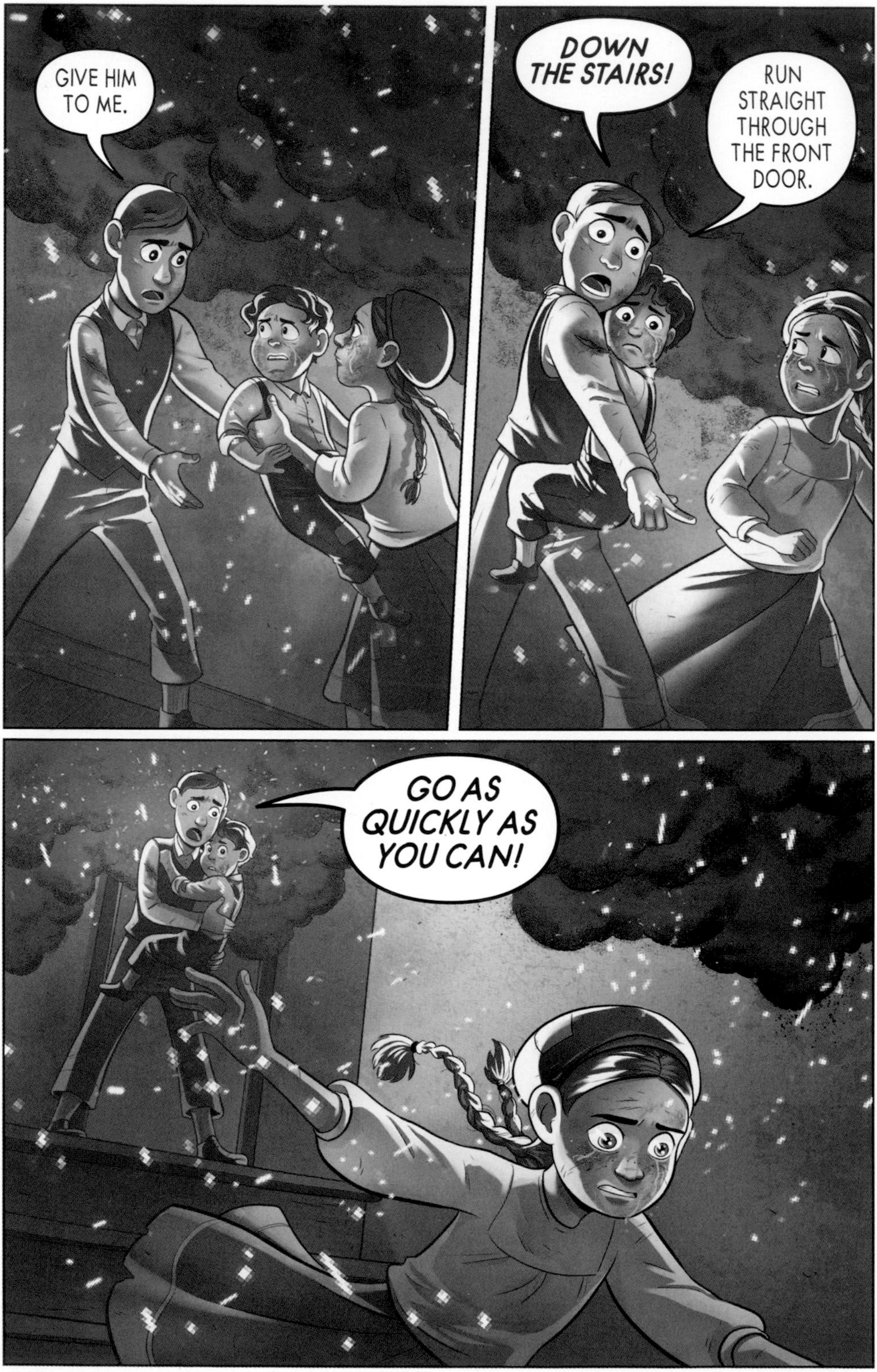
GIVE HIM TO ME.
DOWN THE STAIRS!
RUN STRAIGHT THROUGH THE FRONT DOOR.
GO AS QUICKLY AS YOU CAN!

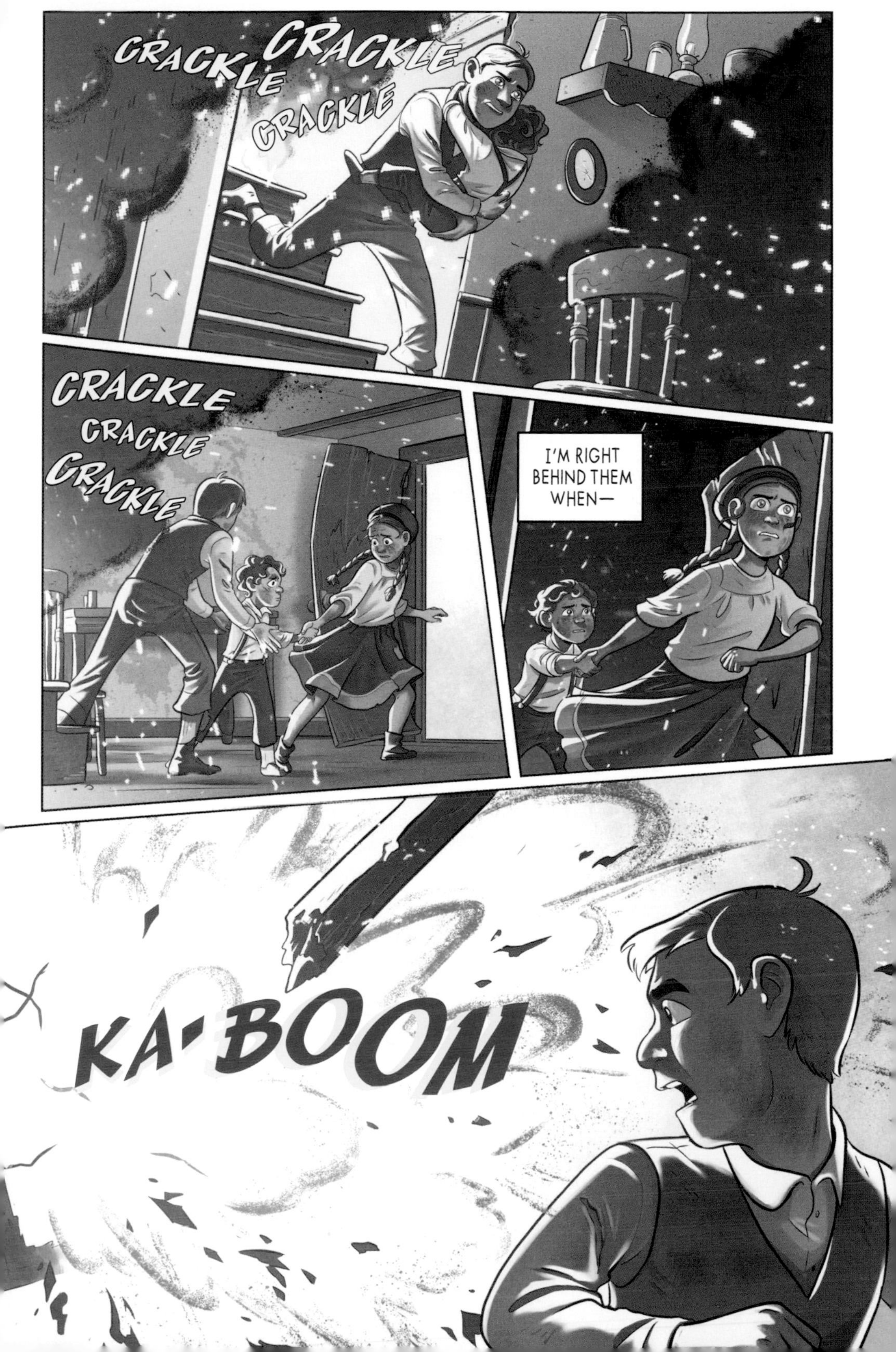
CRACKLE
CRACKLE
CRACKLE
CRACKLE
CRACKLE
CRACKLE
I'M RIGHT BEHIND THEM WHEN—
KA-BOOM

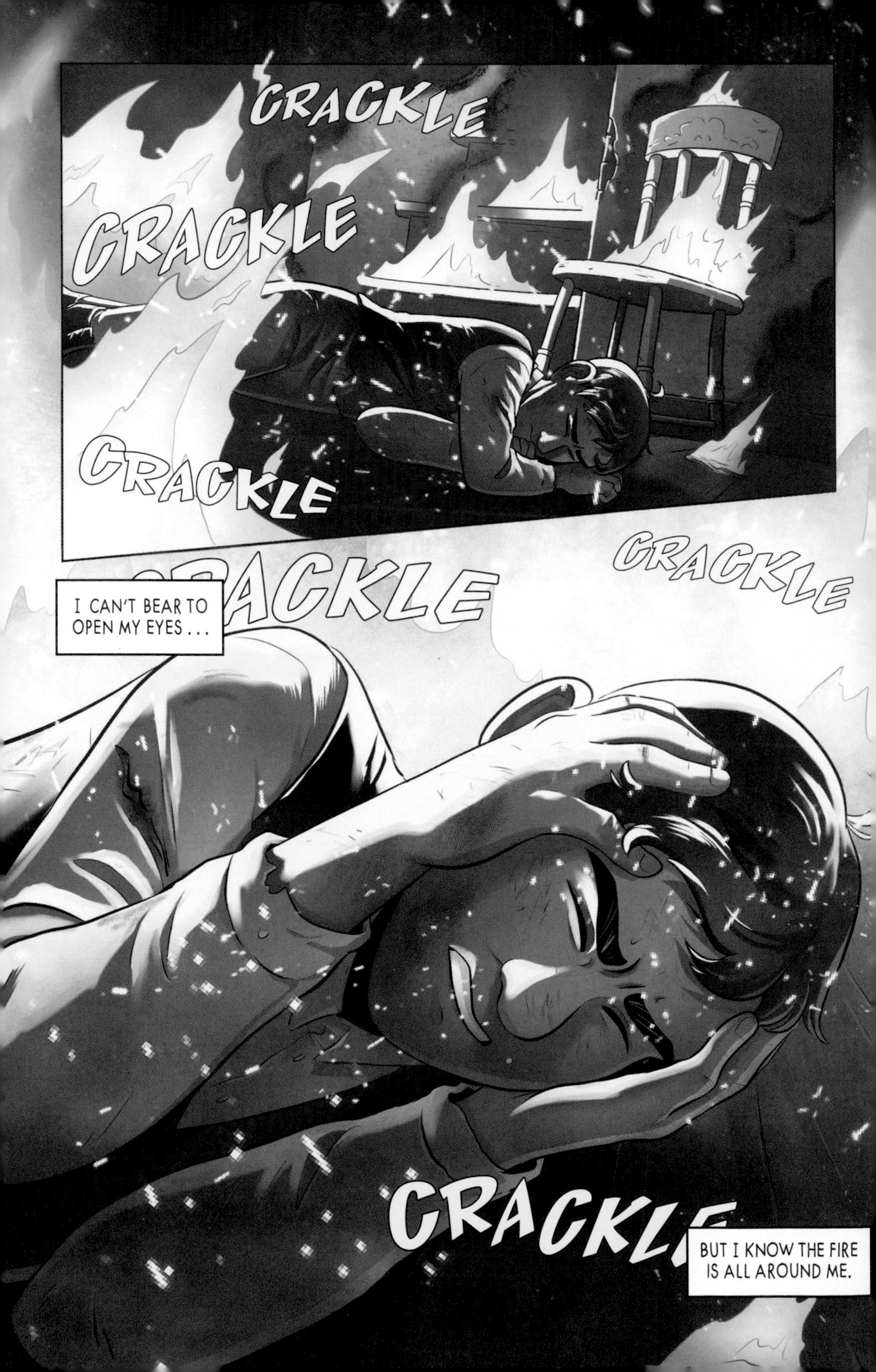
CRACKLE
CRACKLE
CRACKLE
CRACKLE
CRACKLE
I CAN'T BEAR TO OPEN MY EYES . . .
CRACKLE
BUT I KNOW THE FIRE IS ALL AROUND ME.

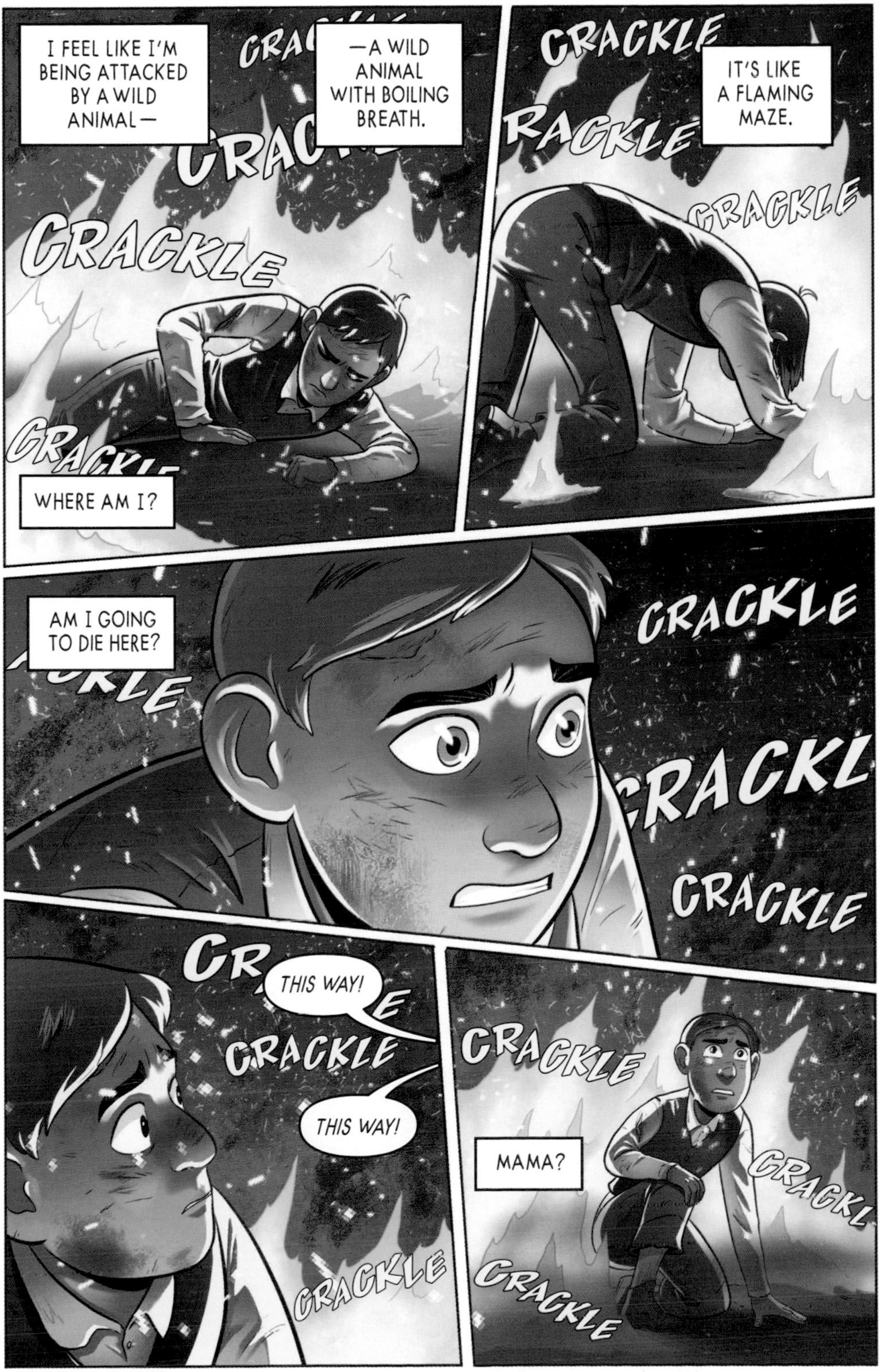
I FEEL LIKE I'M BEING ATTACKED BY A WILD ANIMAL—
CRACKLE
—A WILD ANIMAL WITH BOILING BREATH.
CRACKLE
CRACKLE
WHERE AM I?
CRACKLE
CRACKLE
IT'S LIKE A FLAMING MAZE.
CRACKLE
AM I GOING TO DIE HERE?
CRACKLE
CRACKLE
CRACKLE
THIS WAY!
CRACKLE
THIS WAY!
CRACKLE
CRACKLE
MAMA?
CRACKLE

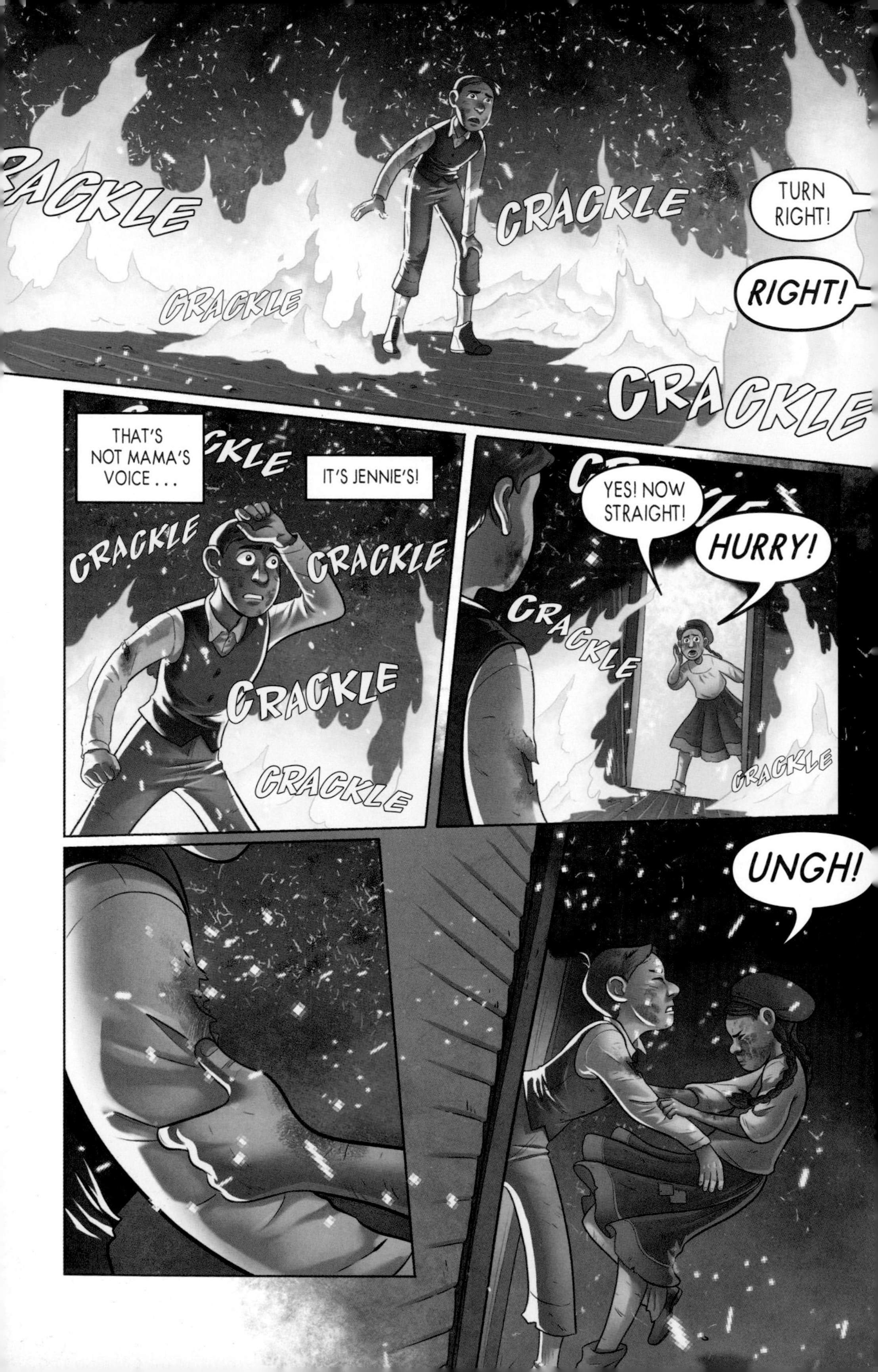
CRACKLE
CRACKLE
CRACKLE
TURN RIGHT!
RIGHT!
CRACKLE
THAT'S NOT MAMA'S VOICE . . .
CRACKLE
IT'S JENNIE'S!
CRACKLE
CRACKLE
CRACKLE
CRACKLE
YES! NOW STRAIGHT!
HURRY!
CRACKLE
CRACKLE
UNGH!

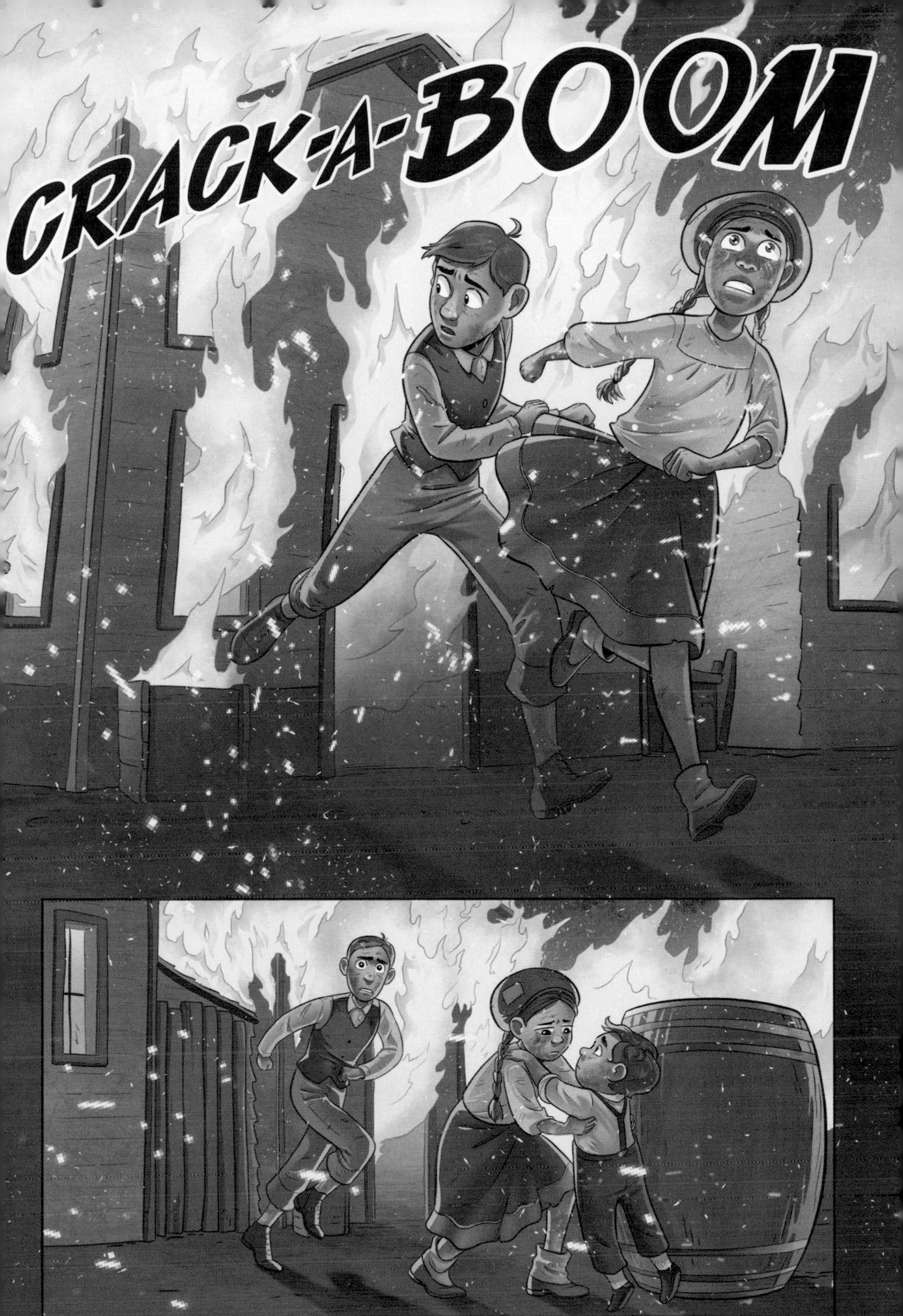
CRACK-A-BOOM

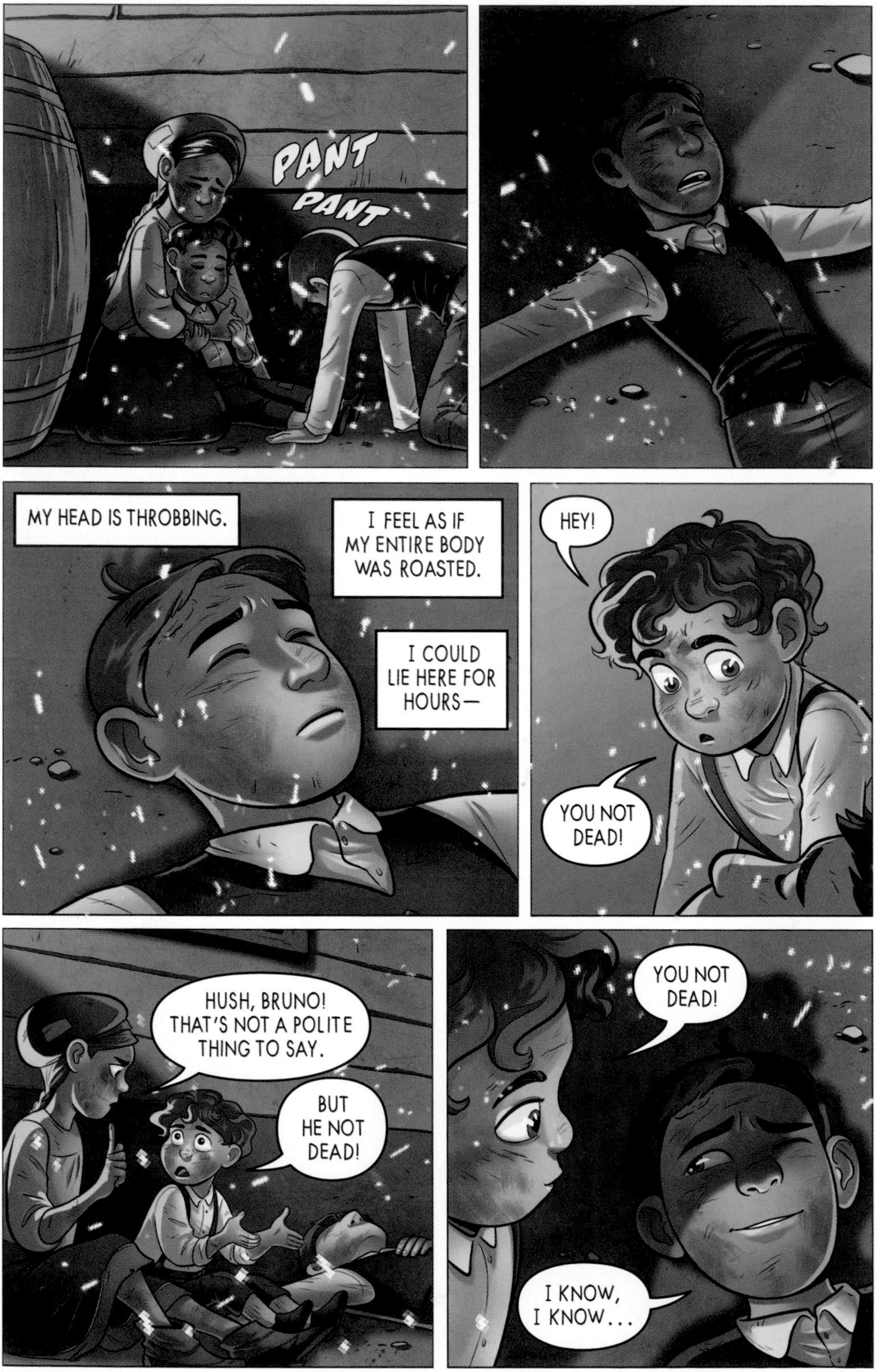
PANT
PANT
MY HEAD IS THROBBING.
I FEEL AS IF MY ENTIRE BODY WAS ROASTED.
I COULD LIE HERE FOR HOURS—
HEY!
YOU NOT DEAD!
HUSH, BRUNO! THAT'S NOT A POLITE THING TO SAY.
BUT HE NOT DEAD!
YOU NOT DEAD!
I KNOW, I KNOW...

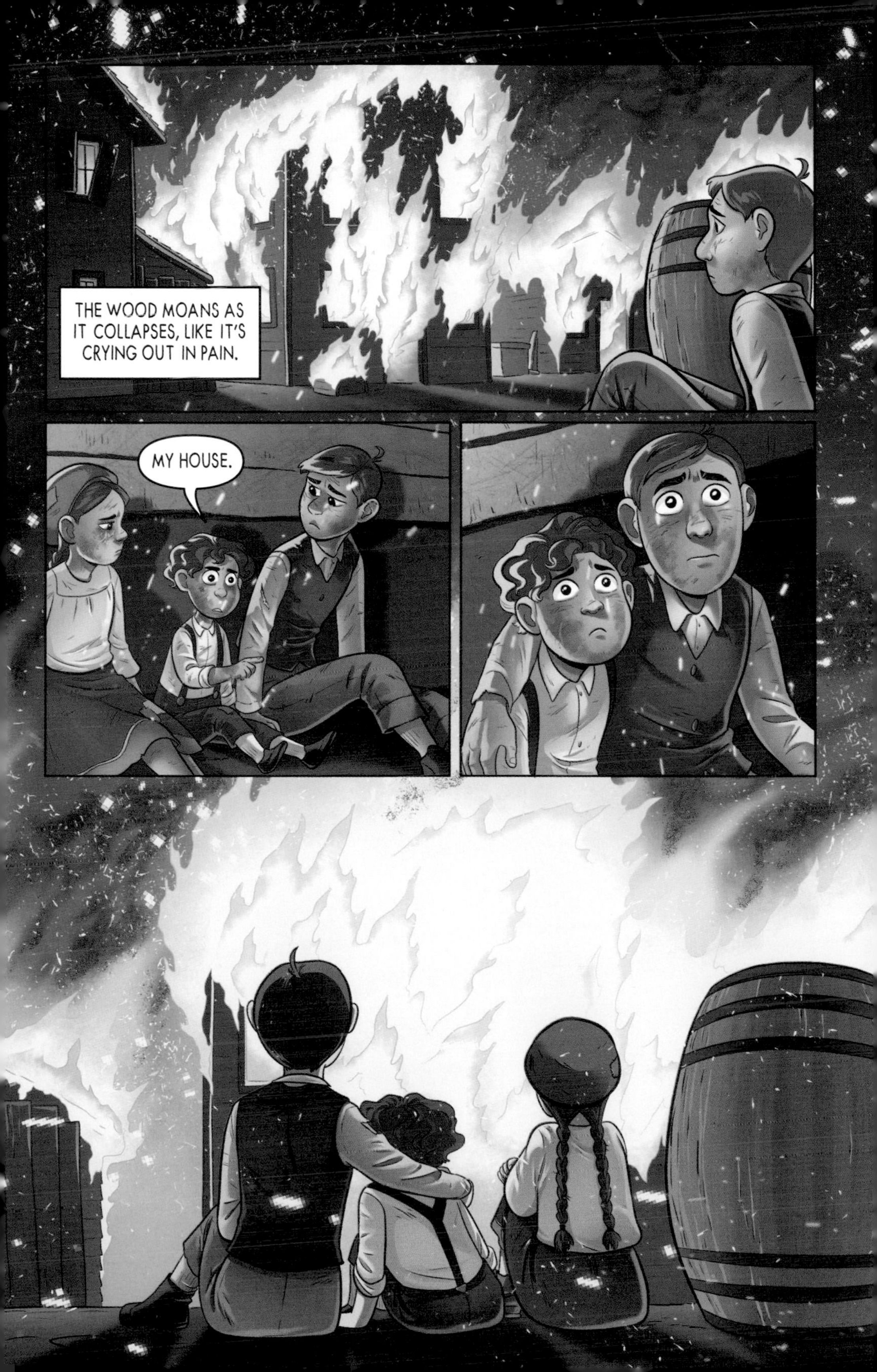
THE WOOD MOANS AS IT COLLAPSES, LIKE IT'S CRYING OUT IN PAIN.
MY HOUSE.

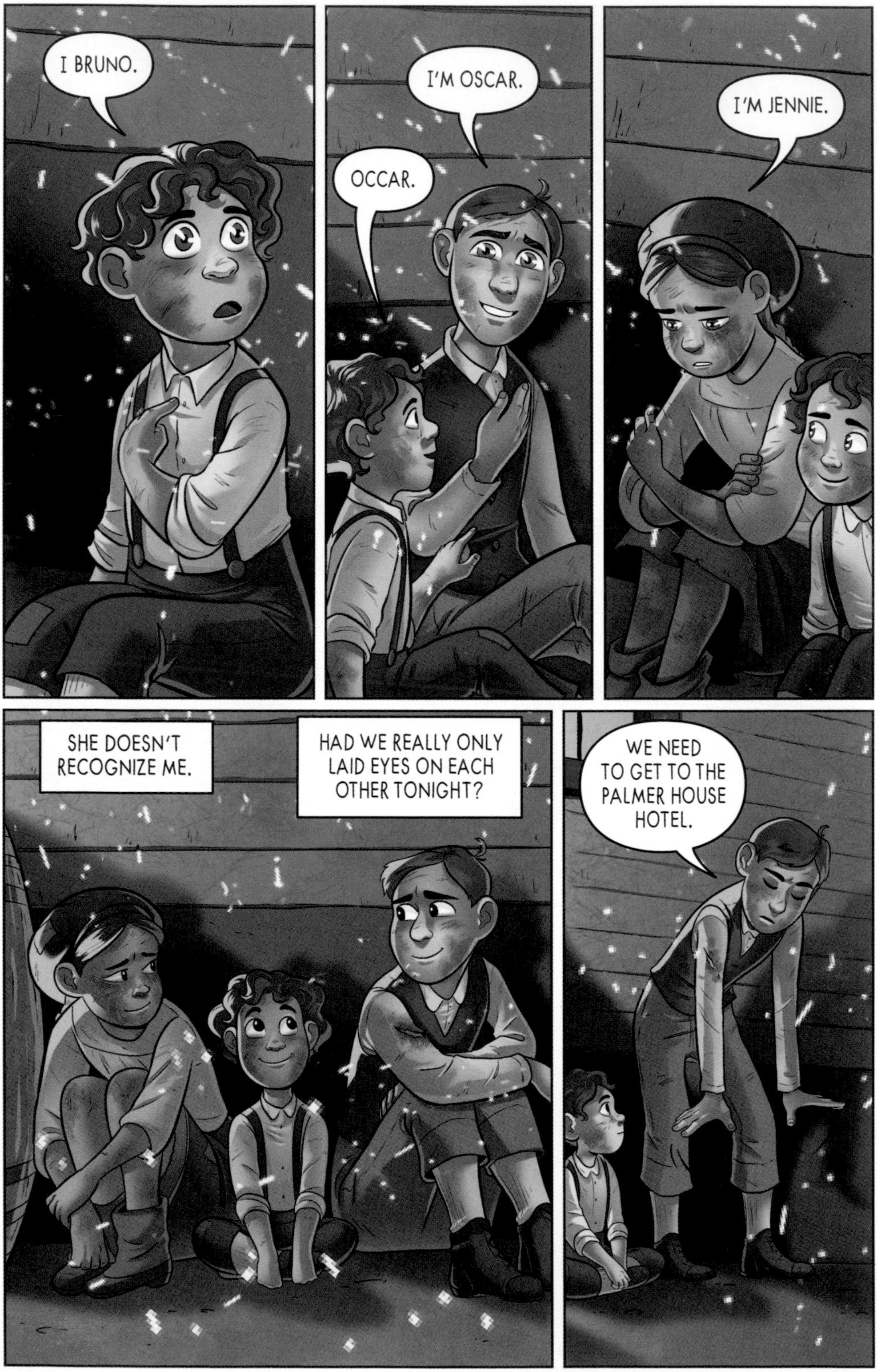
I BRUNO.
I'M OSCAR.
OCCAR.
I'M JENNIE.
SHE DOESN'T RECOGNIZE ME.
HAD WE REALLY ONLY LAID EYES ON EACH OTHER TONIGHT?
WE NEED TO GET TO THE PALMER HOUSE HOTEL.

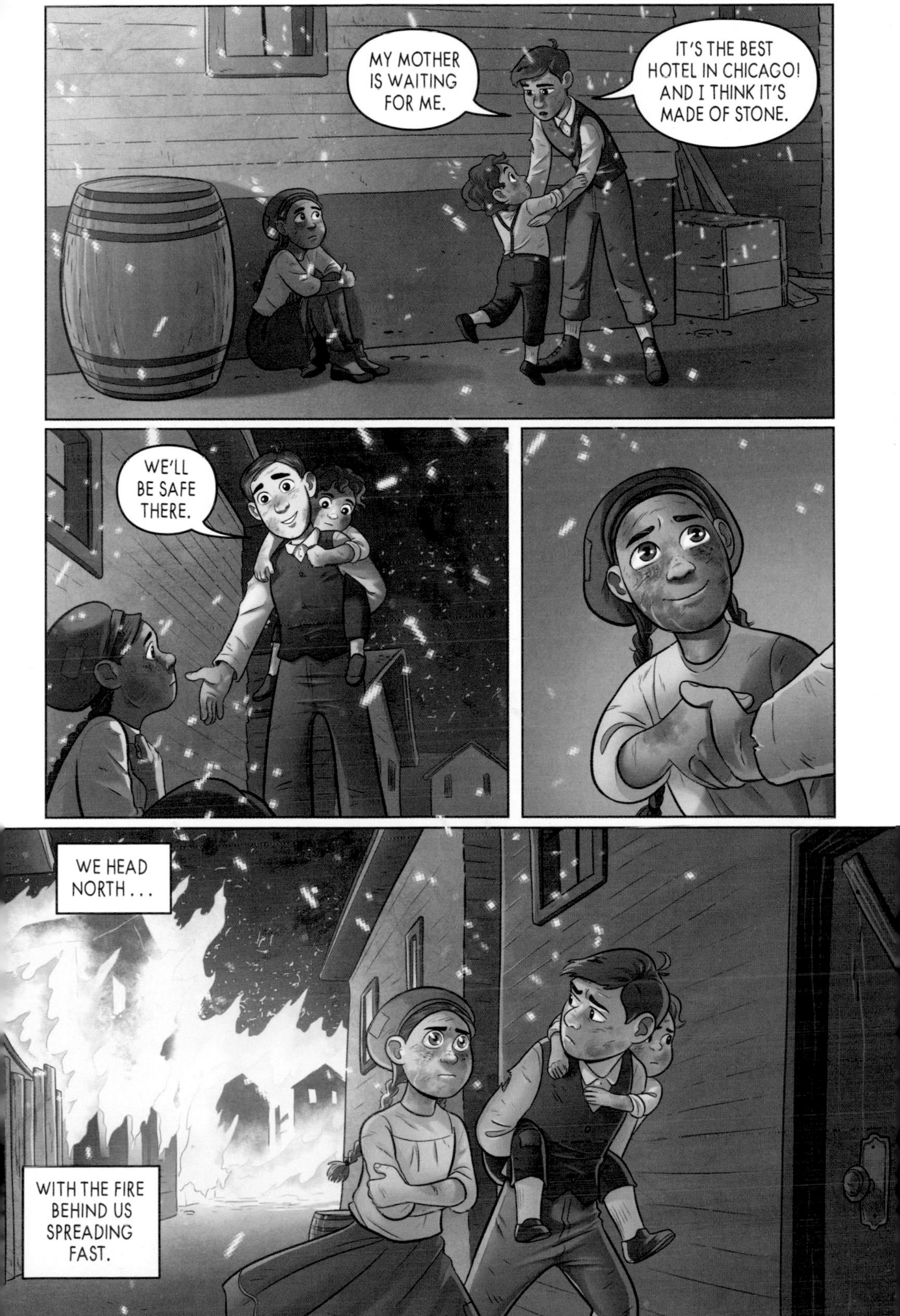
MY MOTHER IS WAITING FOR ME.
IT'S THE BEST HOTEL IN CHICAGO! AND I THINK IT'S MADE OF STONE.
WE'LL BE SAFE THERE.
WE HEAD NORTH . . .
WITH THE FIRE BEHIND US SPREADING FAST.

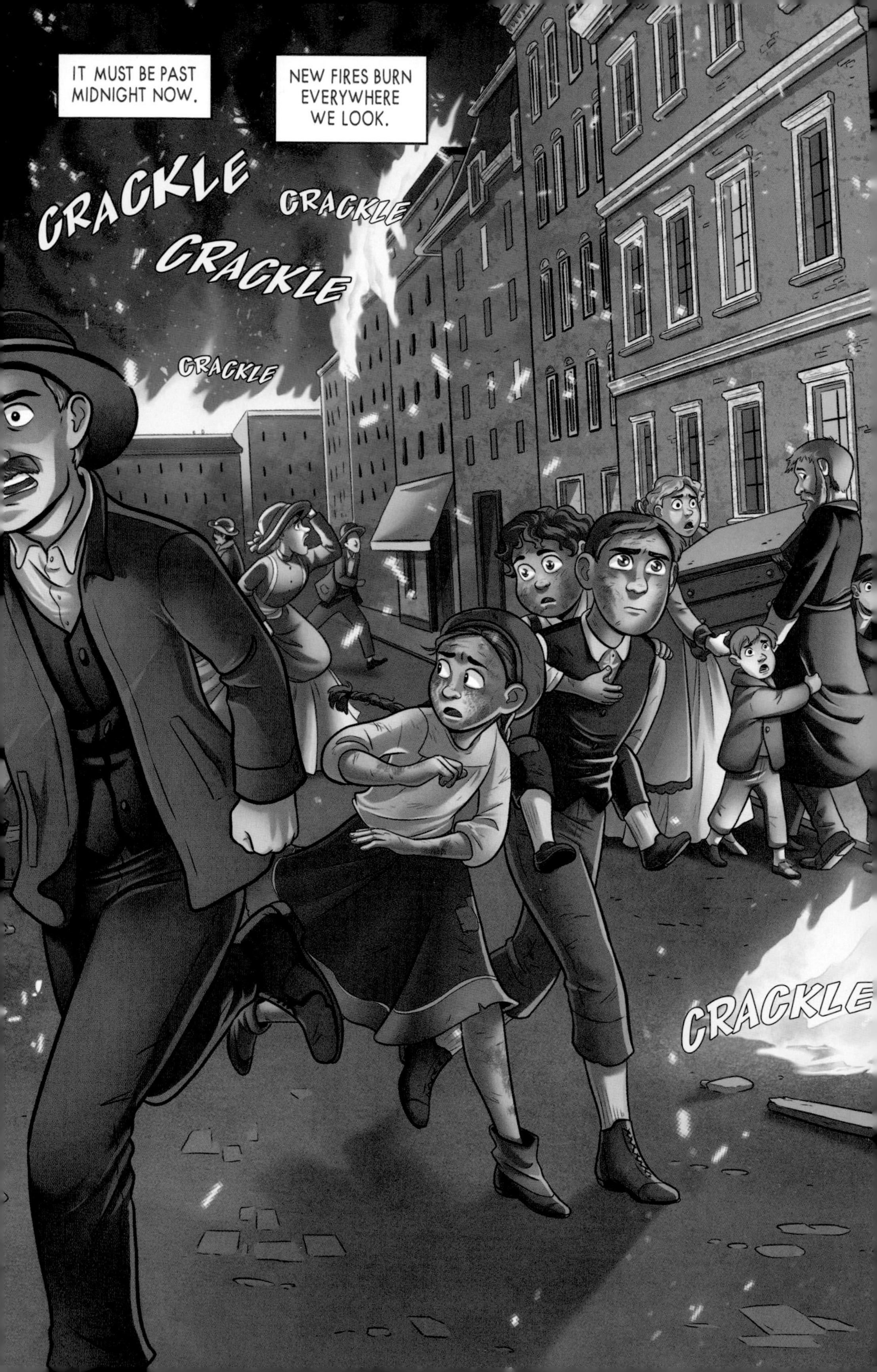
IT MUST BE PAST MIDNIGHT NOW.
NEW FIRES BURN EVERYWHERE WE LOOK.
CRACKLE
CRACKLE
CRACKLE
CRACKLE
CRACKLE

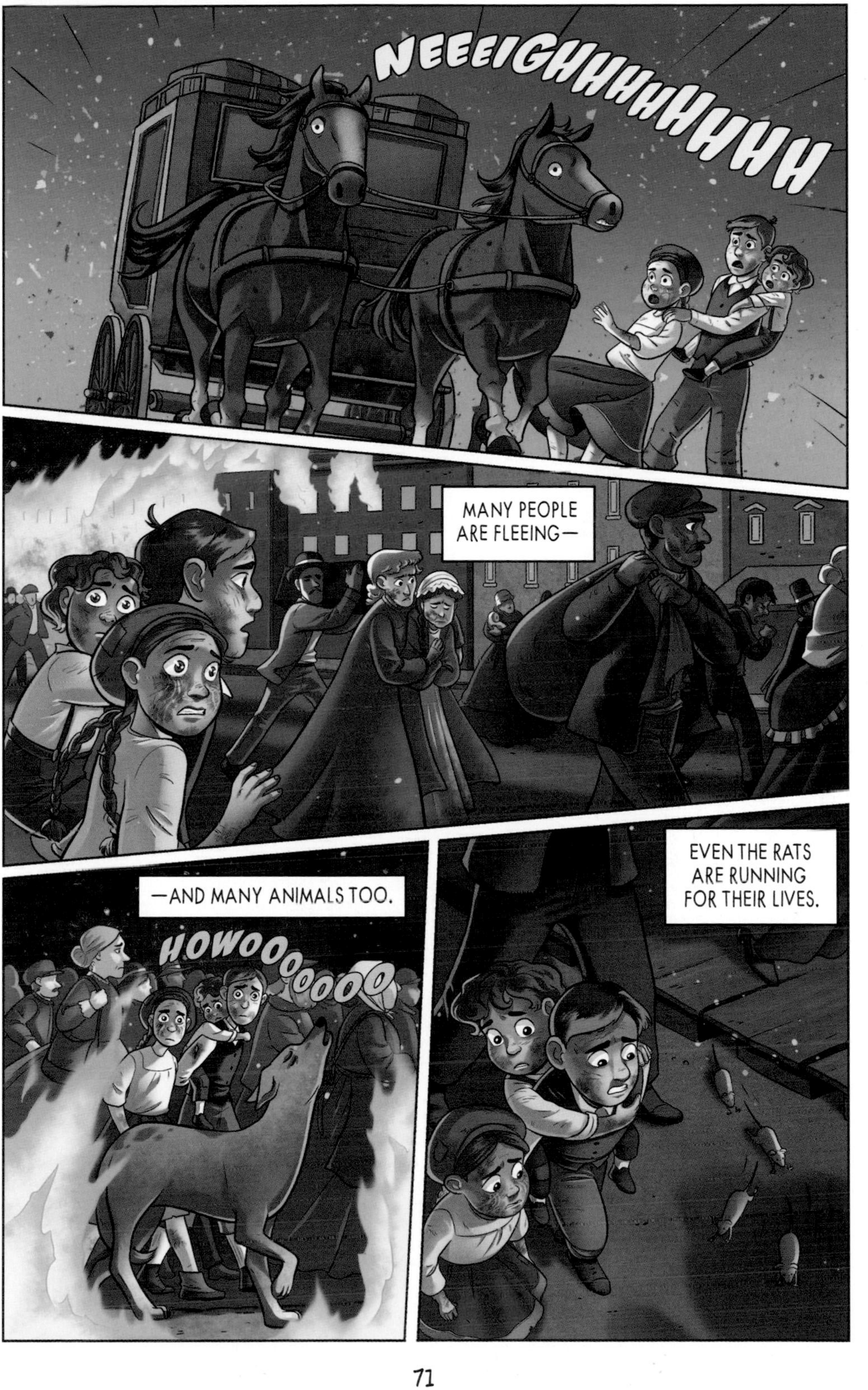
NEEEIGHHHHHHHHH
MANY PEOPLE ARE FLEEING—
—AND MANY ANIMALS TOO.
HOWOOOOOOOO
EVEN THE RATS ARE RUNNING FOR THEIR LIVES.

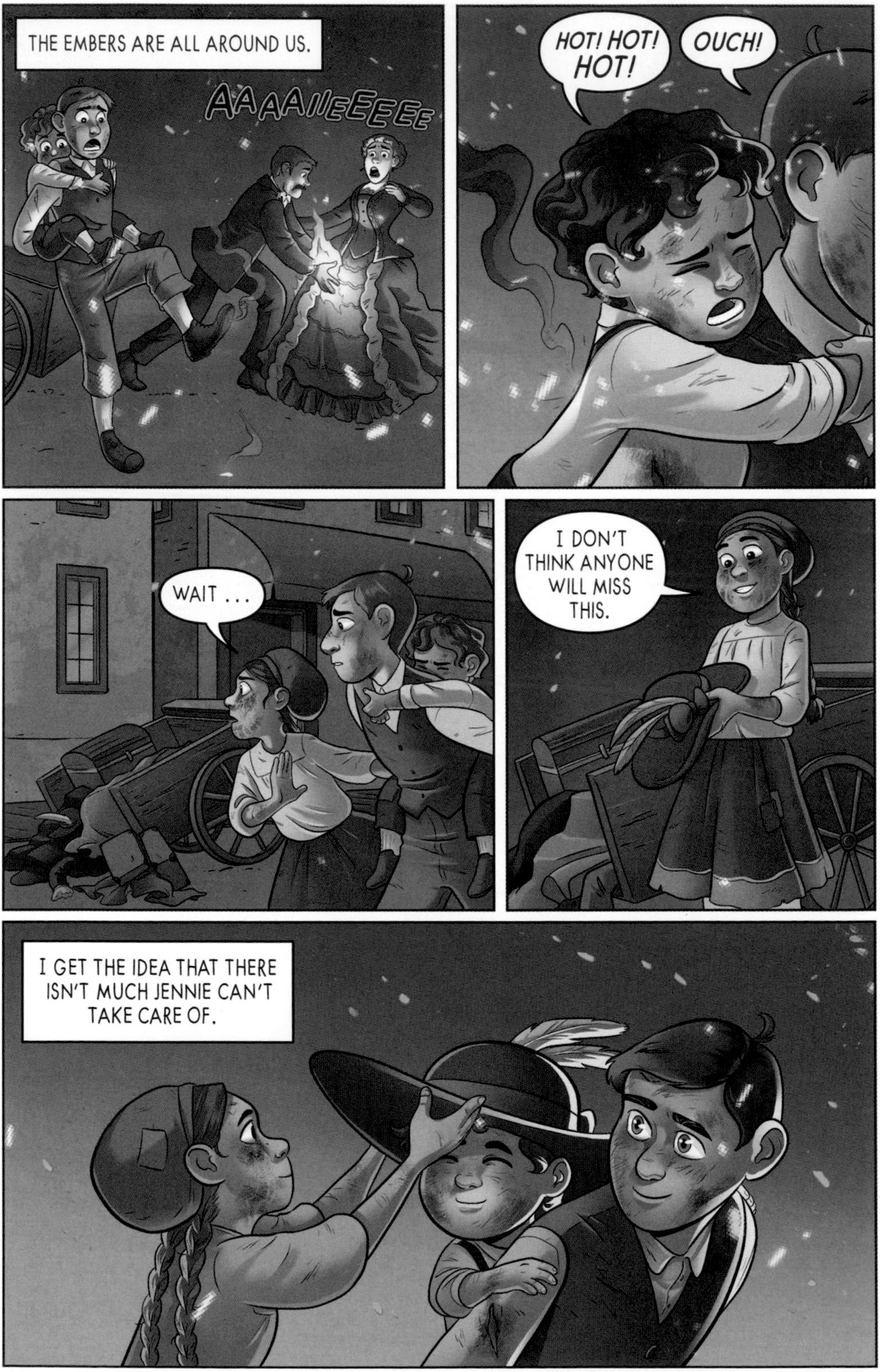
THE EMBERS ARE ALL AROUND US.
AAAAIIEEEEE
HOT! HOT! HOT!
OUCH!
WAIT . . .
I DON'T THINK ANYONE WILL MISS THIS.
I GET THE IDEA THAT THERE ISN'T MUCH JENNIE CAN'T TAKE CARE OF.

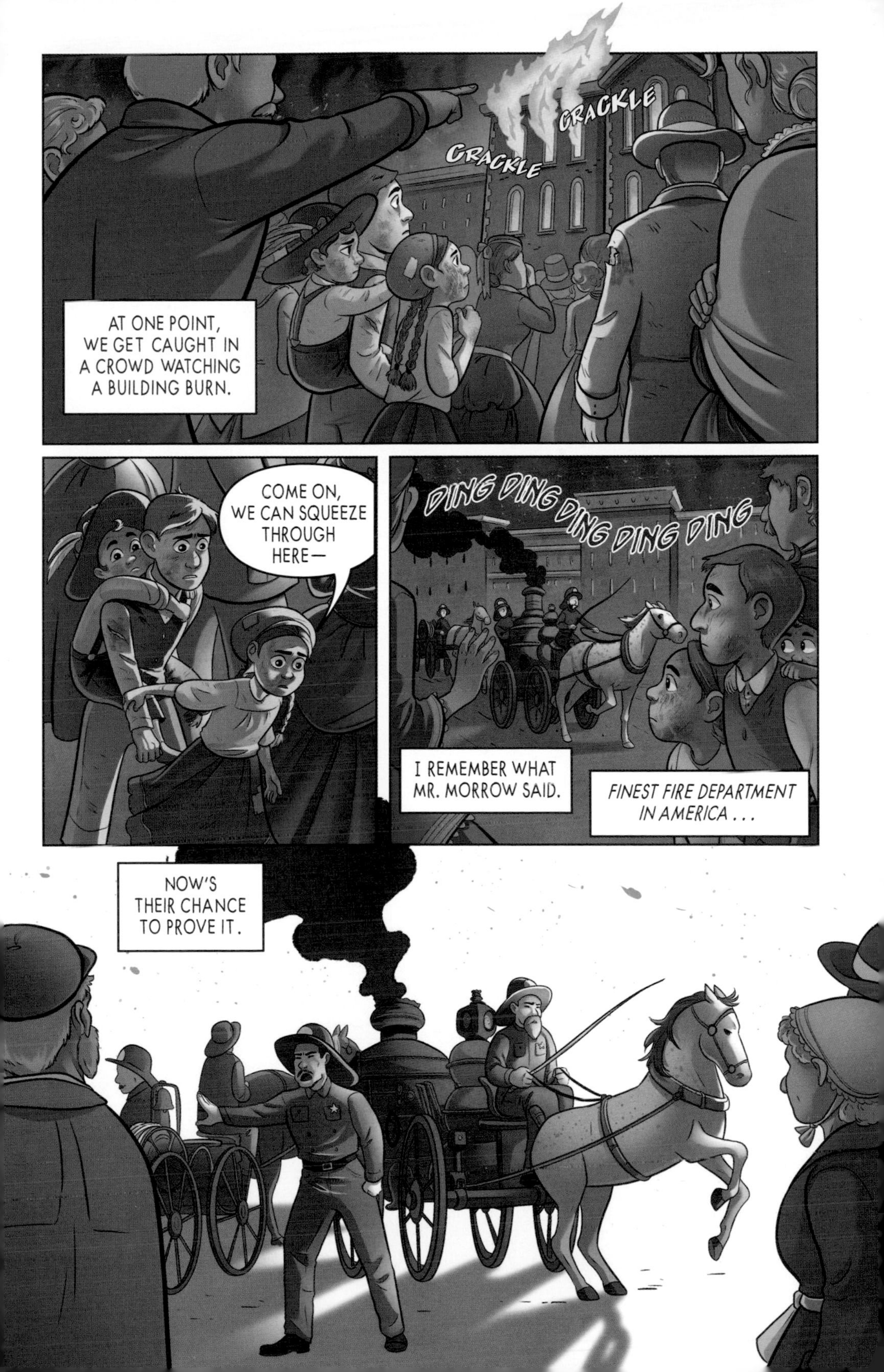
CRACKLE
CRACKLE
AT ONE POINT, WE GET CAUGHT IN A CROWD WATCHING A BUILDING BURN.
COME ON, WE CAN SQUEEZE THROUGH HERE—
DING DING DING DING DING
I REMEMBER WHAT MR. MORROW SAID.
FINEST FIRE DEPARTMENT IN AMERICA . . .
NOW'S THEIR CHANCE TO PROVE IT.

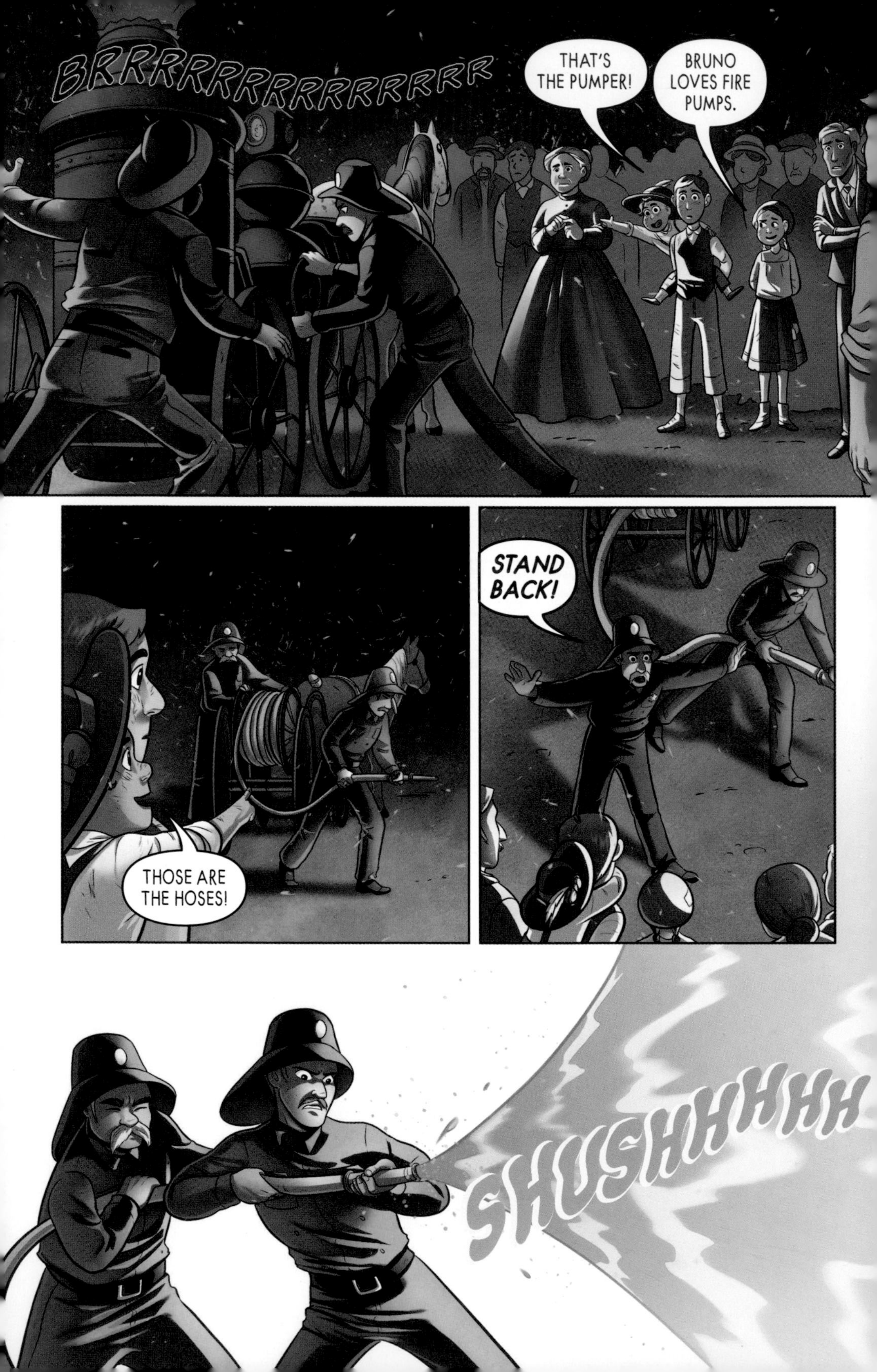
BRRRRRRRRRRRRRRR
THAT'S THE PUMPER!
BRUNO LOVES FIRE PUMPS.
THOSE ARE THE HOSES!
STAND BACK!
SHUSHHHHHH

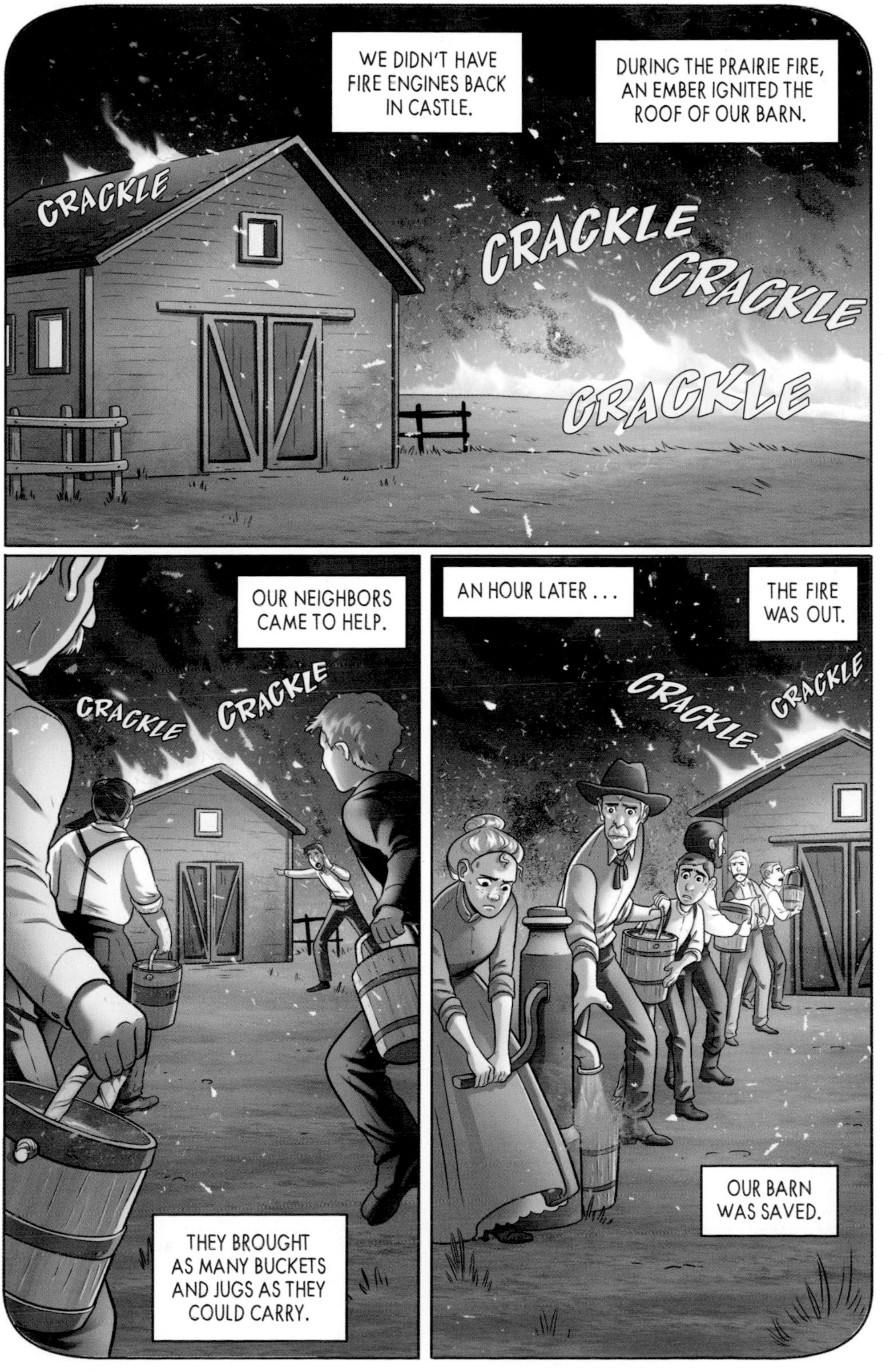
WE DIDN'T HAVE FIRE ENGINES BACK IN CASTLE.
DURING THE PRAIRIE FIRE, AN EMBER IGNITED THE ROOF OF OUR BARN.
CRACKLE
CRACKLE
CRACKLE
CRACKLE
OUR NEIGHBORS CAME TO HELP.
CRACKLE
CRACKLE
THEY BROUGHT AS MANY BUCKETS AND JUGS AS THEY COULD CARRY.
AN HOUR LATER . . .
THE FIRE WAS OUT.
CRACKLE
CRACKLE
OUR BARN WAS SAVED.

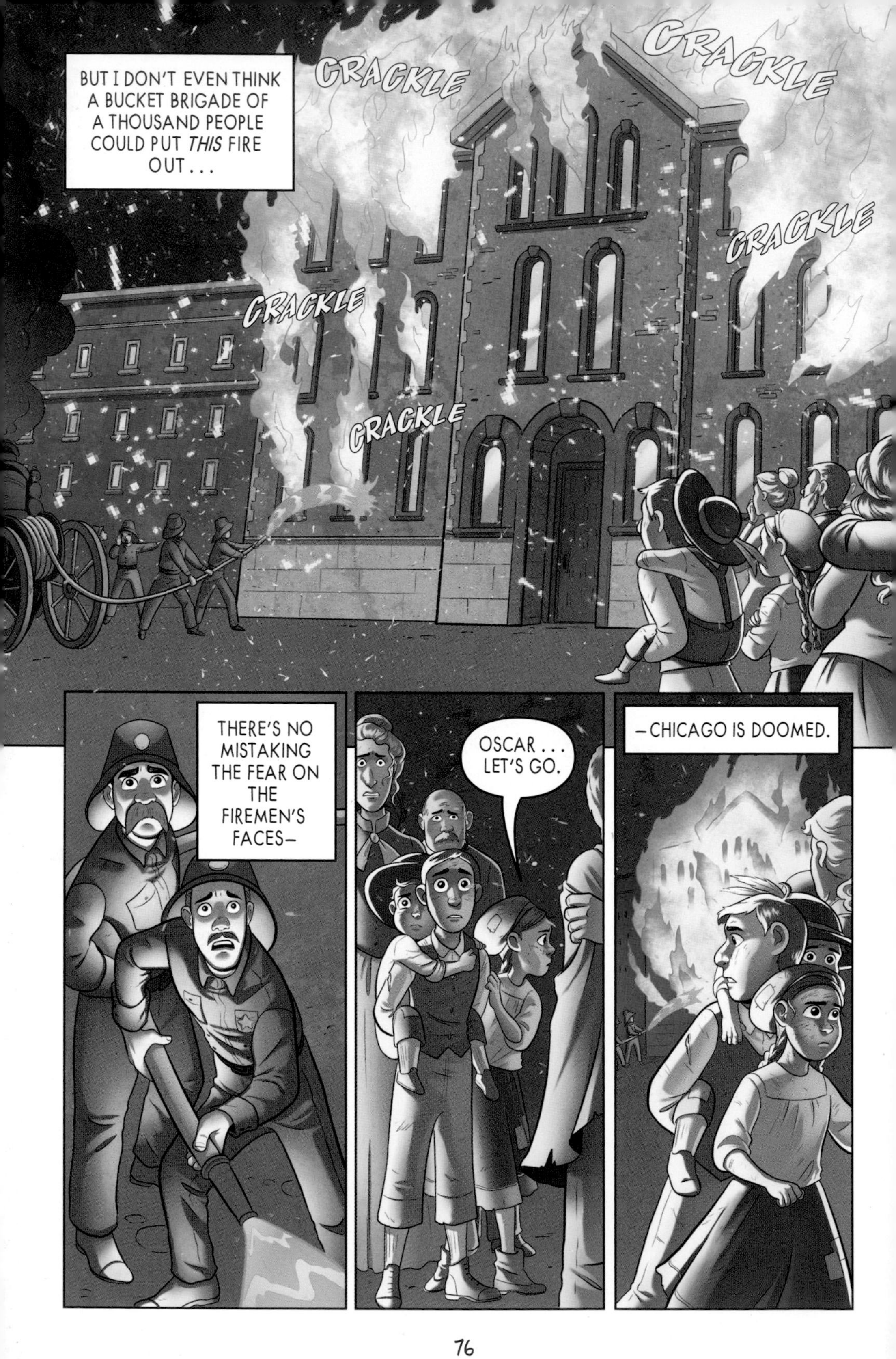
BUT I DON'T EVEN THINK A BUCKET BRIGADE OF A THOUSAND PEOPLE COULD PUT *THIS* FIRE OUT . . .
CRACKLE
CRACKLE
CRACKLE
CRACKLE
CRACKLE
THERE'S NO MISTAKING THE FEAR ON THE FIREMEN'S FACES—
OSCAR . . . LET'S GO.
—CHICAGO IS DOOMED.

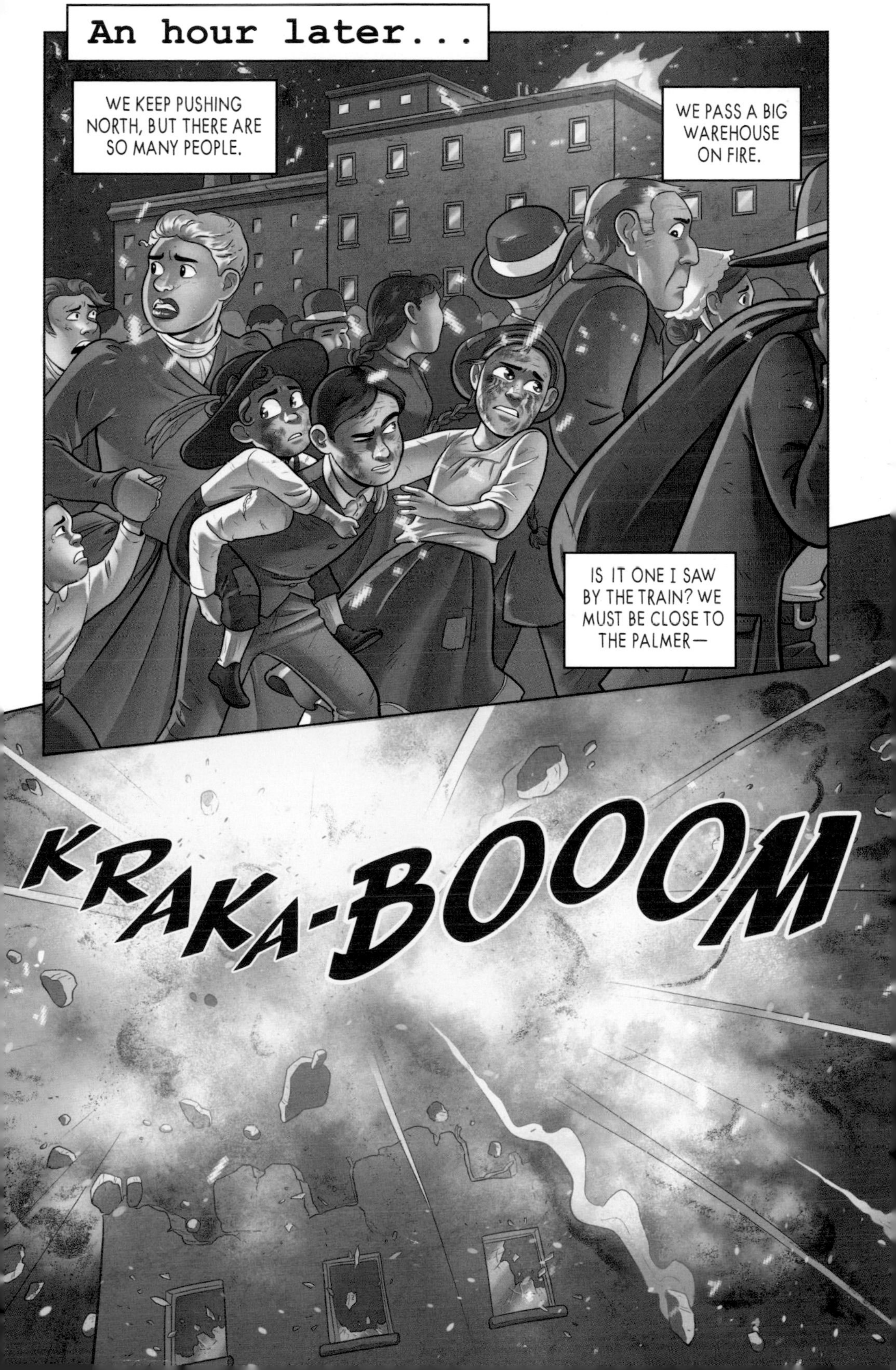
An hour later...
WE KEEP PUSHING NORTH, BUT THERE ARE SO MANY PEOPLE.
WE PASS A BIG WAREHOUSE ON FIRE.
IS IT ONE I SAW BY THE TRAIN? WE MUST BE CLOSE TO THE PALMER—
KRAKA-BOOOM

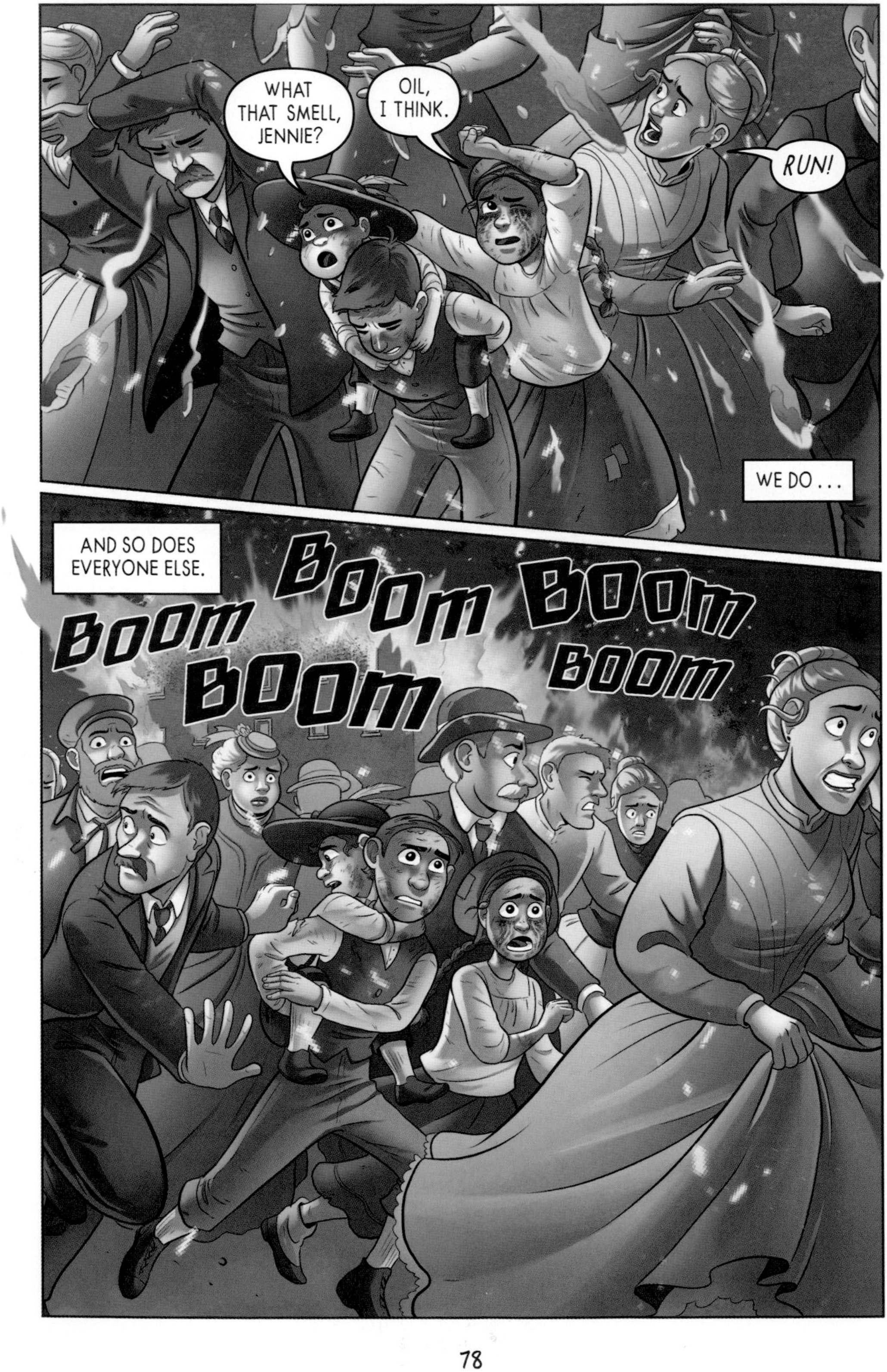
WHAT THAT SMELL, JENNIE?
OIL, I THINK.
RUN!
WE DO . . .
AND SO DOES EVERYONE ELSE.
BOOM
BOOM
BOOM
BOOM
BOOM

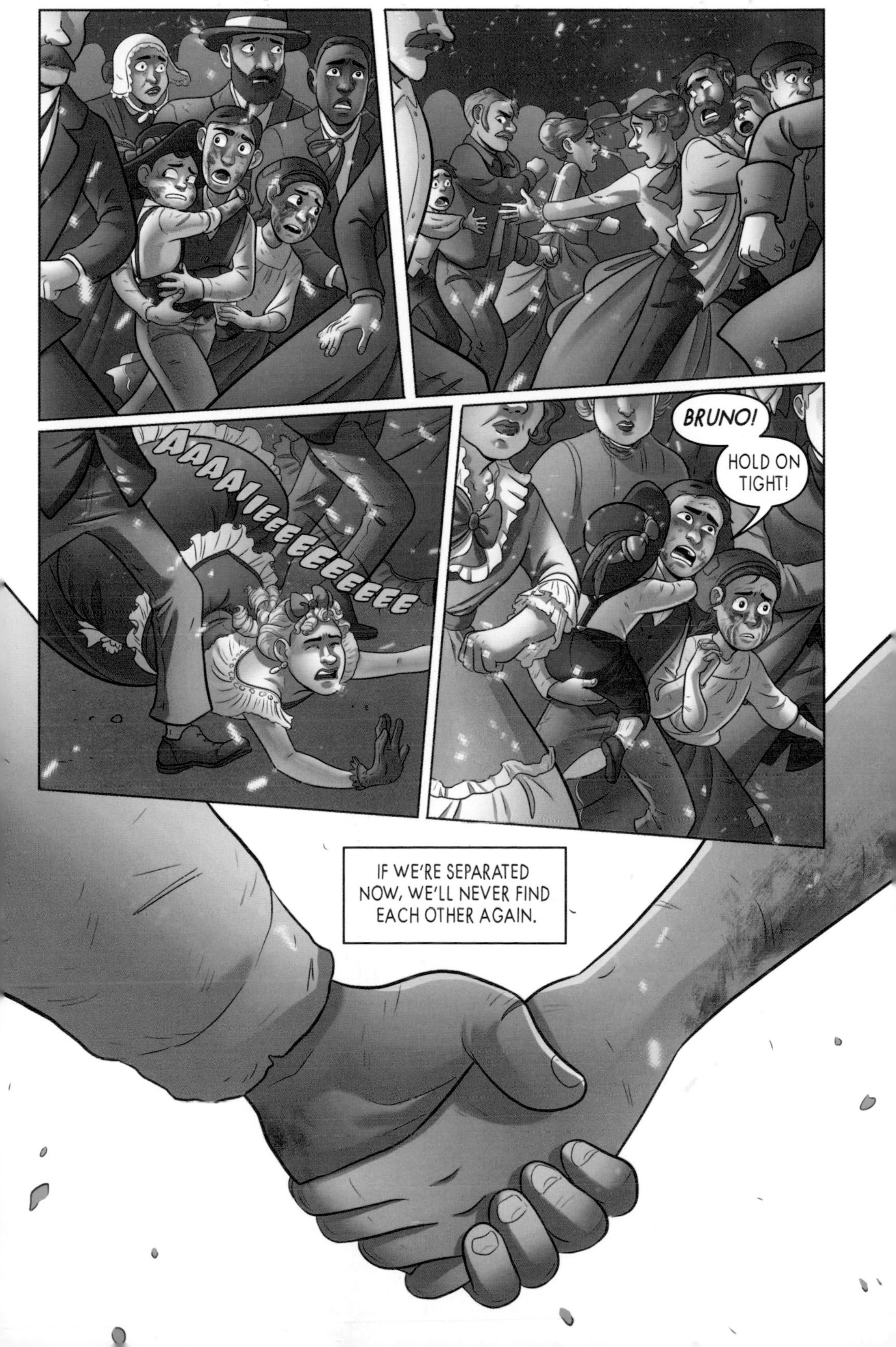
AAAAIIEEEEEEEEEEEEE
BRUNO!
HOLD ON TIGHT!
IF WE'RE SEPARATED NOW, WE'LL NEVER FIND EACH OTHER AGAIN.

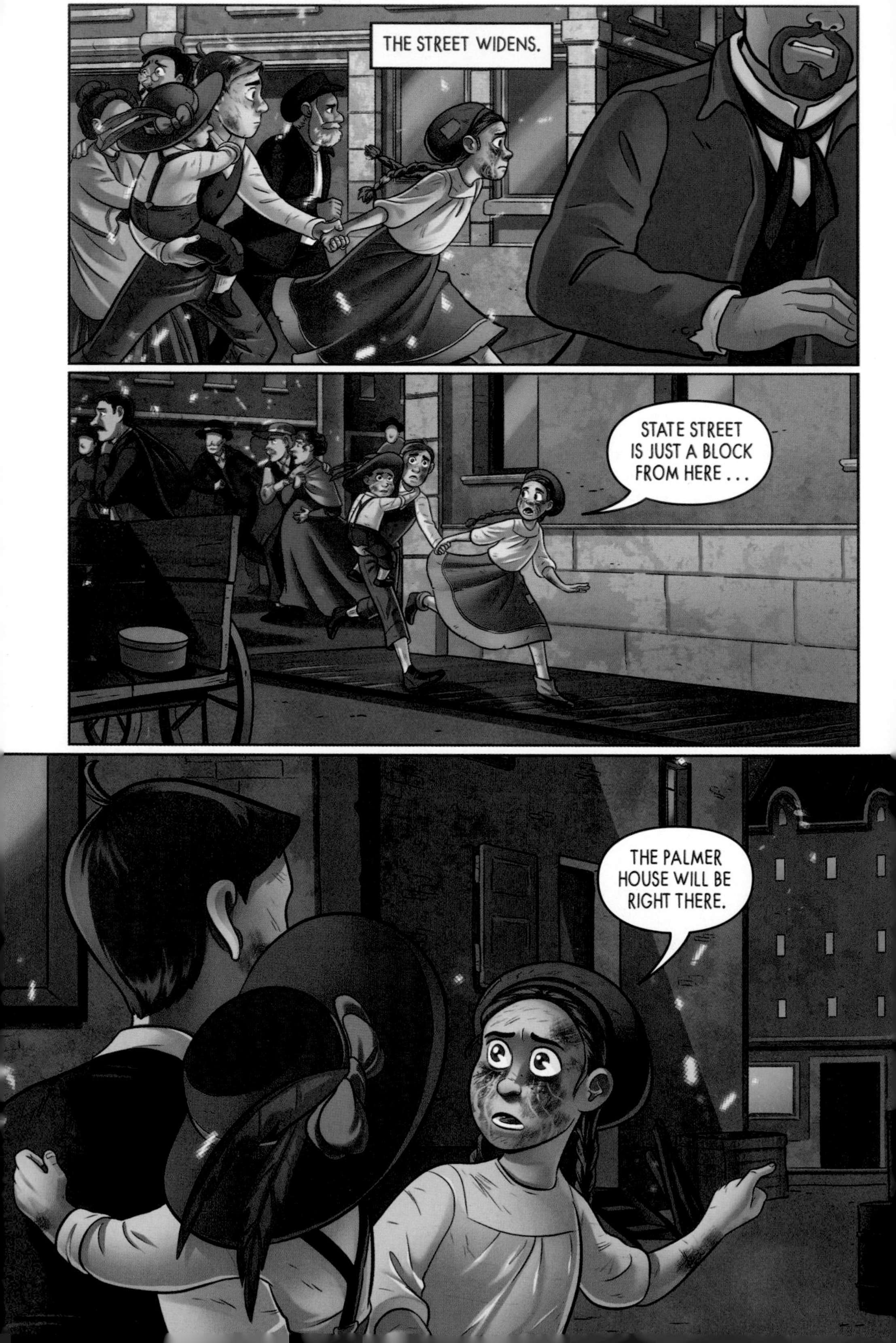
THE STREET WIDENS.
STATE STREET IS JUST A BLOCK FROM HERE . . .
THE PALMER HOUSE WILL BE RIGHT THERE.

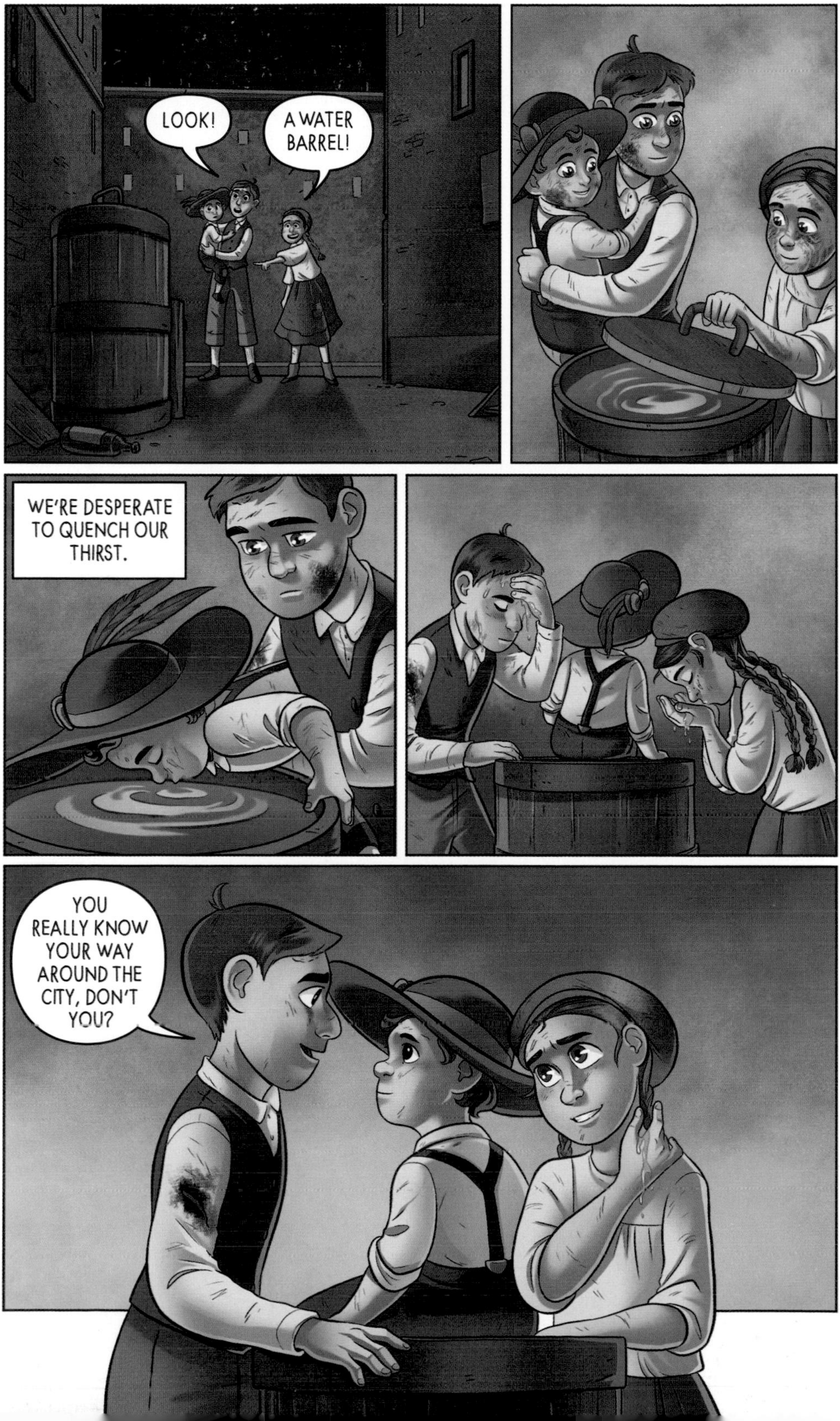
LOOK!
A WATER BARREL!
WE'RE DESPERATE TO QUENCH OUR THIRST.
YOU REALLY KNOW YOUR WAY AROUND THE CITY, DON'T YOU?

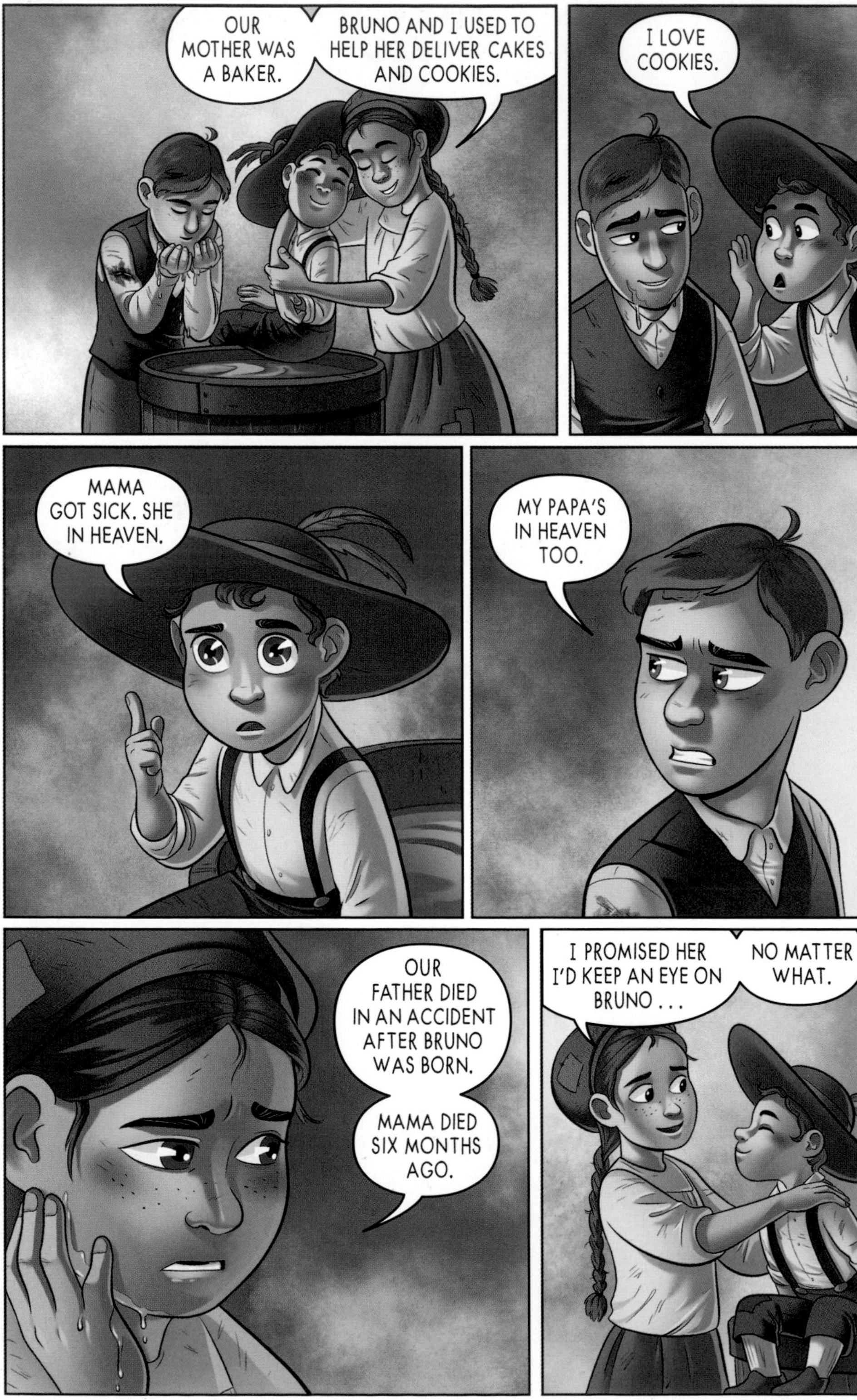
OUR MOTHER WAS A BAKER.
BRUNO AND I USED TO HELP HER DELIVER CAKES AND COOKIES.
I LOVE COOKIES.
MAMA GOT SICK. SHE IN HEAVEN.
MY PAPA'S IN HEAVEN TOO.
OUR FATHER DIED IN AN ACCIDENT AFTER BRUNO WAS BORN.
MAMA DIED SIX MONTHS AGO.
I PROMISED HER I'D KEEP AN EYE ON BRUNO . . .
NO MATTER WHAT.

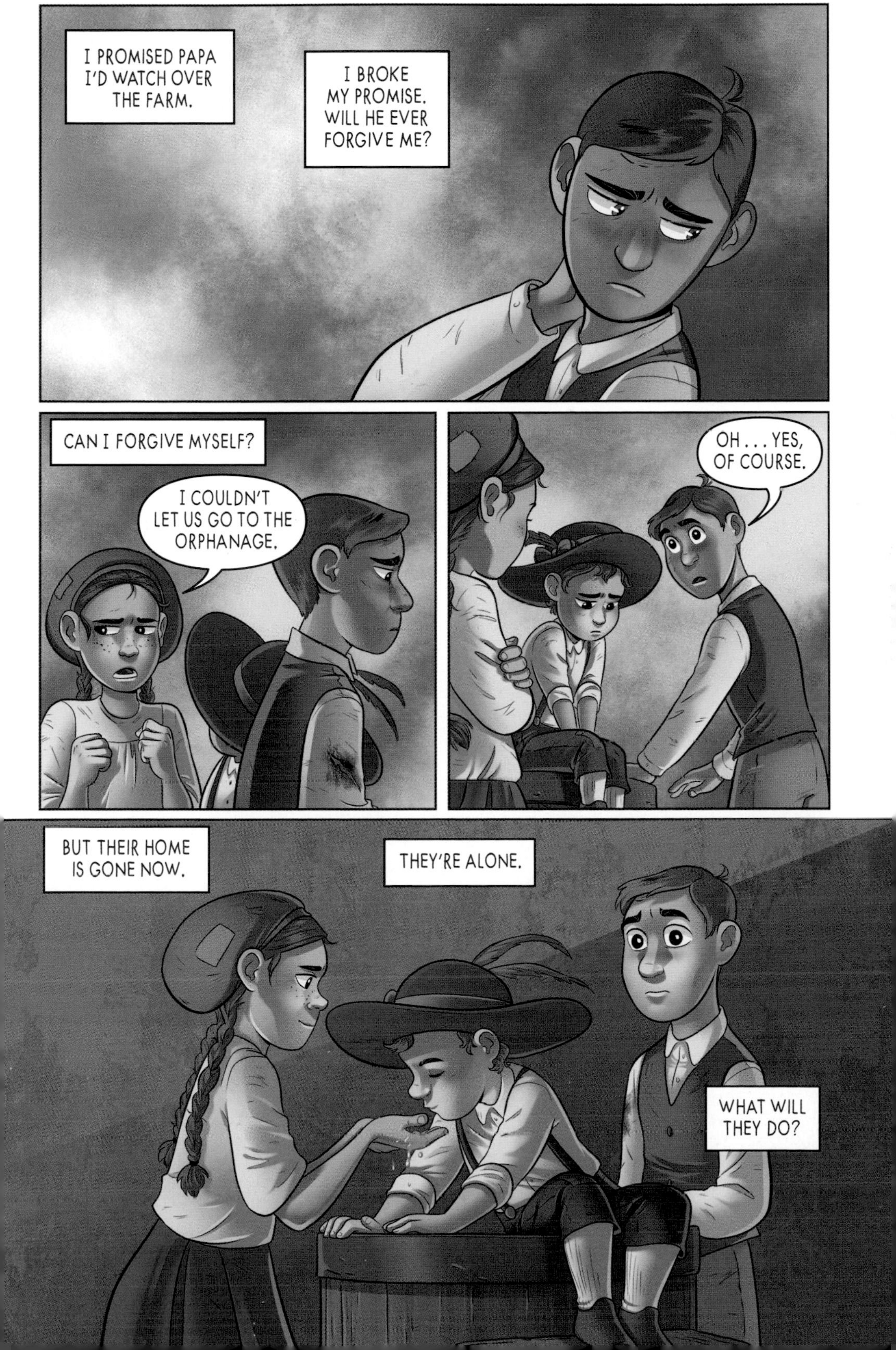
I PROMISED PAPA I'D WATCH OVER THE FARM.
I BROKE MY PROMISE. WILL HE EVER FORGIVE ME?
CAN I FORGIVE MYSELF?
I COULDN'T LET US GO TO THE ORPHANAGE.
OH . . . YES, OF COURSE.
BUT THEIR HOME IS GONE NOW.
THEY'RE ALONE.
WHAT WILL THEY DO?

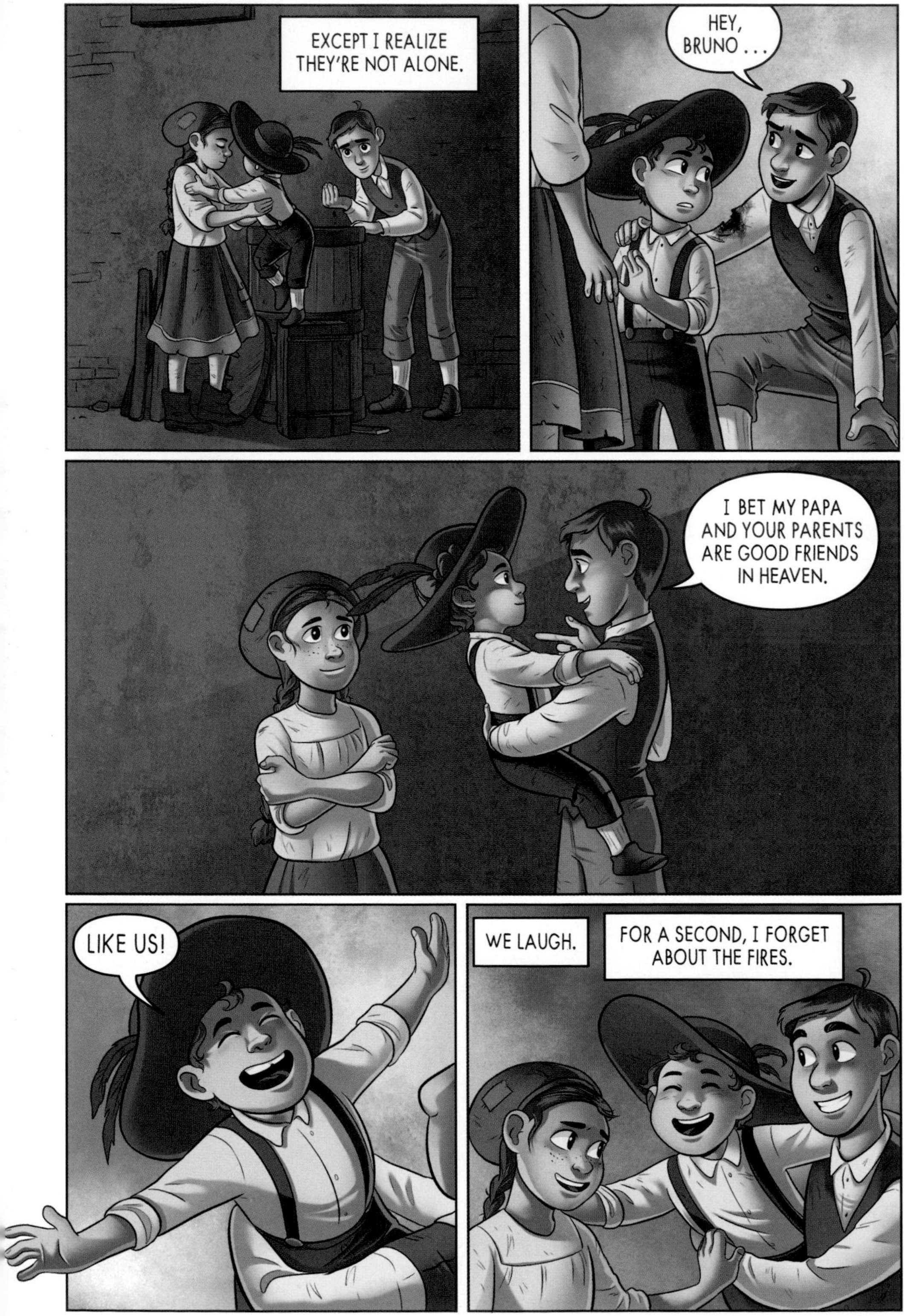
EXCEPT I REALIZE THEY'RE NOT ALONE.
HEY, BRUNO . . .
I BET MY PAPA AND YOUR PARENTS ARE GOOD FRIENDS IN HEAVEN.
LIKE US!
WE LAUGH.
FOR A SECOND, I FORGET ABOUT THE FIRES.

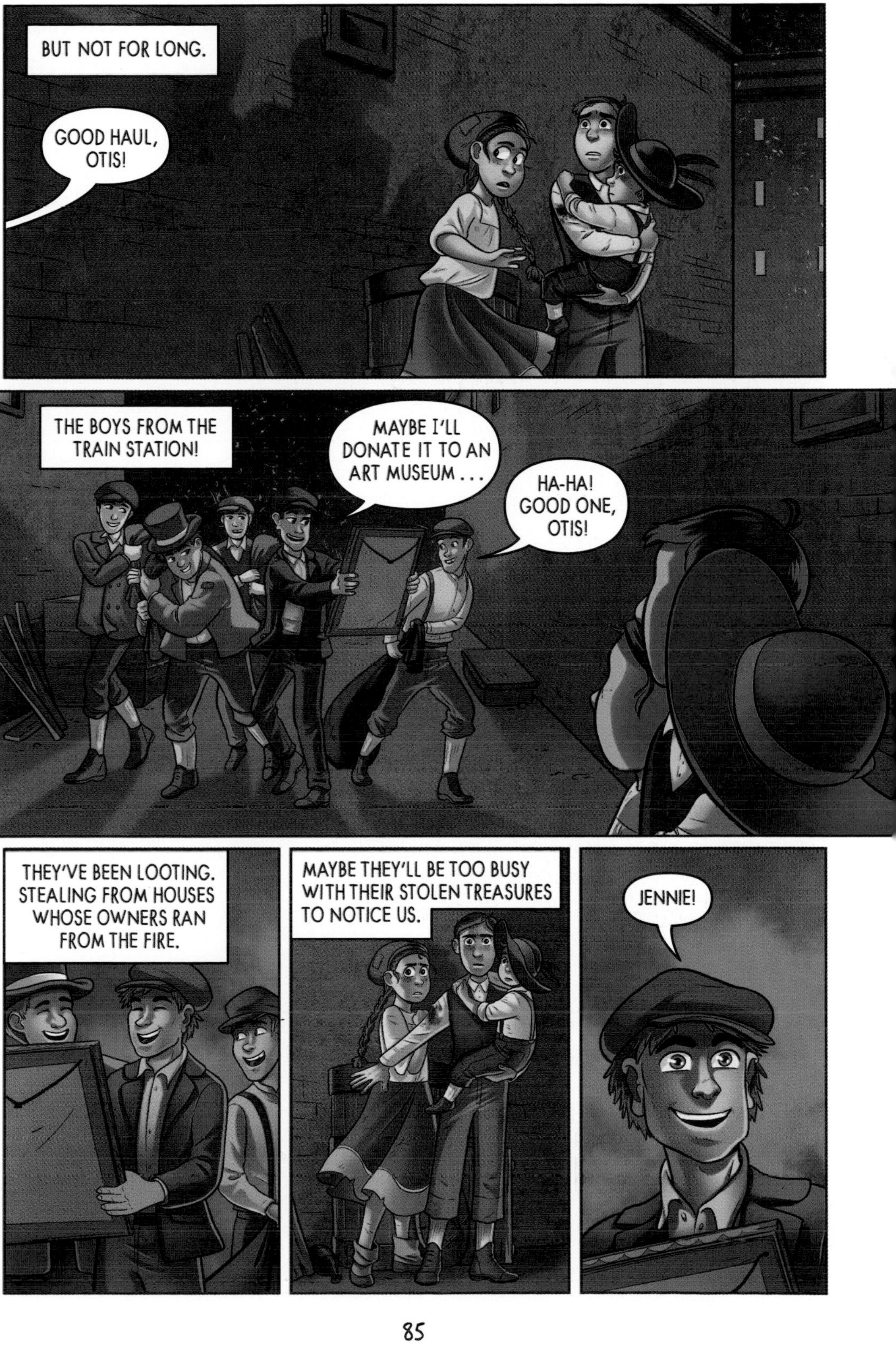
BUT NOT FOR LONG.
GOOD HAUL, OTIS!
THE BOYS FROM THE TRAIN STATION!
MAYBE I'LL DONATE IT TO AN ART MUSEUM . . .
HA-HA! GOOD ONE, OTIS!
THEY'VE BEEN LOOTING. STEALING FROM HOUSES WHOSE OWNERS RAN FROM THE FIRE.
MAYBE THEY'LL BE TOO BUSY WITH THEIR STOLEN TREASURES TO NOTICE US.
JENNIE!

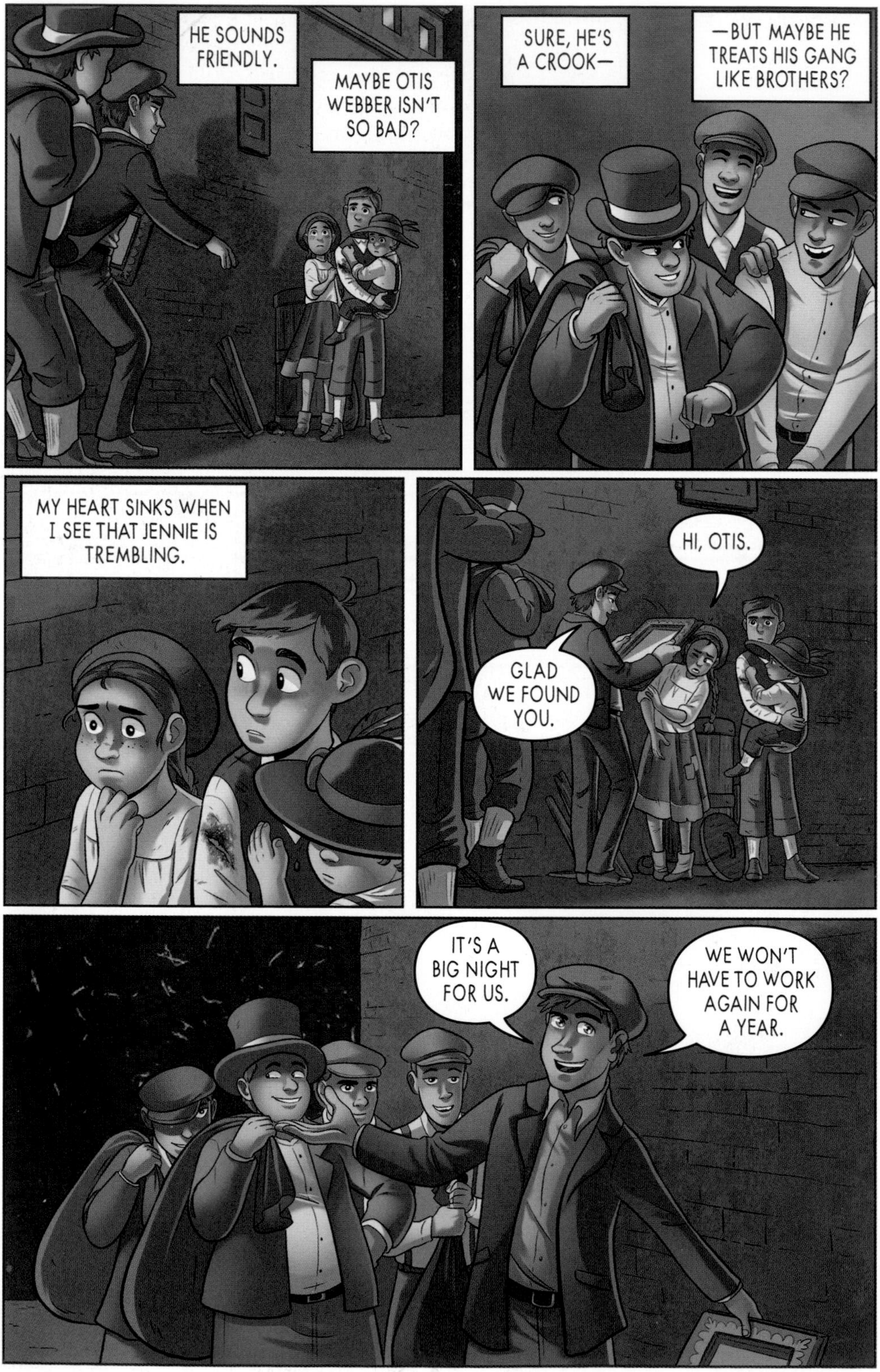
HE SOUNDS FRIENDLY.
MAYBE OTIS WEBBER ISN'T SO BAD?
SURE, HE'S A CROOK—
—BUT MAYBE HE TREATS HIS GANG LIKE BROTHERS?
MY HEART SINKS WHEN I SEE THAT JENNIE IS TREMBLING.
HI, OTIS.
GLAD WE FOUND YOU.
IT'S A BIG NIGHT FOR US.
WE WON'T HAVE TO WORK AGAIN FOR A YEAR.

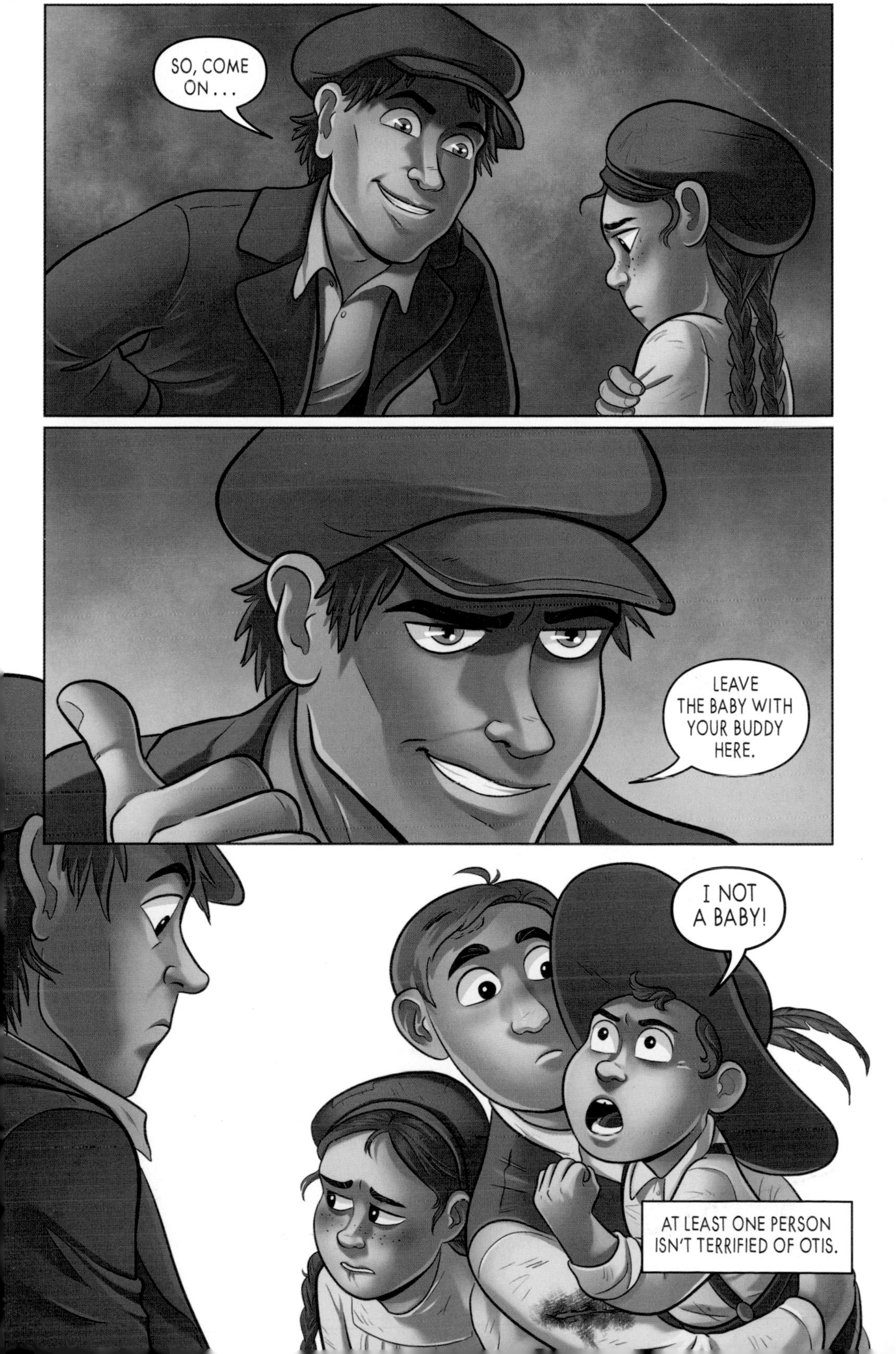
SO, COME ON . . .
LEAVE THE BABY WITH YOUR BUDDY HERE.
I NOT A BABY!
AT LEAST ONE PERSON ISN'T TERRIFIED OF OTIS.

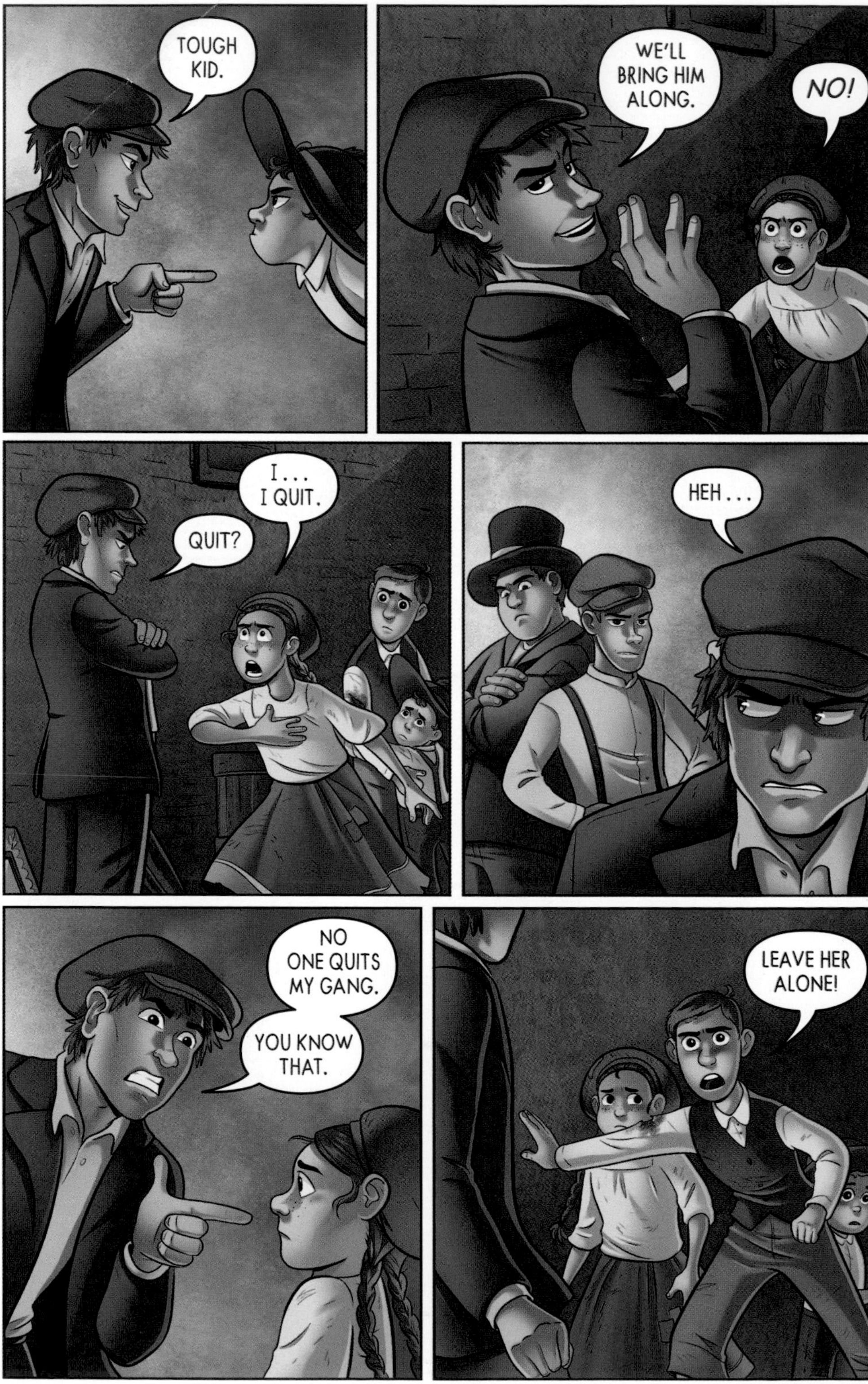
TOUGH KID.
WE'LL BRING HIM ALONG.
NO!
I... I QUIT.
QUIT?
HEH...
NO ONE QUITS MY GANG.
YOU KNOW THAT.
LEAVE HER ALONE!

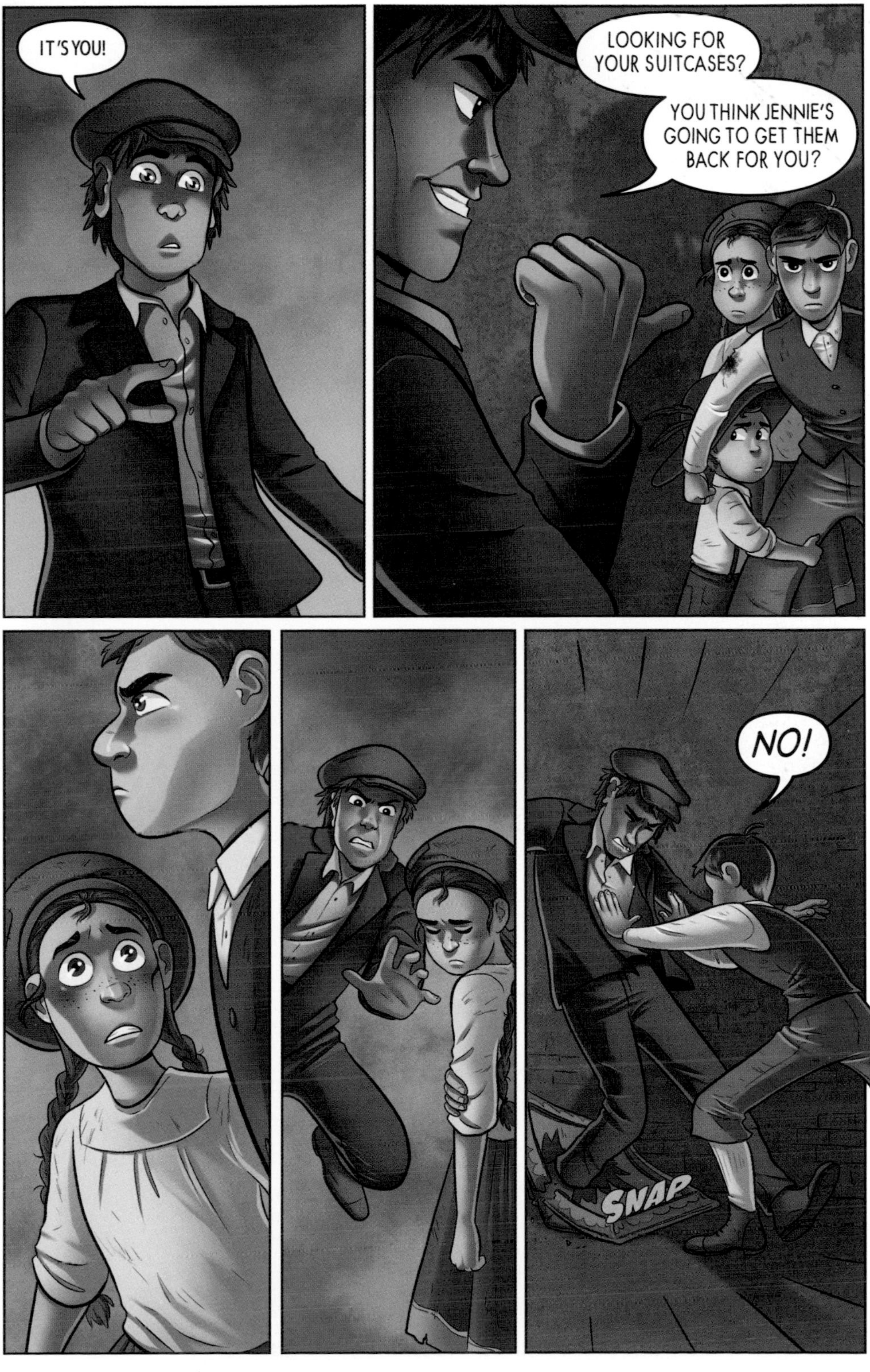
IT'S YOU!
LOOKING FOR YOUR SUITCASES?
YOU THINK JENNIE'S GOING TO GET THEM BACK FOR YOU?
NO!
SNAP

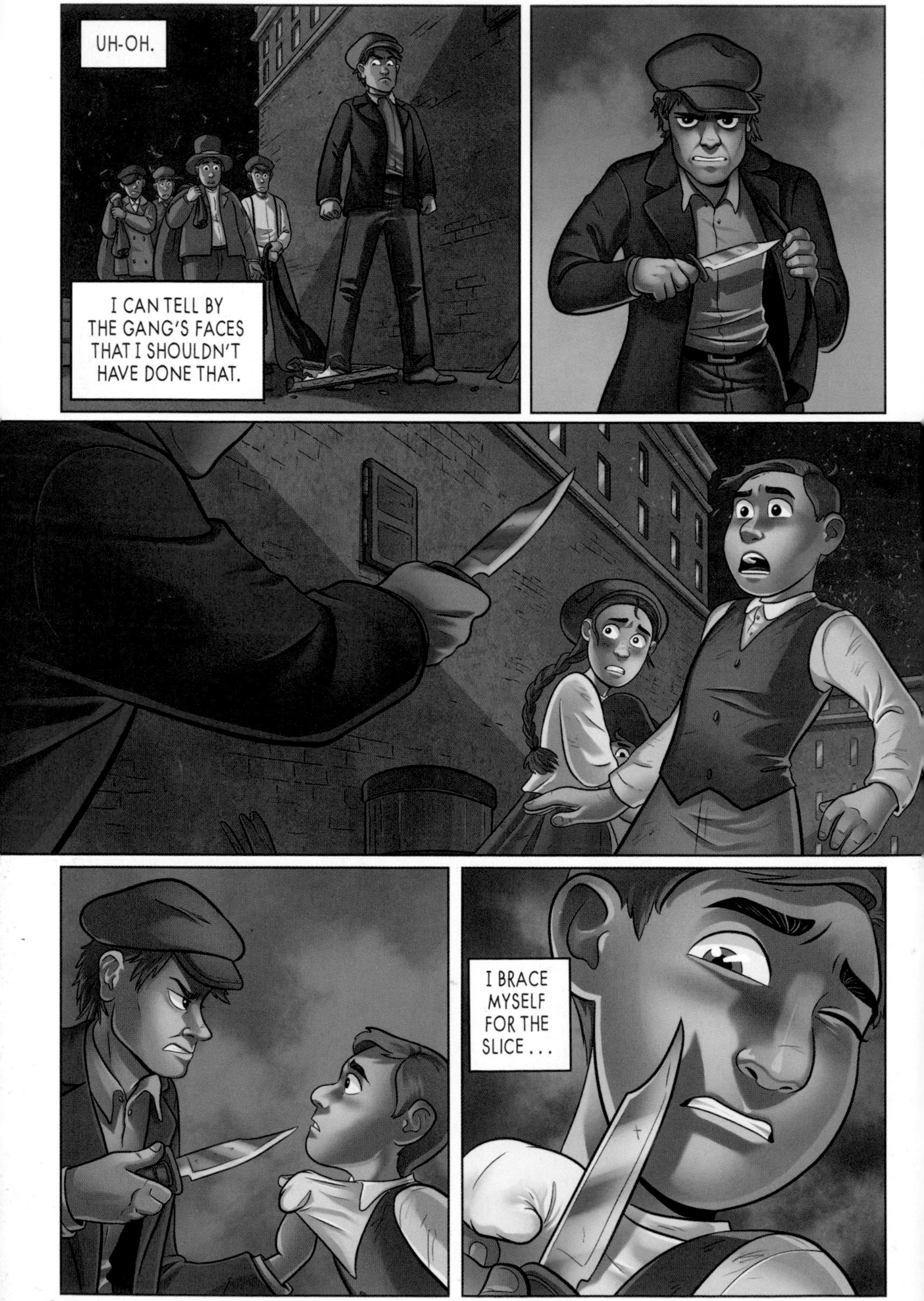
UH-OH.
I CAN TELL BY THE GANG'S FACES THAT I SHOULDN'T HAVE DONE THAT.
I BRACE MYSELF FOR THE SLICE . . .

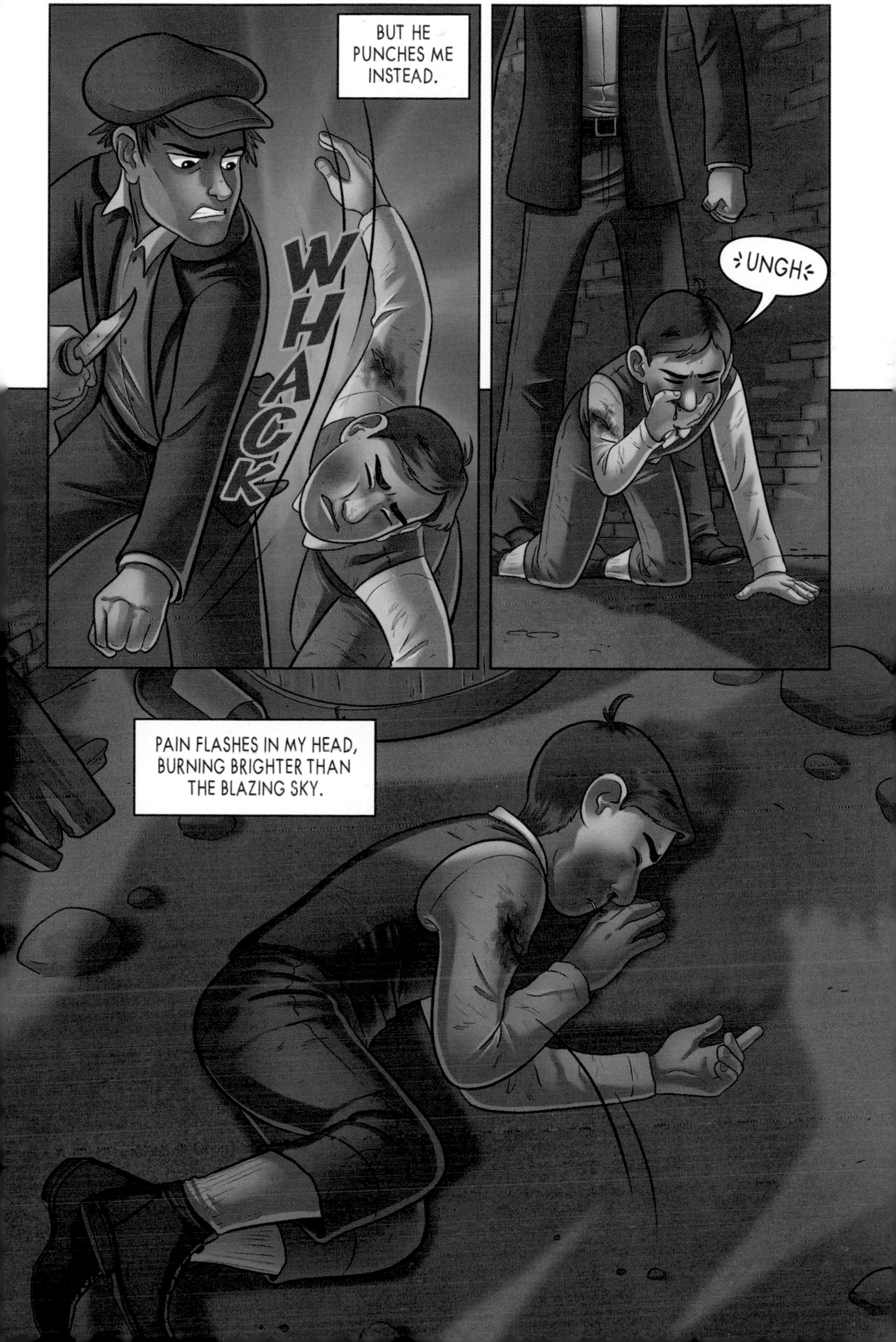
BUT HE PUNCHES ME INSTEAD.
WHACK
UNGH
PAIN FLASHES IN MY HEAD, BURNING BRIGHTER THAN THE BLAZING SKY.

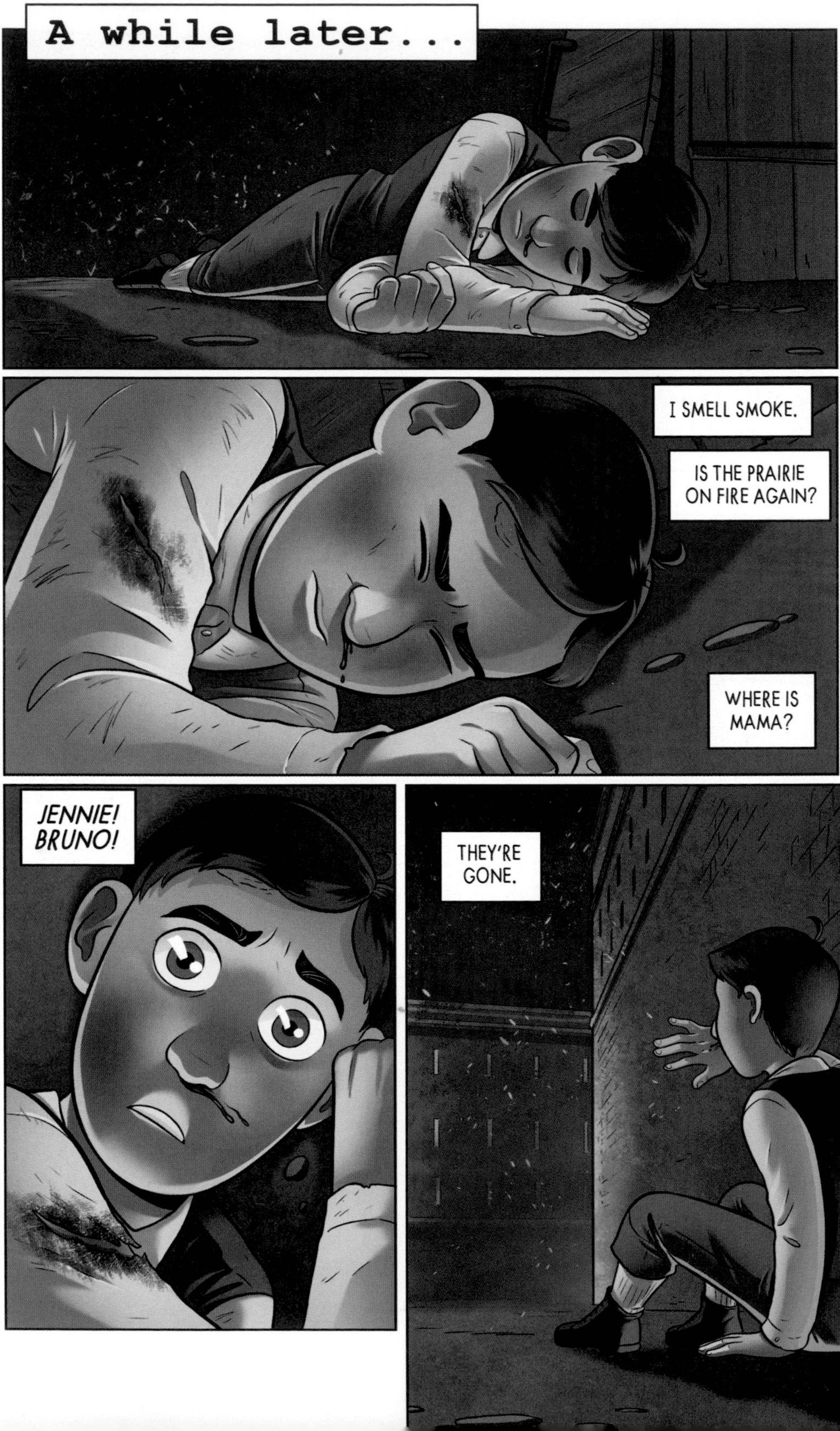
A while later...
I SMELL SMOKE.
IS THE PRAIRIE ON FIRE AGAIN?
WHERE IS MAMA?
JENNIE! BRUNO!
THEY'RE GONE.

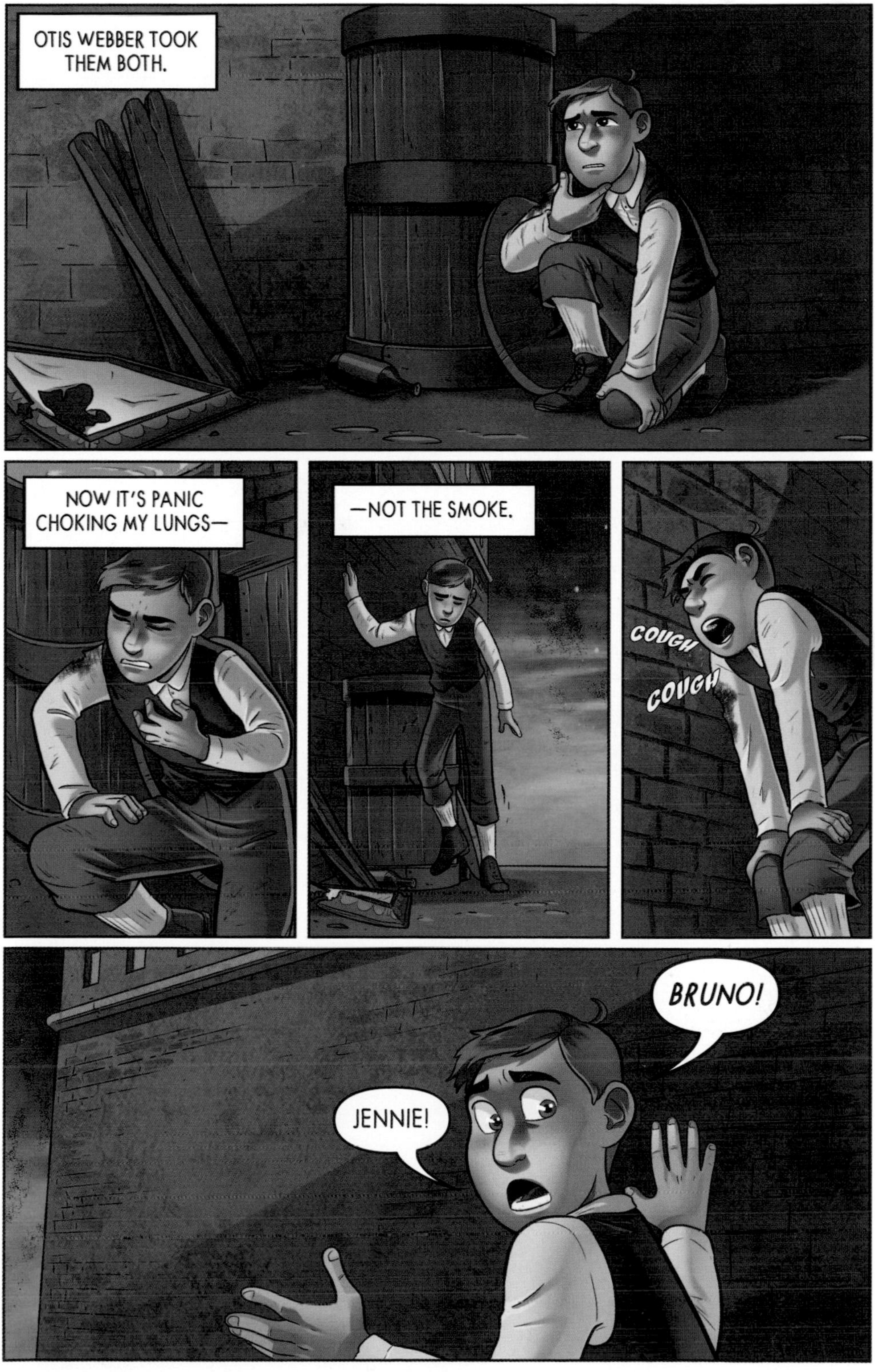
OTIS WEBBER TOOK THEM BOTH.
NOW IT'S PANIC CHOKING MY LUNGS—
—NOT THE SMOKE.
COUGH
COUGH
BRUNO!
JENNIE!

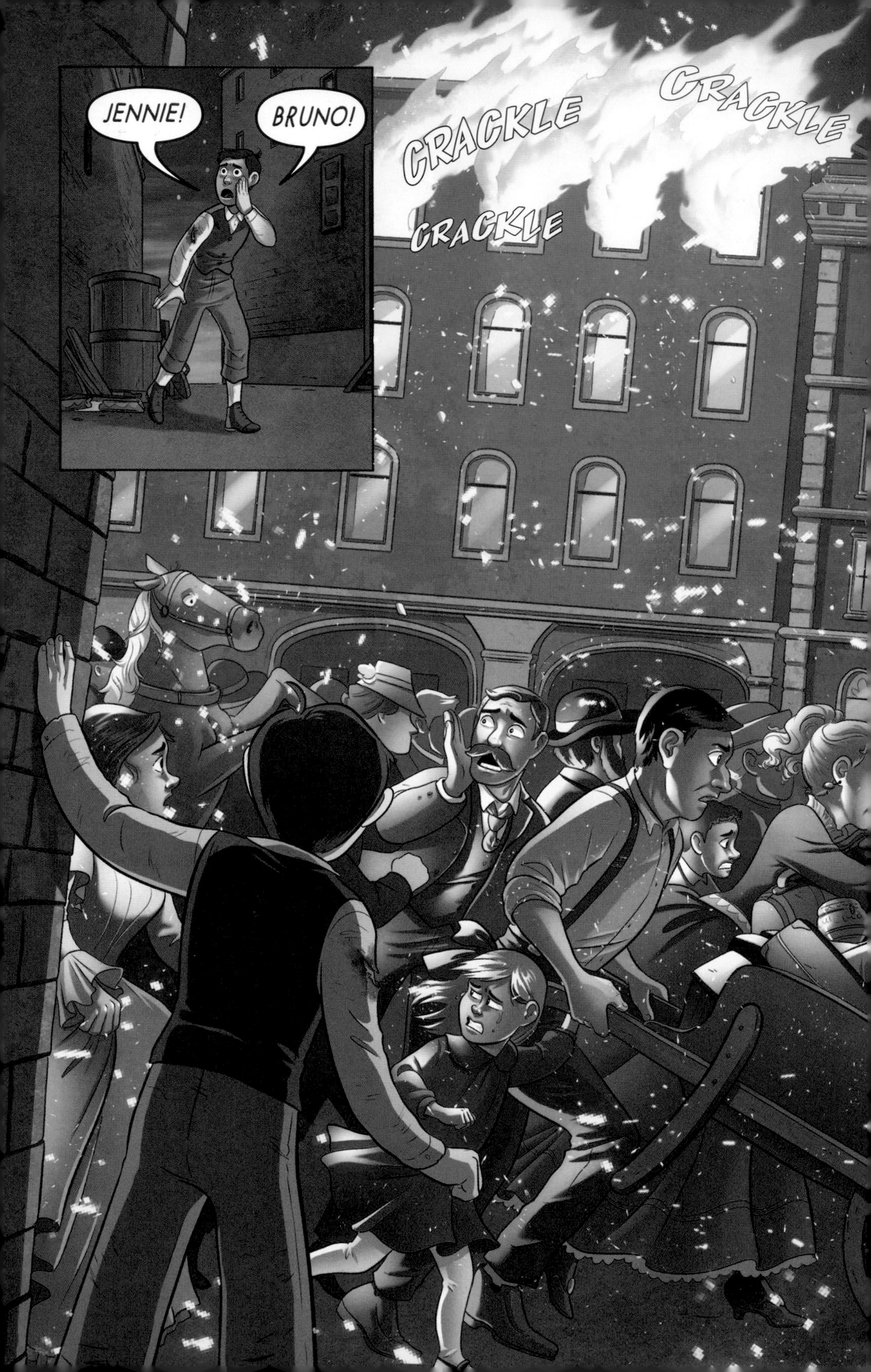
JENNIE!
BRUNO!
CRACKLE
CRACKLE
CRACKLE

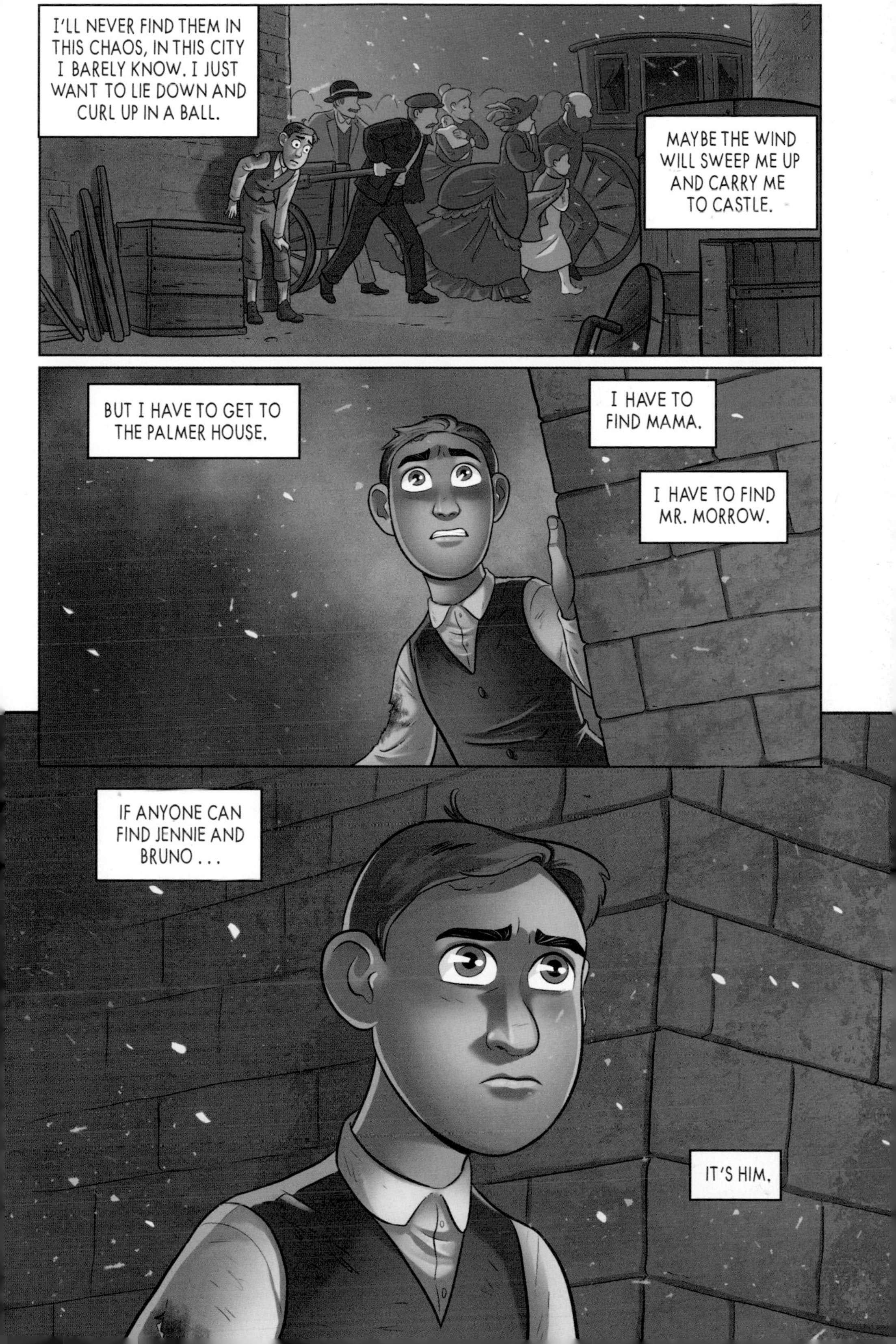
I'LL NEVER FIND THEM IN THIS CHAOS, IN THIS CITY I BARELY KNOW. I JUST WANT TO LIE DOWN AND CURL UP IN A BALL.
MAYBE THE WIND WILL SWEEP ME UP AND CARRY ME TO CASTLE.
BUT I HAVE TO GET TO THE PALMER HOUSE.
I HAVE TO FIND MAMA.
I HAVE TO FIND MR. MORROW.
IF ANYONE CAN FIND JENNIE AND BRUNO . . .
IT'S HIM.

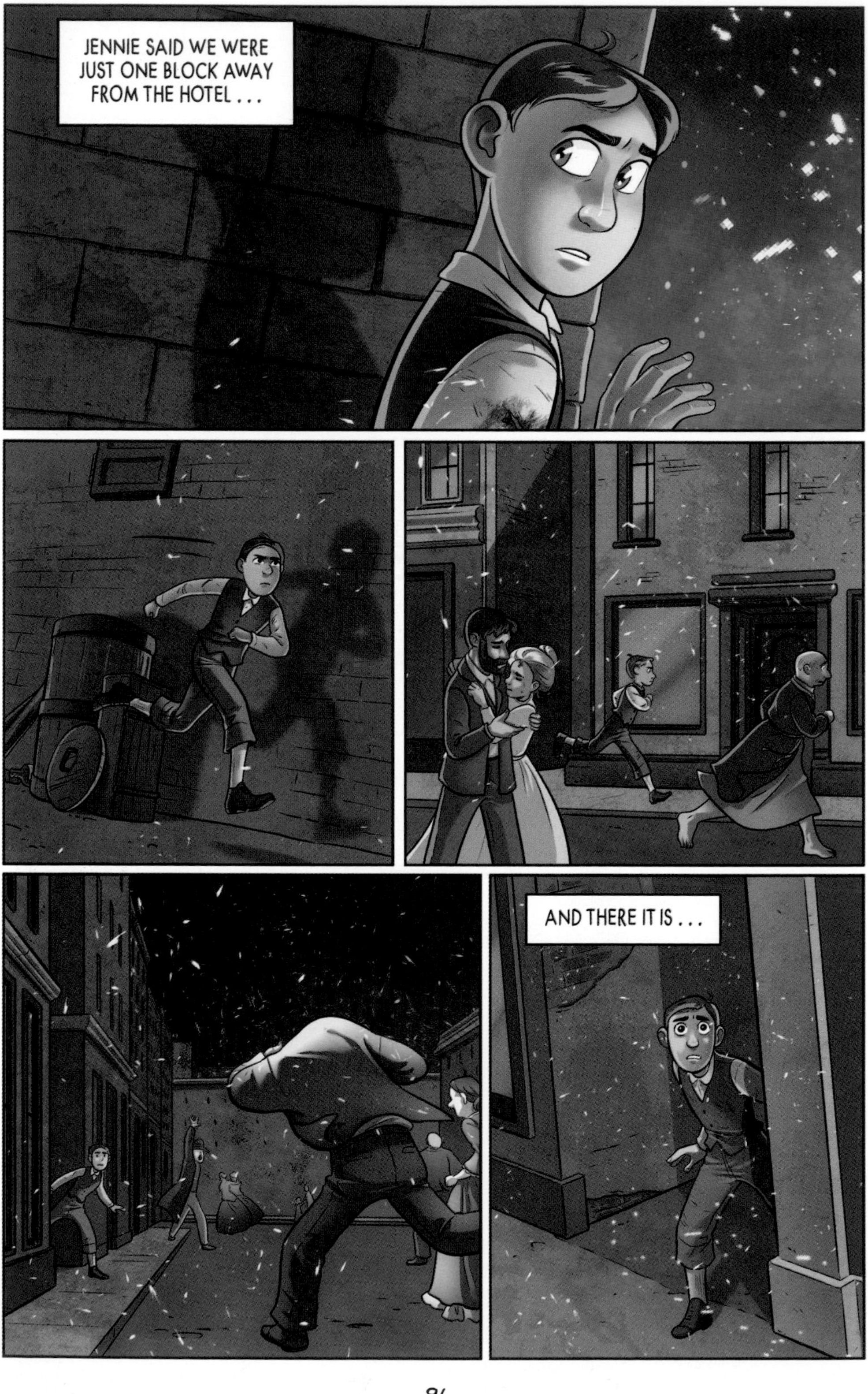
JENNIE SAID WE WERE JUST ONE BLOCK AWAY FROM THE HOTEL . . .
AND THERE IT IS . . .

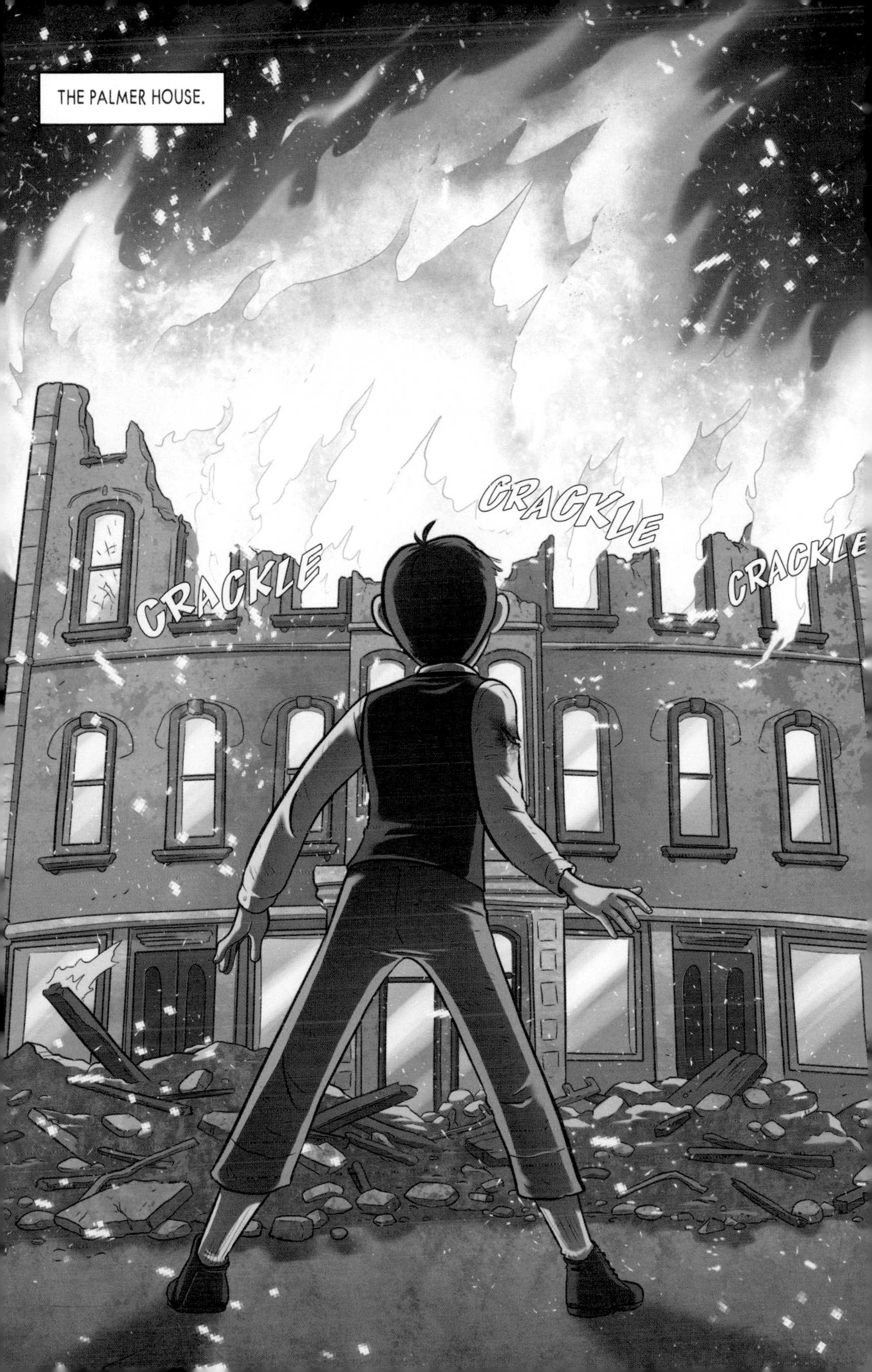
THE PALMER HOUSE.
CRACKLE
CRACKLE
CRACKLE

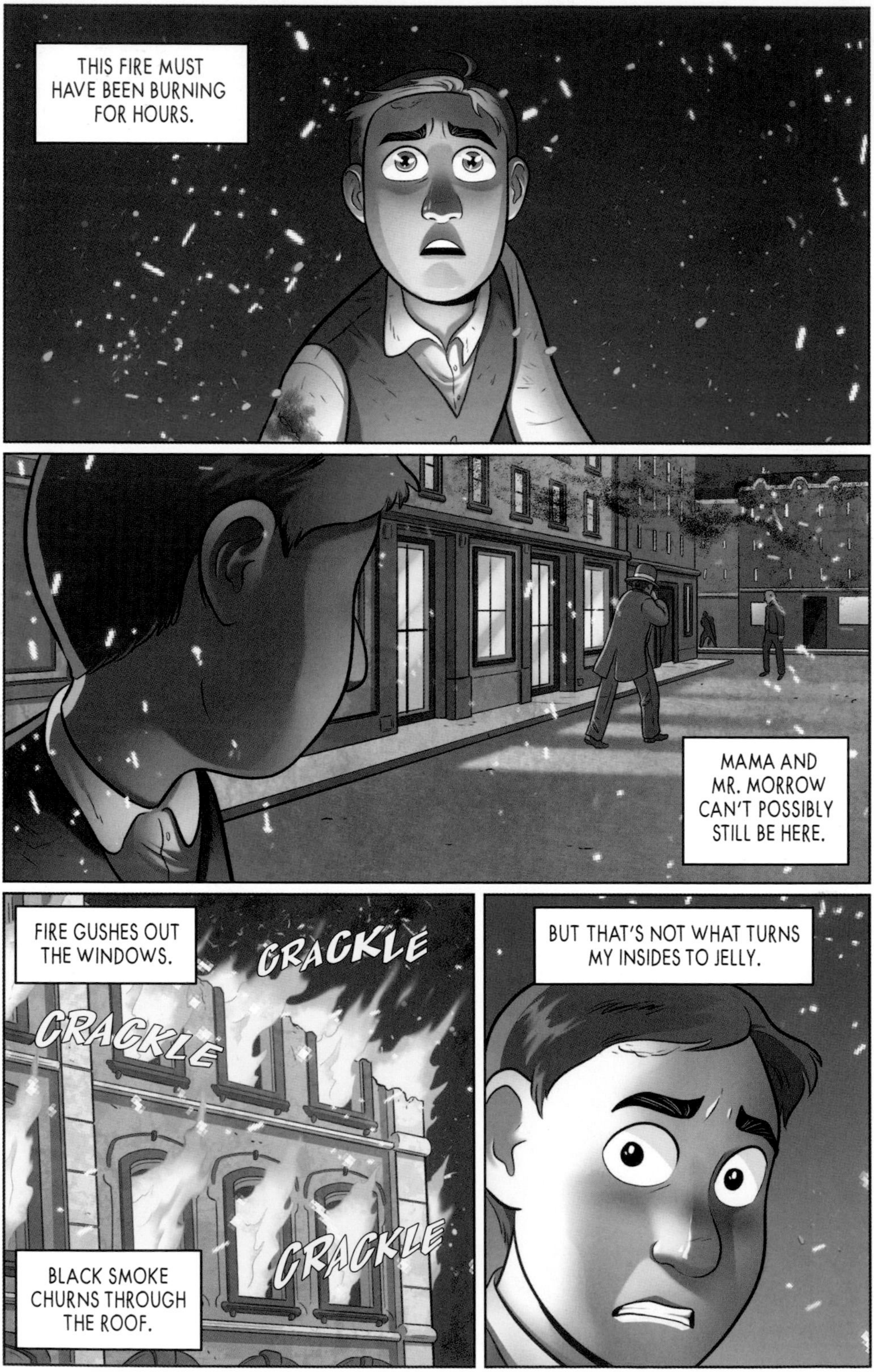
THIS FIRE MUST HAVE BEEN BURNING FOR HOURS.
MAMA AND MR. MORROW CAN'T POSSIBLY STILL BE HERE.
FIRE GUSHES OUT THE WINDOWS.
CRACKLE
CRACKLE
BLACK SMOKE CHURNS THROUGH THE ROOF.
CRACKLE
BUT THAT'S NOT WHAT TURNS MY INSIDES TO JELLY.

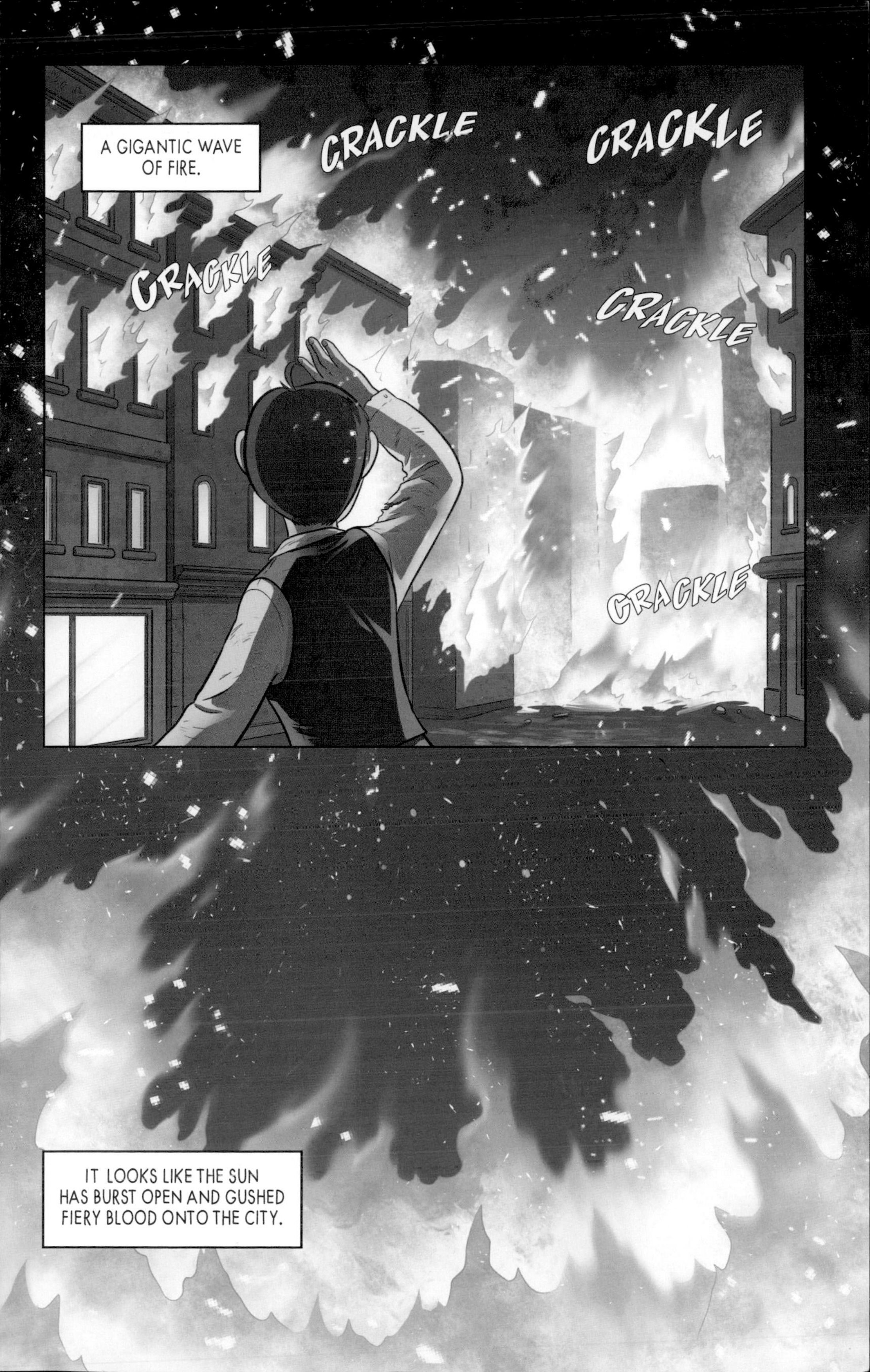
A GIGANTIC WAVE OF FIRE.
CRACKLE
CRACKLE
CRACKLE
CRACKLE
CRACKLE
IT LOOKS LIKE THE SUN HAS BURST OPEN AND GUSHED FIERY BLOOD ONTO THE CITY.

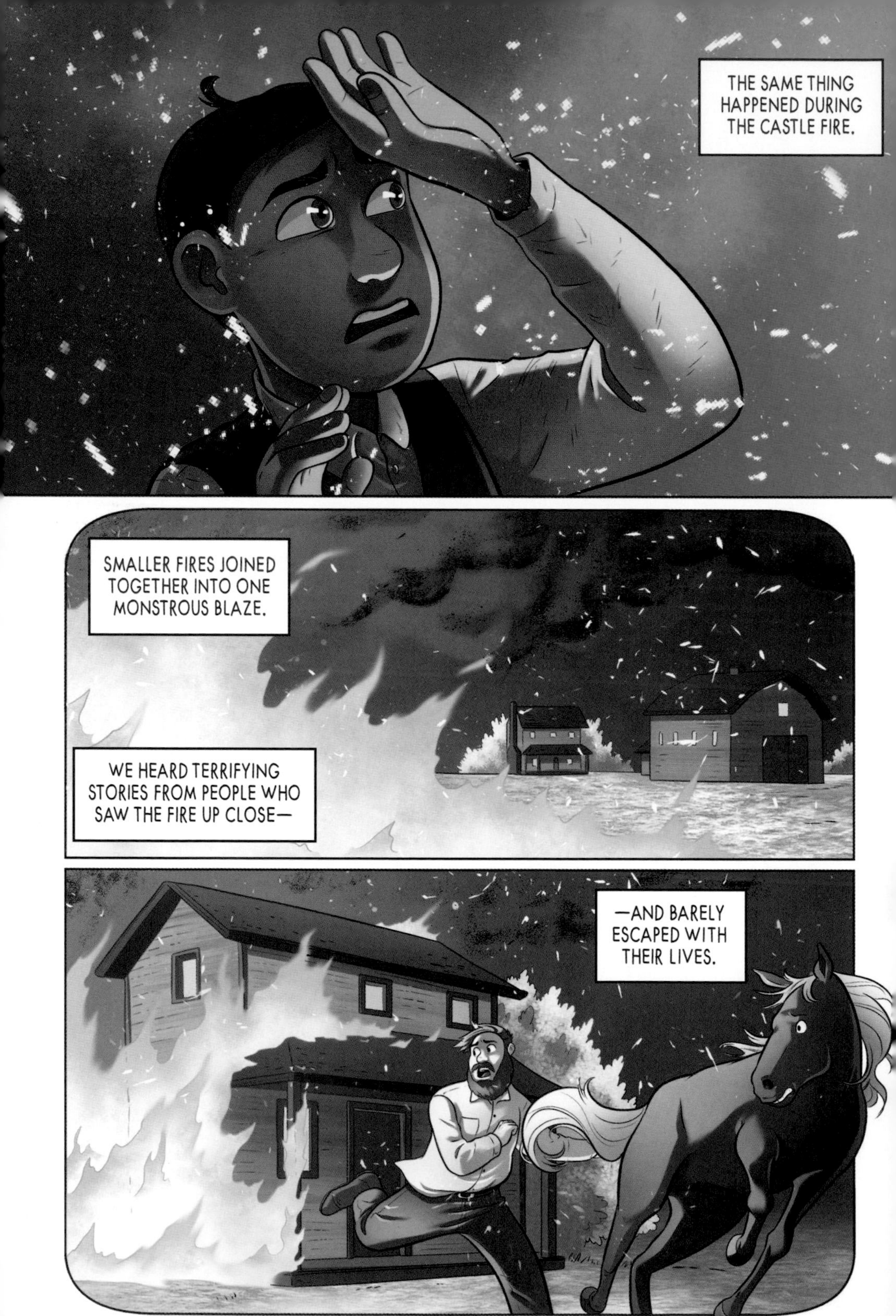
THE SAME THING HAPPENED DURING THE CASTLE FIRE.
SMALLER FIRES JOINED TOGETHER INTO ONE MONSTROUS BLAZE.
WE HEARD TERRIFYING STORIES FROM PEOPLE WHO SAW THE FIRE UP CLOSE—
—AND BARELY ESCAPED WITH THEIR LIVES.

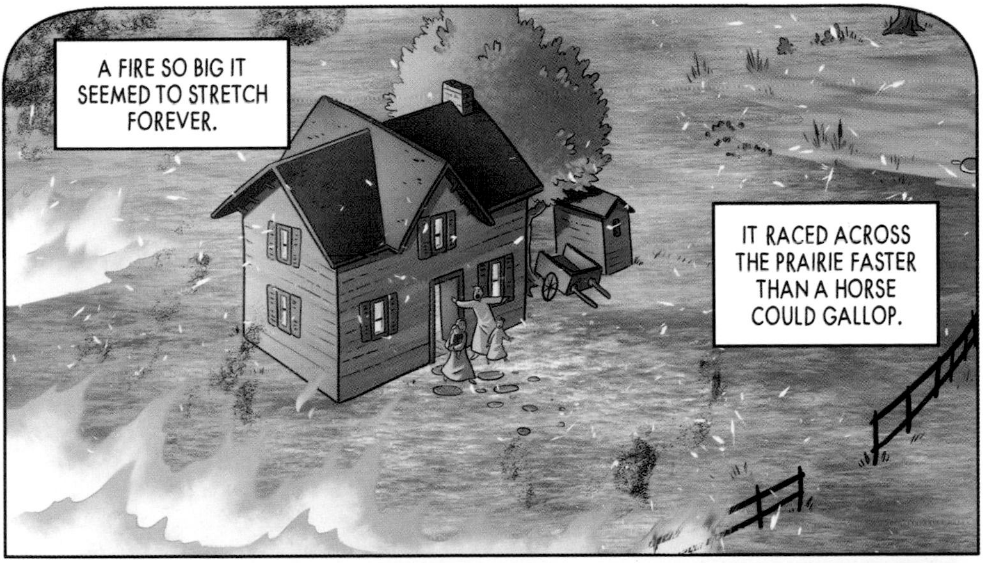
A FIRE SO BIG IT SEEMED TO STRETCH FOREVER.
IT RACED ACROSS THE PRAIRIE FASTER THAN A HORSE COULD GALLOP.

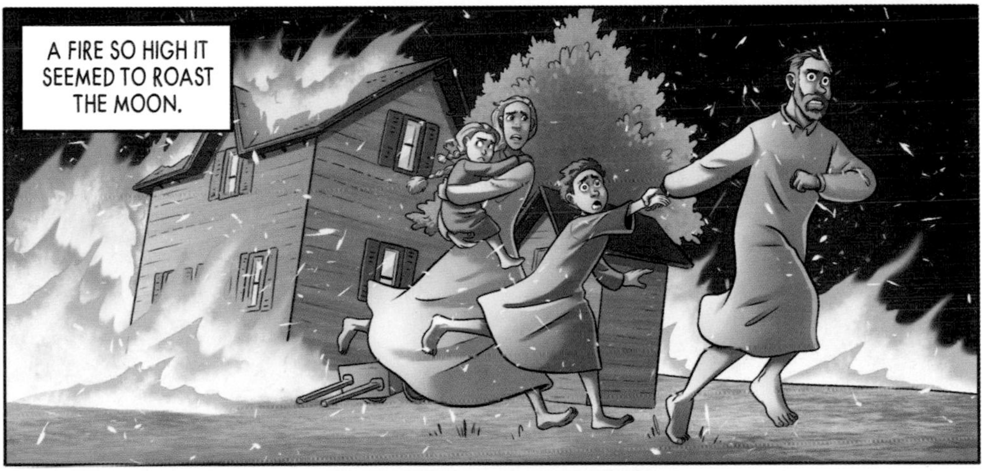
A FIRE SO HIGH IT SEEMED TO ROAST THE MOON.

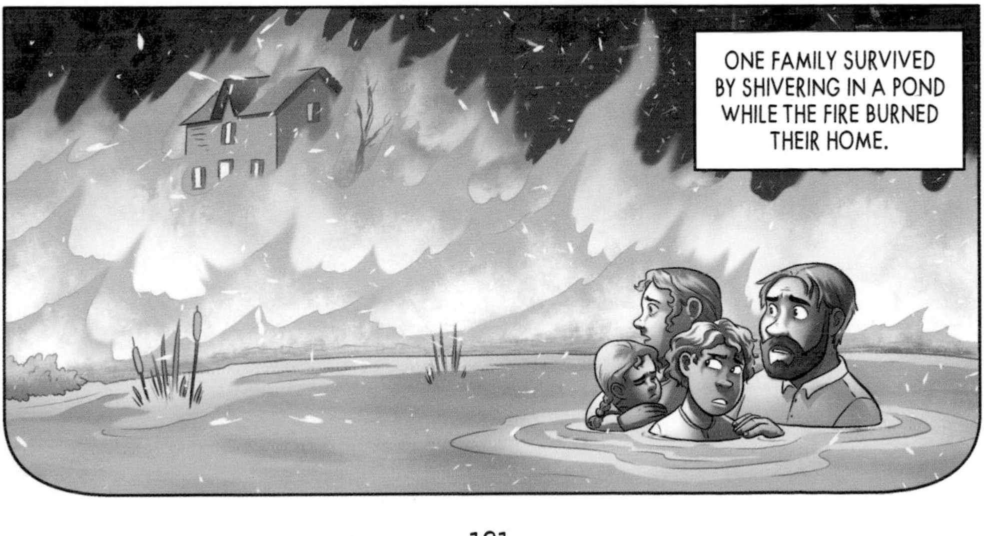
ONE FAMILY SURVIVED BY SHIVERING IN A POND WHILE THE FIRE BURNED THEIR HOME.

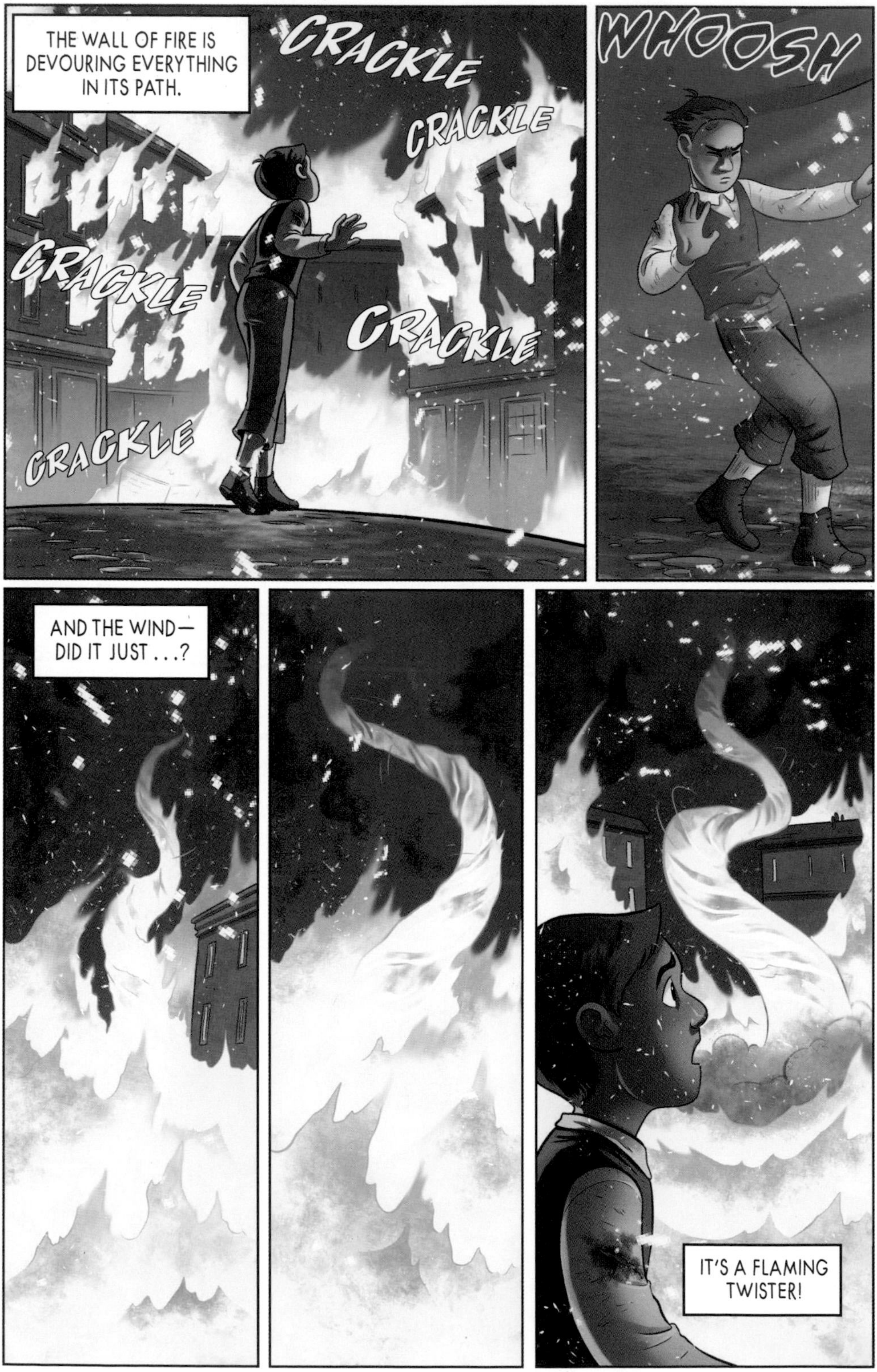
THE WALL OF FIRE IS DEVOURING EVERYTHING IN ITS PATH.
CRACKLE
CRACKLE
CRACKLE
CRACKLE
CRACKLE
WHOOSH
AND THE WIND— DID IT JUST . . .?
IT'S A FLAMING TWISTER!

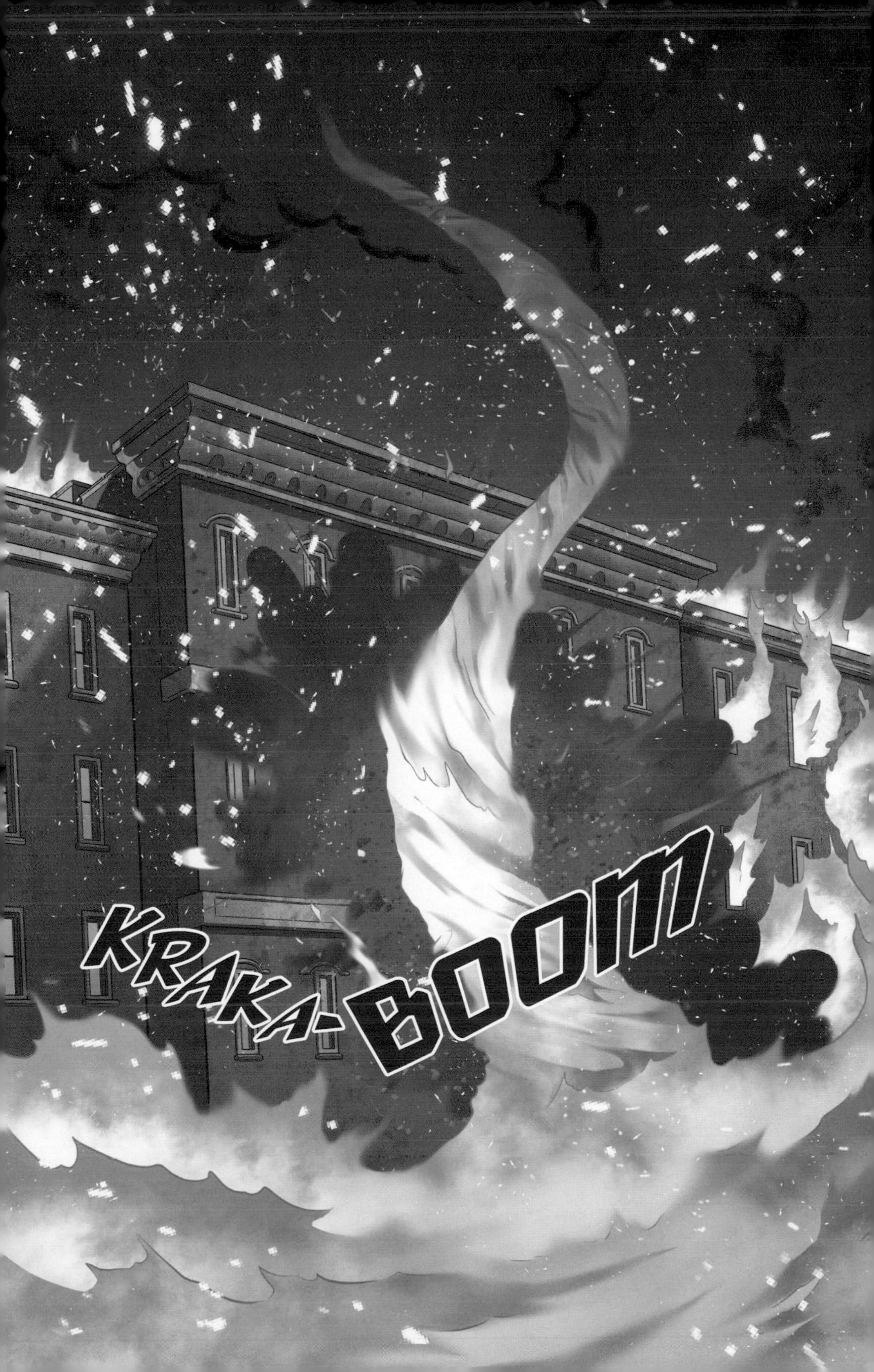
KRAKA-BOOM

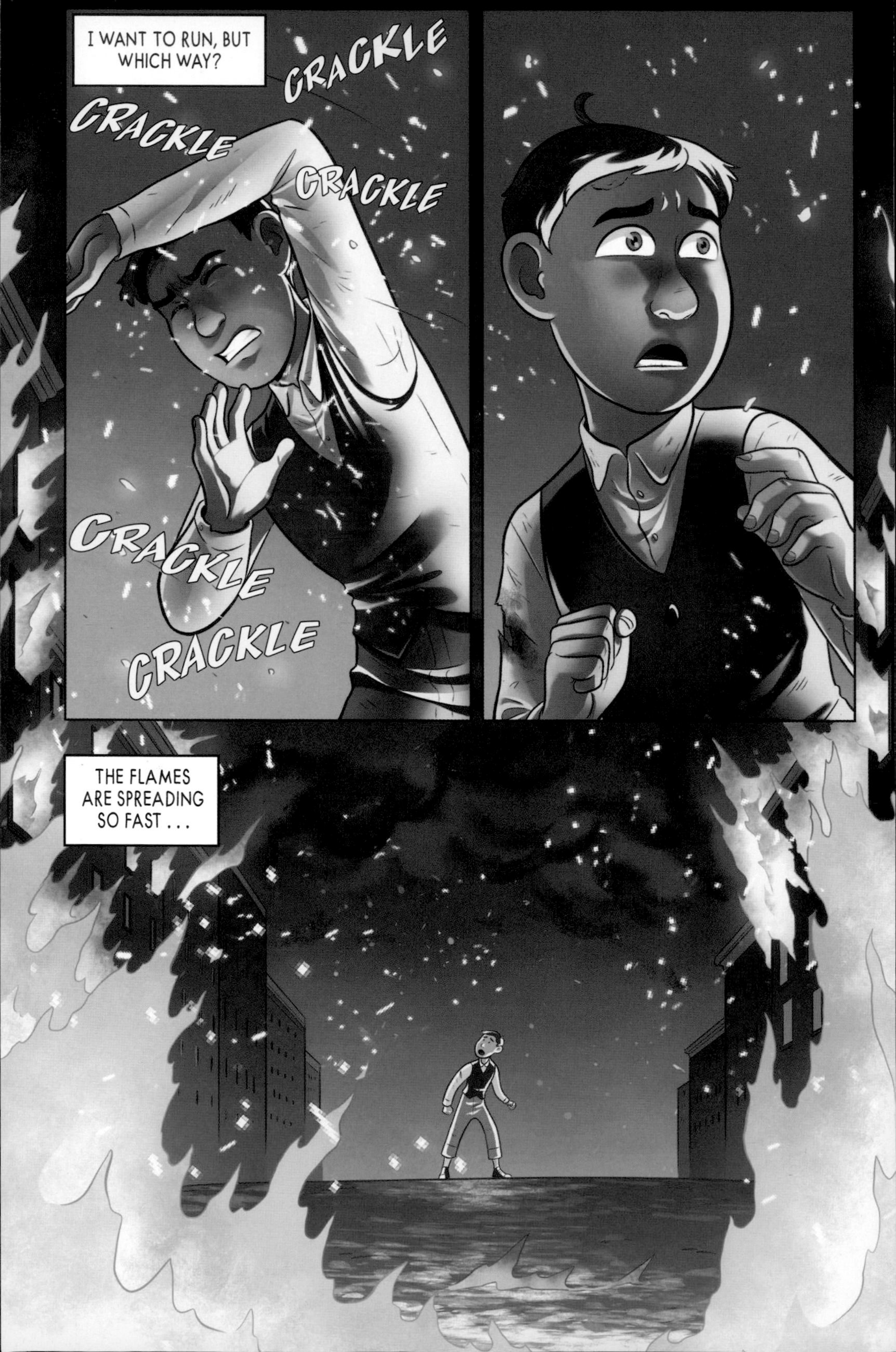
I WANT TO RUN, BUT WHICH WAY?
CRACKLE
CRACKLE
CRACKLE
CRACKLE
CRACKLE
THE FLAMES ARE SPREADING SO FAST . . .

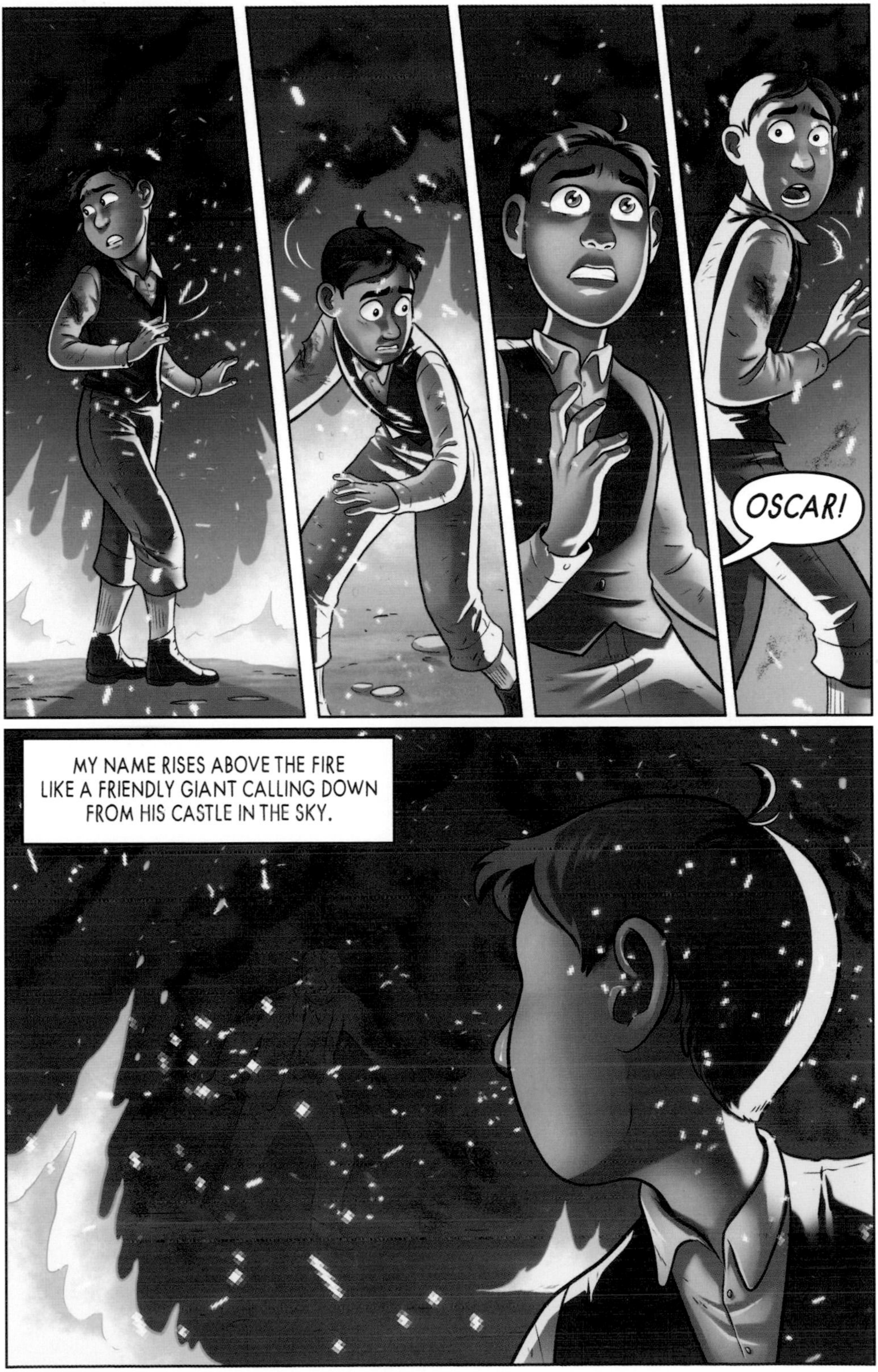
OSCAR!
MY NAME RISES ABOVE THE FIRE LIKE A FRIENDLY GIANT CALLING DOWN FROM HIS CASTLE IN THE SKY.

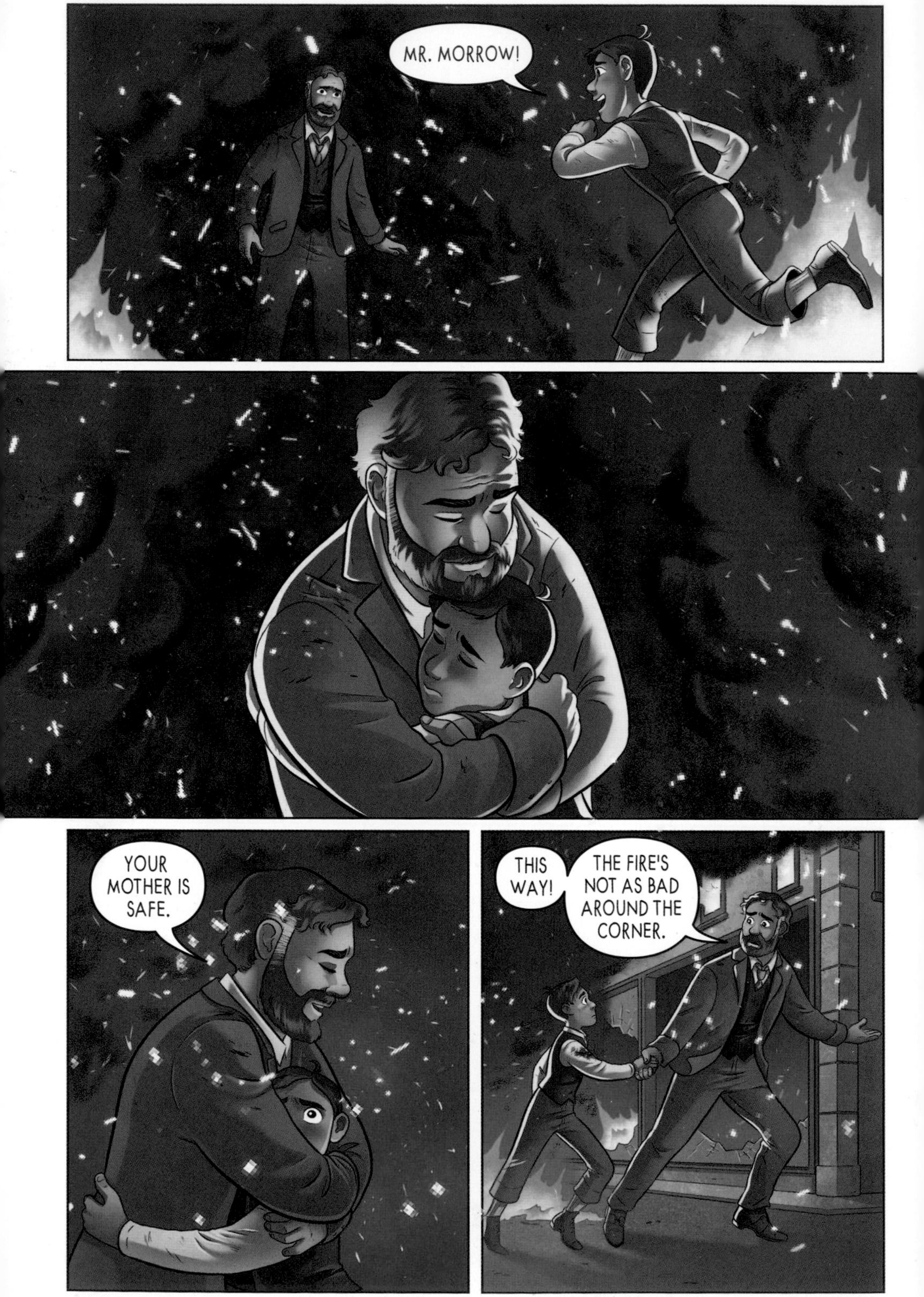
MR. MORROW!
YOUR MOTHER IS SAFE.
THIS WAY!
THE FIRE'S NOT AS BAD AROUND THE CORNER.

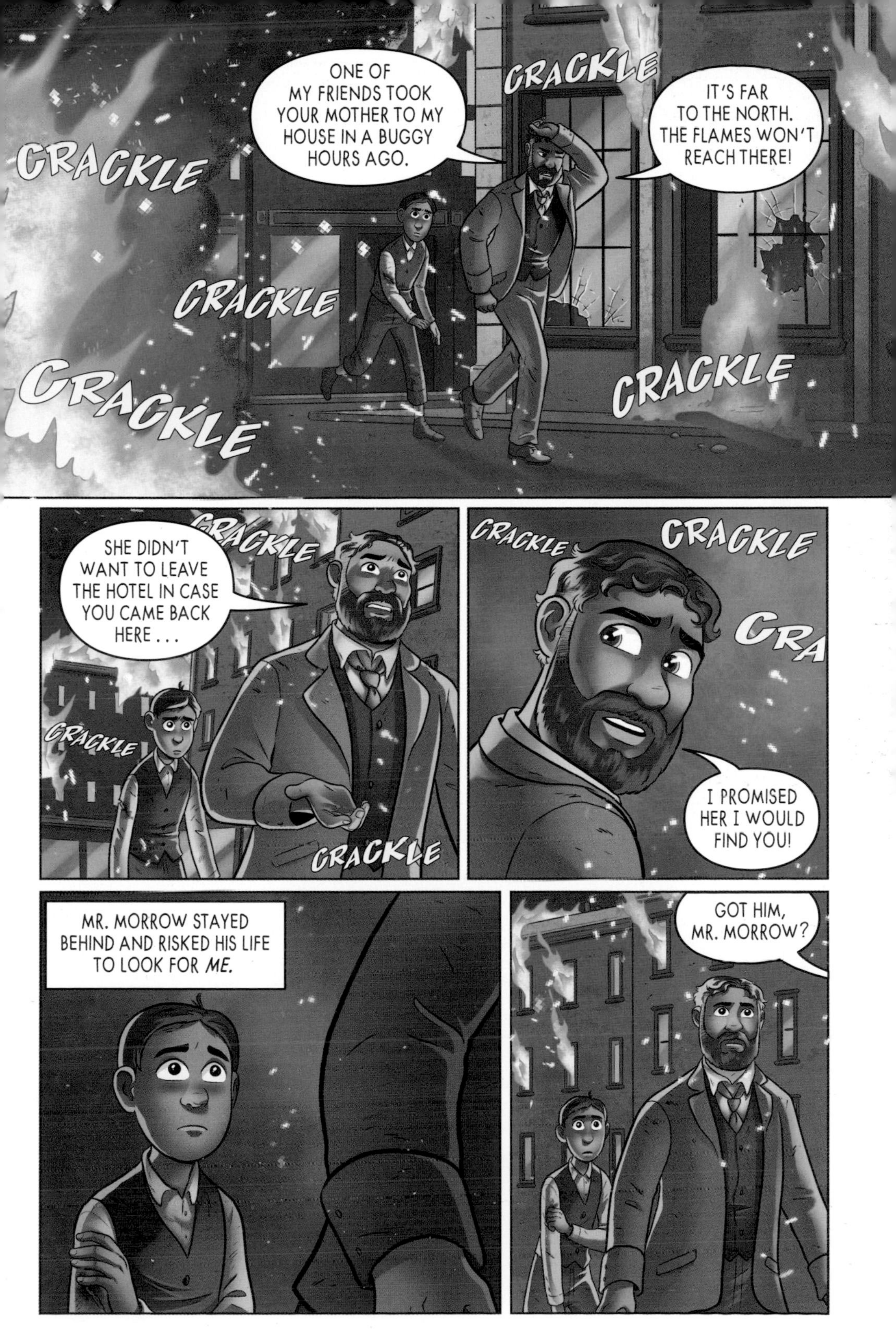
ONE OF MY FRIENDS TOOK YOUR MOTHER TO MY HOUSE IN A BUGGY HOURS AGO.
CRACKLE
IT'S FAR TO THE NORTH. THE FLAMES WON'T REACH THERE!
CRACKLE
CRACKLE
CRACKLE
CRACKLE
CRACKLE
SHE DIDN'T WANT TO LEAVE THE HOTEL IN CASE YOU CAME BACK HERE . . .
CRACKLE
CRACKLE
CRACKLE
CRACKLE
CRA
I PROMISED HER I WOULD FIND YOU!
MR. MORROW STAYED BEHIND AND RISKED HIS LIFE TO LOOK FOR *ME.*
GOT HIM, MR. MORROW?

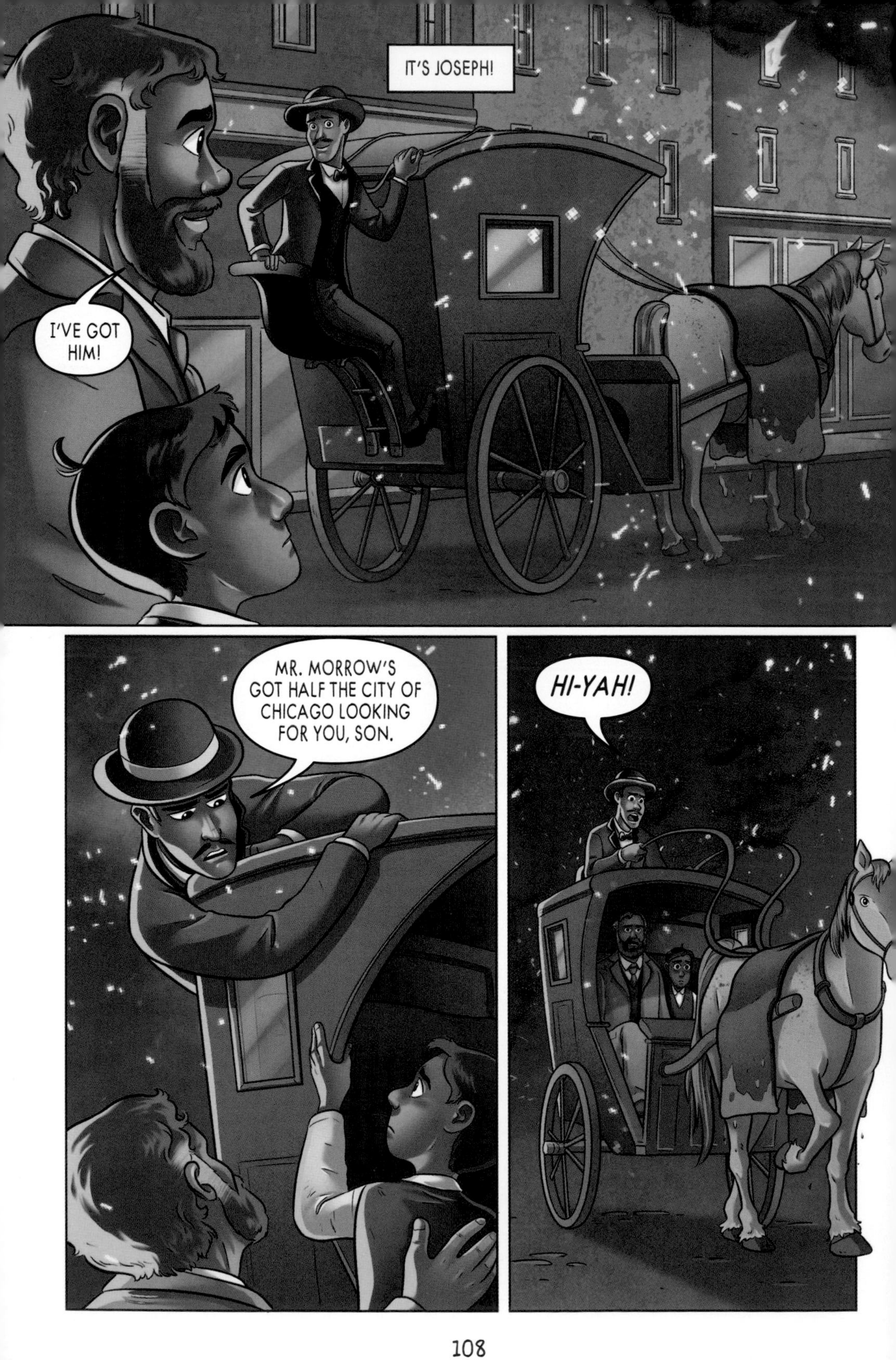
IT'S JOSEPH!
I'VE GOT HIM!
MR. MORROW'S GOT HALF THE CITY OF CHICAGO LOOKING FOR YOU, SON.
HI-YAH!

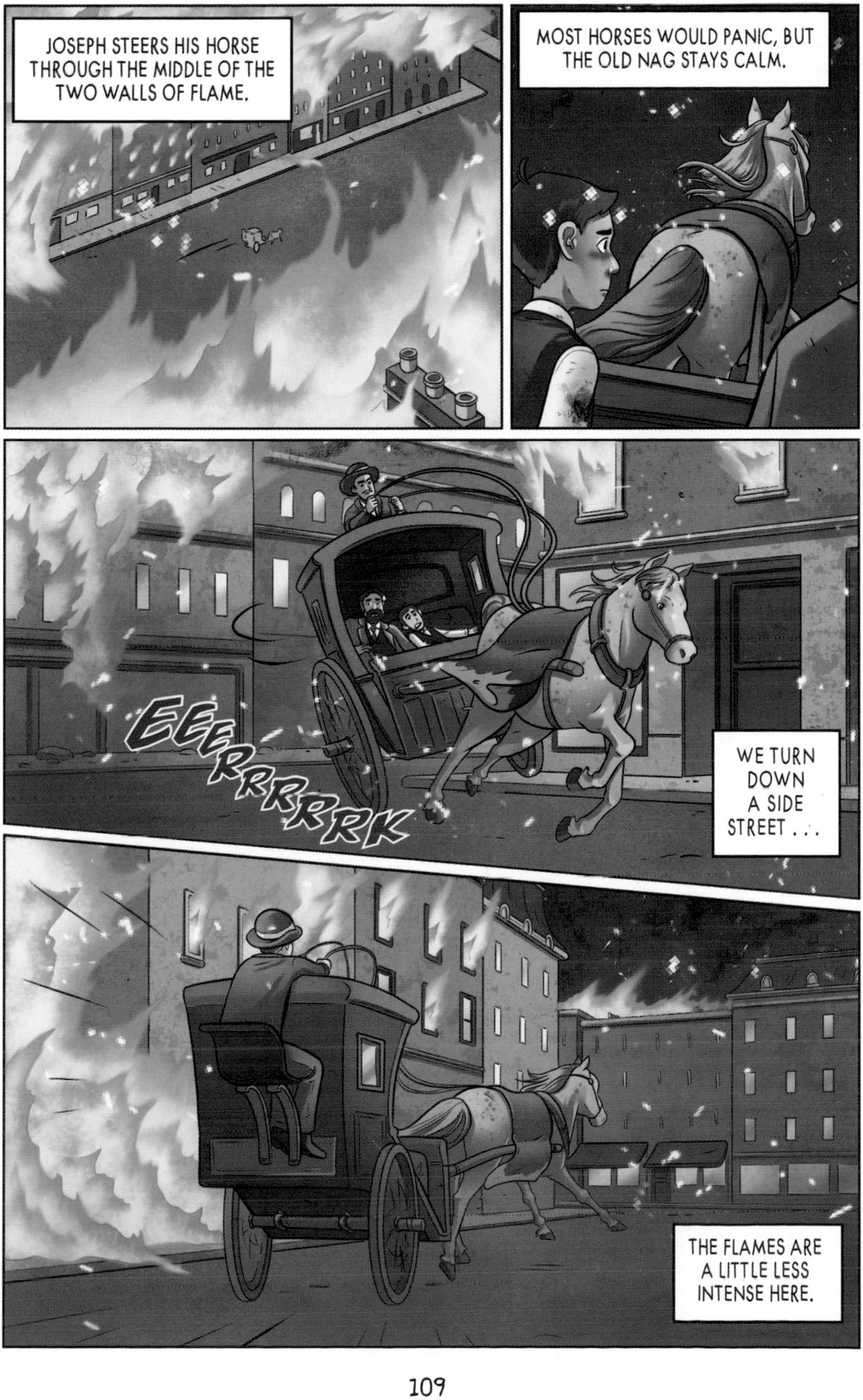
JOSEPH STEERS HIS HORSE THROUGH THE MIDDLE OF THE TWO WALLS OF FLAME.
MOST HORSES WOULD PANIC, BUT THE OLD NAG STAYS CALM.
EEERRRRRK
WE TURN DOWN A SIDE STREET . . .
THE FLAMES ARE A LITTLE LESS INTENSE HERE.

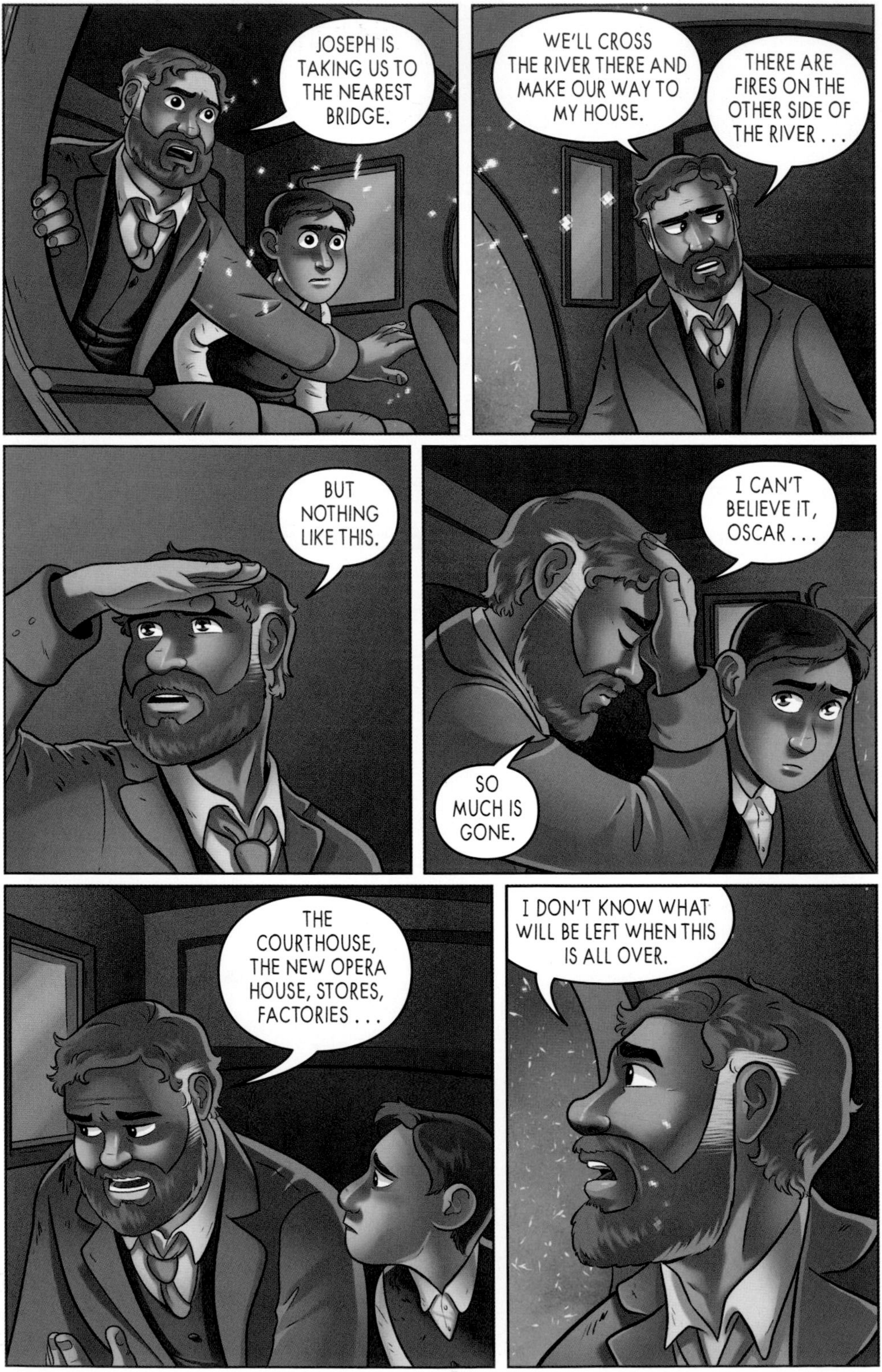
JOSEPH IS TAKING US TO THE NEAREST BRIDGE.
WE'LL CROSS THE RIVER THERE AND MAKE OUR WAY TO MY HOUSE.
THERE ARE FIRES ON THE OTHER SIDE OF THE RIVER . . .
BUT NOTHING LIKE THIS.
I CAN'T BELIEVE IT, OSCAR . . .
SO MUCH IS GONE.
THE COURTHOUSE, THE NEW OPERA HOUSE, STORES, FACTORIES . . .
I DON'T KNOW WHAT WILL BE LEFT WHEN THIS IS ALL OVER.

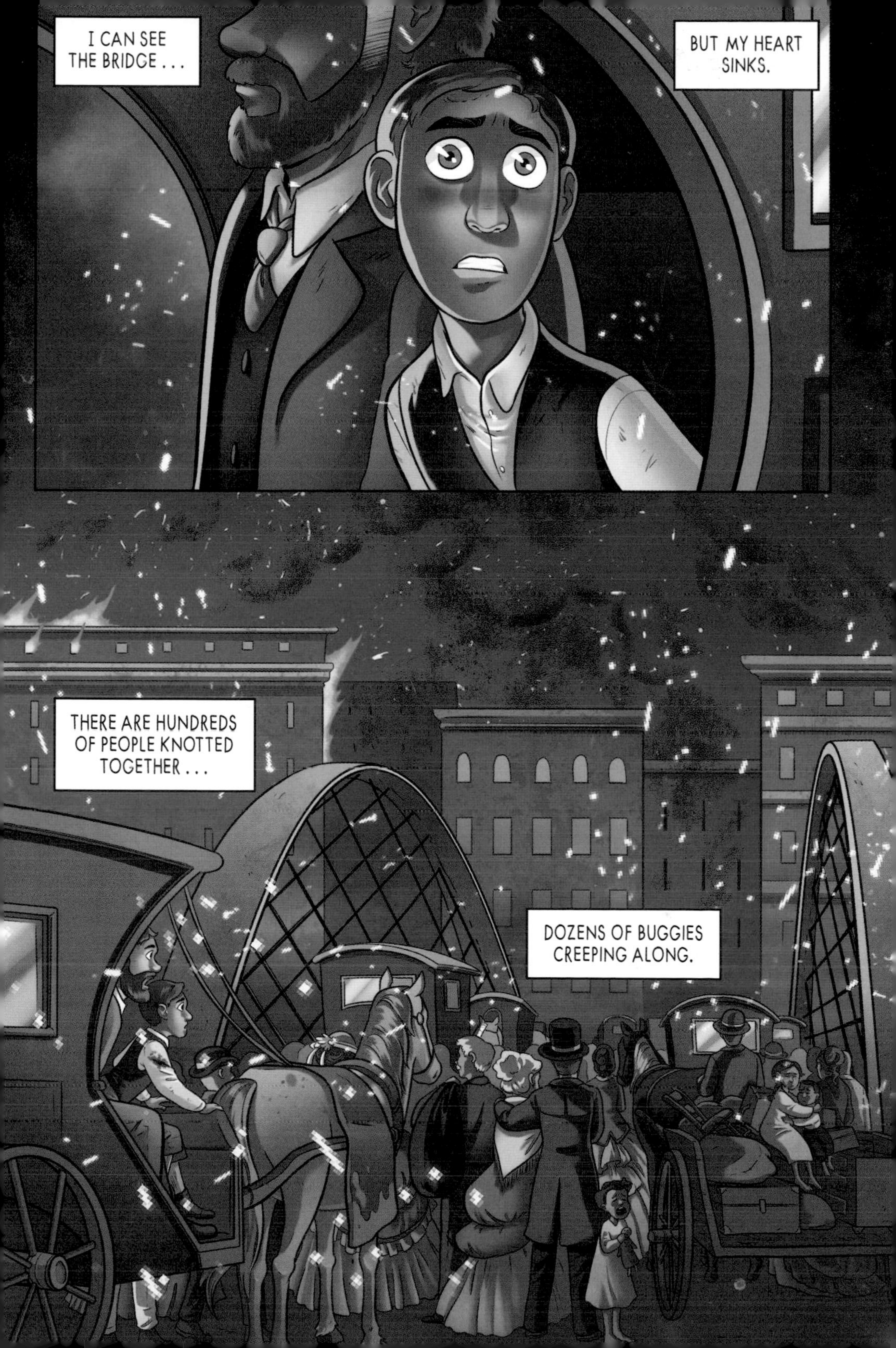
I CAN SEE THE BRIDGE . . .
BUT MY HEART SINKS.
THERE ARE HUNDREDS OF PEOPLE KNOTTED TOGETHER . . .
DOZENS OF BUGGIES CREEPING ALONG.

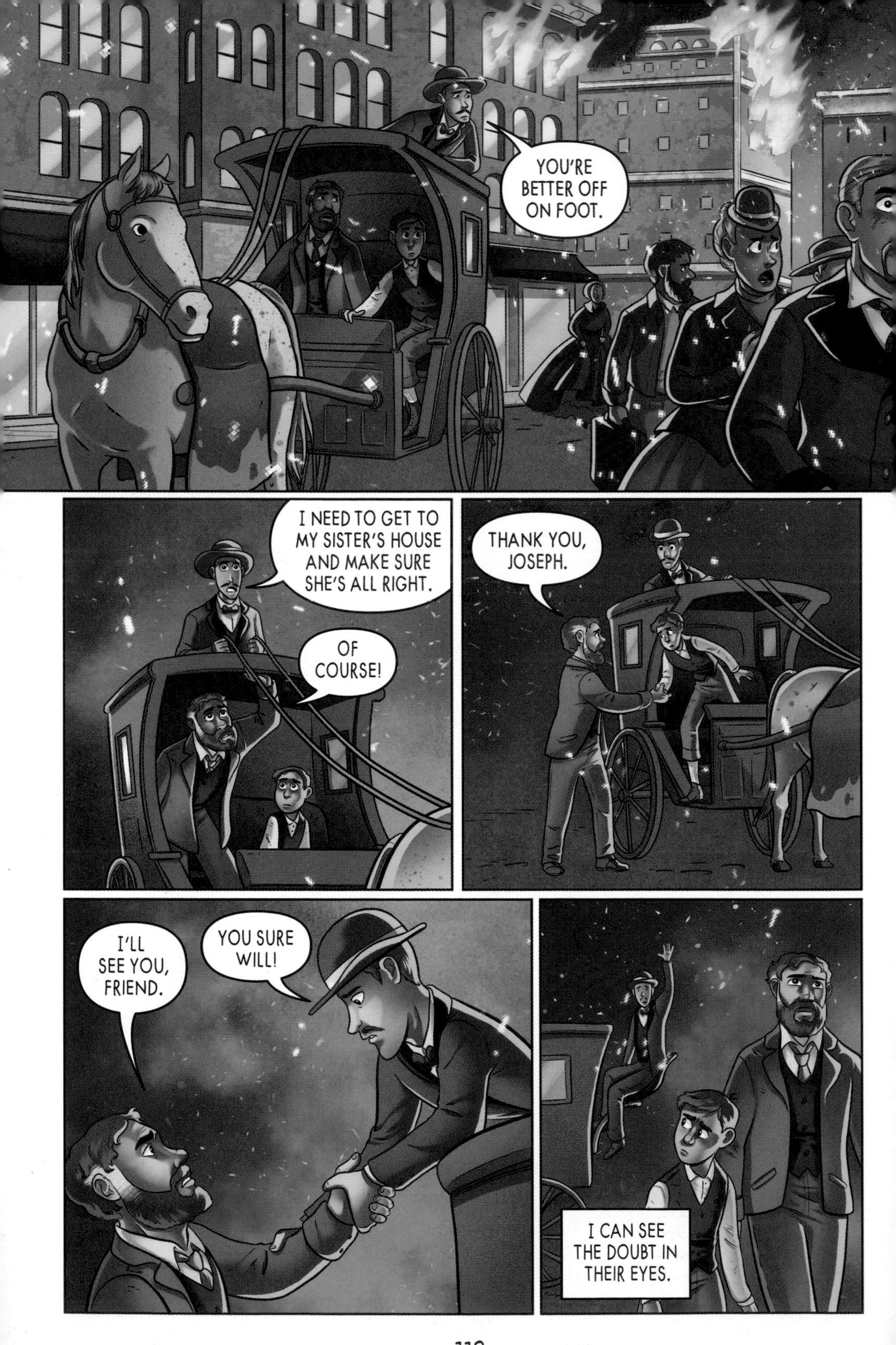
YOU'RE BETTER OFF ON FOOT.
I NEED TO GET TO MY SISTER'S HOUSE AND MAKE SURE SHE'S ALL RIGHT.
OF COURSE!
THANK YOU, JOSEPH.
I'LL SEE YOU, FRIEND.
YOU SURE WILL!
I CAN SEE THE DOUBT IN THEIR EYES.

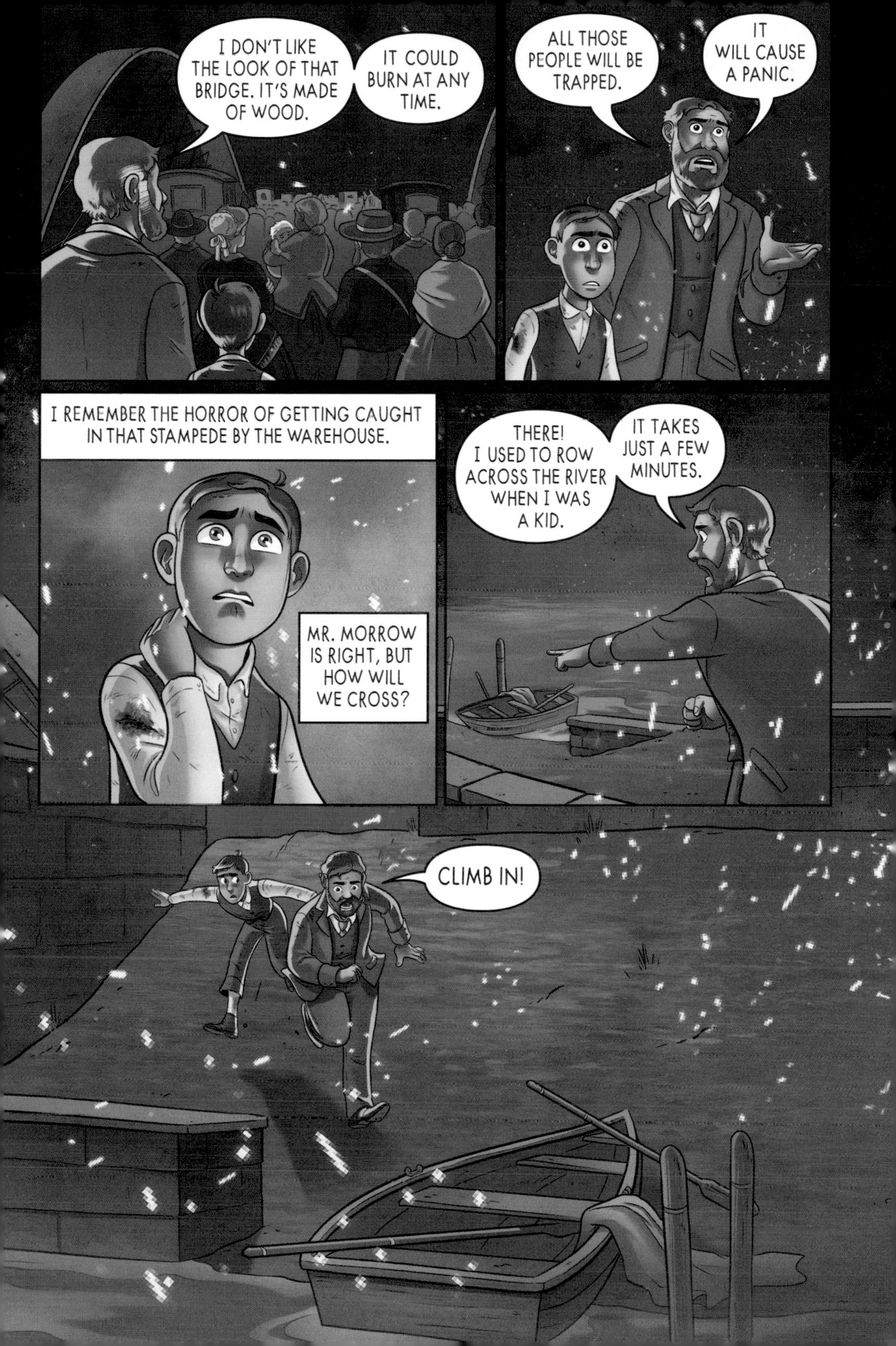

I DON'T LIKE THE LOOK OF THAT BRIDGE. IT'S MADE OF WOOD.
IT COULD BURN AT ANY TIME.
ALL THOSE PEOPLE WILL BE TRAPPED.
IT WILL CAUSE A PANIC.
I REMEMBER THE HORROR OF GETTING CAUGHT IN THAT STAMPEDE BY THE WAREHOUSE.
MR. MORROW IS RIGHT, BUT HOW WILL WE CROSS?
THERE! I USED TO ROW ACROSS THE RIVER WHEN I WAS A KID.
IT TAKES JUST A FEW MINUTES.
CLIMB IN!

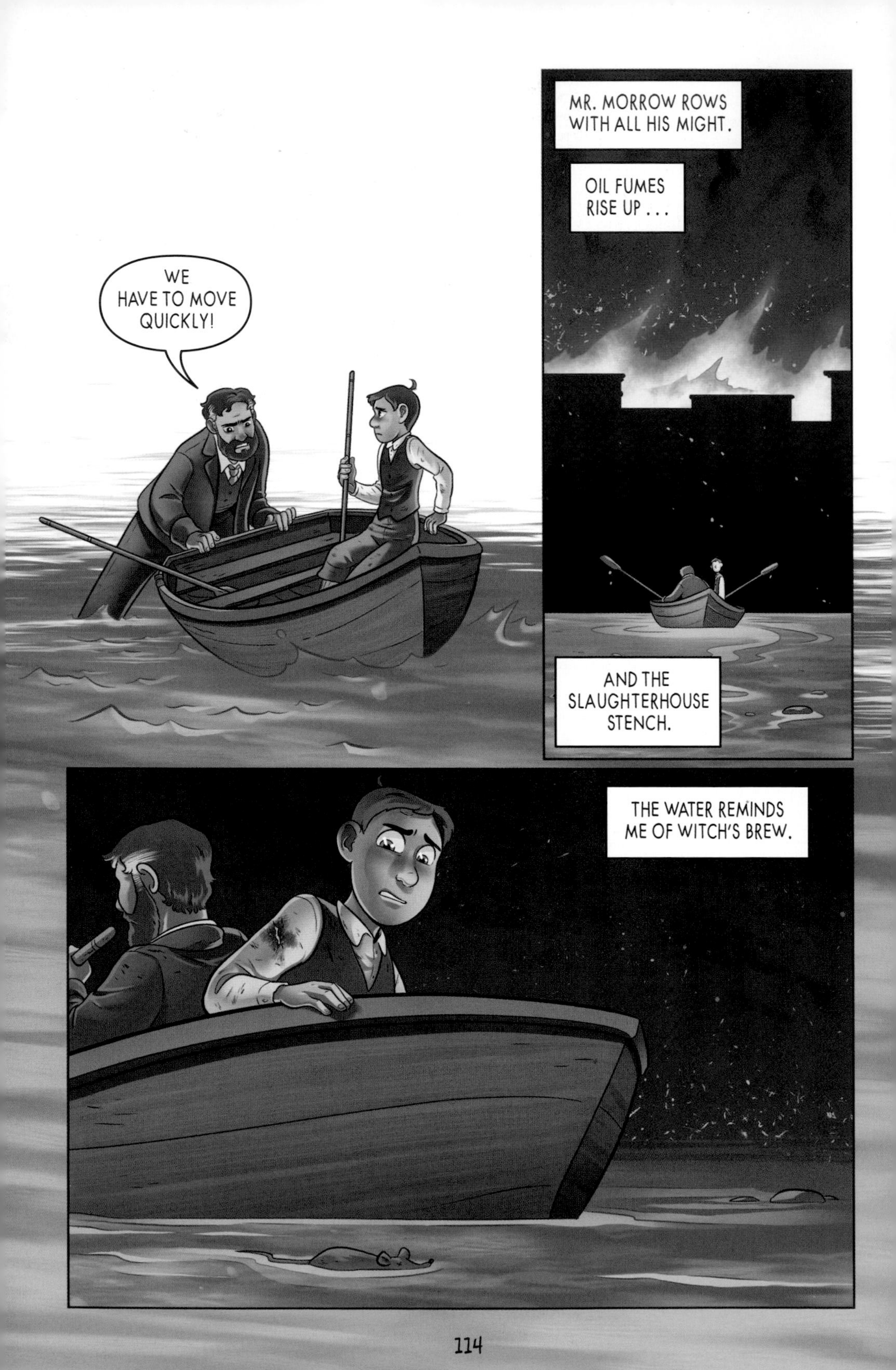
WE HAVE TO MOVE QUICKLY!
MR. MORROW ROWS WITH ALL HIS MIGHT.
OIL FUMES RISE UP . . .
AND THE SLAUGHTERHOUSE STENCH.
THE WATER REMINDS ME OF WITCH'S BREW.

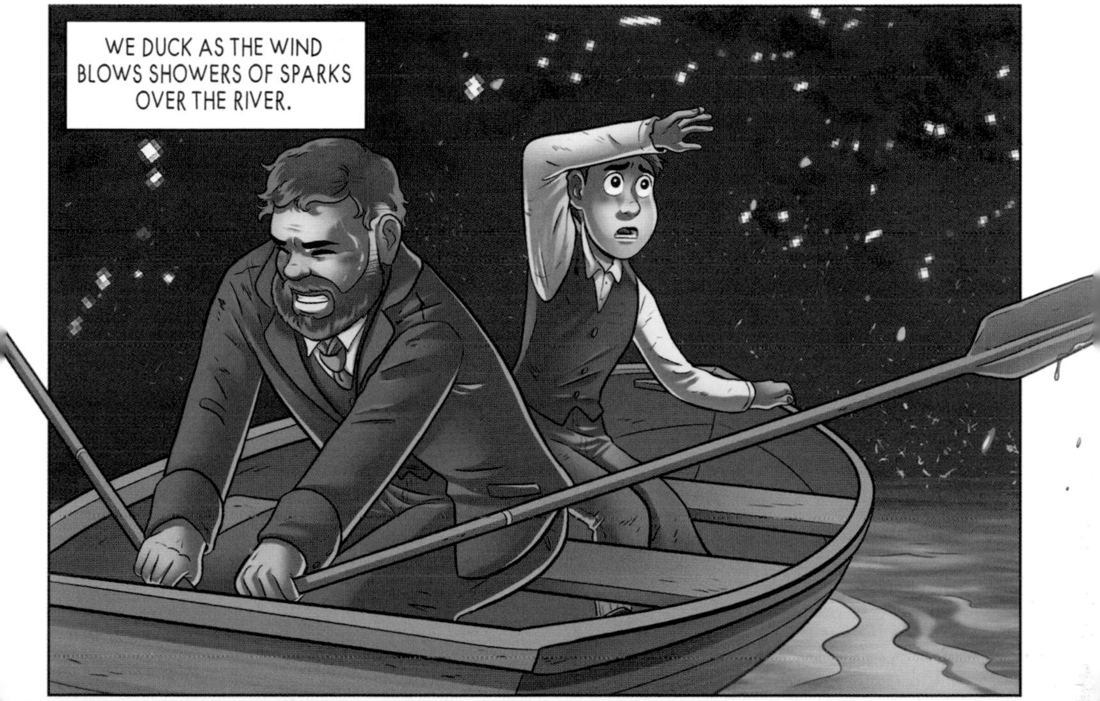
WE DUCK AS THE WIND BLOWS SHOWERS OF SPARKS OVER THE RIVER.

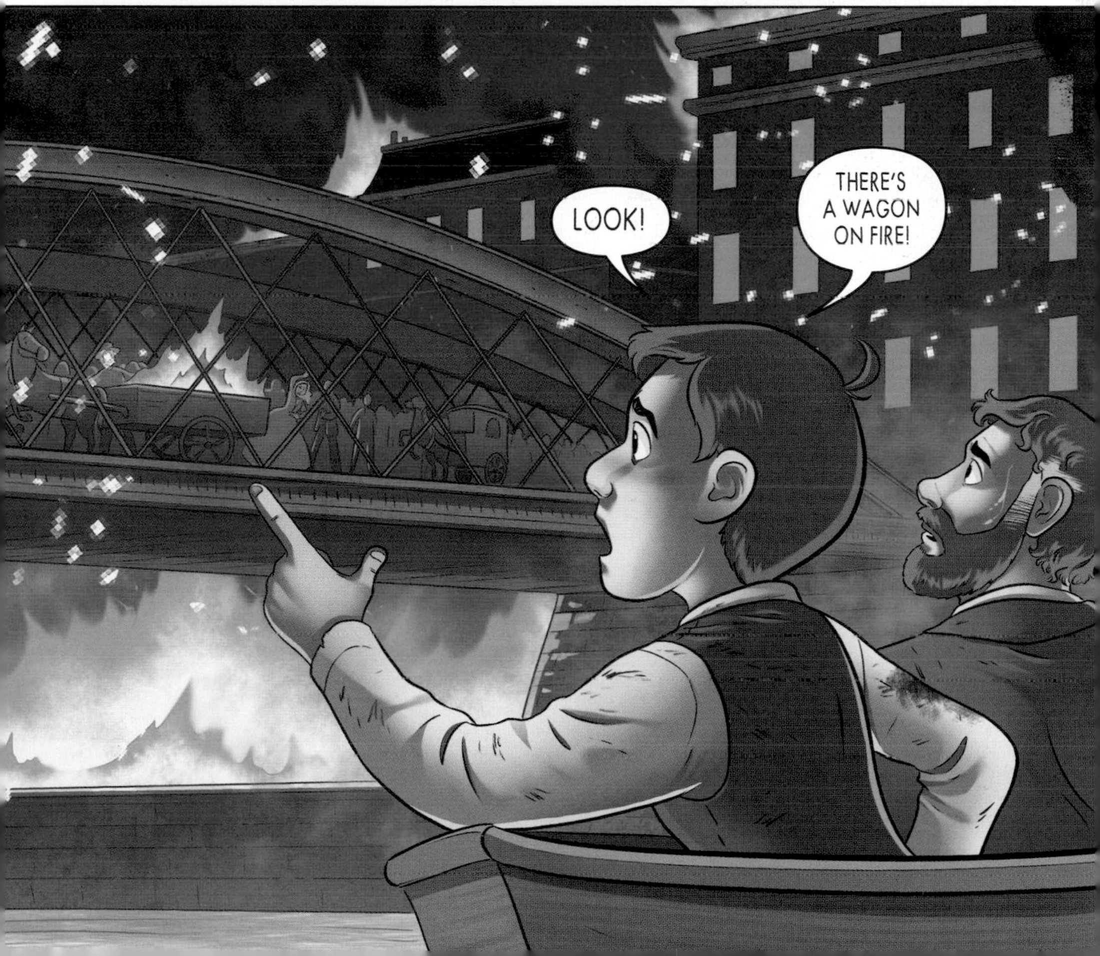
LOOK!
THERE'S A WAGON ON FIRE!

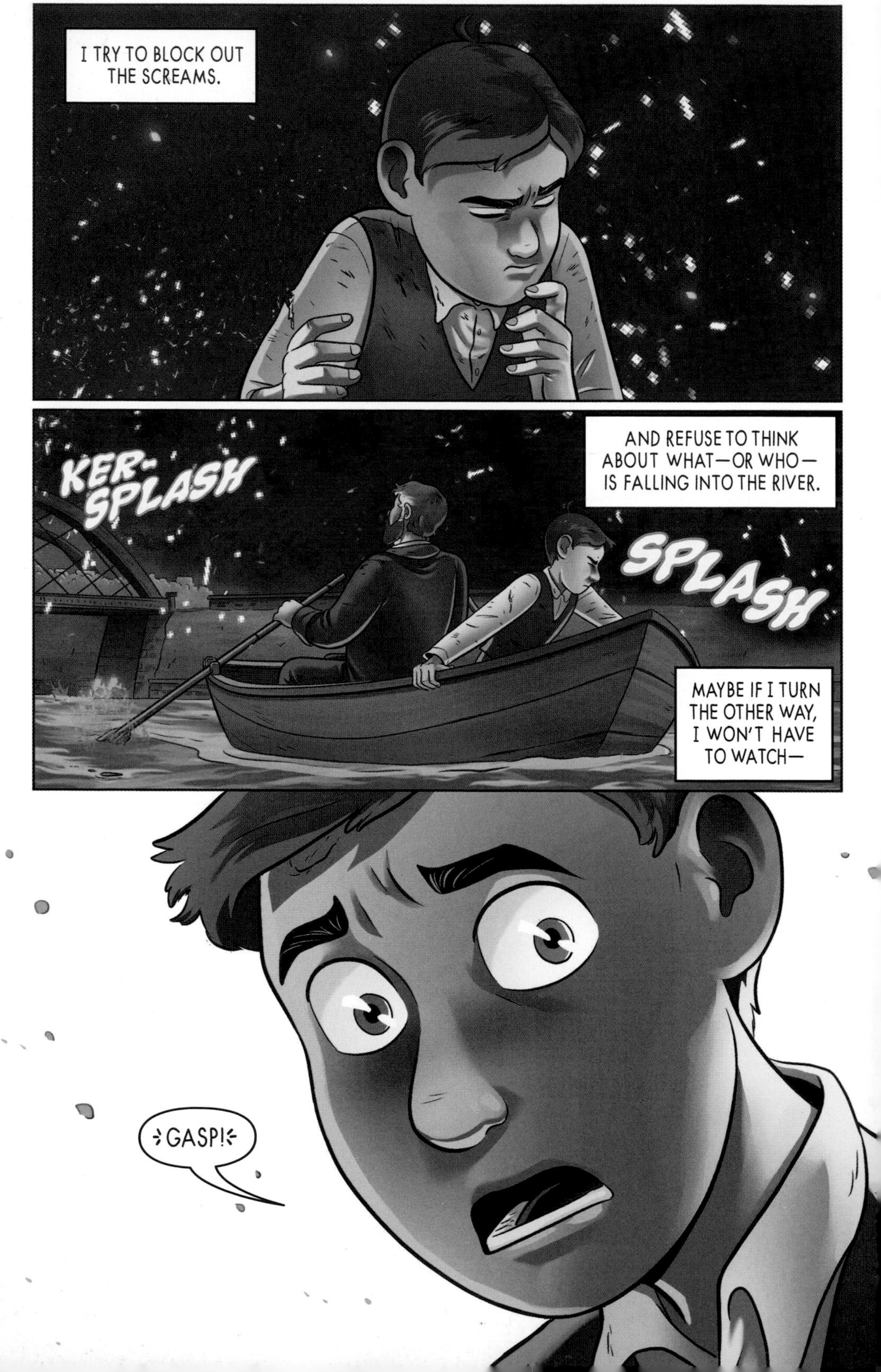
I TRY TO BLOCK OUT THE SCREAMS.
KER-SPLASH
AND REFUSE TO THINK ABOUT WHAT—OR WHO—IS FALLING INTO THE RIVER.
SPLASH
MAYBE IF I TURN THE OTHER WAY, I WON'T HAVE TO WATCH—
GASP!

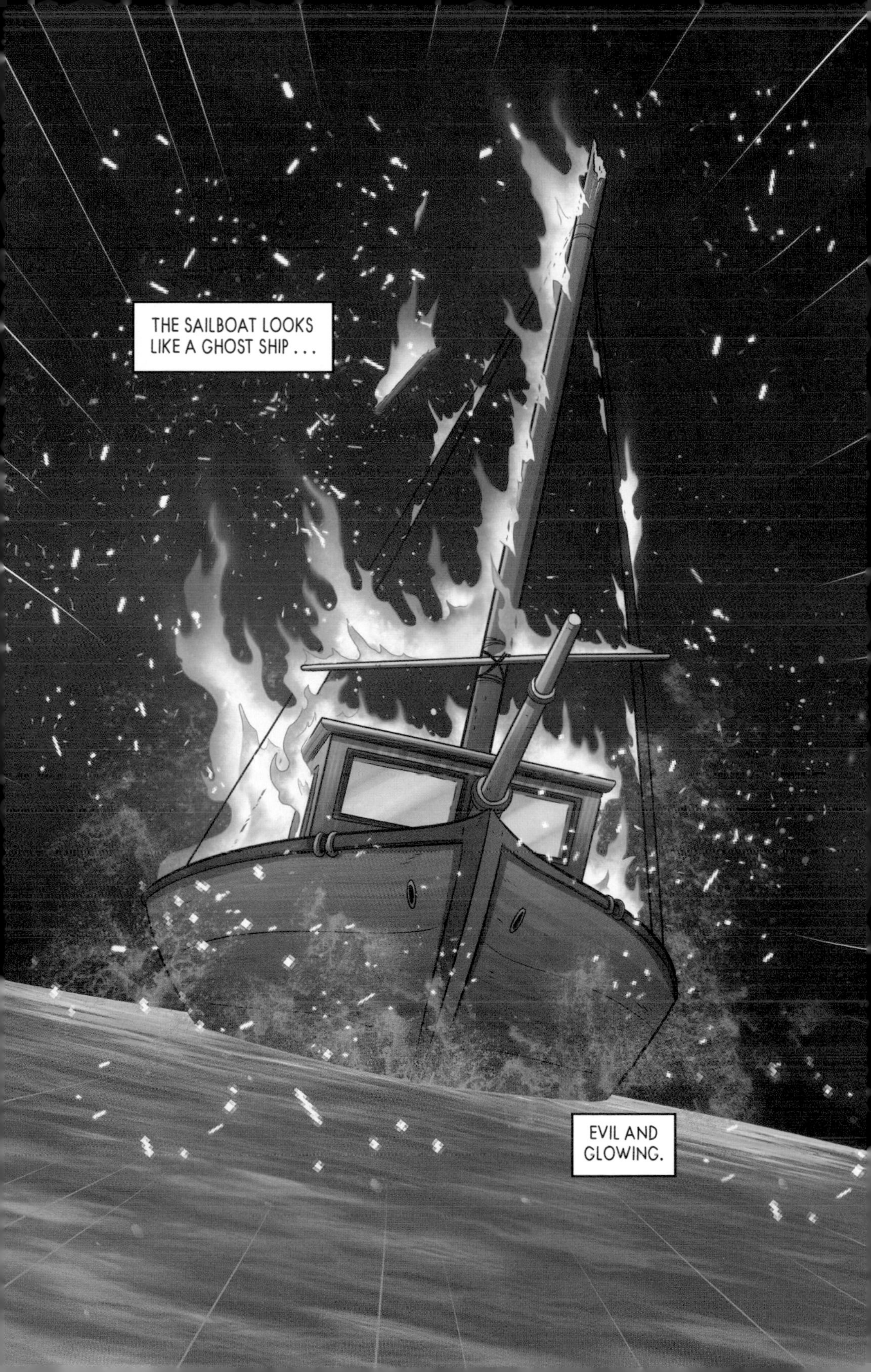
THE SAILBOAT LOOKS LIKE A GHOST SHIP . . .
EVIL AND GLOWING.

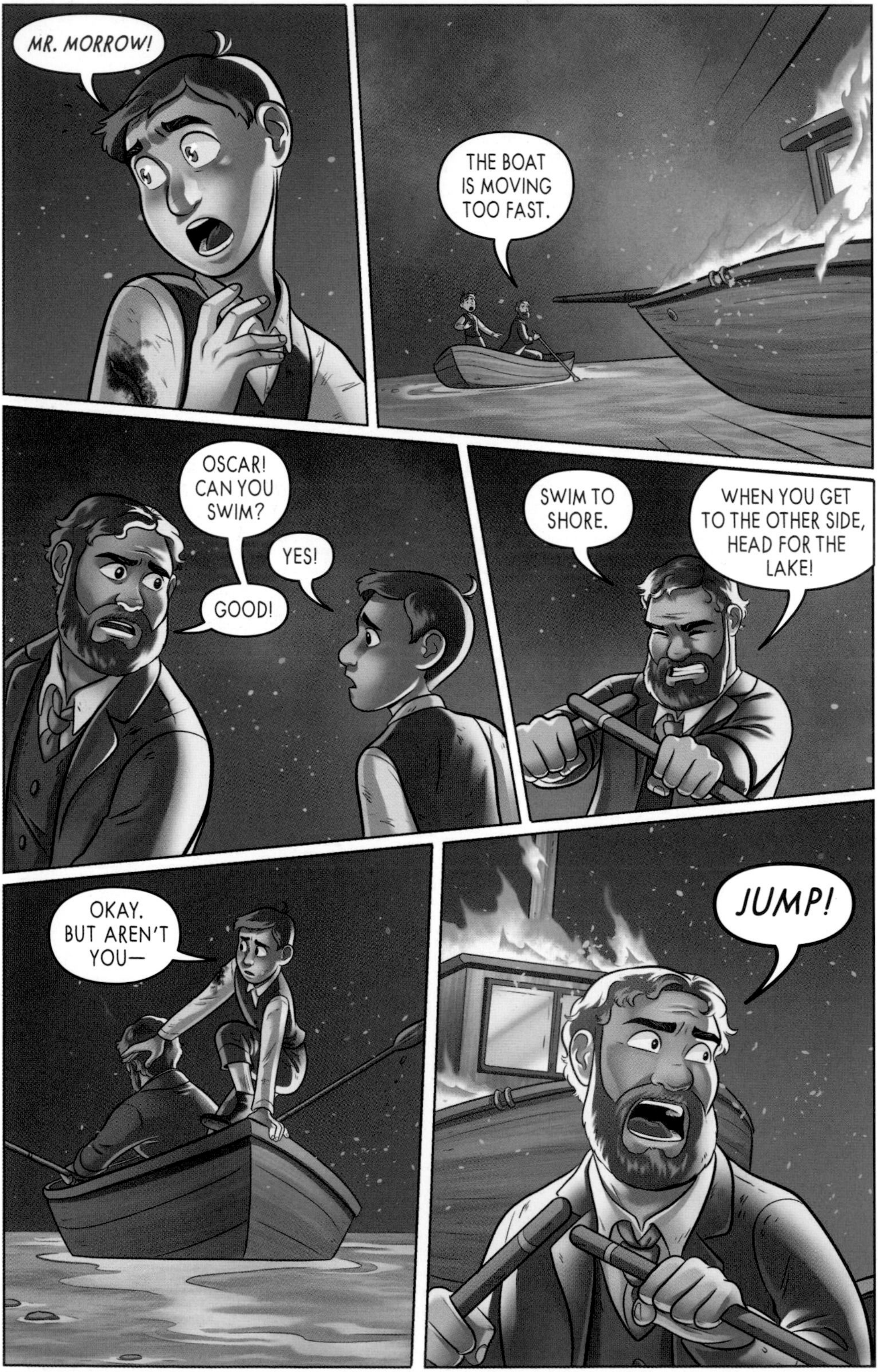
MR. MORROW!
THE BOAT IS MOVING TOO FAST.
OSCAR! CAN YOU SWIM?
YES!
GOOD!
SWIM TO SHORE.
WHEN YOU GET TO THE OTHER SIDE, HEAD FOR THE LAKE!
OKAY. BUT AREN'T YOU—
JUMP!

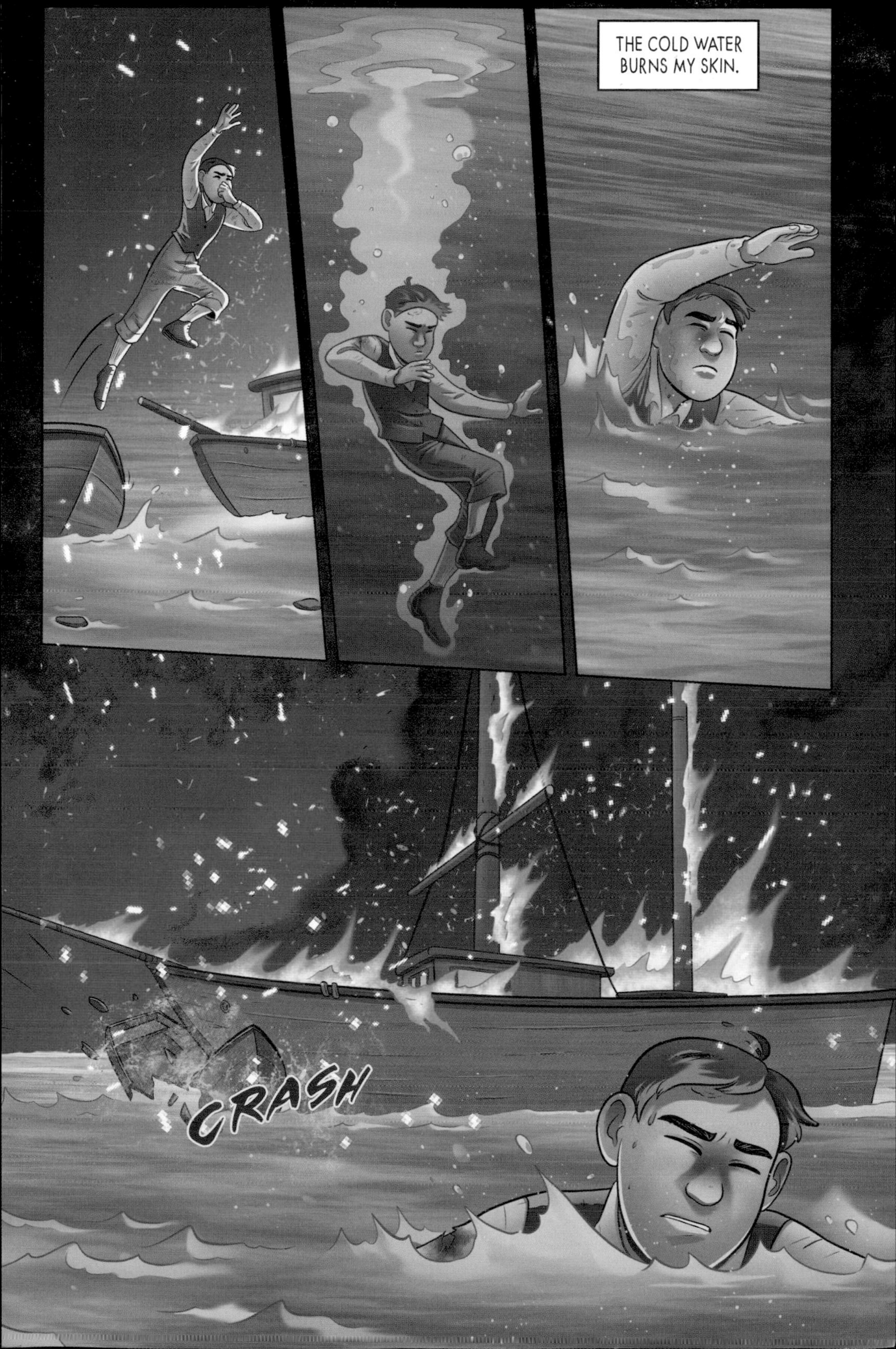
THE COLD WATER BURNS MY SKIN.
CRASH

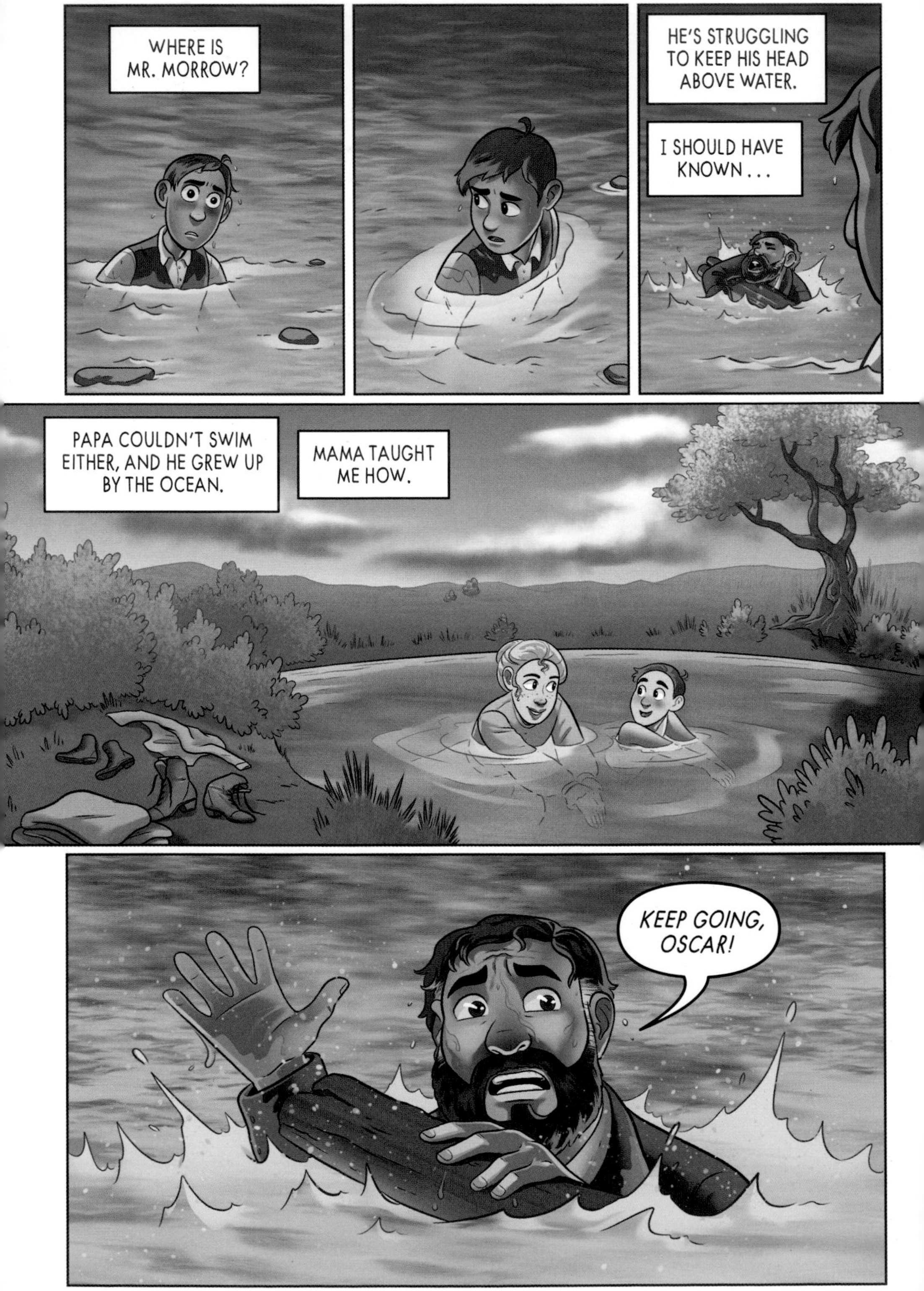
WHERE IS MR. MORROW?
HE'S STRUGGLING TO KEEP HIS HEAD ABOVE WATER.
I SHOULD HAVE KNOWN . . .
PAPA COULDN'T SWIM EITHER, AND HE GREW UP BY THE OCEAN.
MAMA TAUGHT ME HOW.
KEEP GOING, OSCAR!

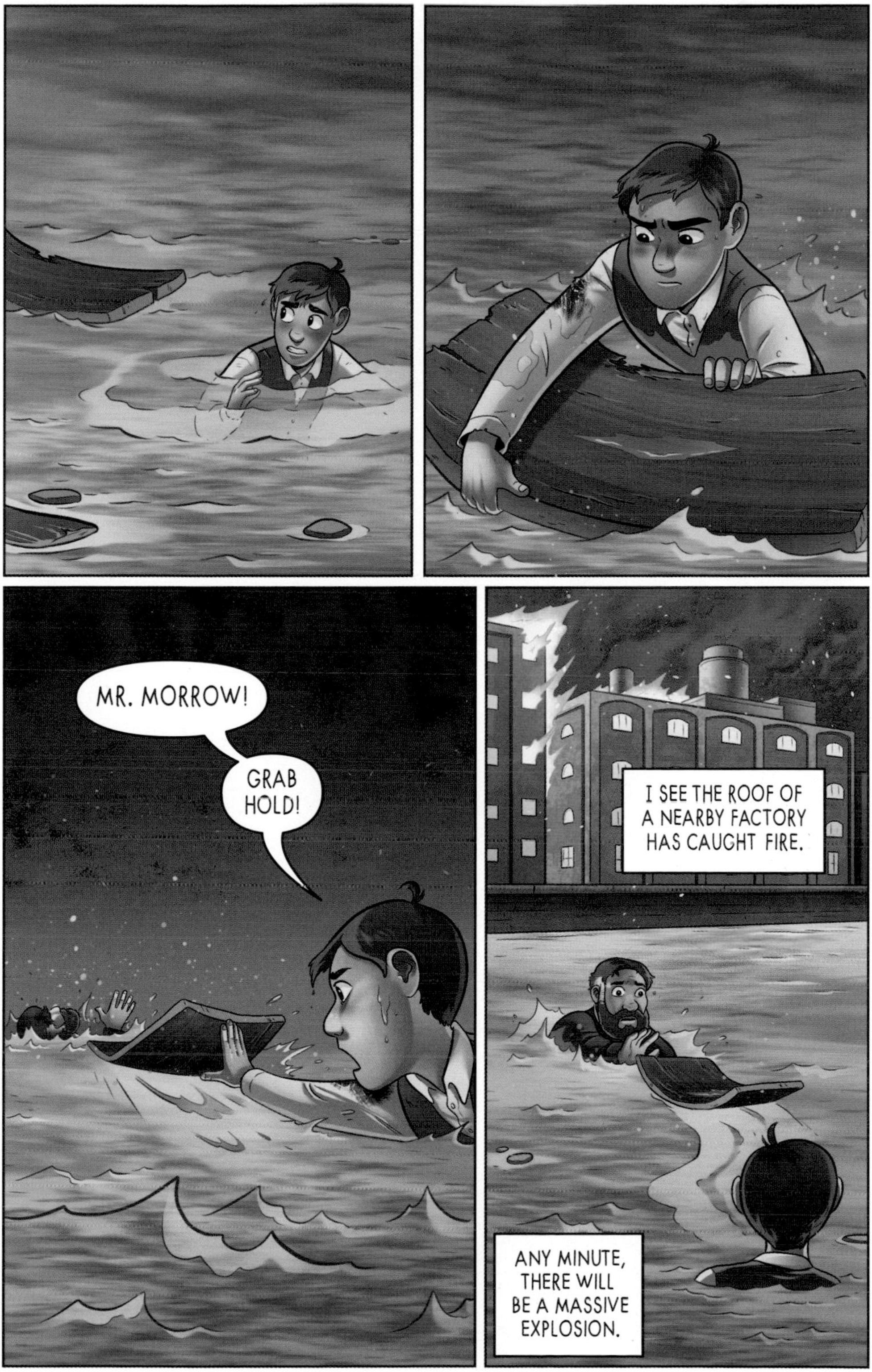
MR. MORROW!
GRAB HOLD!
I SEE THE ROOF OF A NEARBY FACTORY HAS CAUGHT FIRE.
ANY MINUTE, THERE WILL BE A MASSIVE EXPLOSION.

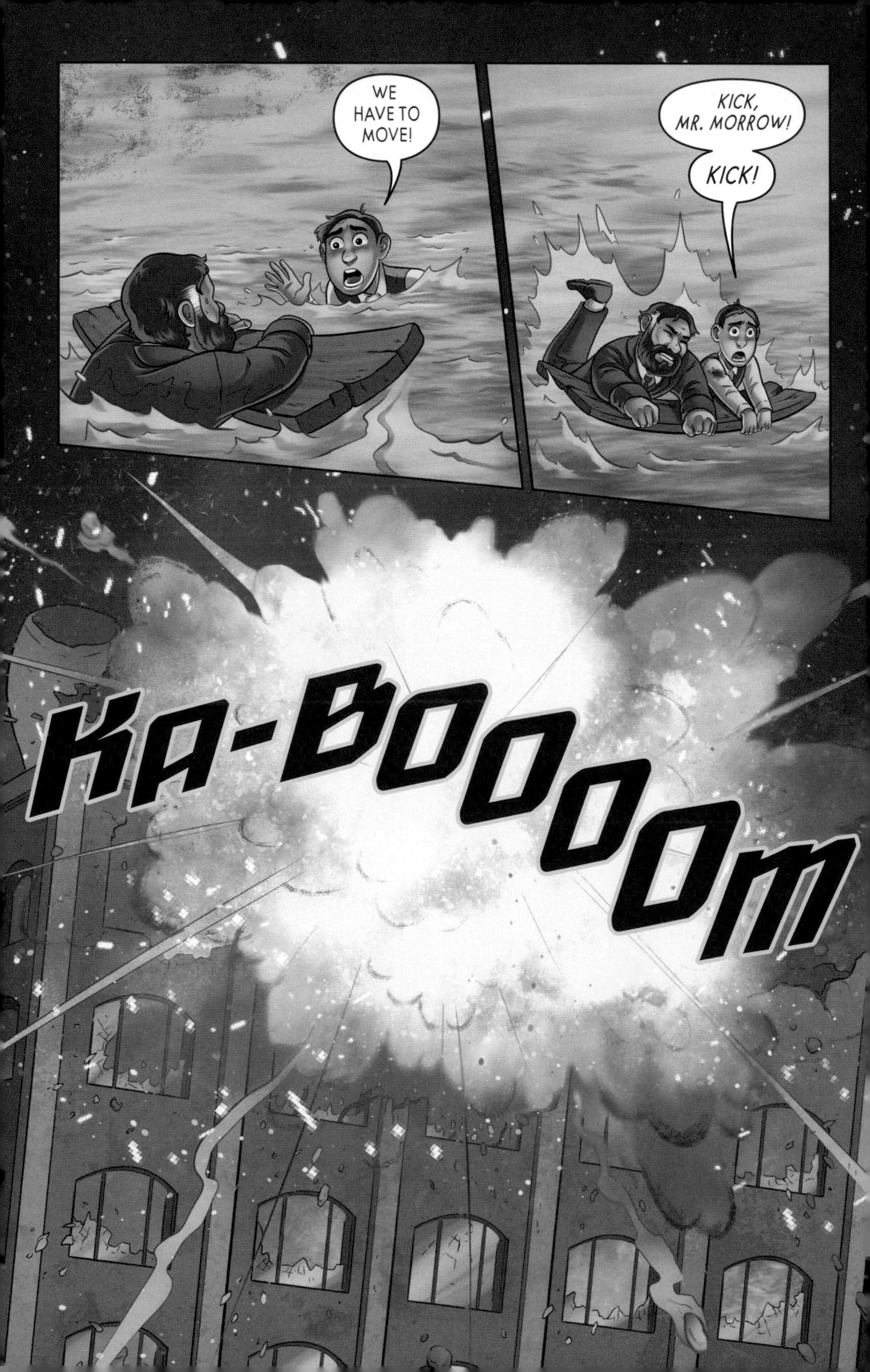
WE HAVE TO MOVE!
KICK, MR. MORROW!
KICK!
KA-BOOOOOM

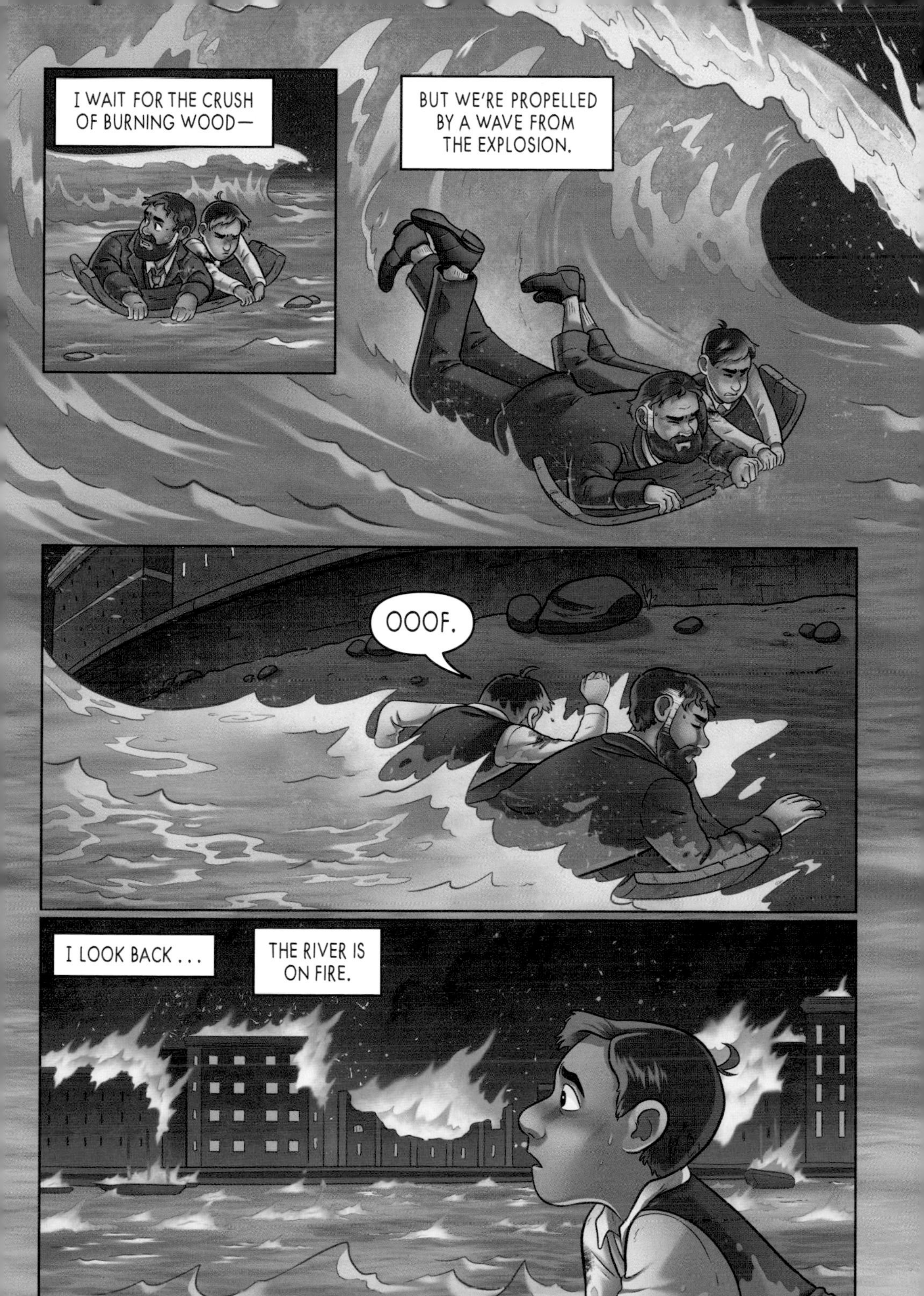
I WAIT FOR THE CRUSH OF BURNING WOOD—
BUT WE'RE PROPELLED BY A WAVE FROM THE EXPLOSION.
OOOF.
I LOOK BACK . . .
THE RIVER IS ON FIRE.

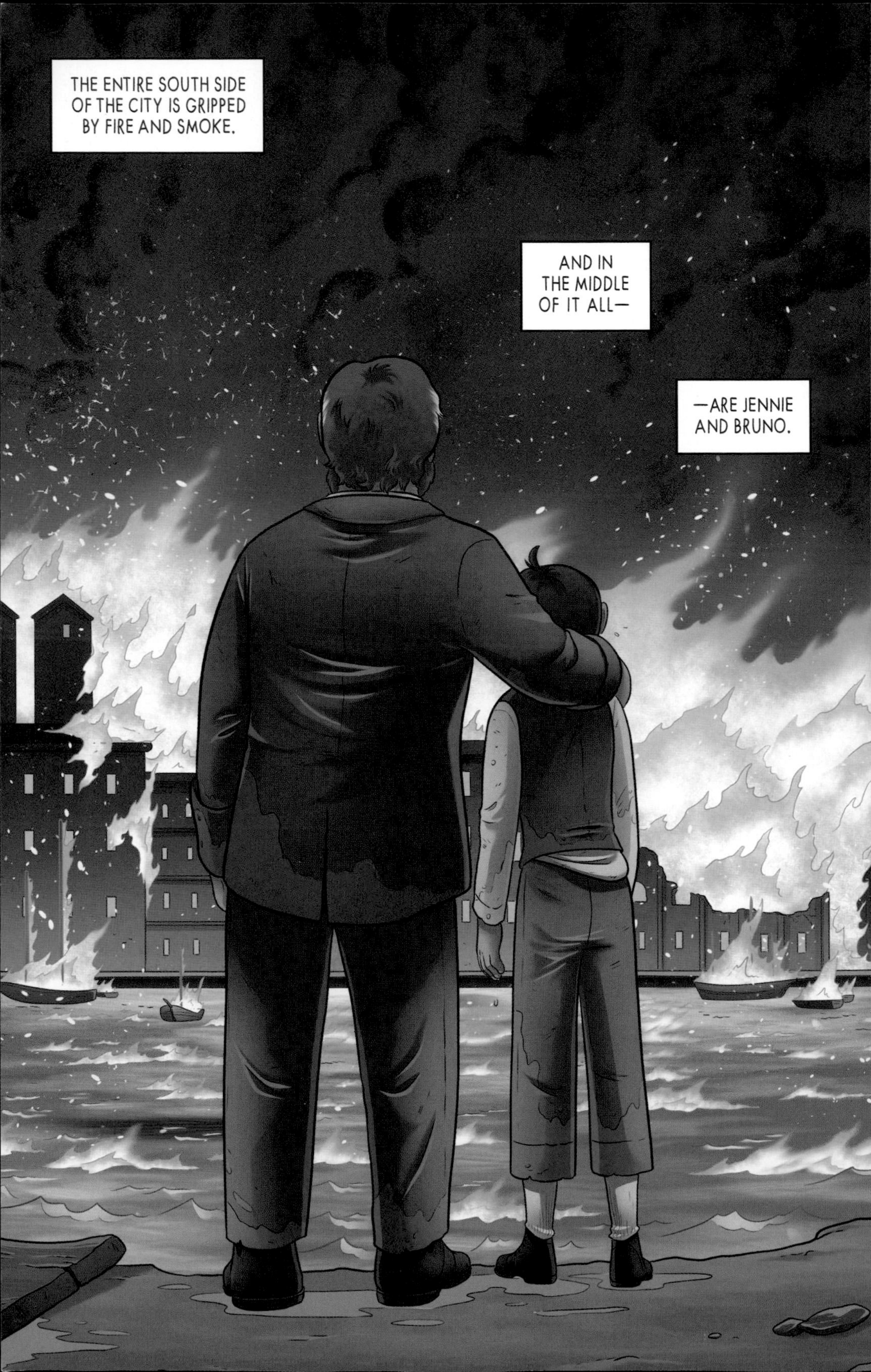
THE ENTIRE SOUTH SIDE OF THE CITY IS GRIPPED BY FIRE AND SMOKE.
AND IN THE MIDDLE OF IT ALL—
—ARE JENNIE AND BRUNO.

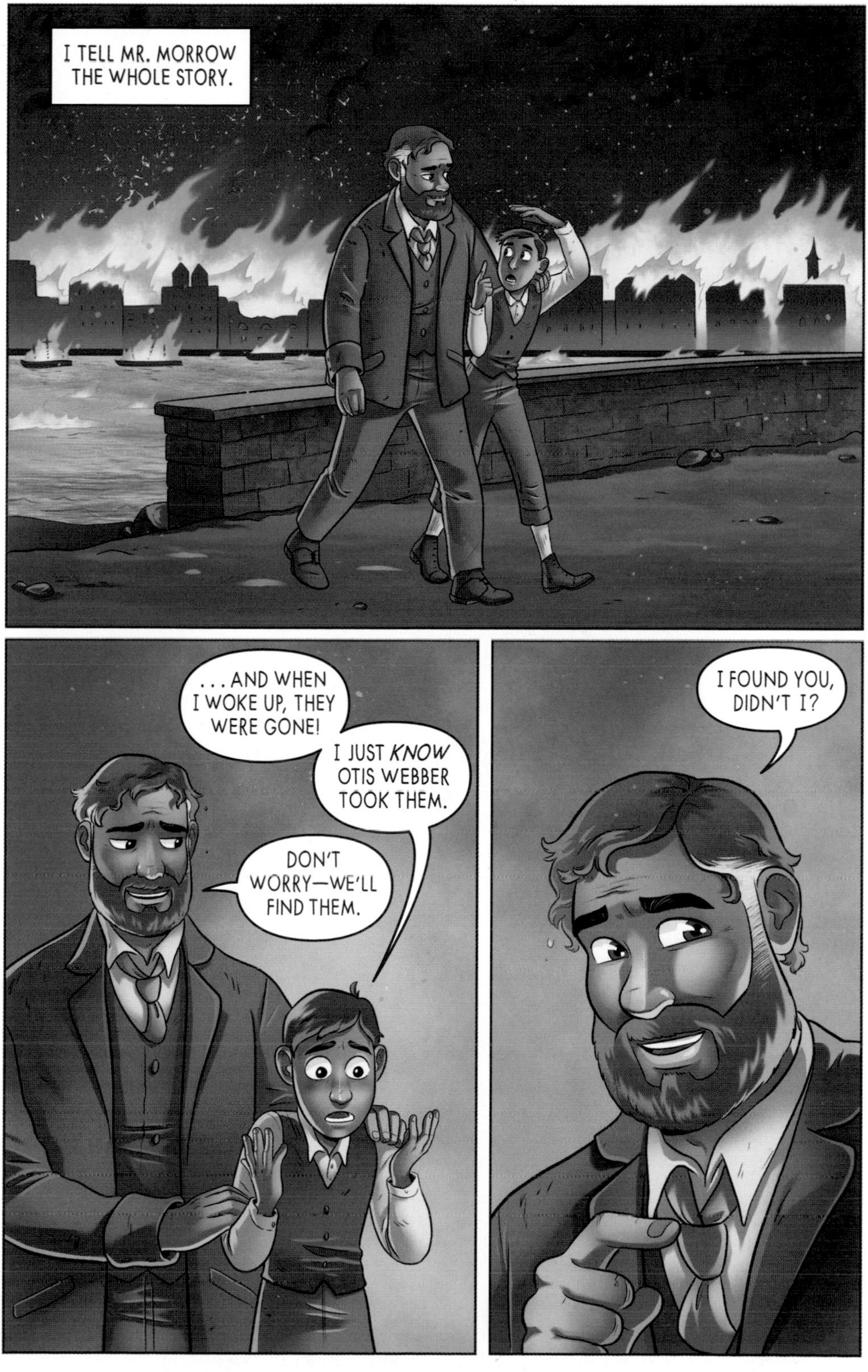
I TELL MR. MORROW THE WHOLE STORY.
. . . AND WHEN I WOKE UP, THEY WERE GONE!
I JUST *KNOW* OTIS WEBBER TOOK THEM.
DON'T WORRY—WE'LL FIND THEM.
I FOUND YOU, DIDN'T I?

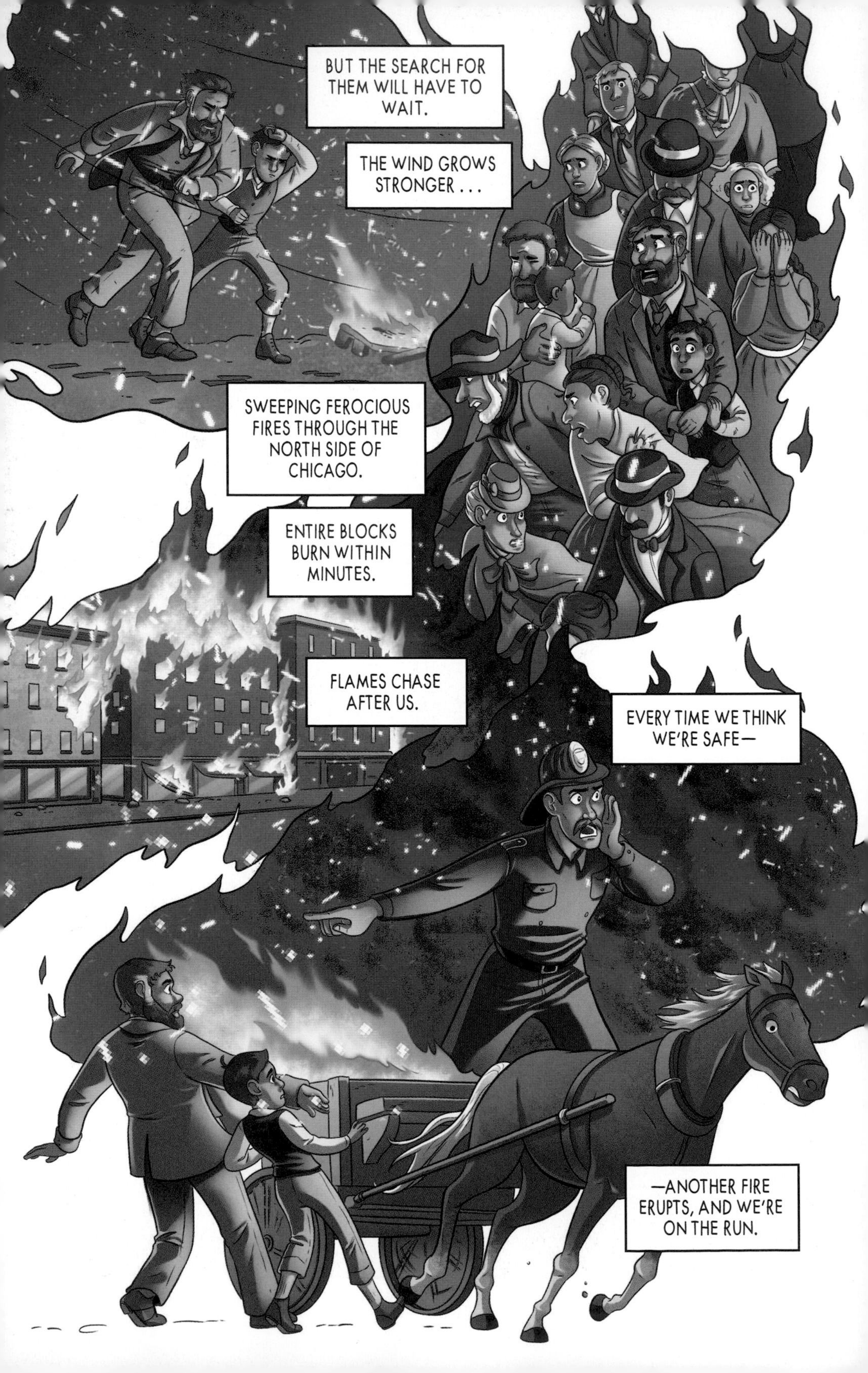
BUT THE SEARCH FOR THEM WILL HAVE TO WAIT.
THE WIND GROWS STRONGER . . .
SWEEPING FEROCIOUS FIRES THROUGH THE NORTH SIDE OF CHICAGO.
ENTIRE BLOCKS BURN WITHIN MINUTES.
FLAMES CHASE AFTER US.
EVERY TIME WE THINK WE'RE SAFE—
—ANOTHER FIRE ERUPTS, AND WE'RE ON THE RUN.

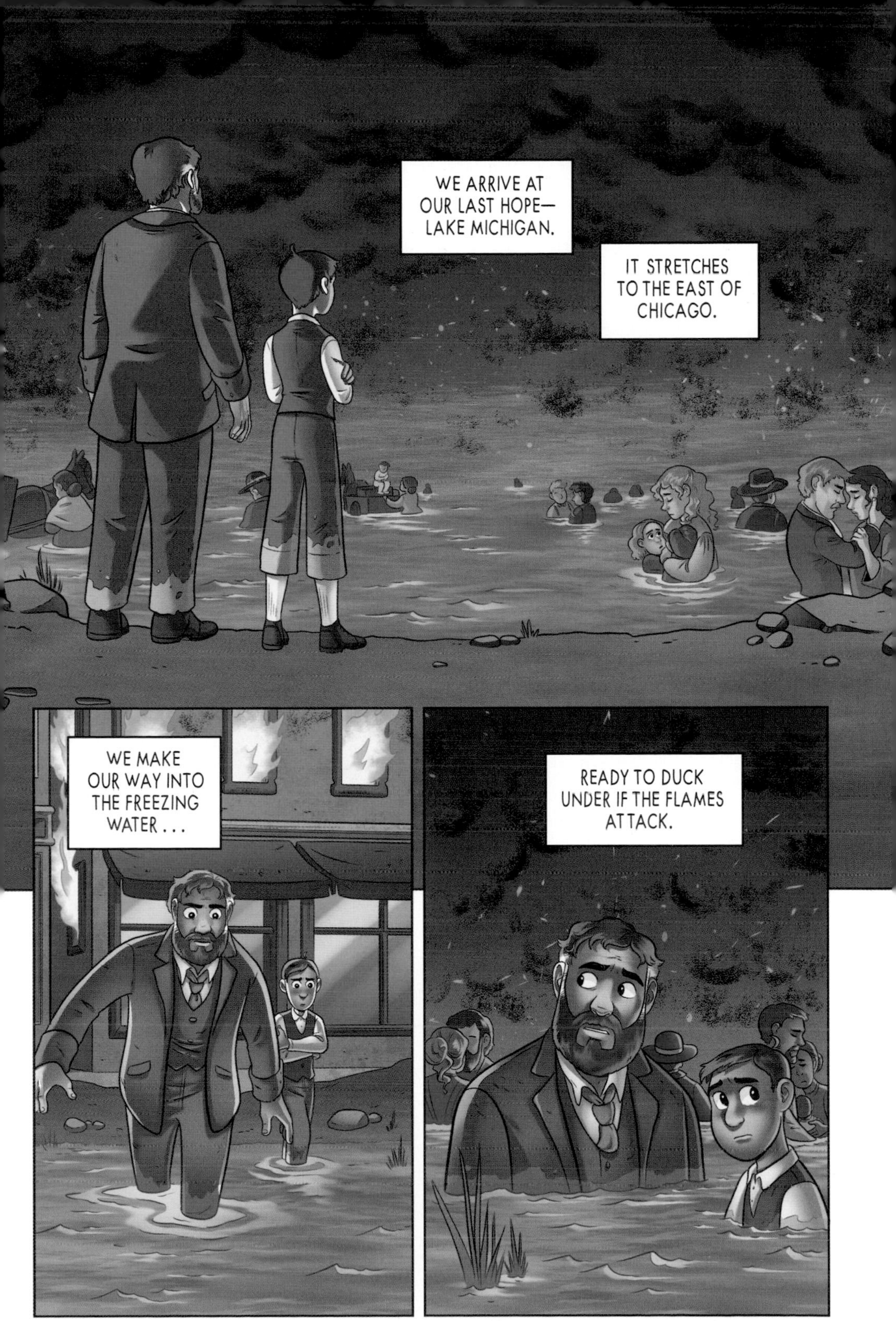
WE ARRIVE AT OUR LAST HOPE—LAKE MICHIGAN.
IT STRETCHES TO THE EAST OF CHICAGO.
WE MAKE OUR WAY INTO THE FREEZING WATER . . .
READY TO DUCK UNDER IF THE FLAMES ATTACK.

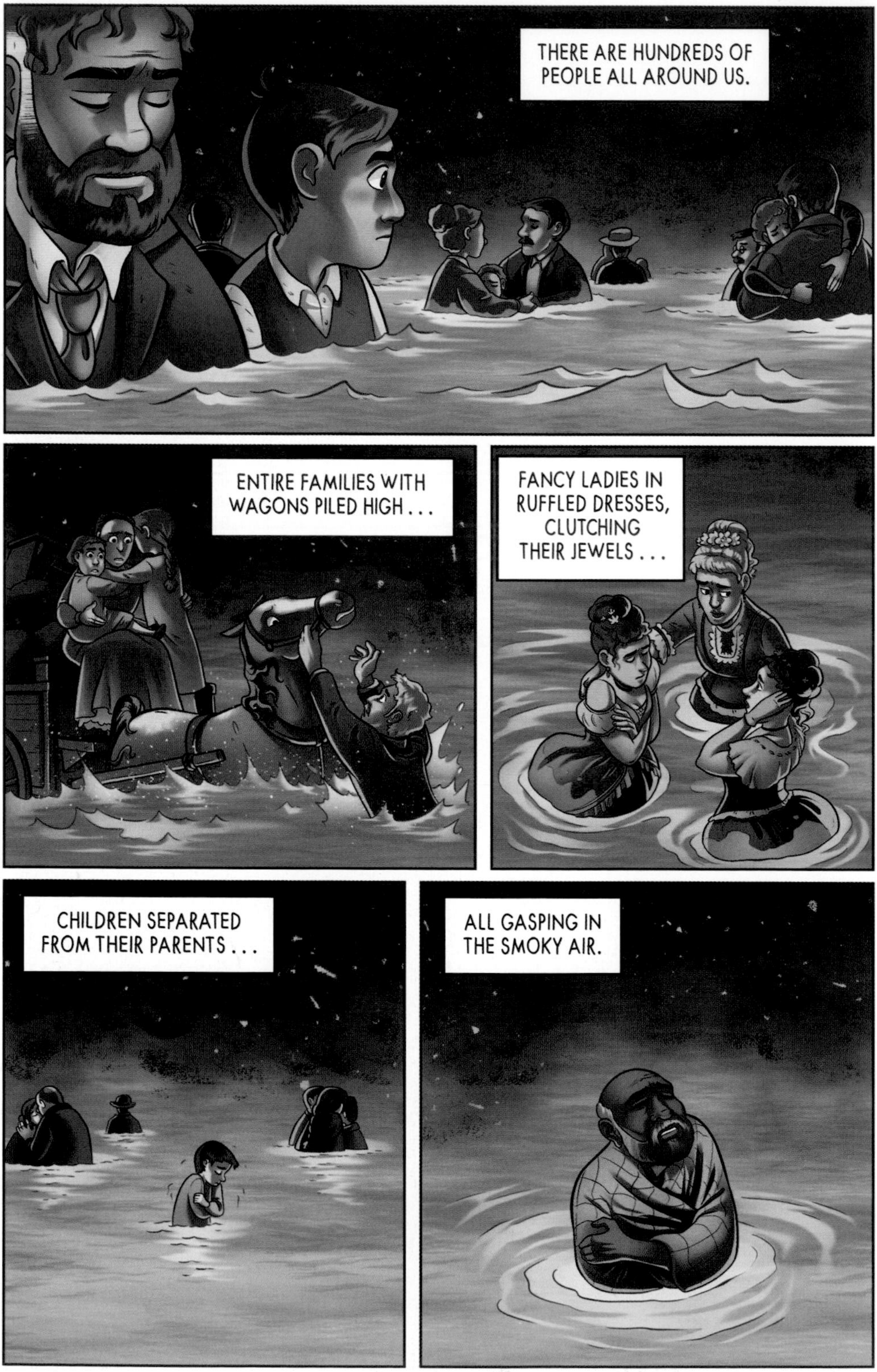
THERE ARE HUNDREDS OF PEOPLE ALL AROUND US.
ENTIRE FAMILIES WITH WAGONS PILED HIGH . . .
FANCY LADIES IN RUFFLED DRESSES, CLUTCHING THEIR JEWELS . . .
CHILDREN SEPARATED FROM THEIR PARENTS . . .
ALL GASPING IN THE SMOKY AIR.

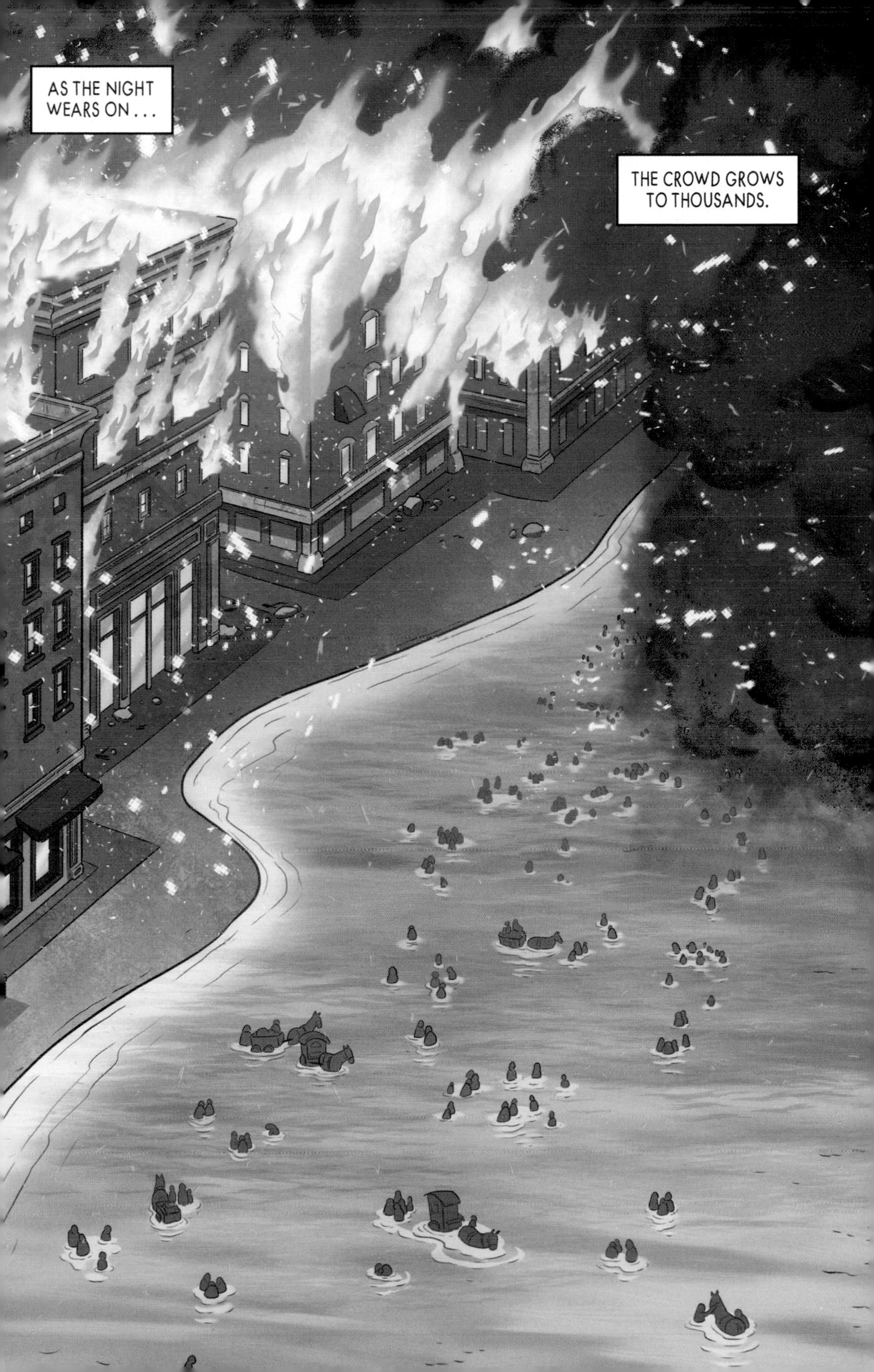
AS THE NIGHT WEARS ON . . .
THE CROWD GROWS TO THOUSANDS.

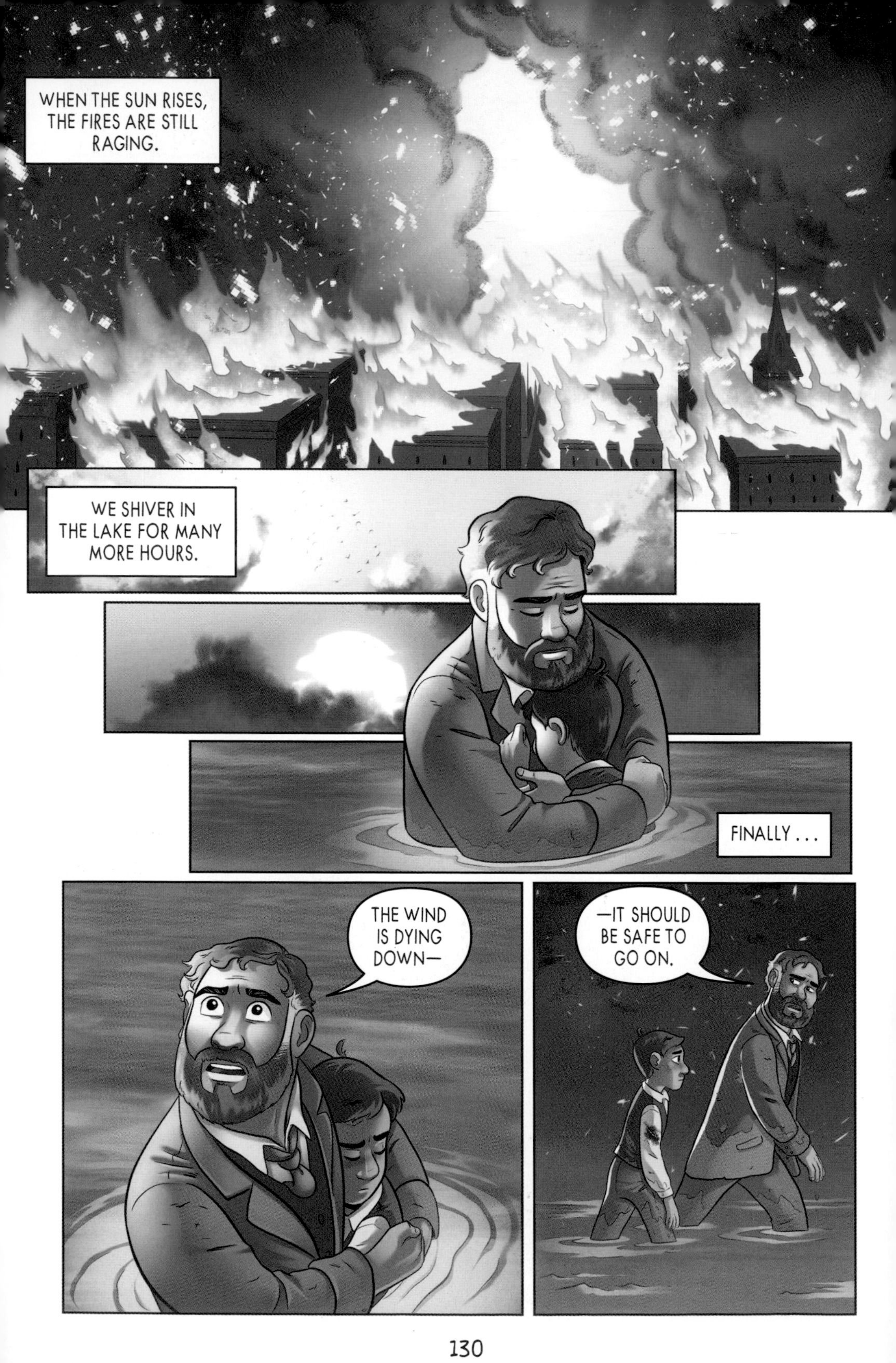
WHEN THE SUN RISES, THE FIRES ARE STILL RAGING.
WE SHIVER IN THE LAKE FOR MANY MORE HOURS.
FINALLY . . .
THE WIND IS DYING DOWN—
—IT SHOULD BE SAFE TO GO ON.

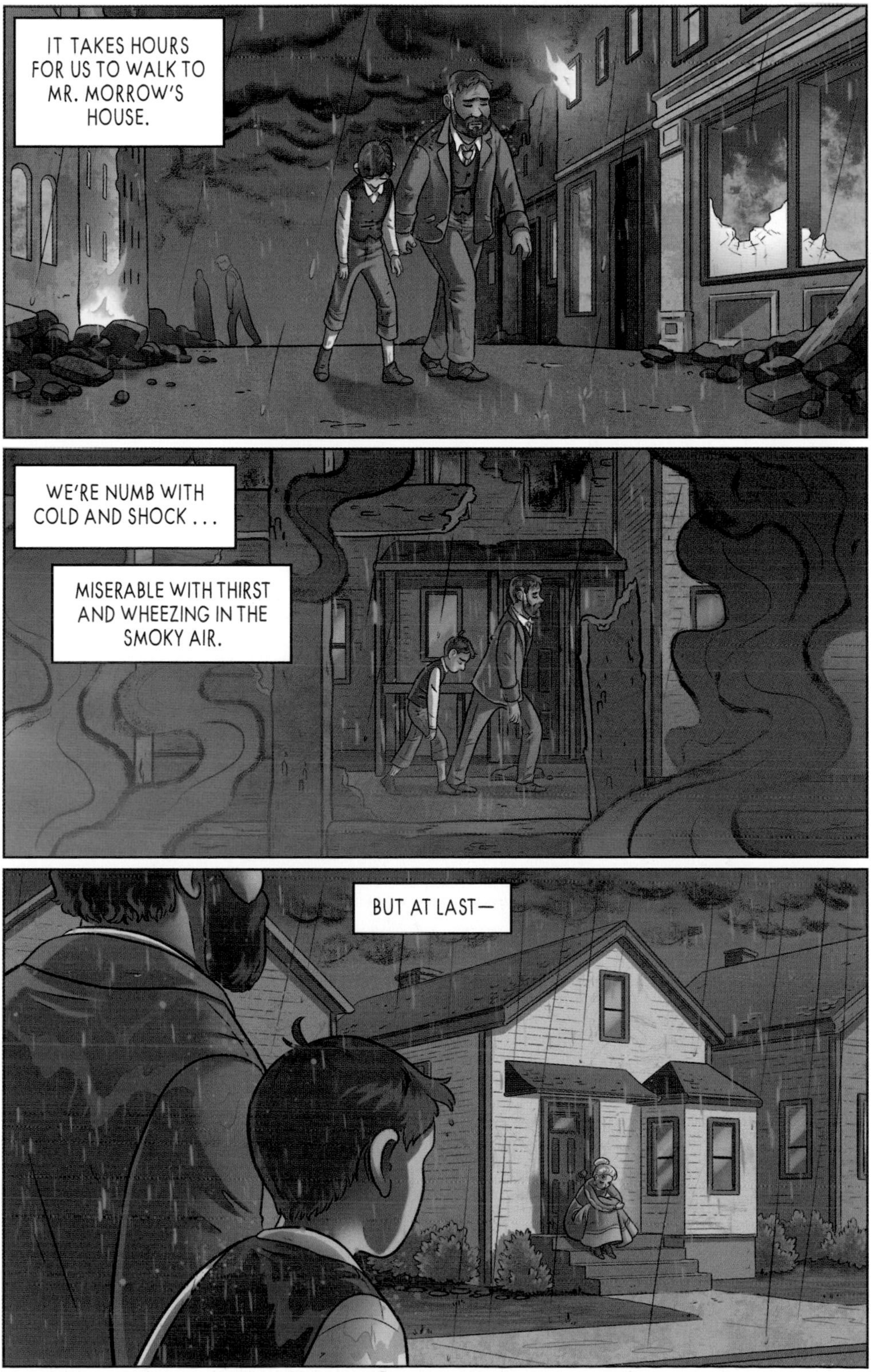
IT TAKES HOURS FOR US TO WALK TO MR. MORROW'S HOUSE.
WE'RE NUMB WITH COLD AND SHOCK . . .
MISERABLE WITH THIRST AND WHEEZING IN THE SMOKY AIR.
BUT AT LAST—

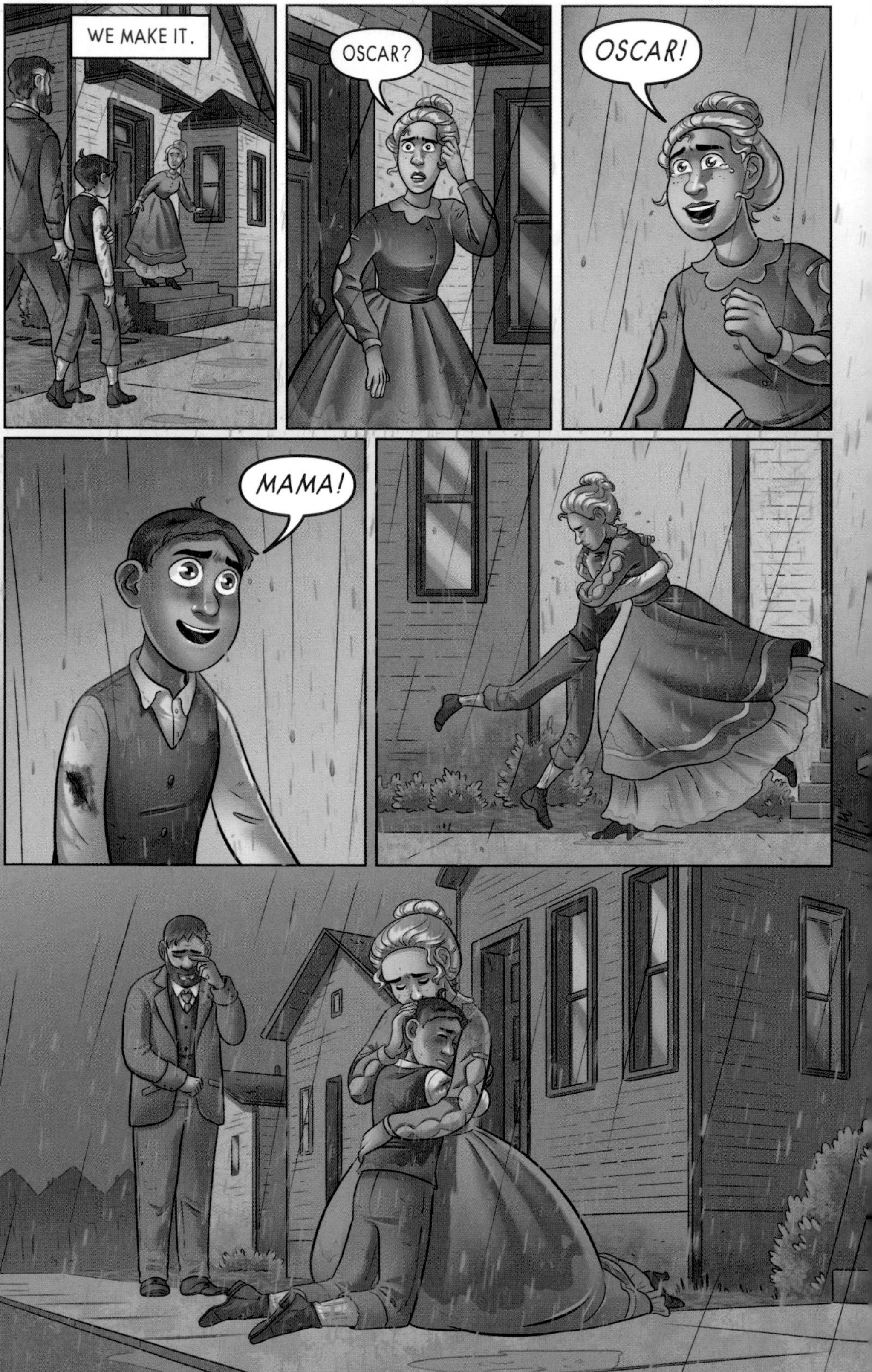
WE MAKE IT.
OSCAR?
OSCAR!
MAMA!

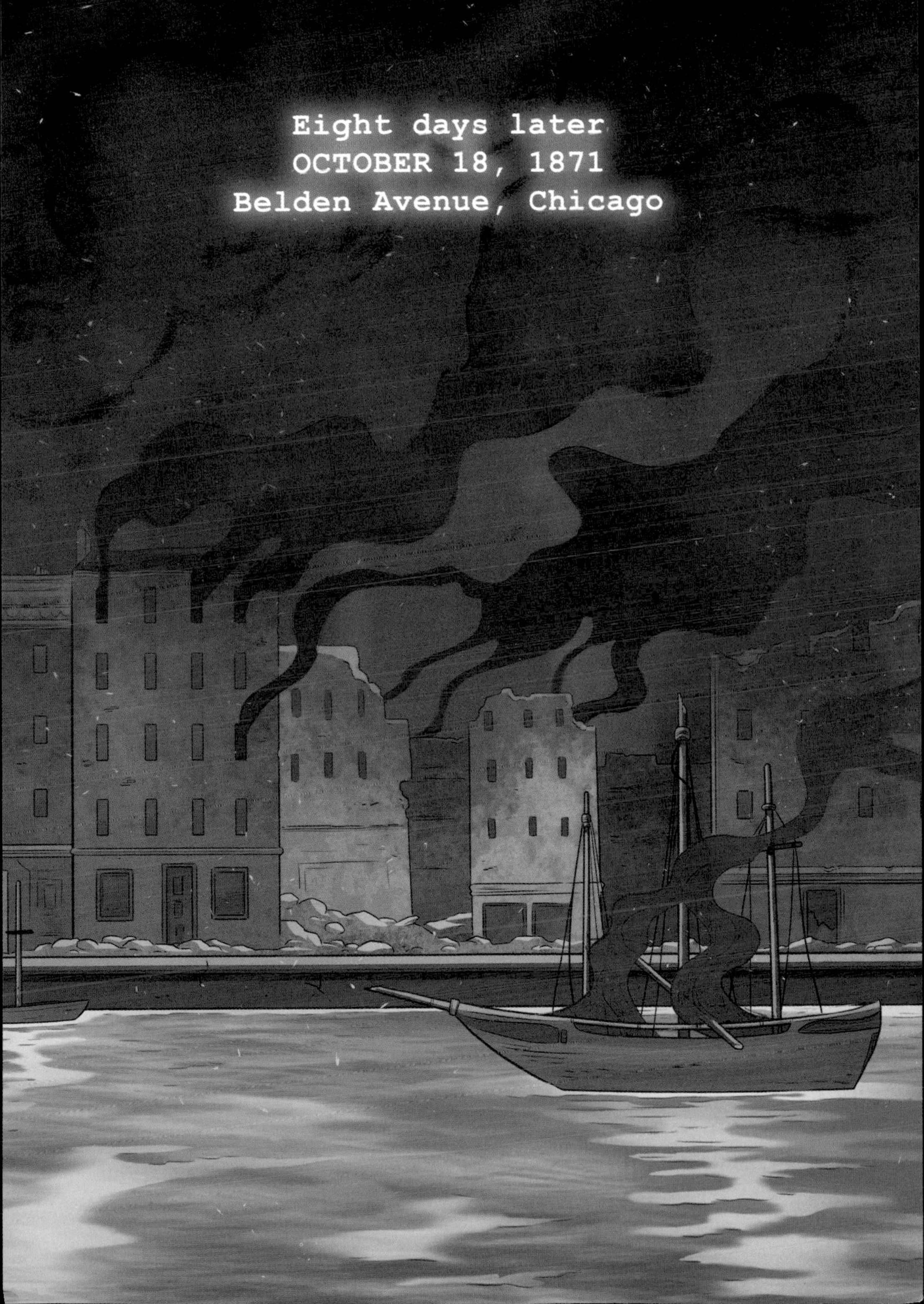
Eight days later
OCTOBER 18, 1871
Belden Avenue, Chicago

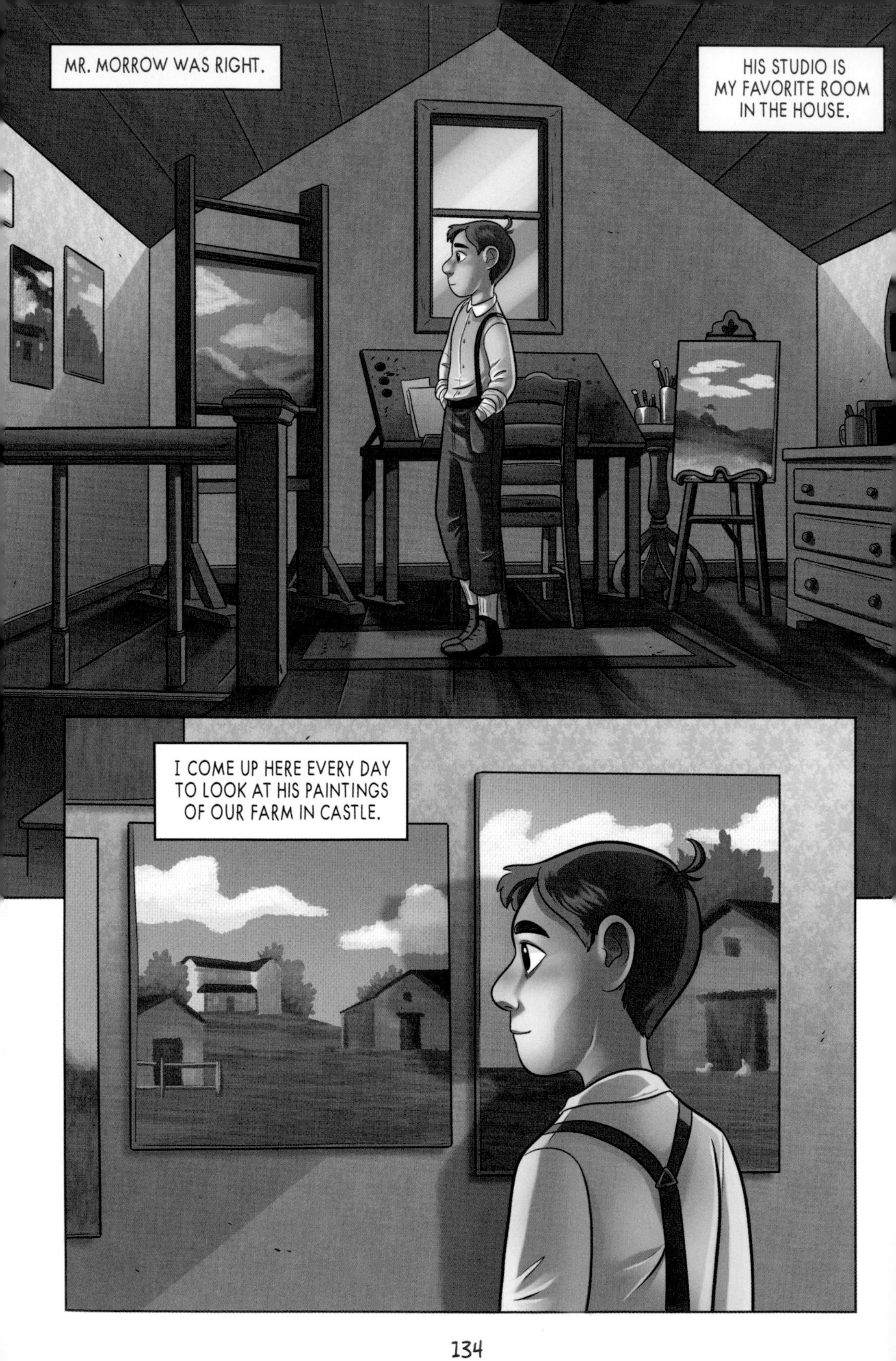
MR. MORROW WAS RIGHT.
HIS STUDIO IS MY FAVORITE ROOM IN THE HOUSE.
I COME UP HERE EVERY DAY TO LOOK AT HIS PAINTINGS OF OUR FARM IN CASTLE.

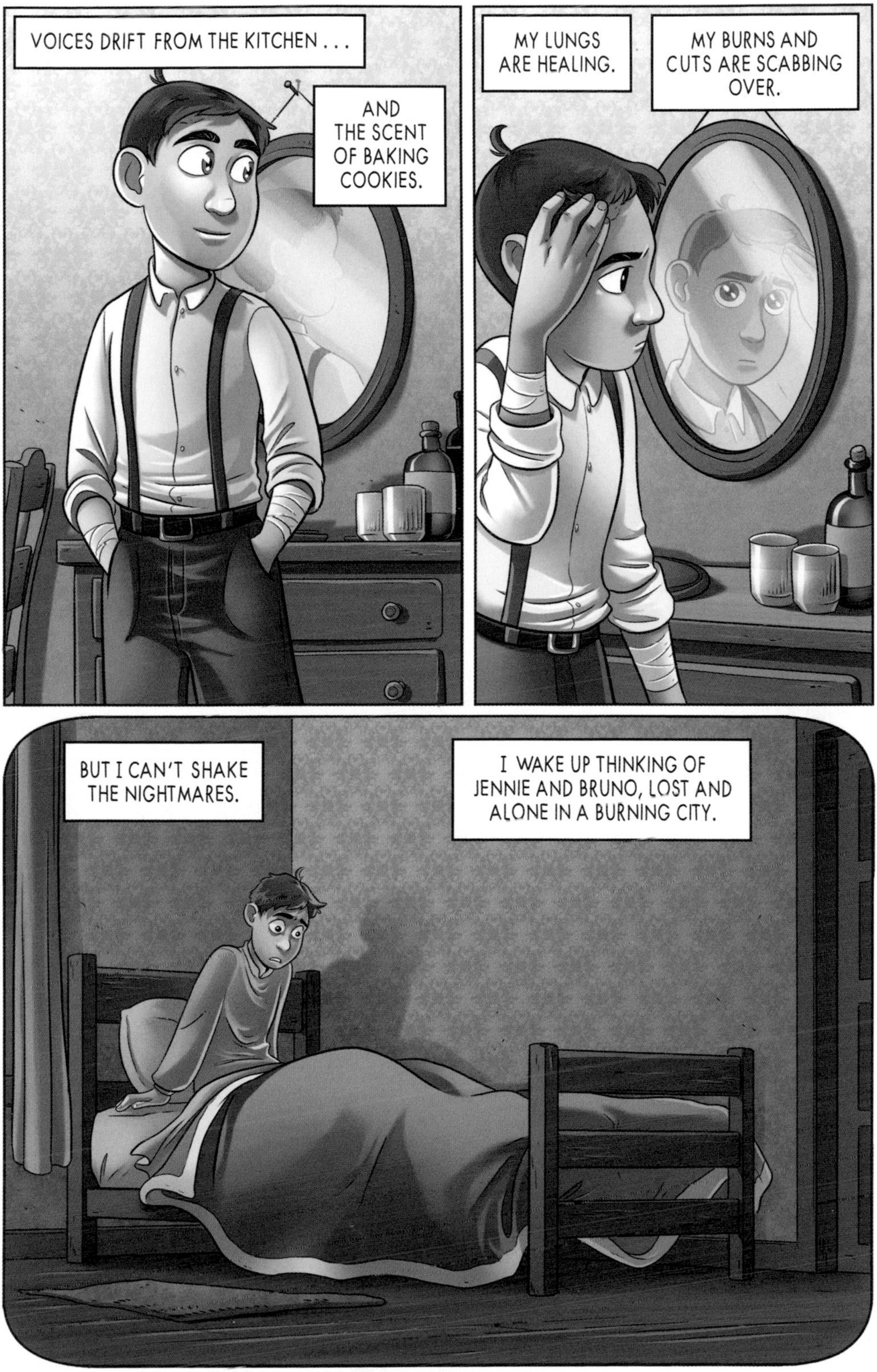
VOICES DRIFT FROM THE KITCHEN . . .
AND THE SCENT OF BAKING COOKIES.
MY LUNGS ARE HEALING.
MY BURNS AND CUTS ARE SCABBING OVER.
BUT I CAN'T SHAKE THE NIGHTMARES.
I WAKE UP THINKING OF JENNIE AND BRUNO, LOST AND ALONE IN A BURNING CITY.

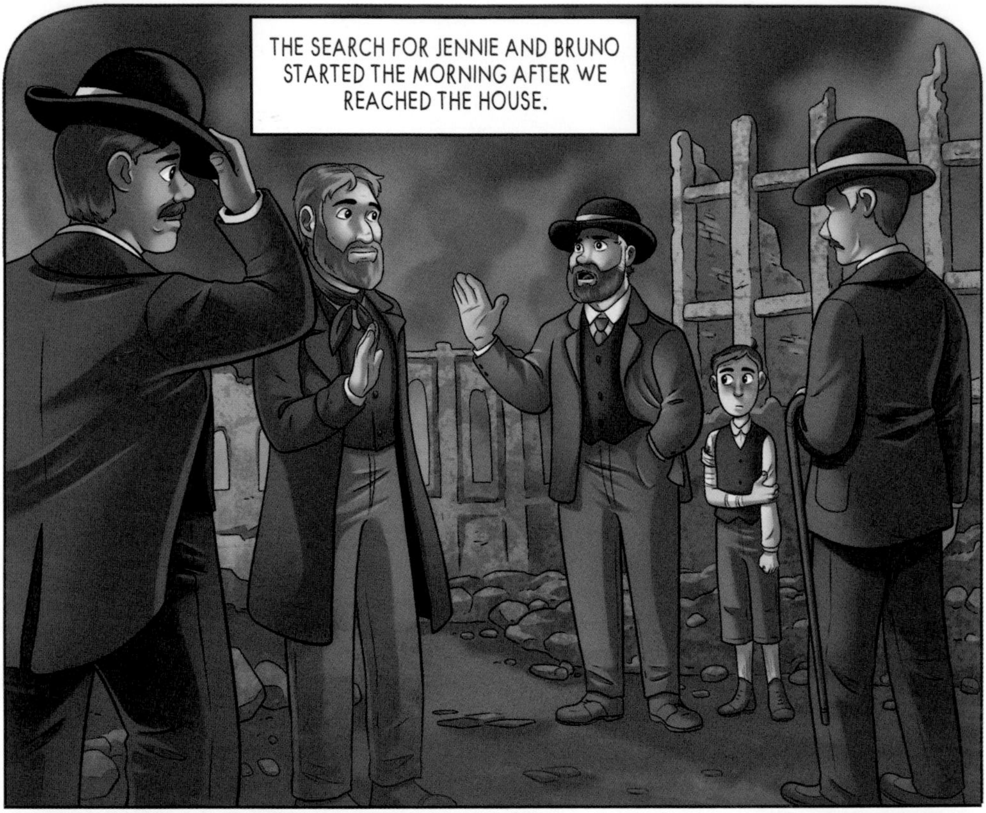
THE SEARCH FOR JENNIE AND BRUNO STARTED THE MORNING AFTER WE REACHED THE HOUSE.

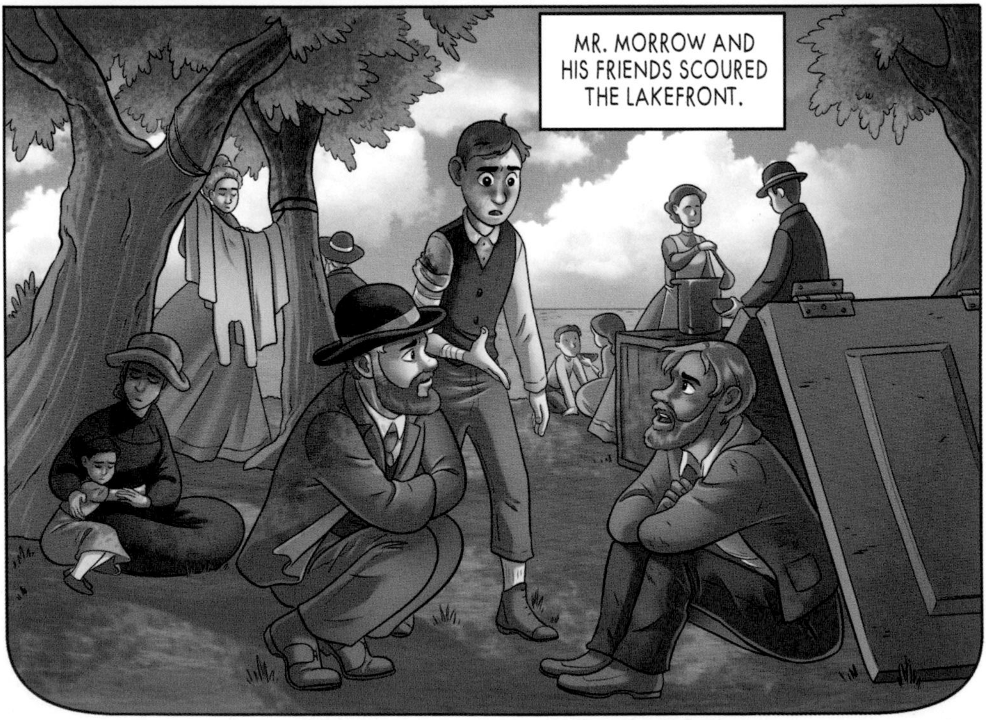
MR. MORROW AND HIS FRIENDS SCOURED THE LAKEFRONT.

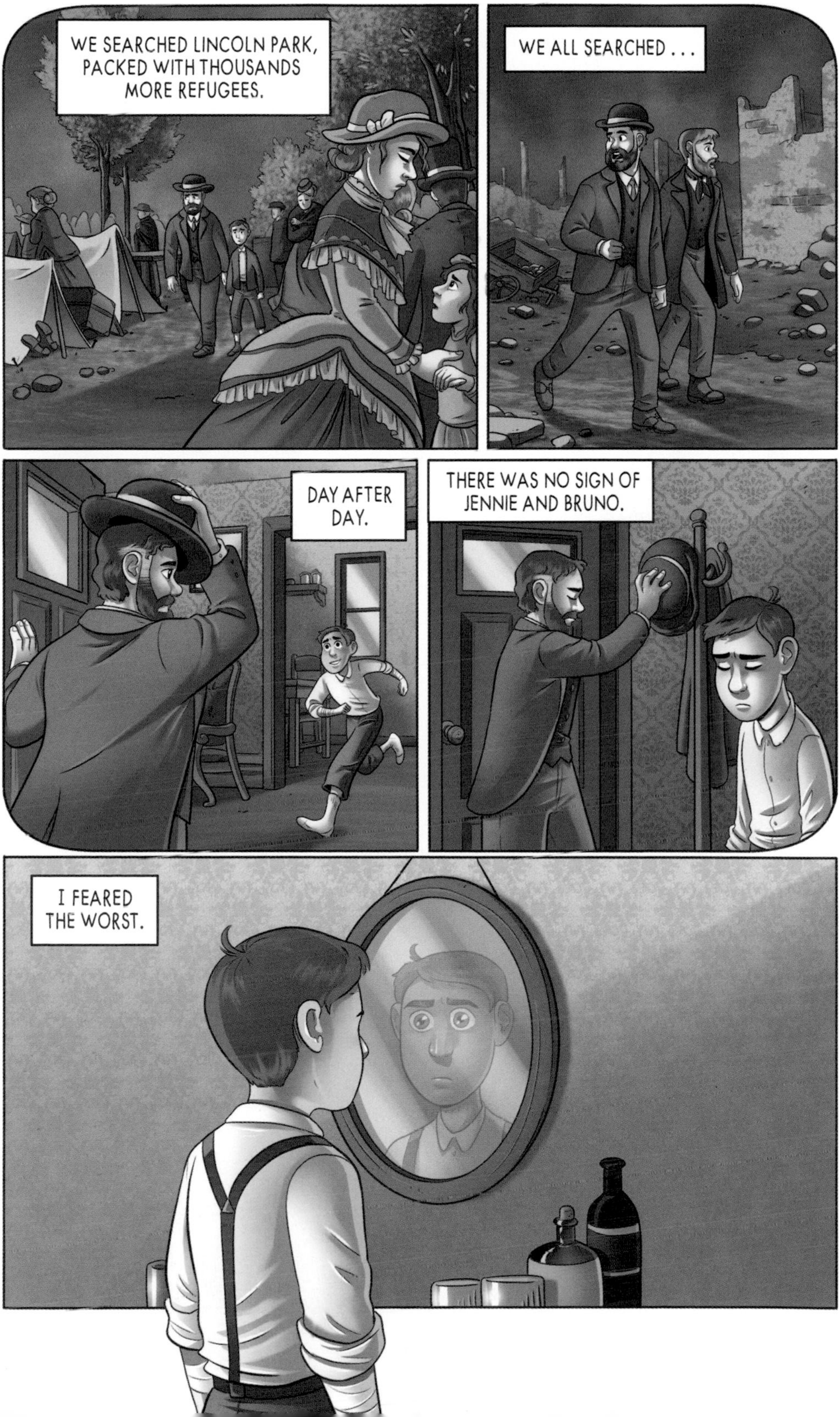
WE SEARCHED LINCOLN PARK, PACKED WITH THOUSANDS MORE REFUGEES.
WE ALL SEARCHED . . .
DAY AFTER DAY.
THERE WAS NO SIGN OF JENNIE AND BRUNO.
I FEARED THE WORST.

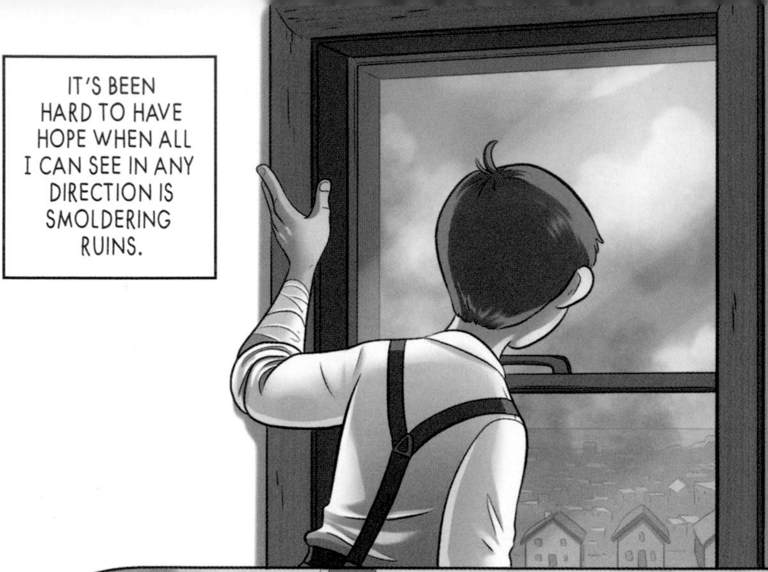
IT'S BEEN HARD TO HAVE HOPE WHEN ALL I CAN SEE IN ANY DIRECTION IS SMOLDERING RUINS.

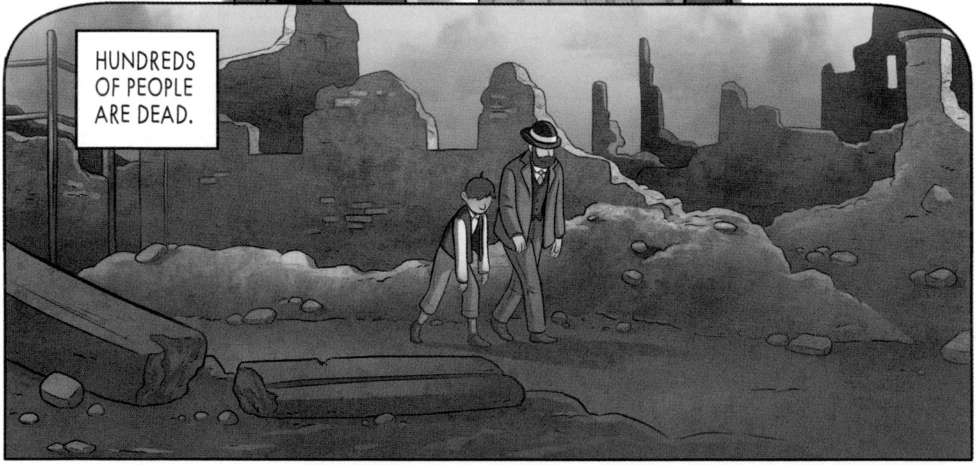
HUNDREDS OF PEOPLE ARE DEAD.

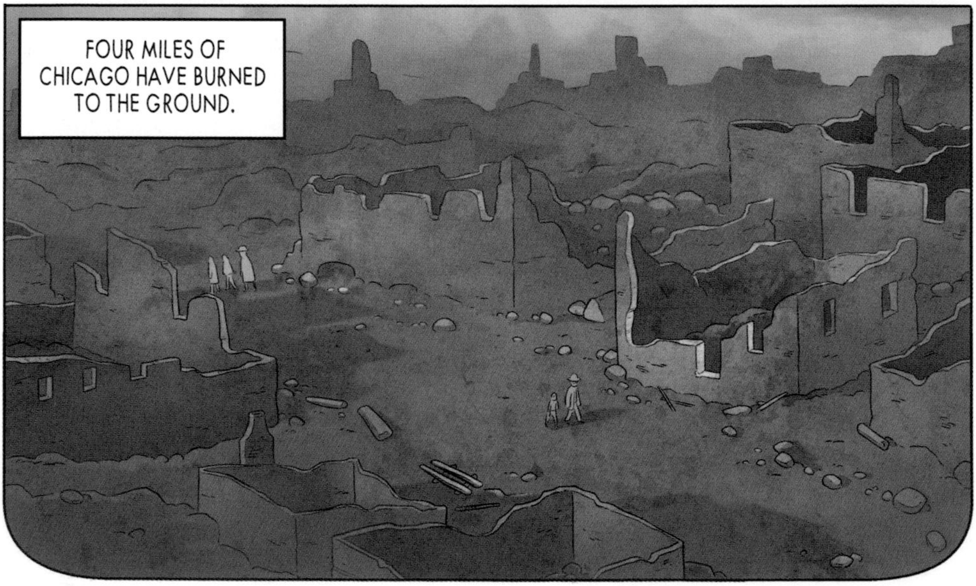
FOUR MILES OF CHICAGO HAVE BURNED TO THE GROUND.

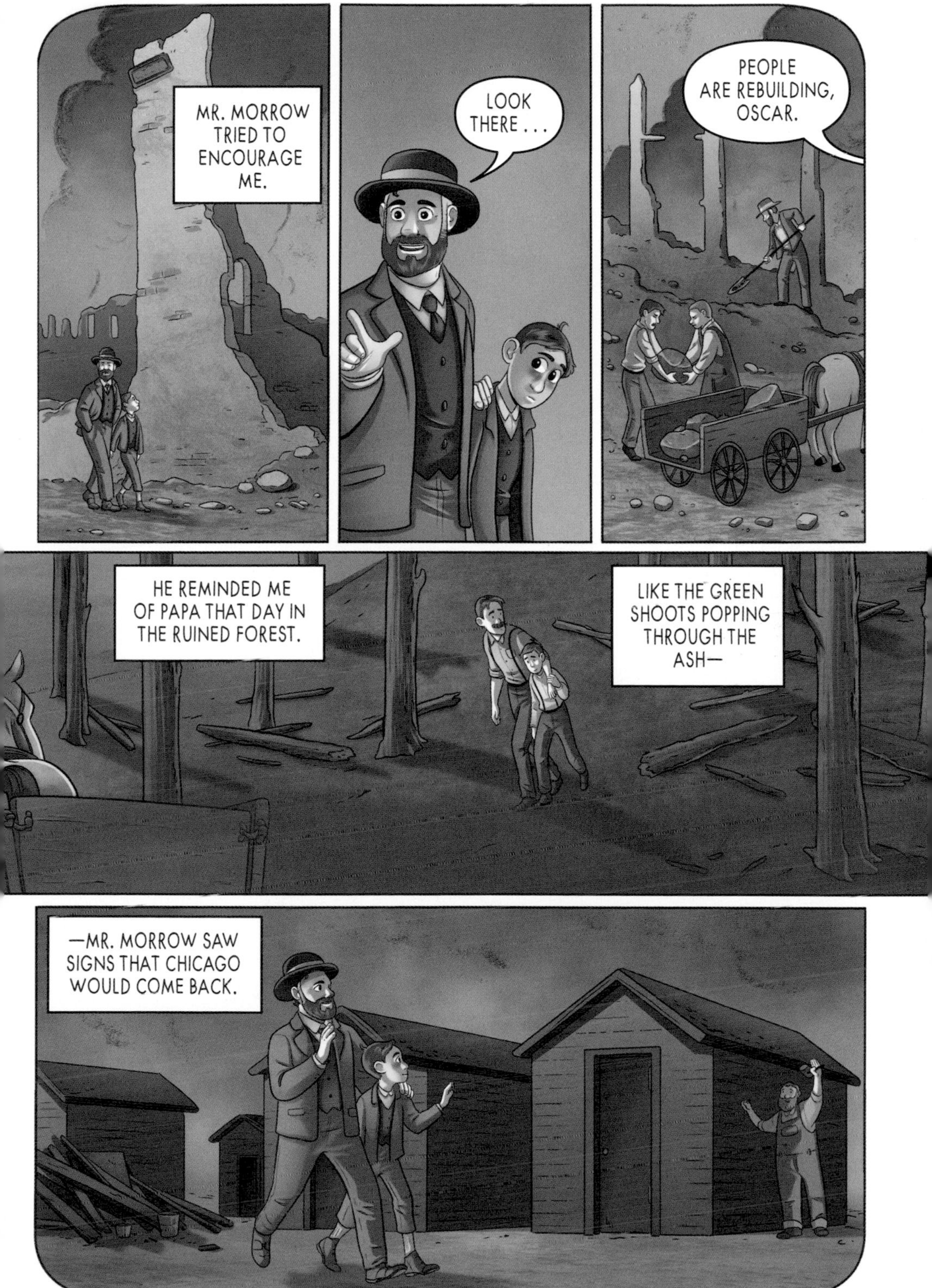

MR. MORROW TRIED TO ENCOURAGE ME.
LOOK THERE . . .
PEOPLE ARE REBUILDING, OSCAR.
HE REMINDED ME OF PAPA THAT DAY IN THE RUINED FOREST.
LIKE THE GREEN SHOOTS POPPING THROUGH THE ASH—
—MR. MORROW SAW SIGNS THAT CHICAGO WOULD COME BACK.

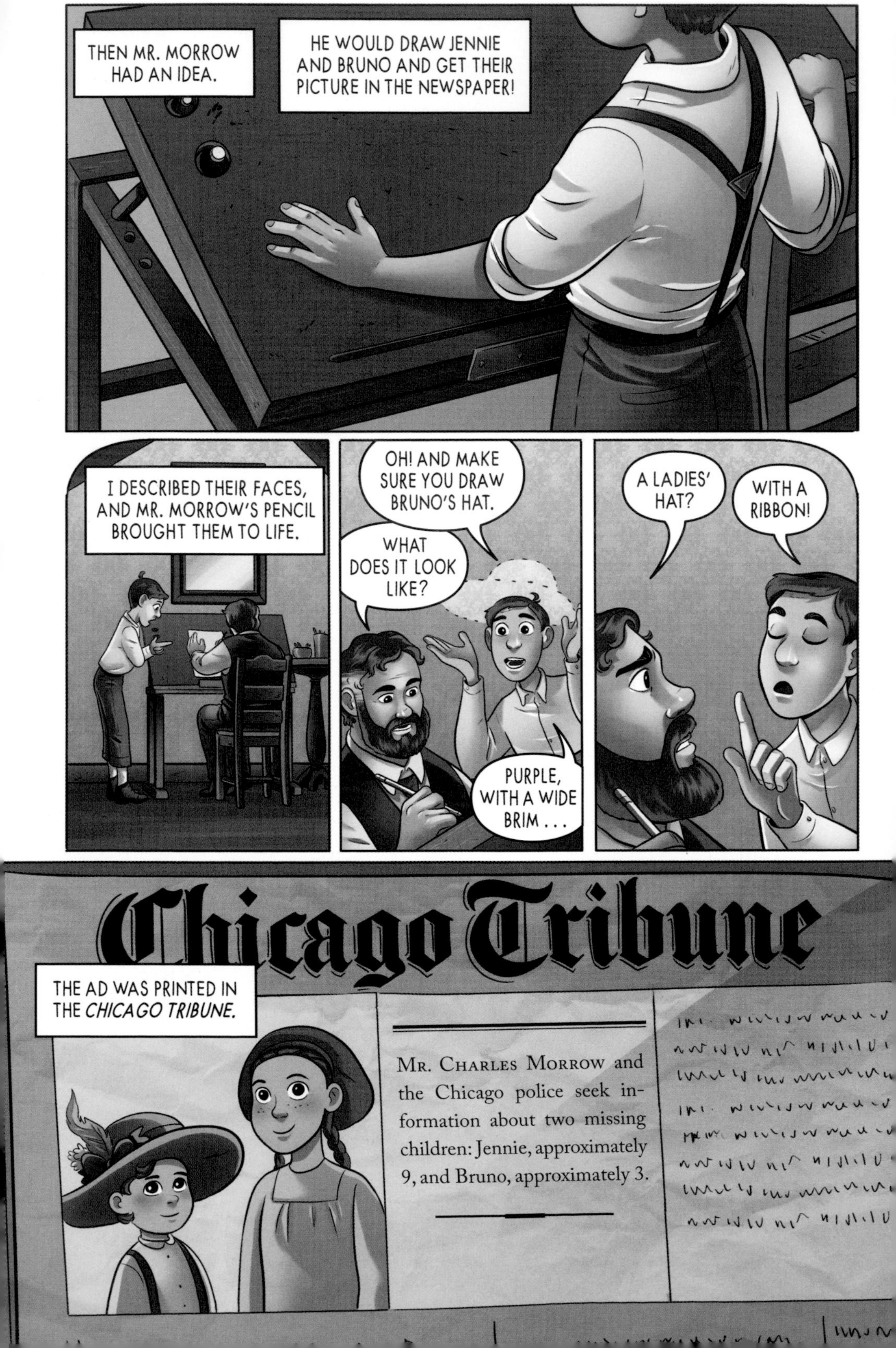
THEN MR. MORROW HAD AN IDEA.
HE WOULD DRAW JENNIE AND BRUNO AND GET THEIR PICTURE IN THE NEWSPAPER!
I DESCRIBED THEIR FACES, AND MR. MORROW'S PENCIL BROUGHT THEM TO LIFE.
OH! AND MAKE SURE YOU DRAW BRUNO'S HAT.
WHAT DOES IT LOOK LIKE?
PURPLE, WITH A WIDE BRIM . . .
A LADIES' HAT?
WITH A RIBBON!
Chicago Tribune
THE AD WAS PRINTED IN THE *CHICAGO TRIBUNE.*
Mr. Charles Morrow and the Chicago police seek information about two missing children: Jennie, approximately 9, and Bruno, approximately 3.

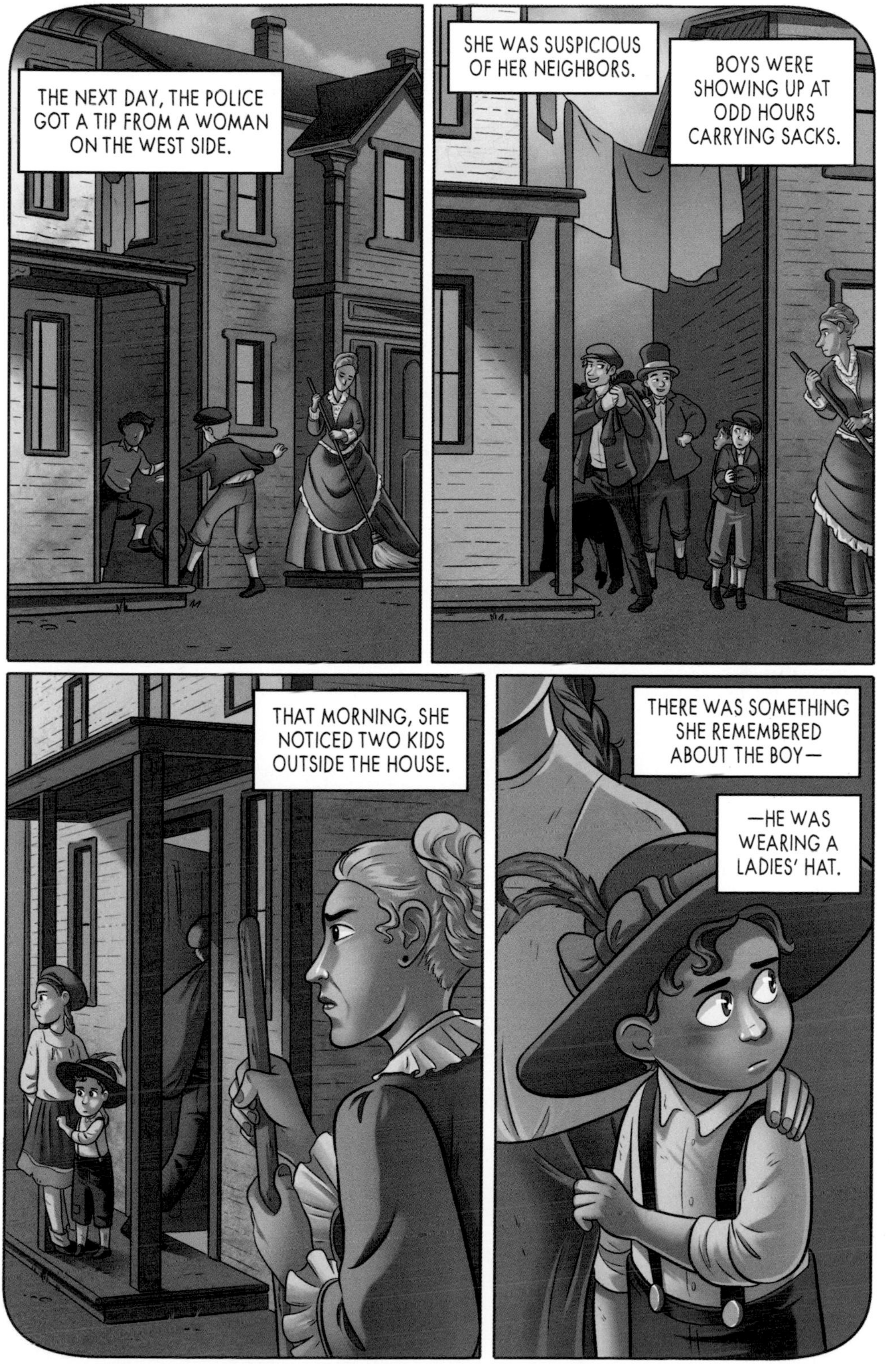
THE NEXT DAY, THE POLICE GOT A TIP FROM A WOMAN ON THE WEST SIDE.
SHE WAS SUSPICIOUS OF HER NEIGHBORS.
BOYS WERE SHOWING UP AT ODD HOURS CARRYING SACKS.
THAT MORNING, SHE NOTICED TWO KIDS OUTSIDE THE HOUSE.
THERE WAS SOMETHING SHE REMEMBERED ABOUT THE BOY—
—HE WAS WEARING A LADIES' HAT.

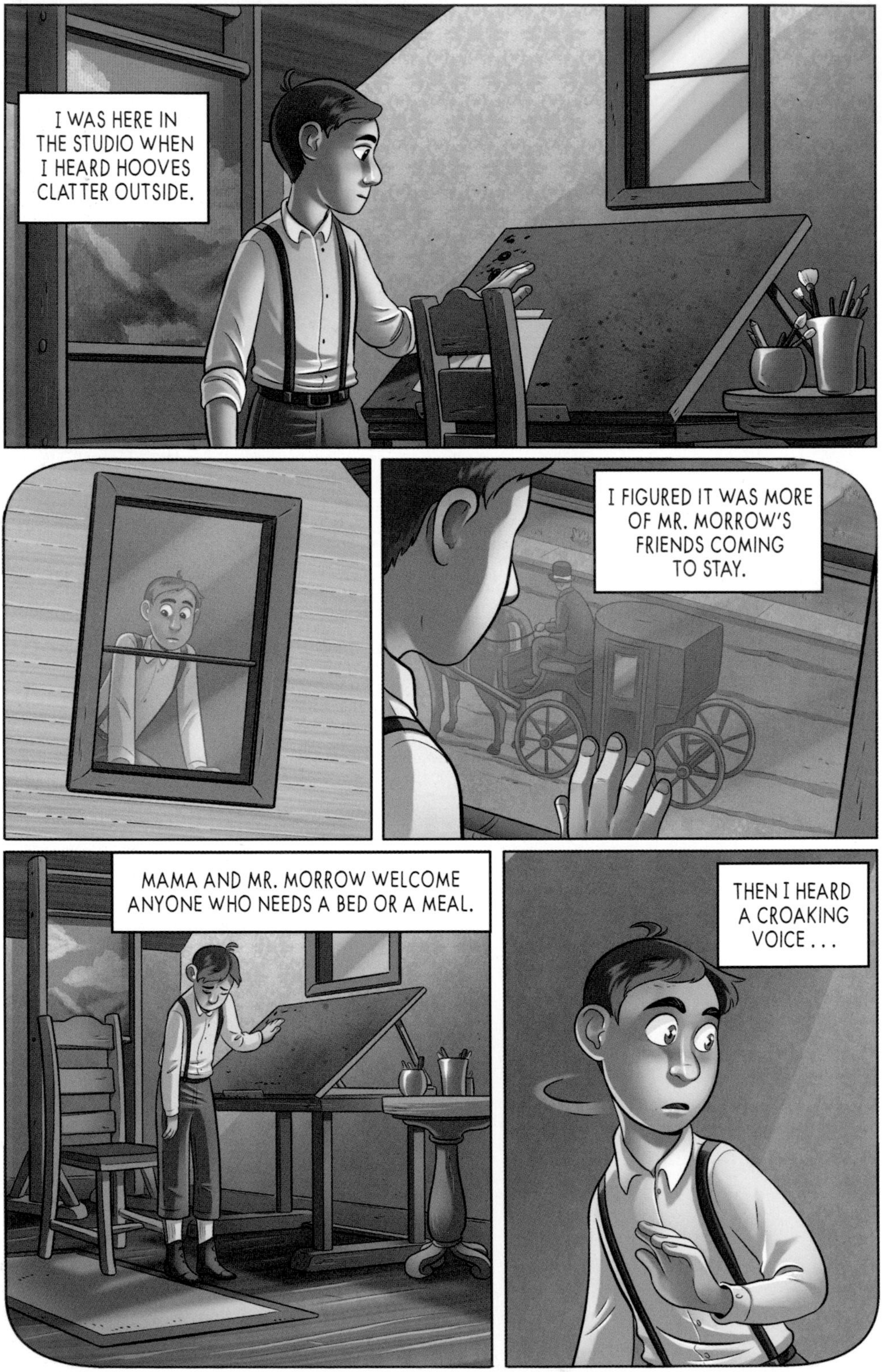
I WAS HERE IN THE STUDIO WHEN I HEARD HOOVES CLATTER OUTSIDE.
I FIGURED IT WAS MORE OF MR. MORROW'S FRIENDS COMING TO STAY.
MAMA AND MR. MORROW WELCOME ANYONE WHO NEEDS A BED OR A MEAL.
THEN I HEARD A CROAKING VOICE . . .

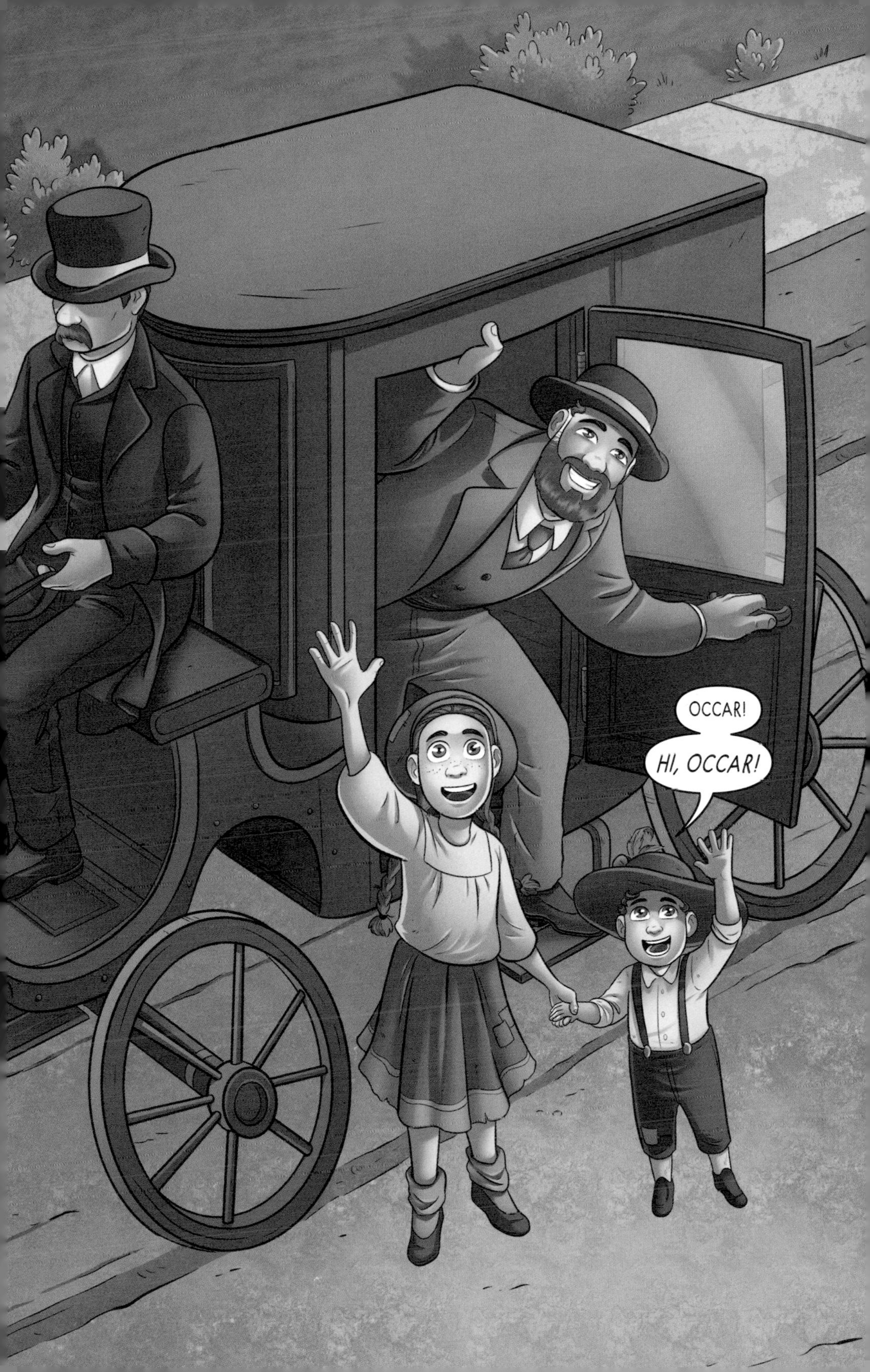
OCCAR!
HI, OCCAR!

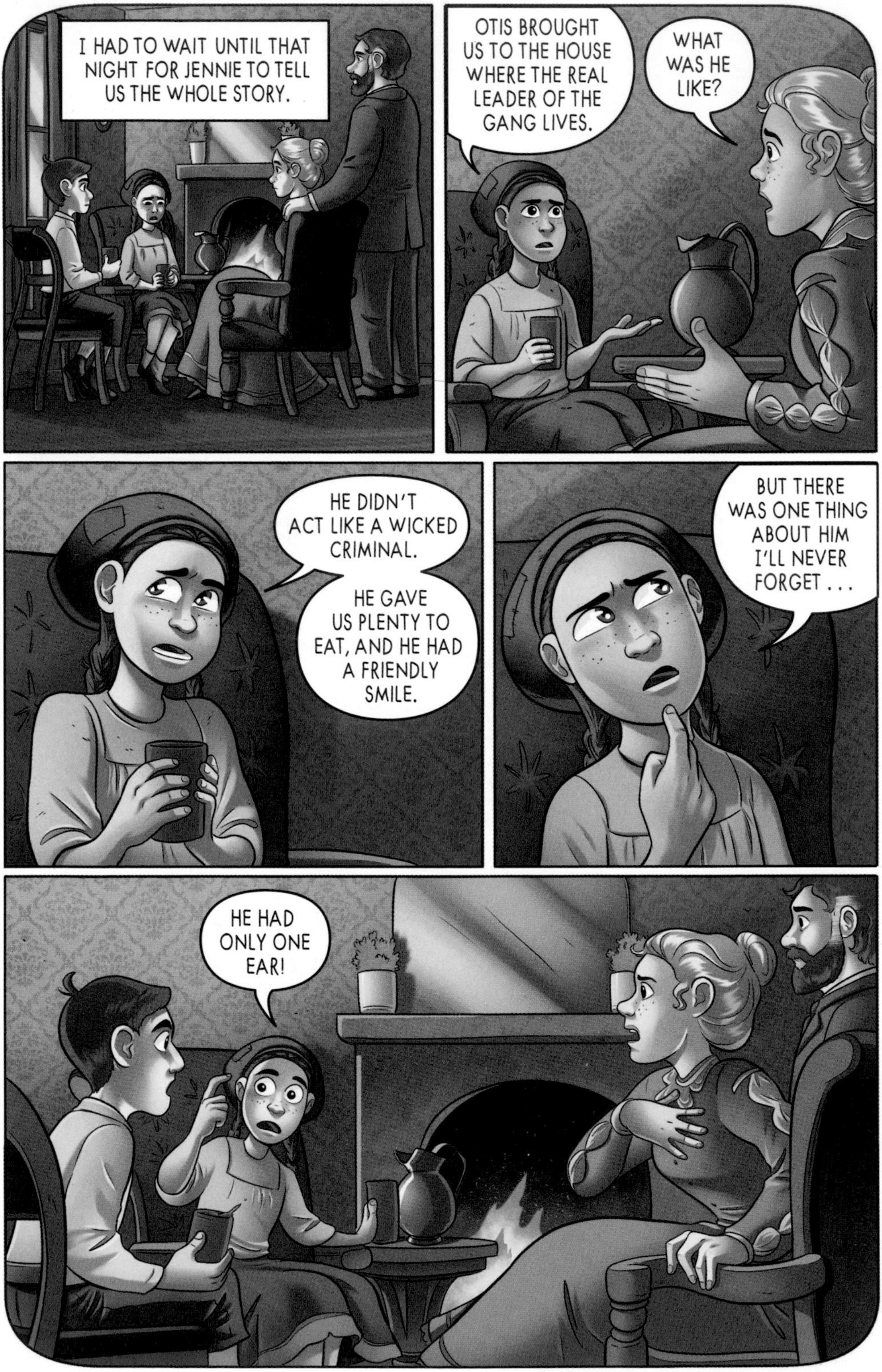
I HAD TO WAIT UNTIL THAT NIGHT FOR JENNIE TO TELL US THE WHOLE STORY.
OTIS BROUGHT US TO THE HOUSE WHERE THE REAL LEADER OF THE GANG LIVES.
WHAT WAS HE LIKE?
HE DIDN'T ACT LIKE A WICKED CRIMINAL.
HE GAVE US PLENTY TO EAT, AND HE HAD A FRIENDLY SMILE.
BUT THERE WAS ONE THING ABOUT HIM I'LL NEVER FORGET . . .
HE HAD ONLY ONE EAR!

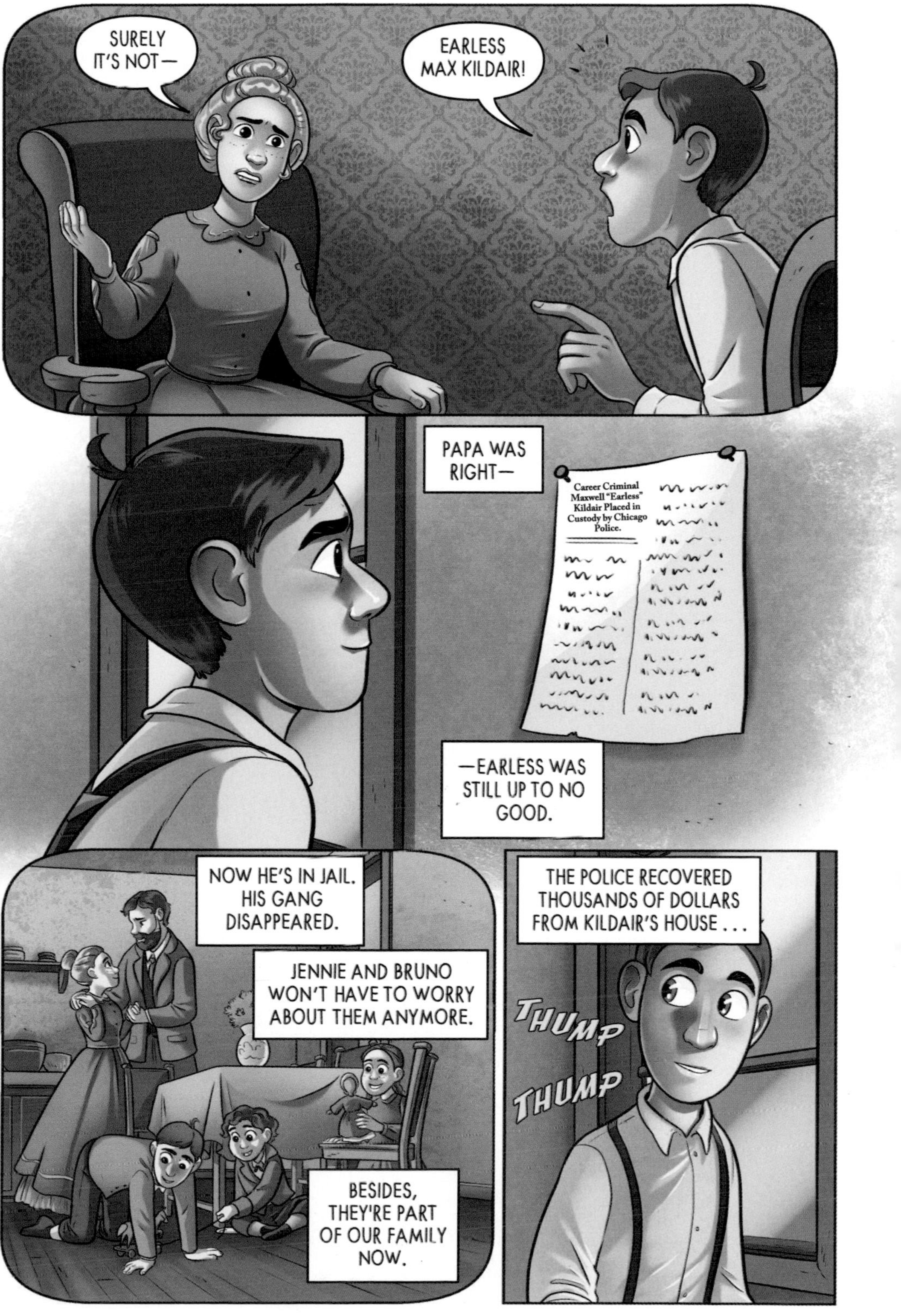
SURELY IT'S NOT—
EARLESS MAX KILDAIR!
PAPA WAS RIGHT—
Career Criminal Maxwell "Earless" Kildair Placed in Custody by Chicago Police.
—EARLESS WAS STILL UP TO NO GOOD.
NOW HE'S IN JAIL. HIS GANG DISAPPEARED.
JENNIE AND BRUNO WON'T HAVE TO WORRY ABOUT THEM ANYMORE.
BESIDES, THEY'RE PART OF OUR FAMILY NOW.
THE POLICE RECOVERED THOUSANDS OF DOLLARS FROM KILDAIR'S HOUSE . . .
THUMP
THUMP

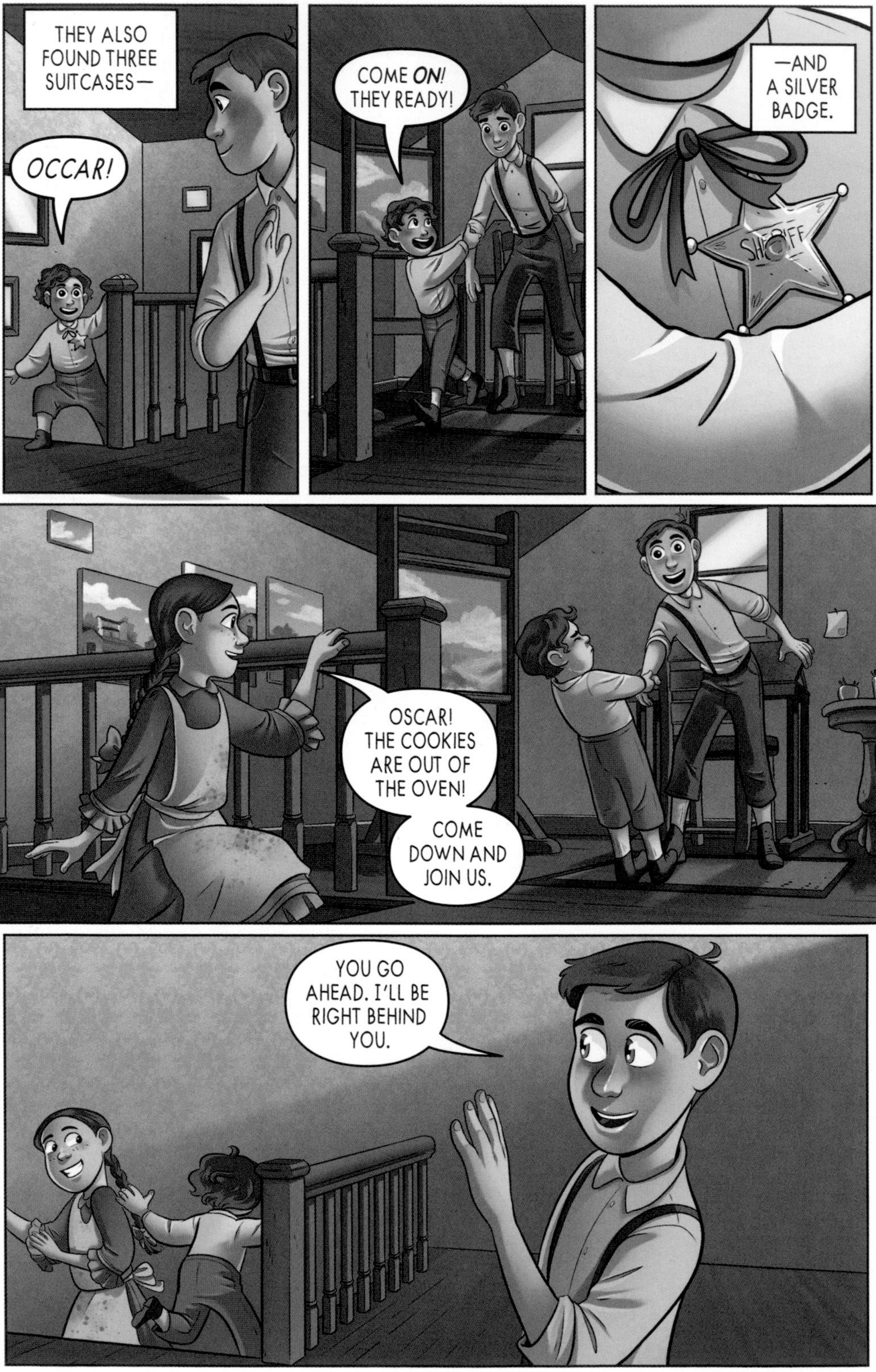
THEY ALSO FOUND THREE SUITCASES—
OCCAR!
COME ON! THEY READY!
—AND A SILVER BADGE.
SHERIFF
OSCAR! THE COOKIES ARE OUT OF THE OVEN!
COME DOWN AND JOIN US.
YOU GO AHEAD. I'LL BE RIGHT BEHIND YOU.

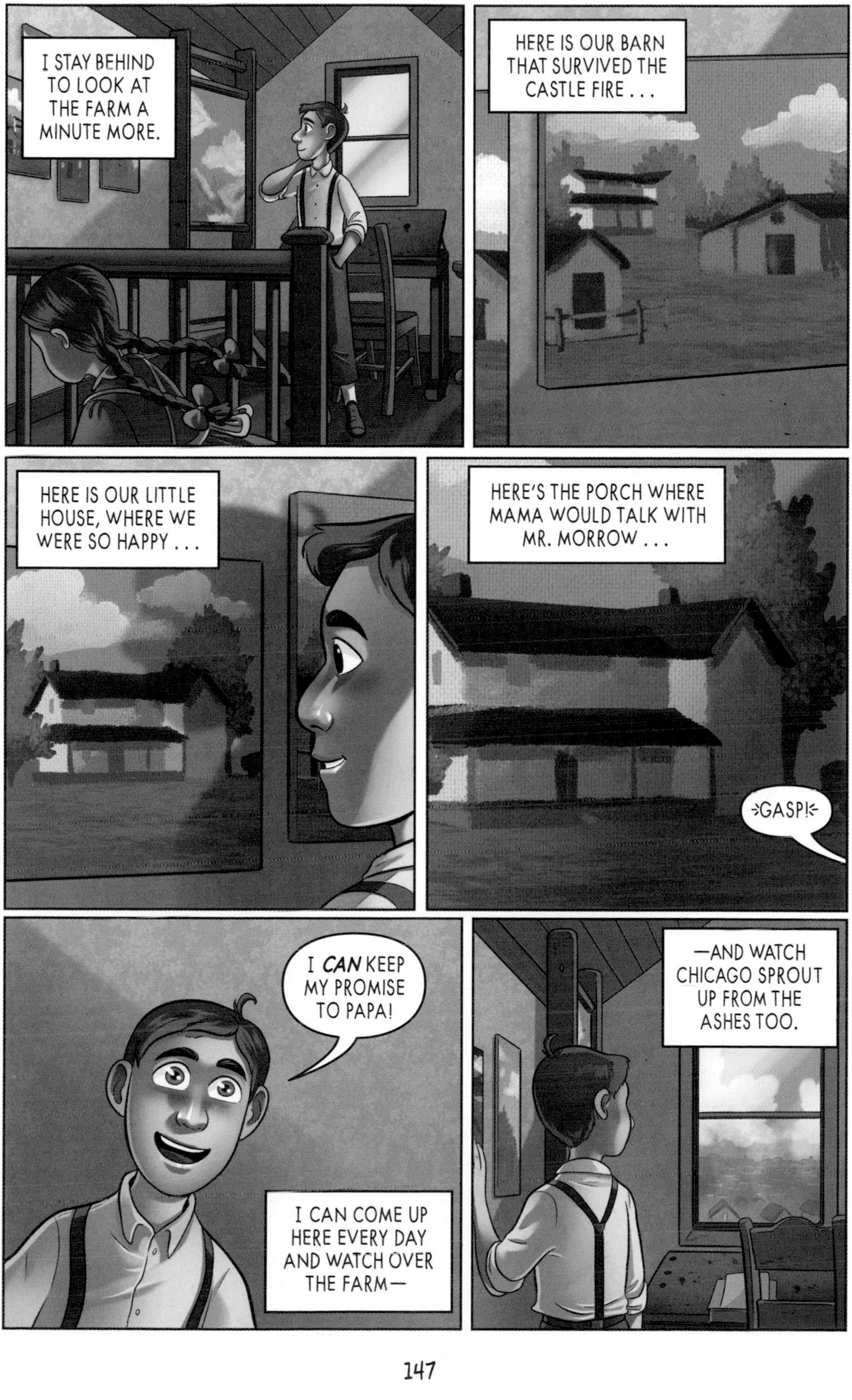
I STAY BEHIND TO LOOK AT THE FARM A MINUTE MORE.
HERE IS OUR BARN THAT SURVIVED THE CASTLE FIRE . . .
HERE IS OUR LITTLE HOUSE, WHERE WE WERE SO HAPPY . . .
HERE'S THE PORCH WHERE MAMA WOULD TALK WITH MR. MORROW . . .
GASP!
I *CAN* KEEP MY PROMISE TO PAPA!
I CAN COME UP HERE EVERY DAY AND WATCH OVER THE FARM—
—AND WATCH CHICAGO SPROUT UP FROM THE ASHES TOO.

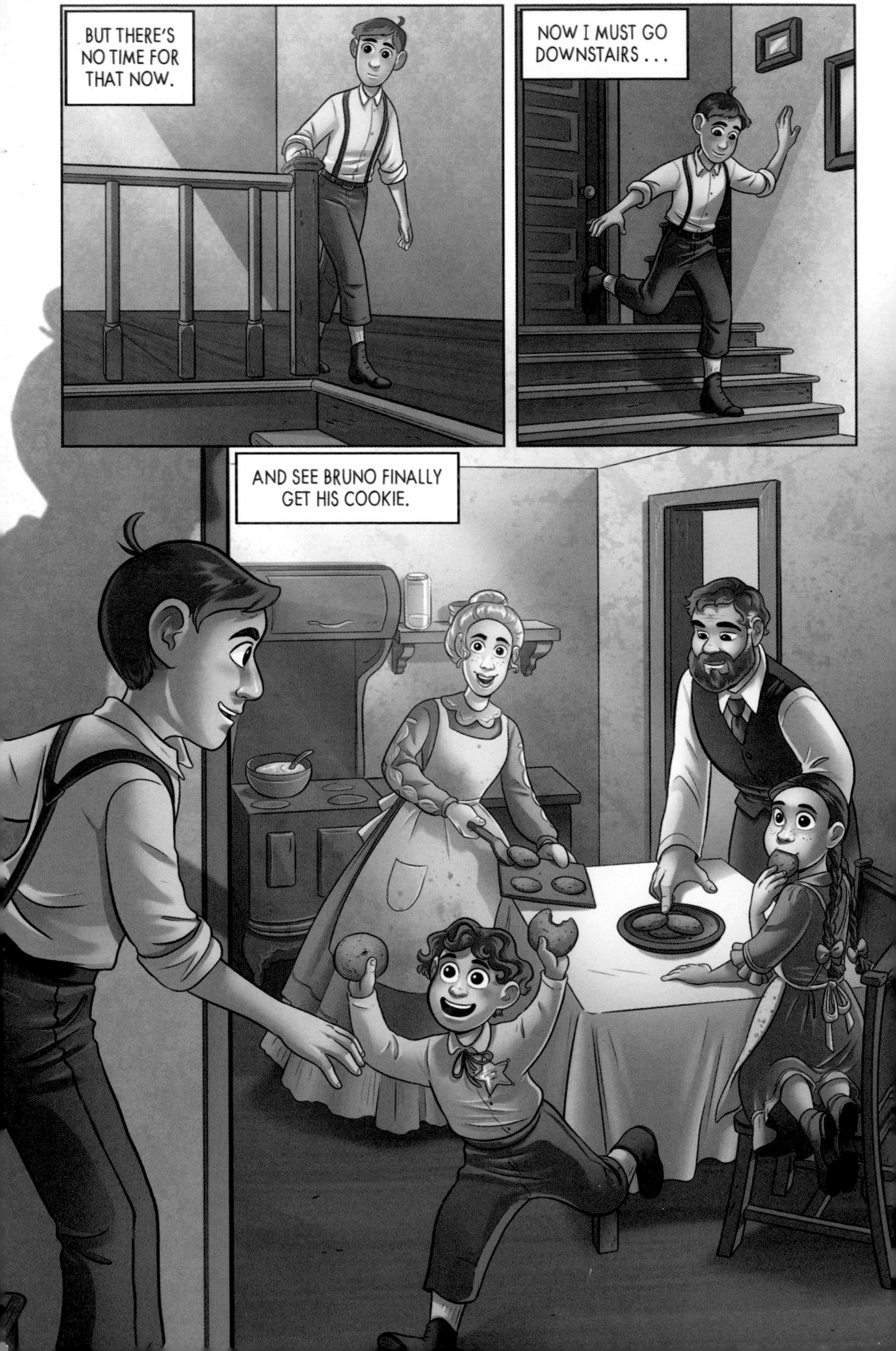
BUT THERE'S NO TIME FOR THAT NOW.
NOW I MUST GO DOWNSTAIRS . . .
AND SEE BRUNO FINALLY GET HIS COOKIE.

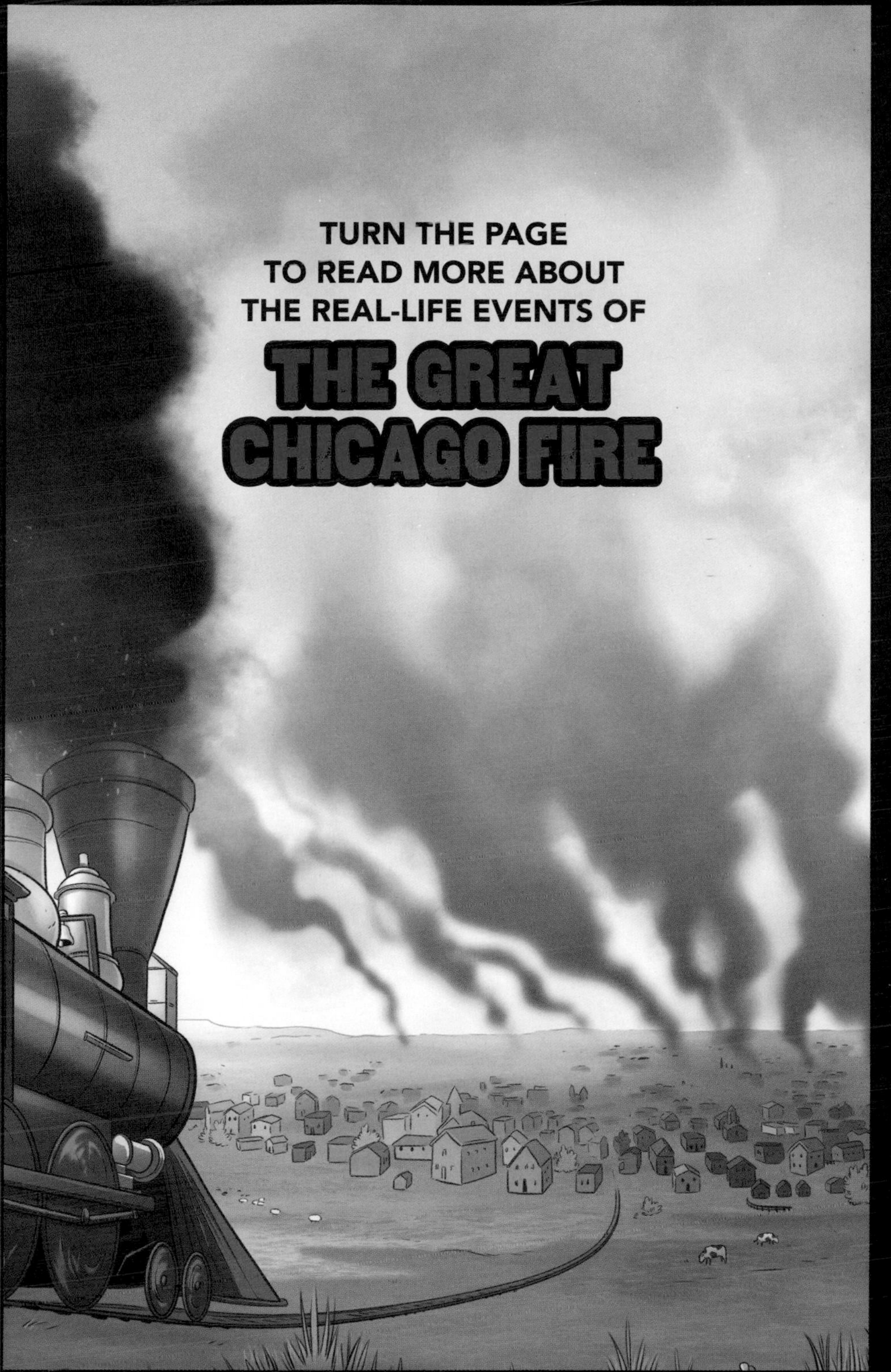
TURN THE PAGE
TO READ MORE ABOUT
THE REAL-LIFE EVENTS OF
THE GREAT
CHICAGO FIRE

Dear Readers,

Have you ever been to Chicago? It's a beautiful, modern city of towering skyscrapers, unique neighborhoods, and many delicious restaurants. I have been there many times, including while researching my original *I Survived the Great Chicago Fire, 1871* book.

While walking the streets with my family, I kept trying to imagine the city as Oscar would have seen it in 1871. It wasn't so beautiful back then. The streets were packed with buggies, wagons, and streetcars pulled by horses. Dozens of trains passed through the city every day. Grisly accidents were common. And then there was the stomach-turning stink from slaughterhouses, stockyards filled with animals, and coal smoke from factories and steam trains. Some days it was bad enough to make people sick.

But even in those long-ago, smelly days, Chicago and its people had a unique energy. Many who lived there at the time were new immigrants from places like Germany and Ireland. They had braved long voyages in hopes of finding new lives for their families.

This spirit made Chicago into the fastest-growing city in the world and helped its people to recover from the Great Fire. Just twenty years after that terrible disaster, Chicago had been completely rebuilt, and this time it was truly beautiful (and better-smelling!).

If you haven't been there, I hope you can visit one day. You won't meet Oscar or Jennie or Bruno (although the events of the fire are all true, the characters are from my imagination). But you will surely have a memorable trip to a dazzling city.

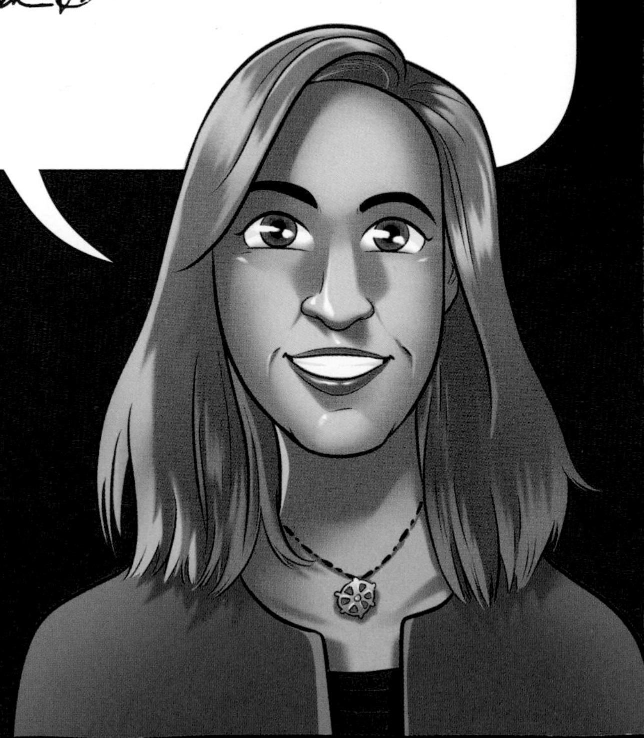

HOW CHICAGO GREW

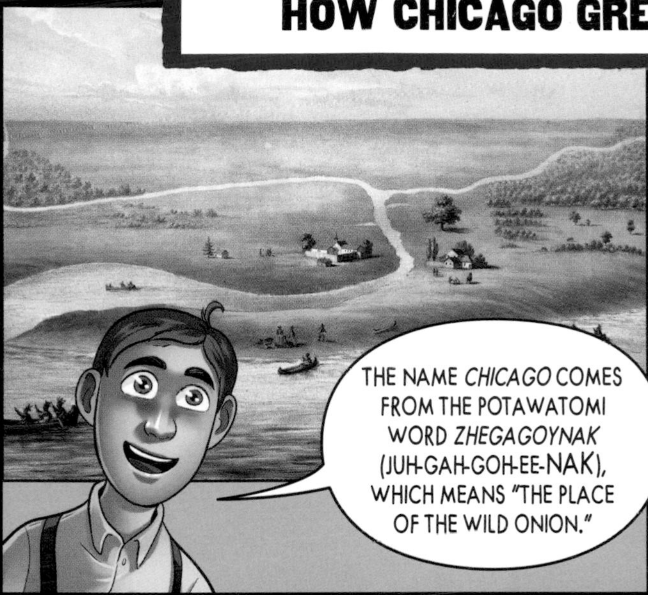
THE NAME *CHICAGO* COMES FROM THE POTAWATOMI WORD *ZHEGAGOYNAK* (JUH-GAH-GOH-EE-NAK), WHICH MEANS "THE PLACE OF THE WILD ONION."

BEFORE THE 1800S, THE AREA WE NOW CALL CHICAGO WAS A **SWAMPY WILDERNESS**. THE POTAWATOMI PEOPLE AND MEMBERS OF OTHER INDIGENOUS NATIONS HUNTED AND FISHED IN THE AREA'S MARSHES AND RIVERBANKS.

BUT BY THE 1830S, MANY OF THE POTAWATOMI PEOPLE, LIKE TENS OF THOUSANDS OF OTHER **NATIVE AMERICANS**, HAD BEEN FORCED OFF THEIR LANDS BY THE U.S. GOVERNMENT.

BY THE EARLY 1870S, CHICAGO HAD GROWN INTO A BUSTLING CITY OF **330,000 PEOPLE**. POWERING THE GROWTH WAS A NEW FORM OF TRANSPORTATION: TRAINS.

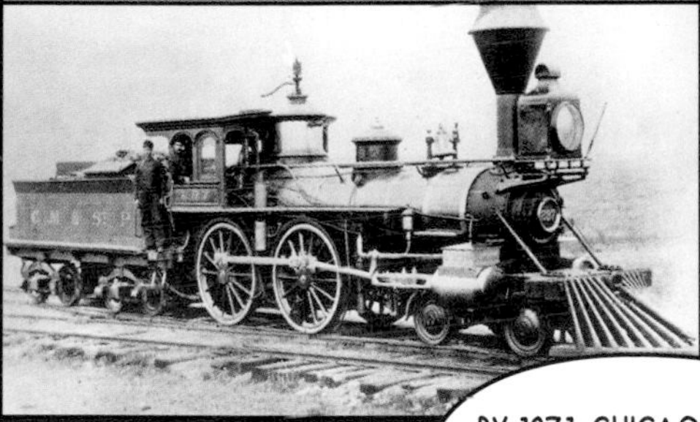

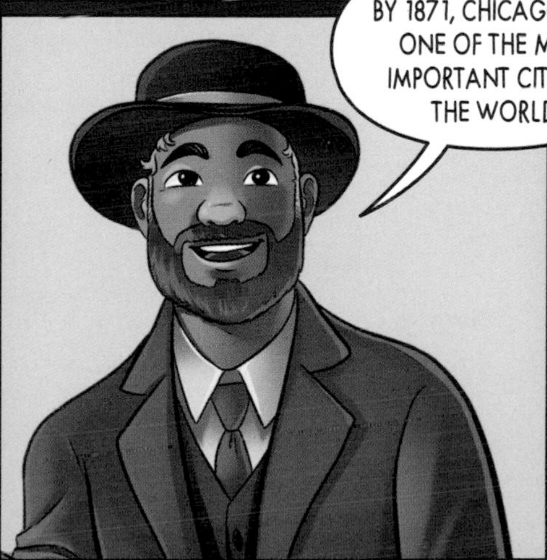
BY 1871, CHICAGO WAS ONE OF THE MOST IMPORTANT CITIES IN THE WORLD.

SUDDENLY, AMERICANS COULD EASILY TRAVEL **LONG DISTANCES**. MORE TRAINS STEAMED IN AND OUT OF CHICAGO THAN ANYWHERE IN THE UNITED STATES. NEW BUSINESSES BOOMED AND NEIGHBORHOODS GREW.

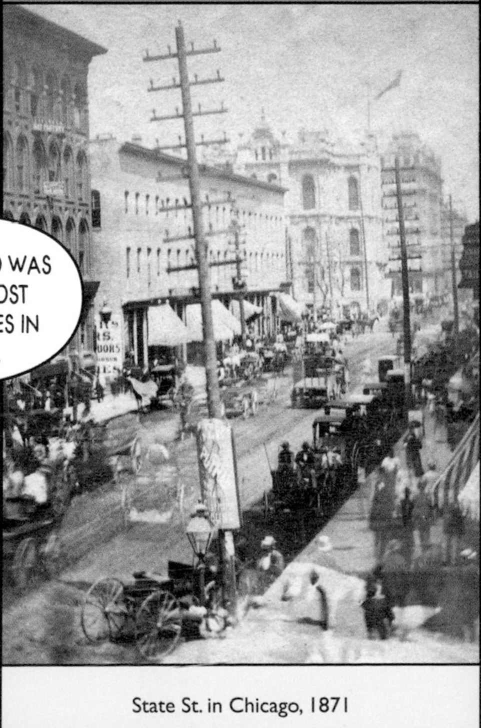

State St. in Chicago, 1871

FIERY DANGERS

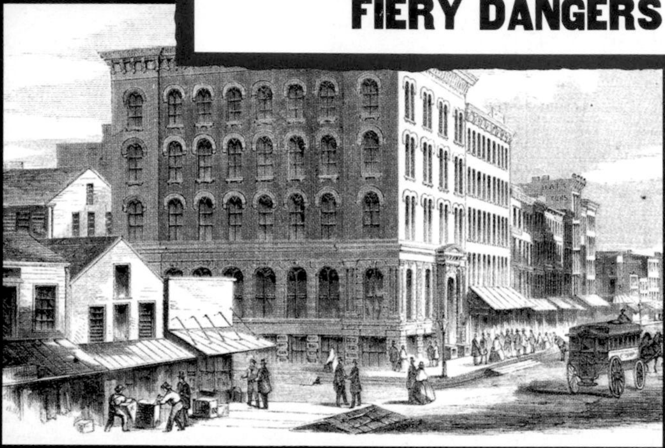

AS CHICAGO GREW, SO DID THE RISK OF HUGE FIRES. MOST BUILDINGS, MILES OF SIDEWALK, AND EVEN SOME STREETS WERE **MADE OF WOOD**.

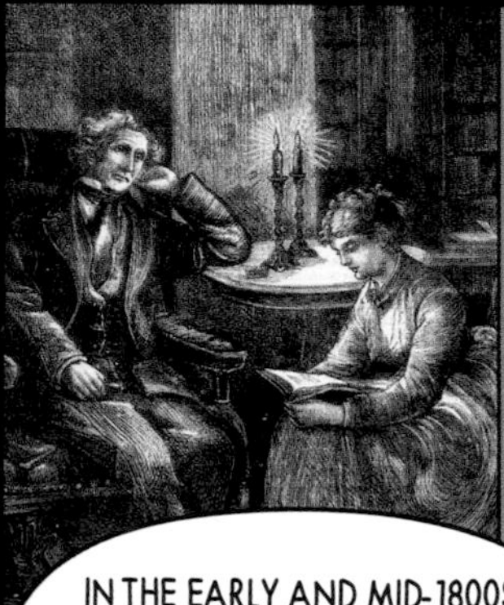

PEOPLE READ BY THE LIGHT OF CANDLES AND LANTERNS. THEY COOKED MEALS ON STOVES HEATED WITH WOOD OR HOT COALS. ONE **SPARK** COULD TORCH A WHOLE NEIGHBORHOOD.

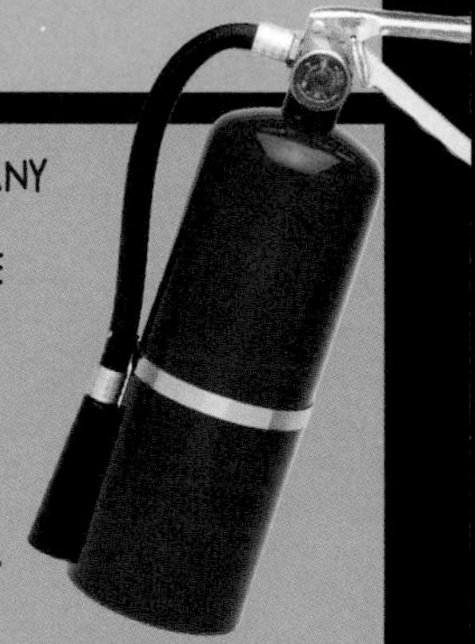

TODAY WE HAVE MANY TOOLS, LIKE SMOKE DETECTORS AND FIRE EXTINGUISHERS, FOR PREVENTING AND FIGHTING FIRES. BUILDINGS ARE CONSTRUCTED WITH FIRE SAFETY IN MIND.

BUT MODERN FIREFIGHTING TOOLS AND MATERIALS DIDN'T EXIST IN THE 1800S. AND CHICAGO WASN'T THE ONLY CITY THAT FACED **FIRE RISKS** AT THAT TIME.

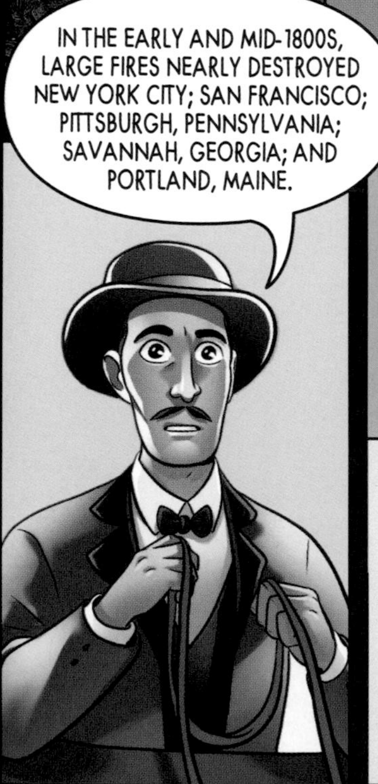
IN THE EARLY AND MID-1800S, LARGE FIRES NEARLY DESTROYED NEW YORK CITY; SAN FRANCISCO; PITTSBURGH, PENNSYLVANIA; SAVANNAH, GEORGIA; AND PORTLAND, MAINE.

CHICAGO ACTUALLY HAD ONE OF THE BEST **FIRE DEPARTMENTS** IN THE UNITED STATES. BY 1871, THE CITY HAD 185 FIREFIGHTERS. THEY RACED TOWARD FIRES IN SEVENTEEN HORSE-DRAWN PUMPER TRUCKS.

BUT THE FIRE DEPARTMENT WAS STILL **TOO SMALL**. CITY LEADERS WOULDN'T SPEND MORE MONEY TO HIRE MORE FIREFIGHTERS AND BUY NEW EQUIPMENT. FOR YEARS, MANY HAD FEARED THAT A MAJOR FIRE COULD TORCH THE WHOLE CITY.

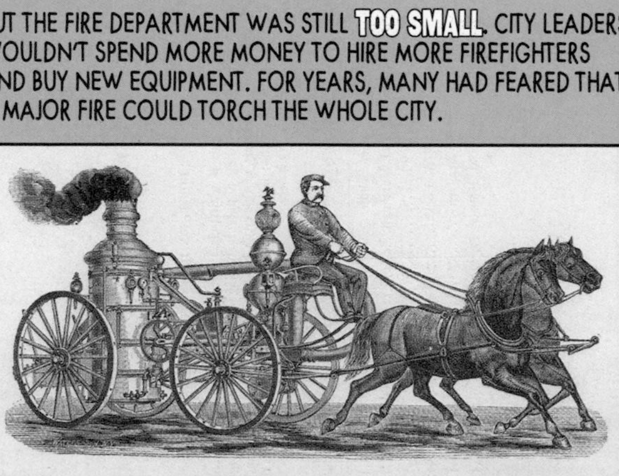

THE FIRE STARTS

THE **GREAT CHICAGO FIRE** BEGAN ON SUNDAY, OCTOBER 8, 1871, AROUND 9:00 P.M., IN A BARN OWNED BY CATHERINE AND PATRICK O'LEARY.

THE FIRE QUICKLY SPREAD. THE ENTIRE MIDWEST HAD BEEN IN A DROUGHT. **STRONG WINDS** SENT EMBERS AND BURNING DEBRIS ACROSS THE CITY.

FIREFIGHTERS WERE DELAYED IN REACHING THE FIRE, GIVING IT MORE TIME TO SPREAD ACROSS THE RIVER AND THROUGHOUT THE CITY.

THE FIRE DEPARTMENT HAD JUST FINISHED BATTLING ANOTHER BIG FIRE THE NIGHT BEFORE. THEY WERE EXHAUSTED.

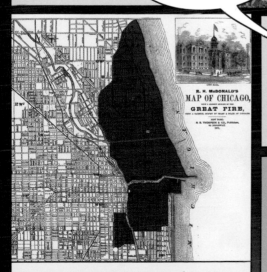

R. H. McDONALD'S
MAP OF CHICAGO,
GREAT FIRE,

The yellow dot shows the location of the O'Leary barn, the source of the fire.

THE FIRE BURNED ALL NIGHT AND THE NEXT DAY. IT WASN'T UNTIL EARLY TUESDAY MORNING THAT THE FIRE BURNED ITSELF OUT, WITH HELP FROM A RAIN SHOWER. AN AREA **FOUR MILES WIDE AND ONE MILE LONG** WAS DESTROYED.

WHAT CAUSED THE FIRE?

WHERE THE FIRE STARTED—IN THE **O'LEARYS' BARN**—WAS NEVER IN DOUBT. NOBODY KNOWS EXACTLY WHAT SPARKED IT. THE WEATHER WAS SO HOT AND DRY THAT EVEN A TINY SPARK COULD HAVE IGNITED THE HAY IN THE BARN.

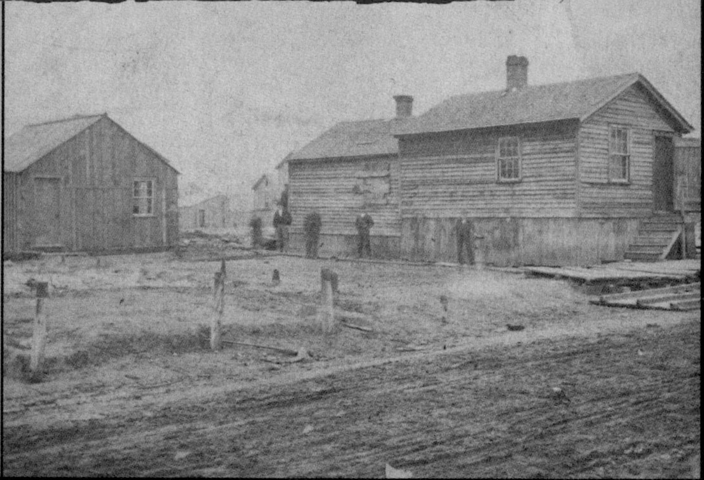

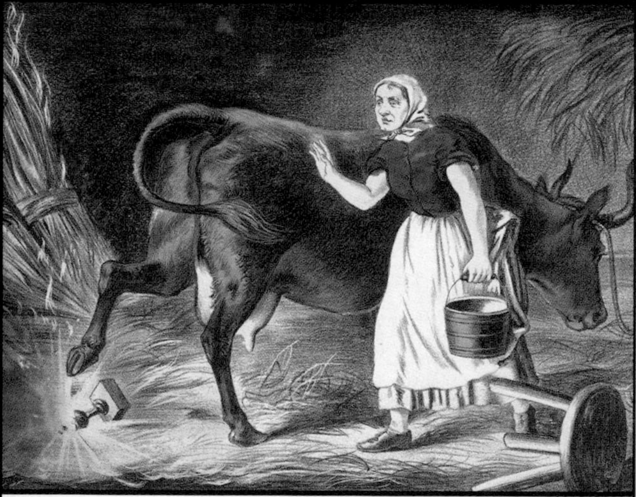

Illustrations of the story about Mrs. O'Leary helped it spread.

BUT A NEWSPAPER REPORTER WROTE A STORY BLAMING MRS. O'LEARY, SAYING A **COW KICKED OVER A LANTERN** THAT SHE'D LEFT ON THE FLOOR.

THE STORY WAS A LIE—THE REPORTER EVEN ADMITTED THAT. THE POLICE INTERVIEWED THE O'LEARYS AND SAID IT WAS NOT THEIR FAULT. BUT LIKE THE FLAMES OF THE FIRE, **THE LIE SPREAD**, AND EVEN TODAY, MANY BELIEVE THAT MRS. O'LEARY WAS TO BLAME.

IN TRUTH, CATHERINE O'LEARY WAS THE HARDWORKING OWNER OF A SMALL DAIRY. SHE HAD FIVE CHILDREN AND OWNED SIX COWS, WHICH SHE MILKED EVERY MORNING, NEVER AT NIGHT. **SHE AND HER FAMILY WERE ASLEEP** WHEN THE FIRE STARTED.

LIKELY, MRS. O'LEARY WAS BLAMED PARTLY BECAUSE SHE WAS AN **IMMIGRANT FROM IRELAND**. AT THE TIME, MANY WERE PREJUDICED AGAINST NEWCOMERS FROM IRELAND AND OTHER COUNTRIES. SHE NEVER GOT OVER THE HURT AND SHAME OF BEING UNFAIRLY BLAMED.

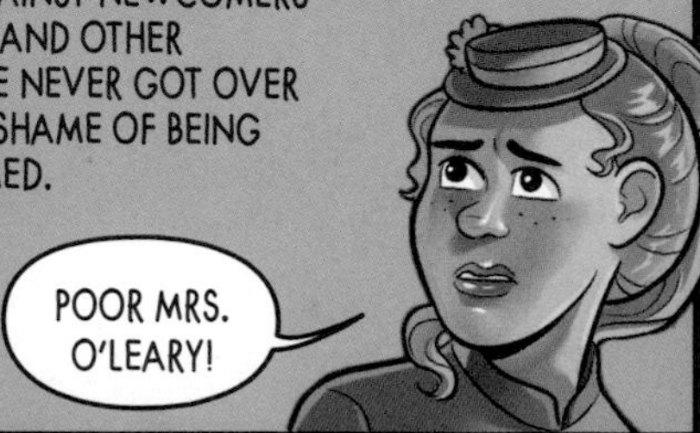
POOR MRS. O'LEARY!

ESCAPING THE FLAMES

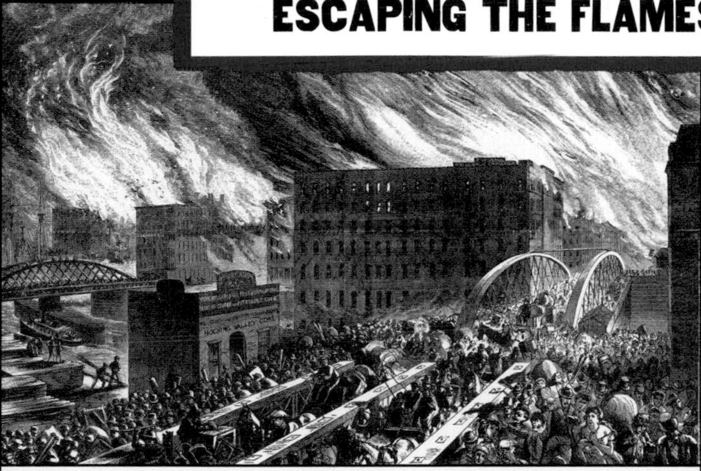

The rush to escape over Randolph Street Bridge

APPROXIMATELY **300 PEOPLE DIED** IN THE CHICAGO FIRE—THE EXACT NUMBER IS NOT KNOWN.

SURVIVORS **ESCAPED** BY RUSHING ACROSS BURNING BRIDGES, WADING INTO LAKE MICHIGAN, AND EVEN LOWERING THEIR CHILDREN OUT OF BUILDINGS IN BUNDLES OF BLANKETS.

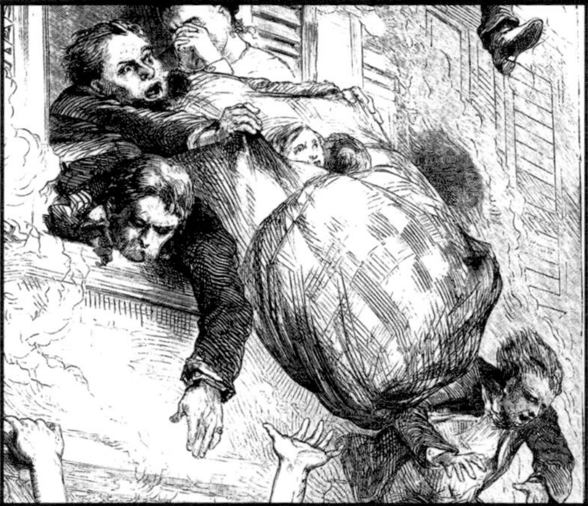

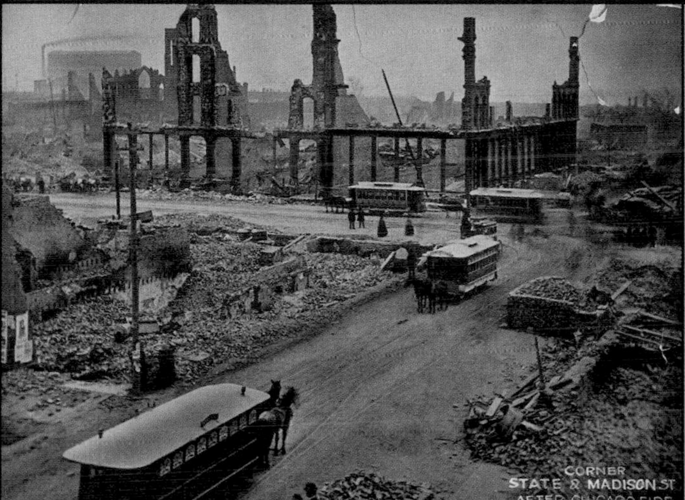
CORNER
STATE & MADISON ST
AFTER CHICAGO FIRE

NEARLY 100,000 PEOPLE LOST THEIR HOMES. BECAUSE SO MANY FACTORIES AND BUSINESSES WERE DESTROYED, **THOUSANDS WERE WITHOUT JOBS** AND COULDN'T BUY FOOD OR SUPPLIES TO REBUILD THEIR HOMES. MANY SURVIVORS LIVED IN TENTS AND SHACKS IN PARKS.

THE CITY IS REBORN

MANY BELIEVED THAT CHICAGO WOULD NEVER RECOVER FROM THE FIRE. BUT CITY LEADERS AND RESIDENTS WERE DETERMINED TO **REBUILD**.

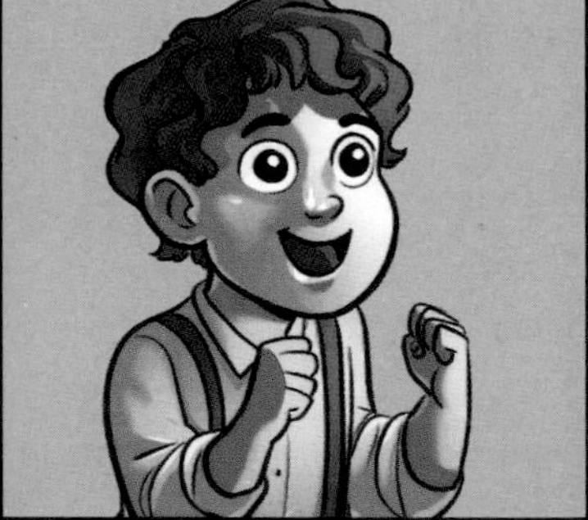

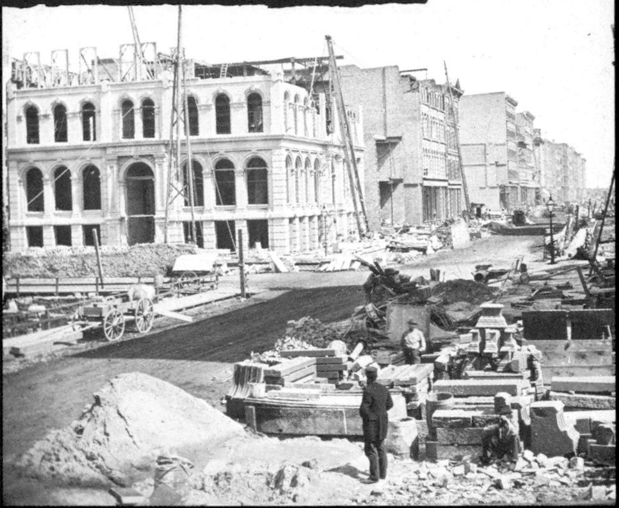

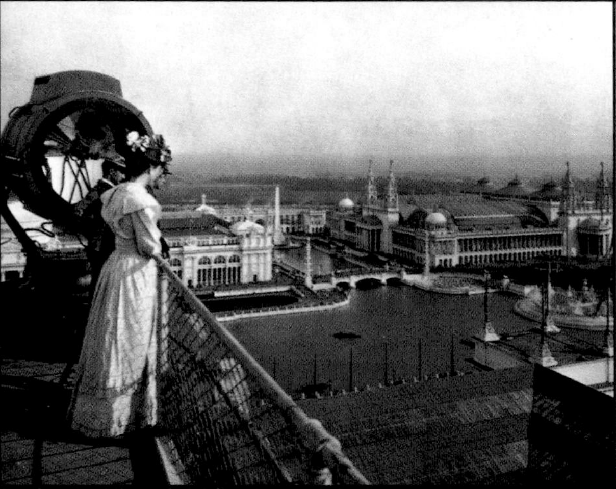

BY THE EARLY 1880S, THE CITY WAS BUSTLING AGAIN. NEW BRICK, STONE, AND STEEL BUILDINGS REPLACED THE SHODDILY BUILT WOODEN STRUCTURES THAT HAD BURNED SO QUICKLY IN THE FIRE. **STRICT BUILDING LAWS** MADE THE PEOPLE LIVING IN CHICAGO—AND OTHER CITIES—MUCH SAFER.

IN 1893, 27 MILLION PEOPLE FROM AROUND THE WORLD WENT TO CHICAGO FOR THE **WORLD'S FAIR**. THE EVENT SHOWED PEOPLE HOW FAR THE CITY HAD COME SINCE THE GREAT FIRE.

TODAY, CHICAGO IS THE **THIRD-LARGEST CITY** IN THE UNITED STATES.

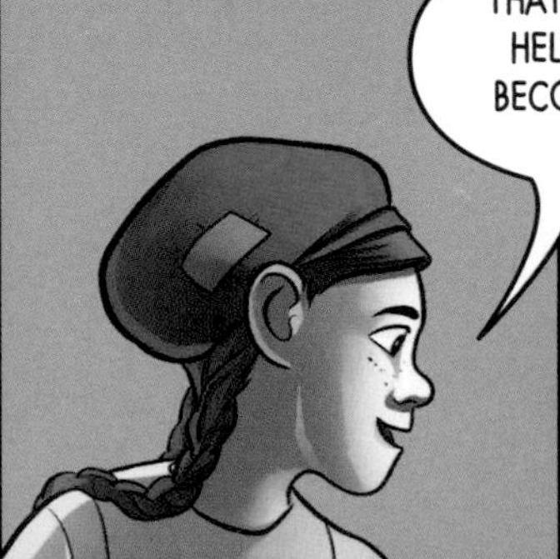
THAT FIRE ACTUALLY HELPED CHICAGO BECOME THE CITY IT IS TODAY!

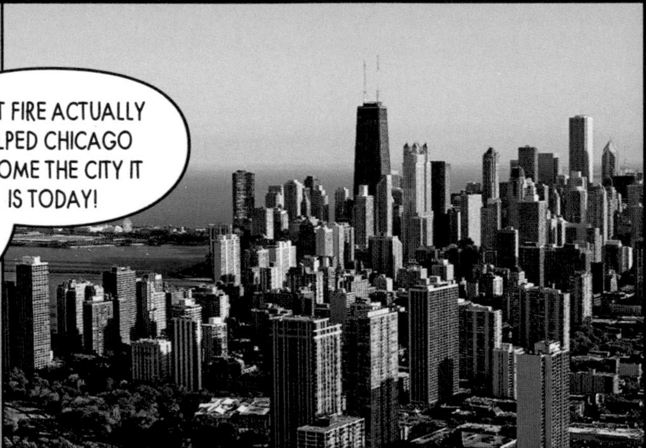

TO LEARN MORE

The Great Fire by Jim Murphy (Scholastic, 1995) is one of Lauren Tarshis's favorite books about history. It helped with her research and is full of fascinating info.

To dig deeper into the Chicago Fire, go to www.greatchicagofire.org to see all kinds of photographs, artifacts, and true stories from the fire.

FURTHER READING

Lauren Tarshis has written other I Survived books on topics related to this one. Some are about fires and accidents that taught us important lessons. Others are events that happened in the 1800s, during the same time period as the Chicago Fire. Lauren always likes making connections between different books and ideas, and she knows that you will too!

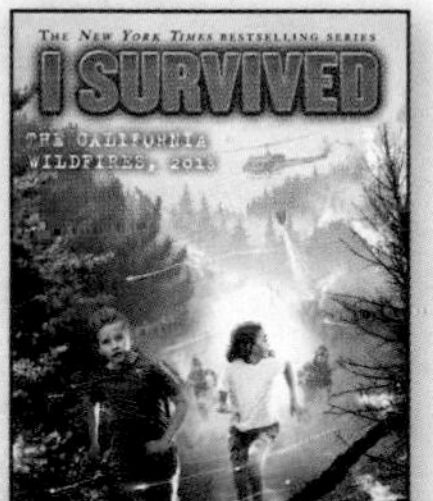
THE NEW YORK TIMES BESTSELLING SERIES
I SURVIVED
THE CALIFORNIA WILDFIRES, 2018
by LAUREN TARSHIS
SCHOLASTIC

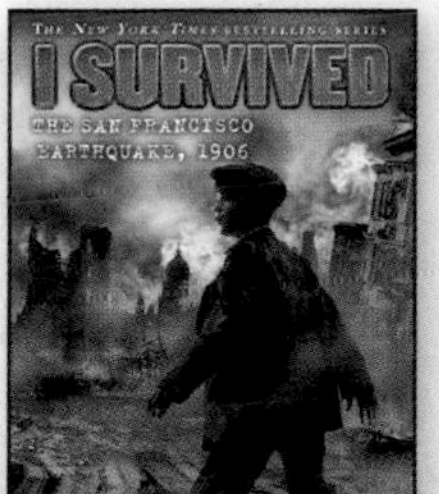
THE NEW YORK TIMES BESTSELLING SERIES
I SURVIVED
THE SAN FRANCISCO EARTHQUAKE, 1906
by Lauren Tarshis
SCHOLASTIC

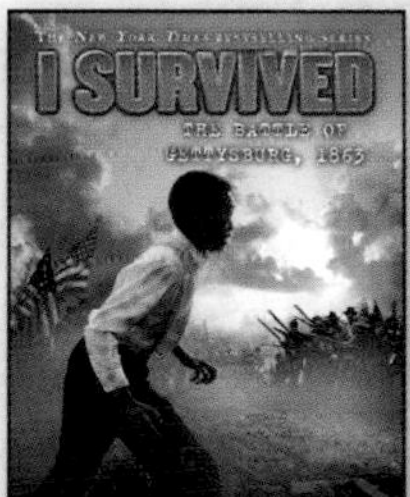
THE NEW YORK TIMES BESTSELLING SERIES
I SURVIVED
THE BATTLE OF GETTYSBURG, 1863
by Lauren Tarshis
SCHOLASTIC

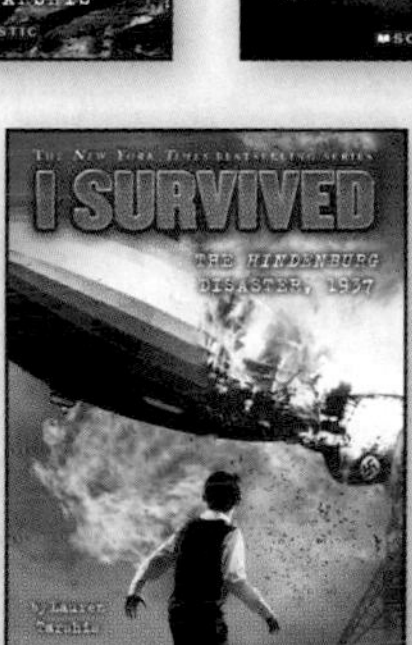
THE NEW YORK TIMES BESTSELLING SERIES
I SURVIVED
THE HINDENBURG DISASTER, 1937
by Lauren Tarshis
SCHOLASTIC

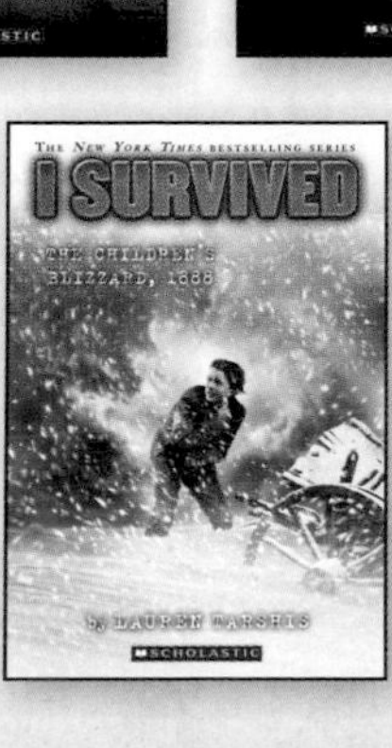
THE NEW YORK TIMES BESTSELLING SERIES
I SURVIVED
THE CHILDREN'S BLIZZARD, 1888
by LAUREN TARSHIS
SCHOLASTIC

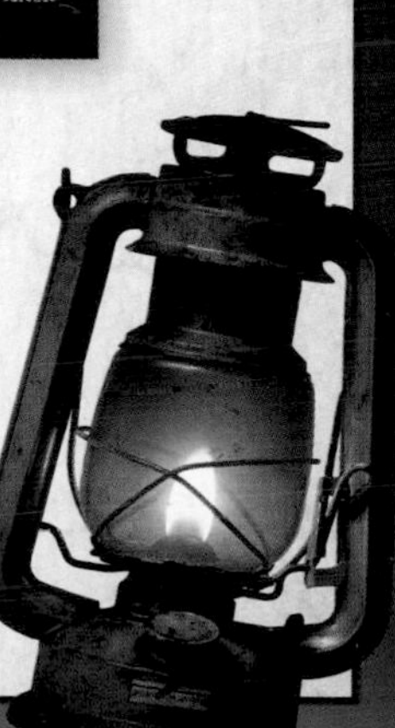

LAUREN TARSHIS'S

NEW YORK TIMES BESTSELLING I SURVIVED SERIES TELLS STORIES OF YOUNG PEOPLE AND THEIR RESILIENCE AND STRENGTH IN THE MIDST OF UNIMAGINABLE DISASTERS AND TIMES OF TURMOIL. LAUREN HAS BROUGHT HER SIGNATURE WARMTH, INTEGRITY, AND EXHAUSTIVE RESEARCH TO TOPICS SUCH AS THE BATTLE OF D-DAY, THE AMERICAN REVOLUTION, HURRICANE KATRINA, THE BOMBING OF PEARL HARBOR, AND OTHER WORLD EVENTS. LAUREN LIVES IN CONNECTICUT WITH HER FAMILY, AND CAN BE FOUND ONLINE AT LAURENTARSHIS.COM.

GEORGIA BALL

HAS WRITTEN COMICS FOR MANY OF HER FAVORITE CHILDHOOD CHARACTERS, INCLUDING STRAWBERRY SHORTCAKE, TRANSFORMERS, LITTLEST PET SHOP, MY LITTLE PONY, AND THE DISNEY PRINCESSES. IN ADDITION TO ADAPTING LAUREN TARSHIS'S I SURVIVED SERIES TO GRAPHIC NOVELS, GEORGIA WRITES ABOUT HISTORICAL EVENTS SUCH AS THE WORLD WAR II BATTLES OF KURSK AND GUADALCANAL. GEORGIA LIVES WITH HER HUSBAND, DAUGHTER, AND RAMBUNCTIOUS PETS IN FLORIDA. VISIT HER ONLINE AT GEORGIABALLAUTHOR.COM.

CASSIE ANDERSON

IS A FREELANCE COMIC ARTIST WHO LOVES TELLING STORIES AND DRAWING PICTURES. SHE IS THE ILLUSTRATOR BEHIND THE LIFEFORMED SERIES AS WELL AS THE CREATOR OF *EXTRAORDINARY: A STORY OF AN ORDINARY PRINCESS*. WHEN SHE'S NOT DRAWING COMICS, YOU CAN FIND HER READING A GOOD BOOK, BAKING SOME TASTY TREATS, OR EXPLORING THE OUTDOORS WITH HER ADVENTURE-LOVING HUSBAND.

JUANMA AGUILERA

IS A COMIC ILLUSTRATOR AND COLORIST BASED IN JAÉN, SPAIN. HIS WORK CAN BE FOUND IN MORE THAN TWENTY COMICS AND GRAPHIC NOVELS PUBLISHED IN SPAIN, CANADA, AUSTRALIA, AND THE UNITED STATES.